EXPLICIT MEMORY

SCARLETT FINN

Also by Scarlett Finn

TO DIE FOR...
TO DIE FOR TRUTH
TO DIE FOR HONOR
TO DIE FOR VIRTUE
TO DIE FOR DUTY
TO DIE FOR LOVE

GO NOVELS
GO WITH IT
GO IT ALONE
GO ALL OUT
GO ALL IN
GO FULL CIRCLE

KINDRED SERIES
RAVEN
SWALLOW
CUCKOO
SWIFT
FALCON
FINCH

LOVE AGAINST THE ODDS STANDALONE COLLECTION
SWEET SEAS
HEIR'S AFFAIR
RESCUED
MAESTRO'S MUSE
GETTING TRICKY
THIRTEEN
REMEMBER WHEN...
RELUCTANT SUSPICION
XY FACTOR

EXILE
HIDE & SEEK
KISS CHASE

THE EXPLICIT SERIES
EXPLICIT INSTRUCTION
EXPLICIT DETAIL
EXPLICIT MEMORY

WRECK & RUIN
RUIN ME
RUIN HIM

MISTAKE DUET
MISTAKE ME NOT
SLEIGHT MISTAKE

NOTHING TO...
NOTHING TO HIDE
NOTHING TO LOSE
NOTHING TO DECLARE
NOTHING TO US
NOTHING TO SAY
NOTHING TO GAIN
NOTHING TO YOU
NOTHING TO THIS

THE BRANDED SERIES
BRANDED
SCARRED
MARKED

RISQUÉ & HARROW INTERTWINED
TAKE A RISK
FIGHTING FATE
RISK IT ALL
FIGHTING BACK
GAME OF RISK

FORBIDDEN PREQUEL DUET
ALL. ONLY.
ONLY YOURS

THE FORBIDDEN NOVELS
FORBIDDEN DESIRE
FORBIDDEN WANT
FORBIDDEN WISH
FORBIDDEN NEED

LOST & FOUND
LOST
FOUND

ONE

"DON'T YOU AGREE?"

"Yes," Flick answered her brother-in-law's brother, her attention over his shoulder.

Coming back to her parents' house, the Hughes' family home, hadn't been on her list of top ten burning desires. But her sister had reached out to include her. After being estranged from her family for over a year, snubbing the invitation wouldn't have been right.

The Hughes family was old money and well established in society. Her mother, Beverly, loved to boast about the house, it was her pride and joy. Everything she wanted. An extravagant display of wealth and taste; the envy of many other wives in their circle.

"You weren't at the wedding, though, were you?"

What was this guy's name? In her defense, she wasn't sure they'd ever been formally introduced. "No."

"Are you married?"

Dusk had long since gone but outdoor lighting kept the patio abuzz with all those gathered to celebrate the wedding anniversaries of both her sisters. The eldest,

Lucia, was married on the twenty-second, and the middle daughter Vivian on the twenty-fourth of the same month in different years. They'd chosen the twenty-third for their joint anniversary celebration.

Groups of people stood around chatting politely, sipping expensive champagne, admiring the gardens that had been re-designed especially for this occasion. She was less interested in the grounds and more interested in the folding glass door at the back of the house. The party's gateway between the internal and external.

"No," Flick said.

"I'm divorced myself."

"I'm not in the market."

The stuttering man with the receding hairline blanched. Her patience was wearing thin. It wasn't his fault, she was preoccupied with the door for a reason and her impatient anticipation was reaching critical mass.

"Flick?"

Turning in the direction of her name, she saw Robert Morse, the man her father, her whole family, wanted her to marry.

"Hi," she said.

Her brother in-law's brother walked away, but this encounter with Robert didn't offer any reprieve from the safety of the benign conversation she'd shared with the retreating man.

Robert's suave demeanor remained the same. His perfectly coiffed brown hair and baby blue eyes were as she remembered. Hurting him hadn't been fun, he wasn't a bad guy. But knowing herself as she did now, it was clear that had been exactly the problem.

"Look at this," Lucia said, rushing in at her side. "You two reunited."

If it wouldn't be considered impolite, she would've rolled her eyes. "I've seen many people tonight I haven't seen in a year and a half."

Since she left.

"Are you nostalgic?" Lucia asked.

Her tension level rose as Robert maintained eye contact. Was this about to get interesting or had her recent experiences set her on edge?

"Problem?" This new male voice came from the rear.

Relief was instant. She'd only taken her eyes off the doorway for a few seconds, but it wouldn't have mattered. His arm lolled over her shoulder to rest along her clavicle, meaning his angle of approach was from behind. He hadn't come from through the house. Of course not. She should've known better than to expect a conventional entrance from her lover.

"I don't know if you ever met," she said, knowing they hadn't. "This is my sister Lucia, and Robert, who has only said one word to me tonight."

"One word too many."

Rushe was Rushe. No airs or graces. Certainly no feigned civility. He didn't acknowledge either of the beautiful people before them any further. While he pressured her to walk backward, she smiled in farewell and let Rushe take her in the direction of the walled rose garden. Bringing her body around his, her love urged her back against the tree at the garden entrance.

"Did you get it?"

"Yeah," he said, retrieving a folded piece of paper from his back pocket.

She took it from him and eagerly opened it to read the promised new birth certificate. "Jones?" she read and let her disappointment shine. "I get a new identity, and this is the name you give me? Why don't I get your name?"

"Because, Kitten," he said, removing the sheet of paper to tuck it away again. "There are folks out there who don't like me. I don't want anyone who looks for me to find you."

"Maybe you could rescue me this time," she said. "You know, for once."

She teased because he let her. Also because the more she pushed, the further his brow came down, so the darker his eyes became. He growled at her and she sighed, letting her hands sink into his pockets now that she'd achieved her aim of riling him a little.

"Couldn't you have gone with something slightly more exotic?"

"Don't want you exotic," he said. "Want you plain, boring, and very difficult to trace. Your family, and their money, make you a target."

"Technically, so do you because there are people out to get you. Our job does too, we don't always make many friends."

"Yeah," he said. "But you're not gonna give up me or the job. I can only limit your vulnerability where you let me."

Getting over her sulk, the more pressing discussion remained pending. "Did you see him?" she asked.

"I went to the hospital and copied some notes, but he's still out of it. I didn't go near his room. We don't know who's watching."

"And Serendipity?"

Rushe shook his head. "She's not there."

"We have to find her," she said. "Jansen was there for me when I needed him. He freed you. I would never have been able to—"

"You wouldn't have been there in the first place if it wasn't for him," Rushe said.

"No, actually, you wouldn't have been there if it wasn't for him. Which means I would've walked into Dell's—"

"Yeah, Kitten."

She knew her point hit home by his snarl of discontent.

"You were never going to leave Serendipity out there alone."

"She might be dead."

"You're preparing me," she said.

Rushe could emotionally detach from everything, except her. Over the course of their relationship, she'd tried to follow his example, but she hadn't managed it yet.

"Someone put Jansen in the hospital, and they've abducted his woman, Serendipity," Rushe said. "We were just as complicit in fucking up their operation as them. You better be prepared because we're next."

"If they put you in the hospital and kidnap me—"

"They're not gonna pull the same play twice, or if they were they'd have tried it by now," Rushe said. "They want something else from us."

The night never felt oppressive when Rushe was around, nothing did. He held the world away from her, at least the evil in it, and if he felt it pushing back all his senses went on hyper alert.

"What should we do now?" she asked on a sigh.

The act of bringing her wrists toward each other made her hands, which were still in his pockets, press to his member. It also squeezed her upper arms on either side of her breasts. Rushe's attention slinked down to her cleavage, so she ensured to push forward and enhance his view as best she could.

"Move," he said, grabbing her shoulder.

He tried to pull her forward, but she didn't budge.

"You want to have sex in my parents' garden?"

"I don't give a fuck where."

They had been separated for more than a day. At

lunchtime yesterday, he'd dropped her off at the rear security-gated entrance of the Hughes home. His own destination had been the hospital where Jansen was laid up in critical condition. Right now it had to be closing in on midnight. The idea of a love-in sounded about perfect to her after the stresses of the day.

"My bedroom is upstairs," she said.

Rushe slipped her hand from his jeans and linked their fingers to pull her toward the house. Unfortunately, they didn't get that far because Lucia got in front of them. Rushe tried to avoid her but Charles Hughes, Flick's father, approached from the other side, closing in on them in a pincer move. Although she didn't expect Rushe to be happy about the interception, she was surprised he gave up so easily by coming to an abrupt halt.

When she collided with his back, she tried to skirt around him, but he got in her way, blocking her from something.

"Felicity, there's someone you must meet," her father said. "He just arrived back here a few minutes ago, and he's eager to meet you." Rushe gave her just enough space to show half of herself. Charles Hughes appeared outright disgusted by her love's presence. "Who is this?"

"This is Flick's boyfriend," Lucia said. "I think."

The glitter in Lucia's eyes betrayed a fascination with this feral creature in their staid environment.

"Her what?"

"Who do you want me to meet, Father?" Flick asked.

If it were appropriate, she would personally introduce Rushe to every person there. She'd willingly fall to her knees in front of them all to prove their relationship too. But Rushe thought the fewer people who knew him, the better… and he wouldn't share any of their intimacies with anyone.

"This is Antoine Mercier; he's a client of Roger's."

She didn't need to witness Rushe sizing up the dashing man who reeked of sophistication and arrogance, because she could sense the snarl.

"Nice to meet you, Mr. Mercier," she said, taking Rushe's lead, not attempting to shake hands or make any physical contact.

"Call me Antoine," he drawled, with an accent.

She frowned. "You're European?"

"French," he said.

Rushe remained static, not a single hair on his body moved, but she grew rigid. It couldn't be a coincidence that Antoine was the same nationality as the family involved with the human traffickers. The same people who were no doubt responsible for recent events regarding Jansen and Serendipity. The lack of change in Antoine, despite her visible negative reaction, confirmed it.

"Isn't it wonderful?" Lucia said, taking Antoine's arm. "His family has been here in the States for a decade, but he still has the accent."

"Roger has been advising Antoine about some tech investment," Charles said. "There's a start-up company moving under the umbrella of a larger corporation. They have the prospect, I should say, there's a window and Antoine has the money, but of course, he wants it to grow."

"We've been spending a lot of time together," Antoine said, covering Lucia's hand with his while his eyes bored into her.

"Excuse me," Charles said, and left the group.

"Lucia," Flick said. "Will you show me the new water feature you had installed for tonight? I noticed it behind the buffet."

"What about the—"

"Please," Flick said, spreading a smile and reaching around Rushe toward her sister, without departing from the defense of her Rushe shield. "Let the men talk business."

"Go on," Antoine said.

TWO

LUCIA TOOK FLICK'S hand, and she led her sister away. Rushe wanted to be alone with this new acquaintance, she could tell. Her love didn't betray much in outward appearance, but she was getting better at reading, at anticipating, his maneuvers.

Lucia took her to the new garden feature but didn't say much about it before her own inquisition began.

"He's a brute," her sister said.

"Who?" she asked, with her back to the wall she could observe the partygoers.

Her main focus was far removed from the masses, where Rushe and this new associate spoke.

"Your boyfriend," Lucia said. "We didn't realize when we sent you the invitation that you would bring a guest. What's his name?"

"How well do you know Mercier?" she asked her sister, maintaining her fixation on Rushe.

Sometimes when there were new developments they had to act quickly. If Rushe needed her, then she wanted to be ready.

"Mercier?" Lucia scoffed. "His name is Antoine. Why would you address him by his last name?"

Habit. "Sorry, I forgot it," she fibbed. "How long have you known him?"

"He's been working with Roger for about a month. We were introduced two weeks ago when he began staying here."

"Here?" she asked, losing the subject of her previous attention. "Why is he staying here?"

"He's having his home built, and there was some sort of delay with construction. I don't know the specifics."

"And if he has all this money, why couldn't he afford a hotel room?"

"That's so impersonal, he's European."

"So?" she asked.

"They're hospitable, aren't they? Very family oriented. He was the one who encouraged Viv and me to get in touch with you. He thought this rift was ridiculous, you should be grateful to him. He places a great premium on family and couldn't stay in a hotel all alone."

She didn't buy it for a second, and neither would Rushe. "So his family is staying here as well? Why didn't I meet them last night?"

"His children live in France," Lucia said, her attention floating across the crowd toward Antoine again. "But he and his wife are divorced."

She didn't like the way her sister sought out the men they'd left alone to talk. "I know you're not looking at my boyfriend like that."

"What? Oh, don't be silly."

Rushe might intrigue her sisters, but neither would be adventurous enough to attempt to tame the beast. To them, he was a wild cat in the zoo, beautiful to look at and admire but never to touch. Antoine, on the other hand, was the height of good breeding, definitely enough to turn the heads of societies darlings.

"You're married," she said.

"What has that got to do with anything?" Lucia snapped. "I admire the man, that's all."

"Just remember to admire him from afar," Flick said. "Why didn't I meet him last night?"

"He had business to deal with."

"What business?"

"Now who's interested," Lucia said.

"Does my man look like the type to step out on?"

"Where did you find him?"

Few people would seek or discover love in the place that she had found it. "In the last place I ever would've looked," she said.

"It's not… serious, is it?"

"He's died for me once, and he'd do it again," she said. "Tell me everything you know about Antoine."

"Why? What do you—?"

"You don't think it's odd that he showed up, and now he wants to live in your parents' house?"

"Roger and I stay here all the time, Viv too," Lucia said. "We all socialize and—"

"He's not family," she said. "Before a month ago, had any of you ever heard of Antoine Mercier?"

Lucia's always sparkling eyes tapered. Before getting a response, Rushe and Antoine walked away from each other. She moved through the groups between them until they united. He immediately took her hand and hooked it into his back pocket.

"We're leaving," he said, leading her into the house and through the dining room.

"There's a bedroom upstairs for us," she said, struggling to keep up as they wound through the long hallways toward the exit. "He's staying here. My family could be in danger."

Rushe stopped in the entry lobby to spin on her. "Why do you say that?"

"He's been working with Roger for a month," she said. "He's living in this house, and you know him. Who is he?"

"Exactly who you think he is."

"The danger."

"I don't want you here," Rushe said.

She slipped her hand deeper into his pocket. "Don't let him see you riled, Lover. You know we have to be here to watch out for them. They have no idea who he really is, and if he gets control of them… We can't risk their safety."

"And what about yours?" he growled, thrusting her back against the wall, knocking the wind out of her. "You're asking me to risk you."

She recognized the darkness, the edge he teetered on so precariously. "We talked about this," she whispered. "You have to let me be a part of your work, risks and all."

"I don't know if I can," he admitted on a hushed exhale.

"You're capable of anything, Lover. I've known that since the night we met. As long as I'm with you I'm safe, Rushe."

Footsteps preceded a new feminine tone. "Vivian, we won't have…"

Rushe twisted toward her mother's voice but kept his body on hers, her eternal defender. From how Beverly Hughes' voice trailed away, she'd guess Rushe landed her with that nefarious glare. Her mother must have been calling back to her other daughter because at the moment she remained alone in the entryway.

"What is this?" Beverly asked her daughter, unable to tear her attention away from the alien creature in her lobby.

"We're going to bed," Flick said.

"We?" That did bring Beverly's focus to her daughter. "You know this man?"

"No, we just met," Flick sassed. "I'm a real slut now, ma."

Beverly's jaw fell on a croak of indignation, but Rushe crouched to nuzzle his face in her hair. The action was cover meant to misdirect attention from the hand he scooped up under her dress to fondle her ass.

The enjoyment she got out of shocking her family was inexplicable. Vivian came in at Beverly's back, prepared to speak and see what her mother gawped at. She stopped when she witnessed the unexpected show.

Her smile spread. She didn't know how Rushe read her so well; they'd never been in her family's company together. Playing his role as the animal, he sucked her neck until she gasped at the sting. Her love drew his mouth higher, tracing his teeth along her jaw.

"He gets testy if I don't service him at least five times a day."

"Felicity!"

"This is the guy with the hands!" Vivian exclaimed. "You said he did it himself!"

"That's right," she said, stroking a hand up his arm and down his chest.

Taking hold of Rushe's belt buckle, she sashayed away from the wall and led him toward the staircase.

"You're going to do it in our parents' house?" Vivian gaped like a teenager.

"A bunch of times," Rushe grumbled, and flopped his arms around her.

"Felicity!" Beverly exclaimed.

"Good night!" she called out and took Rushe up to her bedroom. As soon as the door closed, granting them seclusion, she turned out of her love's arms. "Why is Antoine Mercier here with my family? This is about

Jansen, tell me what they did to him, how he looks."

She couldn't bear to think of Rushe in pain. The idea he could go through the same ordeal as Jansen disturbed her.

"I didn't go in," Rushe said.

"Will he wake up?"

"I don't know."

The suspense was unbearable. She was used to things happening quickly, or at least being able to take action. With Antoine there, and connected with this debacle, things had gotten serious not only for her and her love, but her family as well.

"What about Serendipity? Give me the details."

"She was last seen at work eight days ago," he said. "No one's seen her since then."

"Eight... after I got the email."

"You think if we'd mobilized quicker—"

"Don't get defensive," she said, recognizing where his tone was heading. "I made a statement. I'm not blaming you for anything. We couldn't have foreseen this. It took us nearly three days to verify the facts of what happened to Jansen."

"We don't know the facts," Rushe said, shoving her further into the room and turning on the lights to look around.

The space was vast, but basically empty. The bed and the nightstands stood against the head wall with a large window behind it. Looking at it now, Flick was reminded of her prison in Victor's mansion.

She and Rushe met after a sequence of events leading her into the clutches of gangsters led by a man called Victor. In the end, she discovered the chain of command actually went higher than him, presumably to the bankrolling Merciers. Victor's job was to capture women for his superiors to sell. Their trade was human trafficking, and she'd almost been a victim herself.

Rushe had gotten involved with Victor after Victor and his gang learned Jansen was an undercover cop sent to spy on them. When the game was up, Victor snatched Jansen's girlfriend in an effort to force the cop to do his bidding. It worked. Serendipity was that girlfriend. When Jansen had no luck in locating or saving her, he hired Rushe through a third party to do it for him.

When Victor got paranoid about Flick's relationship with Rushe, and of Rushe's identity, Victor imprisoned her lover. On her journey to be sold, Jansen intercepted the shipment and saved her. Together they freed her lover and his. Many lives were lost in that operation, including Victor's. Only the four of them and one other person walked out of that building alive. The other person was Simone, who she assumed was a relation of Antoine. The French woman was responsible for supervising Victor and looking after the women meant to be sold.

"They have Serendipity?"

"Yeah," he said, sitting on the bed to unlace his boots. "Mercier just confirmed it."

"So what now?"

Rushe sat up to stare her down. "Sex."

THREE

"YOU HAD IT made here, Kitten," Rushe said, drying his hands on the towel then throwing it back into the bathroom an hour or two later.

She lay on the soft white linen of the bed brushing her fingers up and down the black leather of Rushe's loose belt lying across her abdomen.

"Don't start that. There's enough money in the bank that we could have a house if we wanted it, but we don't."

Rushe's money might not equal Hughes proportions, but he was no slouch and would always be able to provide for her. While working for various clients through the years, he'd done some very risky jobs for some very wealthy people. Those contracts paid very well.

Rushe joined her on the bed, laying himself out then picking her up to drape over him, tossing the belt aside in the process.

"I've got something you can wrap those fingers around."

"What does Mercier want?" she asked, rolling onto her front so they were chest to chest. "Money?"

"Don't worry about—"

"We're a team," she said. "Remember what happened the last time you shut me out? Does he want money? How much of it? Is it a ransom? Will he let Serendipity go if—"

"He doesn't want money from us. The Merciers are only mid-level. They don't have great funds, not like your folks here. They do okay, but they're not as affluent as they'd like people to believe. But it's not our money they want."

"Victor was selling those women for him, wasn't he?"

While working for Victor, Rushe's mission was to locate and liberate Serendipity. But he'd also played a covert role in freeing the kidnapped women meant to be sold to the highest bidder.

"Mercier works for his uncle, Jerome, he has no kids of his own," Rushe said. "Jerome is Simone's uncle too."

Simone had been at Victor's side throughout the job, watching the gangster's every move to report back to her family, the sponsors of the operation. The refined woman's task might have been to supervise and chronicle, but she actually spent more of her time seducing Victor's men.

Though Rushe was technically one of those men, Simone's attempts to seduce him were never successful. Not that she boasted about that truth to anyone. It suited Rushe's cause to let the other men in the posse believe he was as beguiled with her as they were.

"She's out there? But I thought the police—"

"They had nothing on her," Rushe said. "Nothing physical anyway. I don't know what information Jansen fed back about her. She probably played the victim. I don't know the details of the investigation. I'll find them out, but it will take time. Other than the testimony of the freed women…"

"But Jansen's a cop. He knew what was going on."

"Jansen had his own mess."

She pushed her hands to his chest, propping up her weight. "His superiors found out that Victor kidnapped Serendipity?"

"Yeah," Rushe said. "Looks that way."

Jansen's original assignment had been to infiltrate the gang and gather information on the crook and his cohorts. But once Victor had control of the woman he loved, the cop was stuck and fed all sorts of inaccurate and false information to his superiors to ensure Serendipity's safety. Rushe might have been called in to save the day, but after Flick got involved, she had been used against him just like Serendipity was against Jansen.

"What happened?" she asked.

Rushe grumbled. His hand landed on her crown, losing his fingers in her hair, he pushed her head down onto his chest.

"He was suspended," Rushe said. "Pending investigation."

"But that was months ago, what—"

She tried to lift her head, but he pressured it in place, keeping her pressed to him. She loved the warmth of his skin, the resistance of his muscles, and the pound of his heart that lived encased in the inky resonance of his deep, gravelly voice.

"He went rogue, got obsessed with getting the guys involved in Victor's game, involved in endangering his woman. Jansen's a fucking asshole."

"Would you have done anything differently?" she asked. "They held her for months." She turned her face toward him until her lips met skin. "He loves her, Rushe. I know how much you hate loving me. I know it makes you weak. Is that what they want?"

His hand froze, still knotted in her hair. "What?"

"They blame us for Victor's death. They financed the operation, but you and Jansen… and me… we stopped it from getting off the ground. What's more, we probably sent a whole team of cops to sniff around."

"Jansen's the cop, and I told you then that was his problem."

The boom of his voice vibrated against her cheek. "Is that what they want, Lover? Do they want me? They've already taken Jansen's girl."

"Do you think I would hand you over?"

"No," she said, insulted by the offense in his tone. "That's what scares me, Rushe. I love you, and I've seen you go through enough for me."

"I've endured nothing for you," he said. "I've been taking shit all my life."

"Without you, I have nothing."

"Flick—"

"You have the job, you're great at it. You have purpose."

"I don't like this talk," he said.

"You know if it comes down to a choice… the smart money—"

"Enough!" Casting her body away from his, Rushe pinned her down, snatching her wrists in his fists. "What the fuck do you think you're going to say? Why in the fuck would you—"

"Because we find ourselves in these life and death situations without ever having discussed a course of action. You're the master of forethought, why wouldn't you—"

"I know exactly what to do," he said.

"Sacrifice yourself every time, is that your plan?

I don't need you to prove your love to me. I know you love me. I face that truth every day and it makes me happy. You're the one who has a problem with it. If it's your plan to get yourself hurt in order to validate your feelings, then your plan sucks!"

"You're gonna learn, Kitten," he said. "You're gonna learn to do what you're told. I get between you and danger, always."

"What is it they want? What does Antoine want?"

"There's a guy, Theo Silver. Everyone calls him Silver."

"What about him?"

"He needs some work done," Rushe said. "Mercier will be in touch with him. I have a debt to settle."

"Who is Theo Silver? What does he want with my lover?"

Moving to his side, his hand coasted over her breast when his form drifted away. He grasped, massaging the flesh toward himself and away. The motion attracted a grumble, and his face delved into her hair.

"Don't worry about that." He pinched her nipple, and her calf drifted between his legs. "Your lover has his own wants."

"No sex until we talk," she whispered.

His lips slithered down her body until he kissed her nipple. Lapping it once, he pinched it again, rolling the peak between his fingertips.

"Your tits… you have incredible cans."

Circling her again, he coated one breast then the other in long, lingering kisses.

"You're making out with my breasts," she said on a smile and combed her fingers through his hair. "We have to talk. This is important. But it's been a long day and I'm tired. I'd forgotten how much energy it required to sit up straight all day and smirk at everyone."

"Go to sleep," he said, suckling one pebble then the other.

"If I go to sleep, I'll wake up sore because you'll still be feasting on me."

"Your breasts are mine. I can do whatever the fuck I want with them."

Bringing her leg higher, she elevated her thigh to his groin and began to undulate. Then, elevating her ass, she twisted to grind herself into him. He grunted and grabbed her hip to hold her down flat, so his mouth could continue its worship.

"I wanna play with your dick."

Seizing her hand, he coiled her fingers around the length of him, but she released him to slap her hands onto his shoulders and push him onto his back. He let her throw a leg over him to mount his torso, because she kept her breasts on his face. He hummed out his pleasure and tested her with his teeth.

A joyous shriek leaped from her. "I can only sleep on top of you."

"You stay right where you are, Kitten."

He held her in place. "Rushe!"

"My girls."

"Smothered to death," she said, shimmying herself against him. He buried his face in her cleavage and rolled her to her back, parting her legs with his. "Talk, then sex."

In typical Rushe grouch fashion, he exhaled and flopped onto his back. He tucked her under his arm, ensuring she stayed plastered to the height of him.

"Silver is a pimp," he said, threading his fingers into her hair.

"And Mercier knows him?"

"By association." His fingers trailed down her

spine and back up, then down again. "Silver doesn't hang out on street corners."

"You know him?"

"He has a reputation," Rushe said.

"Do you know Antoine?"

"I did research on Victor, and on the Mercier family. It's how I know their finances aren't that hot."

"Antoine and Simone are cousins, and he's here, so does that mean…?" Her first impression of Simone was that she was superior. Her opinion had only gone downhill from there. "Are we going to…? Will we see her?"

"I don't know," Rushe said. "If you want me to set you up—"

"We work together," she said. "Antoine knew you, downstairs. You knew him too."

"Mercier was at the meeting…"

"In Dell's," she said, in a moment of clarity.

"He worked as a liaison with Victor."

"Why is he here? Why infiltrate my family?"

"Because you care about them," Rushe said, drumming his fingers on the vertebrae above her ass in the groove of her back.

"I got that email ten days ago," she said. "He's been working with Roger for a month; he's been staying here for two weeks. Antoine orchestrated this."

FOUR

IN A RAGE, she tried to shove up.

Rushe got hold of her and slammed her onto her back again. "You gonna run into his bedroom, Kitten?"

"He's using my family as pawns. They should be made aware of—"

"What did Lucia say?"

"About what?" she asked.

"You got all that info; you didn't say nothing about danger?"

"I tried to point out it was odd, but…"

"Their world isn't like ours," Rushe said.

Nudging her nose to his jaw, she kissed his stubble. Something as simple as acknowledging they came from the same world highlighted just how far they'd come as a couple.

She'd once been as naive as her sister. Declaring to her family that Mercier was a criminal would be met with indignation. The sad fact was, given she'd been estranged from her family for close to a year and a half, she could never claim to be a typical, or respected, member of the Hughes family. Most probably she'd be laughed out of the room if she made such a claim to them.

The idea of a criminal in their midst was so outlandish it would be impossible, as far as her father was concerned. He prided himself on being an excellent judge of character. A criminal, in their opinion, looked like Rushe. Though they wouldn't be far wrong by many definitions.

"So what does he want?"

"Mercier wants to make us wait."

"Does he know you?" she asked. "If he thinks he can make you sweat it out, he's misjudged his opponent."

"He didn't know if I'd come here to your parents' house with you," Rushe said. "That's my bet. They didn't make plans for us because he can't anticipate our actions yet."

"So we wait… until he tells us… until he has a job for us."

"Not us, me. They don't know we work together."

"I'm just your bitch," she said. "Letting them continue to believe that could be useful for us further down the road."

Rushe's arms came around her, clamping her body to his. "Let me foresee the problems. Open your legs."

She had said sex after talking. "What do you want to do to me?"

"My dirty 'ho, you want me to spell it out?"

"I want you to talk to me," she whispered. "Tell me about your dick."

"You love my dick."

"I do."

"It's gonna fill that pussy," he said. Taking her hand, he slid it down between her legs. "You're gonna get it all juiced up for me."

Rushe had stretched her sexual boundaries until the elastic snapped from the pressure. Now, as she slid the length of her index finger up and down her clit, she was flooded with the power he gave her.

Shifting to the end of the bed, her love grabbed her knees and forced them wide; those bullet eyes of his fastened their sights on her center.

"Faster," he ordered. "I wanna hear you moan, Kitten. Stroke my pussy. I want you ready. Your empty little cunt wants to be filled up with my fat cock... that hot little pussy gets so wet when I talk."

"Yes," she breathed.

"I want to glide in. You want my cock in there, you gotta make me want it."

She increased her pace, recalling every time they'd had sex, and thinking about the solid mass of him widening her to fit him. About the times Rushe forged into her with such passion and fury. Those memories now made her hips rise into her own caress. Rushe's growl proceeded her panting exhale.

"Rushe."

"Not yet, Kitten. You're gonna take me hard."

Her eyes drifted closed when his hand ran down her shin to her foot. Cocking her leg he positioned her foot against his balls, pushing her toes up against his dick.

"I thought about you," she whispered. "Last night, I was thinking about your cock."

His hand slapped hers away from its task. At the moment she opened her eyes, his body braced above her. "You touched my pussy?"

"Rushe," she exhaled, witnessing the raw anger in him.

"Did you?"

"Maybe."

"You broke the rules," he snarled, his lips

remaining completely still.

Flipping to his back, he lay beside her and scooped his hand under her head. "Wrap your lips round my cock." A tickling shimmer trickled up her waist to her ribcage. "You show me that you're sorry, suck it."

Using his strength, he got her face into his lap and as he pushed her downward, she immediately opened wide to accommodate him. The bold head of his dick reached deep. She inhaled to let him push further into the confines of her throat. Rushe released his pressure when she took him as far as she could, then he let her draw up and down.

"Eager little slut, you can't wait to get my dick in your throat."

Dipping down she took him in, then sucked him out. Kissing the emerging beads from the tip of him, she worked her hand up and down, her eyes drifted to his.

"Don't want your hand, Kit," he said, tugging her wrist to remove it. Taking a handful of her hair, he brought her face over his daunting organ. "You want it? You want to suck it?"

"Yes," she said, and opened her mouth to take him.

He raised her head before she could reach him. "Say it."

"I want to suck it."

"What do you want to suck?" he asked. "Look at me."

Rolling her eyes upward, she did as she was told. "Your dick. I want to suck your dick."

"When you get my dick in your mouth, you're gonna suck it like you mean it. Show me you're sorry. No one touches my pussy without permission."

"Sorry, sir," she said.

On his huffing exhale, she knew she had him. Rushe released her head, letting her face fall against him.

She tasted the length of him with her tongue, circled his head, and sucked him into her mouth again. Up and down, she sucked until her cheeks burned.

Then suddenly, he snatched her hips from the bed and yanked her body away to reposition them. She did her best to keep performing for him while he turned to throw her leg over his shoulder. Now that she straddled his face, he lifted his head to kiss her clit.

She whimpered and her own attention diverted, but he spanked her. "This is for my pleasure, slut. You keep working. Earn your place at my side."

Doing as told, she did her best to keep up the action. It wasn't easy. His tongue probed into her then flickered over her.

"Rushe," she wheezed out, her mouth still full of him.

"Your sweet pussy juice, you're gonna come all over my tongue… You suck my cock into your throat."

Closing her eyes, she did just that. Working him with her hand, she fondled his balls, and tried to ignore the awareness growing in her.

"Rushe," she said again, increasing her pace as his tongue moved faster on her and shoved inside. "Oh, God!"

Orgasm enveloped her at the same moment his hot milk sprayed her mouth. With barely any presence of mind, she swallowed, licking the last remnants from him before she flopped onto him, her cheek landing on his groin.

"You're cruel," she whispered with a broad smile.

He slapped her ass again. "Yeah, punishment by orgasm."

"I'd have asked permission if I had a way to get in touch with you."

"If you had a way to get in touch with me, I'd

have abandoned the job last night and come here to be with you."

The promise of sex always existed between them. Words were as potent as the physical where they were concerned.

"I missed you."

"You never feel right when we're not together," he said, caressing her legs. "Neither do I."

That was a hell of an admission from the man who needed no one. Tipping her head closer, she traced her nose up his length, and down, letting the tip of her tongue join in until she got to his head, and puckering her lips, she kissed him.

"You still hungry?" he asked.

"Showing my appreciation."

"He feels appreciated, believe me."

Her smile widened as she closed her eyes. "I love him. I love you."

"You sleeping down there? I might get cozy with your pussy again."

"That's the hope," she said on a sigh.

His hair tickled her thigh, indicating he'd elevated his head again.

In the next second, he enticed her clit through his lips. "Sweet nectar."

She snapped her legs down and together, bringing her to an almost kneeling position on his abdomen. "I was kidding," she said, smiling.

Twisting her body around, she tucked her head under his chin and linked their fingers on the bed at his sides. When she closed her legs to nestle between his she deliberately caught his member between her thighs, causing it to fill with blood again.

"Rushe."

"I'll give you a five minute break, no more than that," he grumbled, greatly put out by the idea she might want to rest.

"That's not what I was going to say," she said, bringing her head up so she could look him in the eye. "You do trust me now, don't you?"

"With my life."

Though Rushe was capable of lying to her, she didn't see any hint of deception. They'd been through a lot and nearly lost each other more than once, but he was her priority. Could he be ready to accept that?

FIVE

BREAKFAST IN THE HUGHES house traditionally offered everyone a chance to reflect on the previous night's events, and to inform others of all plans for the day ahead. Put another way, it served as an opportunity to bitch and boast.

Although she'd expected Rushe to be hesitant about joining the family around the table, he wasn't. While traversing the hallway on their way to the breakfast room she tried, and failed, to interlink their fingers. Instead, Rushe hooked her digits into his back pocket, and curled his own hand around the back of her neck to direct her into the room.

Her father held prominence at the head of the table, flanked by Roger and Antoine. Martin sat facing Lucia and beside his wife, her other sister, Vivian. Beverly was seated opposite, with an empty chair at her side. All of those present silenced and turned to examine her and Rushe when they entered, but her lover didn't pause for so much as a heartbeat.

He strode across the room and upon reaching

the table, he urged her forward, yanked out the chair next to Beverly, sat, and pulled her down into his lap.

"Good… morning," Beverly Hughes managed to say.

"Morning," Flick said.

Rushe's hand skimmed down her spine to her ass. Scooping his hand underneath, he gave her a boost. "Fruit," Rushe said.

She stood and bent over the table to reach the dish of fruit salad in the center of the spread. As she ladled it into one of the individual bowls, her love grasped her hips to jerk her ass into his direct line of sight.

With his proprietary squeeze, a smile formed on Flick's lips. "What does everyone have planned for today?" she asked.

On scanning the dumbstruck faces at the table, she stuck on Antoine. The European wasn't amused or shocked, but his astute eyes were fixed on hers. She sat down on Rushe's thigh and forked a slice of peach into his mouth.

Something about the act was so sensual that she forgot all about Antoine. Rushe must've sensed her discomfort, though she didn't know how. His gaze remained glued to hers as he took the fork and tossed it down on the table.

If Flick had been able to think of anything else, she might have noted her family had never been so silent. But Rushe parted his lips just enough to give her a silent command.

Blindly selecting another segment with her fingers, she took it up to his mouth. Her lover dipped forward to take both the fruit and her fingertips in the process.

"This is highly irregular, Felicity," Charles Hughes declared, breaking the trance between her and her love.

Turning his head, Rushe planted a glare on her father. She pushed the bowl to the table and draped her arms around his neck. But his head moved again, and she knew Antoine was getting that same scowl.

With a sigh, her cheek rested on her arm, which remained on his shoulder. Somehow, even in that space Rushe had asserted his dominance over every other man. He was the alpha. She would never know how he sized up a room and took control with such ease, but he'd done it again.

AFTER THAT ENCOUNTER with the family, they hadn't lingered over their meal. It wasn't much later when she was sat on the end of their bed, stroking her hands down her thighs, awaiting her love's re-entry to the bedroom.

"I'm not going to the spa with my sisters," Flick called to Rushe in their bathroom.

"I'm not staying here," Rushe called back.

Pointing her toes, she scrutinized her legs. "I'll put out."

"Généreux de votre part."

Antoine came into view in the open bedroom doorway at the same instant Rushe materialized.

"Get outta here," her love said, marching to be equidistance between her and the trespasser, blocking her from Antoine Mercier's line of sight.

"She is très sexy, une belle femme."

"Fuck off or give me the information, messenger boy."

"You are not proud of your woman?" Antoine asked.

"He's très proud, believe me," Flick said.

"Spirited."

Antoine sauntered into the room, prompting Rushe to move in toward him. If Mercier tried to challenge Rushe's superiority, he was going to lose.

But Serendipity was still in trouble. The only way they had a chance of helping her was to play Antoine's game, at least for now.

"Say your piece and get out of here," she said, getting to her feet.

"I am not the one going somewhere, ma chère."

Antoine handed Rushe a folded slip of paper, which her love opened and read. Blinking his attention back up to Antoine, the two men locked focus.

"Oui?" Antoine asked.

Rushe nodded once.

She approached her lover, and though he would be aware of her, she tucked her hand into his back pocket to indicate her proximity. Out of nothing more than provocation, Mercier lingered over checking out her figure. Rushe growled and took a step toward the Frenchman, so Antoine slunk back and disappeared from their turf.

"Lover?" she asked, grazing her lips on his upper arm.

"We're leaving."

This was an order, a command to be obeyed. The specifics of where they were going or why eluded her, but he was taking her along for the ride. She wouldn't argue. No matter the destination or motivation, she wanted to be at Rushe's flank, and for now at least, he was allowing her to be there.

SIX

THE CAR WOULD be untraceable, and their luggage sparse, but Rushe would have everything they could possibly need. During their last adventure, Rushe almost lost his life. There had been no time to recover from that ordeal, either physically or emotionally. Nevertheless, as they drove on for hours, the steely resolve encompassing Rushe intensified. He was ready for anything.

"What do they want us to do?" she asked, for what had to be the tenth time.

Rushe still didn't answer.

Her reluctance to leave her family was appeased when Rushe made it clear Antoine was there to maintain the threat, but physical harm was unlikely. Antoine had ingratiated himself with the Hughes family and wanted that friendship to continue. The longer he was there, maintaining the association, the longer he could have Rushe do his bidding. The life of privilege and luxury he was living in the Hughes home would appeal to him as well.

She could've stayed with her family, but Rushe

wanted her at his side, and she'd fought for that honor. She wasn't going to give up the chance.

Antoine had resided with her family for two weeks and had been part of their lives for a month. If it had been his intention to indiscriminately hurt them, he'd had ample opportunity to do it.

Rushe also highlighted Antoine wasn't the type to do any dirty work himself. His family had employed Victor, and his lowlife thugs, so they wouldn't have to deal with the unseemly side of trafficking. Profits were what the Merciers wanted, not blood spatter on their designer suits.

"Do you know where Serendipity is?" she asked. "Where they're holding her?"

"No."

"Can we be sure that she's still alive?"

"No, but I've asked to see her, for proof of life," Rushe said. "Keeping her alive gives them leverage. They'll be more likely to sell her on when they've finished anyway, rather than killing her outright."

She nodded. Given Serendipity's beauty and grace, she'd definitely fetch a high price.

"I'm not afraid," she said. Rushe glanced from the road to her. "What we're doing is right, Rushe. I'm not afraid of them."

"You keep your mouth shut. I don't want you mouthing off at anyone. You're gonna do what you're told, Kitten. You speak only when I speak to you, only with my permission."

"But—"

"I can get both of us out of this alive. Having you with me is a risk, but it's less of a risk than having you out there unprotected. You can't leave my side and can only speak when I speak to you."

Her love was a stickler for laying out the rules, as emphasized by him saying the same thing twice.

Miscommunication was another of his peeves.

"I trust you, Lover. But I will act in our best interest."

"I've heard that from you before," he grumbled.

His forethought tortured him. Although he would never admit it, sometimes it weakened him. Rushe envisioned scenarios that led to him losing her. Avoiding that outcome was his highest priority. Neither could deny the influence their wellbeing had on the other anymore. They were each other's greatest asset and biggest burden.

Less than an hour later, Rushe drove off the interstate and down a series of residential streets. The journey from her parents' house in New Hampshire was a long one, but they were definitely back in New Jersey, though she didn't recognize the area.

As she was about to ask where they were going, Rushe pulled up to the curb in front of a brown stucco building and yanked a pair of black gloves from the door.

"What are we—"

"Stay here," Rushe said, donning the gloves without turning off the engine.

Ready to question him further, her words lodged in her throat when he reached under his seat and produced a gun.

He checked the clip and chambered a round. "After this job you're gonna know exactly what I'm capable of, Kitten. It's up to you if you stick around after or not."

"Rushe—"

"Stay."

He left the car so rapidly, she had no time to respond. After storming up the path, Rushe went directly into the house without knocking.

Only a short while ago, he was saying he wanted her with him, except there she found herself abandoned out in the cold, alone.

Two solid bangs preceded a distant roar. They could only have come from one place and been one thing. Rushe came out of the building and strode down the path to re-enter the car and hide the gun under his seat again.

"I'm hungry," Rushe said. "We've gotta be at Silver's in an hour."

"Is he local?" she asked, her words stunted. "Will we be late?"

"I don't give a fuck," Rushe said, driving on. "He can wait."

A few streets went by before she spoke. "Lover, who was that?"

"A rapist," he answered.

Though he said it without intonation, she was surprised by how his candor conveyed his anger.

"You killed him?"

"No, but you can guarantee that's gonna sting."

"You did that for Silver? That's part of the job?"

"Antoine told me last night we'd be working for Silver," Rushe said.

"That was the job on the piece of paper?"

His resolve remained on the road ahead of them, and he stayed quiet. Rushe didn't miss a thing. There was no way he hadn't heard her; he'd chosen not to respond. She wouldn't push but was finished hiding her fears. Rushe had a right not to answer her questions, but she had an equal right to ask them anyway.

SEVEN

AFTER A DRIVE-through meal, Rushe drove them into a wooded park. She expected them to pull into a secluded spot because she assumed he wanted sex. An erotic interlude might be needed as a stress reliever after the shooting job. Except Rushe didn't seem stressed, and as it turned out, they didn't stop. The forested area grew thicker, and the road got bumpy as the concrete wore out, but they didn't park.

Eventually a rolled-apart chain link fence offered an opening at the edge of the trees, and they trundled over worn-out grass toward the back of a house. Other homes flanked the detached timber structure, and three other cars were parked in the shabby yard. Rushe pulled in behind the vehicles and shut off the engine.

"How do you know the back way?"

From their position, she could see it was a residential street that backed onto the forest area they'd emerged from.

"I've been here before," Rushe said.

"What should I expect?"

"Stay close to me," he said, and she nodded. "There will be things—"

"Save it for the bedroom when we're alone," she said. "Say whatever you have to. Touch me wherever you need to. I trust you."

With a single nod, he released his seatbelt and turned to exit. She caught hold of his arm to delay him.

"What?" he asked.

"I love you… No matter what, okay?"

"Out."

After he blasted away from the vehicle, she inhaled and closed her eyes. This was going to be the toughest job yet, for both of them. The slam of the trunk bounced the whole car. Rushe's patience was strained.

Before she could follow through on her plan not to show Theo Silver any fear, she first had to prove her mettle to herself and to her love. Breezing out of the car, she rounded it to where Rushe tossed their new duffel over his shoulder. She didn't say a word, only hooked her hand into his back pocket and gathered herself close.

Rushe had told her once he didn't trust her because he couldn't predict her actions. It made sense to her now. If she was erratic or disobedient, he couldn't anticipate her position. Her love relied on his forethought being accurate, and she was an anomaly.

Intent on his path, he took them toward the house, up the narrow back stairs, through the screen and across a wide kitchen. A rabble of jeering voices dulled when she and Rushe came into the living room.

A pool table dominated the center. Couches lined the perimeter, all angled to view the ongoing game. The front window was covered with gray gauze that let in light but prevented them from seeing what was beyond.

Rushe remained just inside the room, zoned in on the black man folded into a Barca-lounger in the corner. Well dressed and cool, the man had no muscle mass, but his knees were raised so high he had to be all height.

"You made it," he said.

"Silver," Rushe replied.

"What's that? You brought me a present?"

"You want me to stay, so I brought my shit."

"Your property?" Silver said. "Is that right?"

"Problem?"

"She's smokin'," a male voice mumbled.

She didn't want to identify the body it went with.

"You know we've got supplies here," Silver said.

"Brought my own."

"Cody, take him up," Silver said. "Five minutes, we gotta talk."

A young guy, in maybe his early twenties, gave his pool cue to another guy and crossed to an internal door in the corner. As she trailed behind Rushe, she noticed the perpendicular door had nine different locks, that had to be the way in and out the front.

The man, Cody, took them through the door and up a set of enclosed stairs to a hallway with various rooms leading off it. He stopped at the second door on the left and shoved it aside.

"Bathroom's next along," Cody said and sloped off.

Rushe led her into the bedroom and tossed the duffel to the bed. She kept hold of the denim until he unlatched her and attached her fingers to the metal of the footrail.

"What now?" she asked, when her love closed the bedroom door. "You have to talk to him? Work for him? Rushe—"

"We're staying here. It's the price we pay."

"For my freedom, or our lives? How does this help Serendipity?"

"Kitten," he said with a tone of warning. "Settle in. This will be just like before, but you're gonna do what you're told this time."

Tension radiated from him; his anger was infuriation. He wasn't the type to run errands for others. The only time he'd be caught doing it was in extreme circumstances. Right then, it was the price for their lives.

Jansen had assured her safety; he'd rescued her and helped her rescue Rushe. Now he lay in a hospital bed, unconscious, with a chance he may never wake again.

Serendipity was Jansen's woman, out there alone and defenseless. Rushe had too much honor to let that slide, to tuck tail and run to save himself. So he'd go after Serendipity, and only Flick's life would be a price too high to pay for her liberation.

He viewed it as his responsibility to ensure her safety above all else, and she saw it as her responsibility to ensure his sanity. Slinking toward him, she laid her hands on his biceps and let them glide up his arms to his shoulders.

"What are you doing?" he grumbled.

"Doesn't this feel nice," she whispered, reminiscent of a time they'd shared in the shack.

Carrying on their journey, she linked her fingers at the back of his neck and with no assistance, levered her weight up until she was off her feet. Winding her legs around his torso, she let the cushion of her lips meet his. He didn't respond, but that didn't deter her. Insinuating the tip of her tongue between the seam of his mouth, he opened before she touched his teeth.

On instinct, his mouth seized hers. Charging forward with his long gait, they crashed against the wall. Robbing her hands from the back of his neck, he smacked them to the wall, far above her head.

"Are you trying to tempt me, Kitten?"

"If I was doing that, I'd be on my knees," she purred.

With a huff, Rushe tilted his head to kiss her again. The potency of the blending of their mouths had her knees trying to ascend, but the weight of him immobilized her.

"You gonna ride my cock good?" he asked. "Speak."

"Yes," she breathed. "Yes, sir."

"How deep can you take me?"

"Lover," she whimpered, and tried to move her hands but he slammed them back.

"When I want it, you spread your legs and take it," he growled. "When I want it."

"I want to help," she said. His feral focus on her mouth drifted upward. "Make you feel good."

"Fuck out the frustration?"

"Yeah," she exhaled and tipped forward to kiss his jaw.

His forehead landed on hers, bumping her head back against the wall. "Kit..." he murmured without elaborating.

"What? What is it, Lover?"

Straightening his form, she saw torture in his eyes. That only usually reared its head when she cried.

Drawing the shutters up over his expression, he backed away. "Stay," he barked.

She stumbled to her feet, and using the wall to catch her balance, she watched him turn and exit the bedroom. What was in his mind? Something else had been on his lips, but he'd chosen not to say it. Pushing him wouldn't necessarily help, and she was used to living in wonder where her love was concerned.

EIGHT

FOR THE REST of the day, she was alone in the bedroom. With its king bed, it was a decent size and had a small window overlooking the same back yard where Rushe parked the car. So overall, the environment was more comfortable than the one they'd existed in at the shack.

Occasional movement outside the door kept her on alert, in part in case of trouble, though she didn't predict any. Rushe was there and he'd never leave her in danger. What she wanted most was her lover to return.

Downstairs had been alive with noise of conversation and the odd shouted command. But she hadn't been able to distinguish Rushe's voice.

Darkness began to descend outside. Should she get ready for bed? Rushe could be down there all night. No point in waiting if he was going to be busy. The noise level increased, indicating more people had arrived. Music started and gradually it got louder, the traffic certainly grew, there was a party going on.

Given their history, she wasn't inclined to go

down and investigate. But she did want to see Rushe, wanted to know he was okay. He had brought her there to protect her. As he'd said, the risk was greater for her to be out in the world alone than to be surrounded by these crooks. But she felt alone. As much as she hated herself for it, she was anxious about the number of people. A party meant alcohol, and this man Silver was a pimp.

Rushe could be down there. He could need help but wouldn't flee without her if there was trouble. Maybe he was stuck. She lay back and propped her feet up on the duffel still at the foot of the bed.

Just as she settled on the decision to stay there and trust Rushe had everything under control, the bedroom door opened. Bracing on her elbows, she expected to see her lover. But it wasn't him. Three men of varying heights and ethnicity bundled into the room. Seeking out a weapon hadn't been a priority, though it probably should have been.

"See..." the shortest one said. "He brought us a present."

"I'm nobody's present," she said.

All three came closer.

The one at the rear flung the door closed. "What's your rate, honey?"

"Too high for you," she said, getting onto her knees.

"I say we get ourselves a free sample."

"You don't wanna do that," the one who hadn't spoken yet said, showing a gold tooth in place of an upper canine. "Rushe say you could?"

"Rushe doesn't say nothing," the short one said.

"That's 'cause he doesn't have to," she said. "He'll rip your dick off for even thinking about bringing it near me."

Luckily, her lingering consideration of leaving

the room to go downstairs meant she hadn't taken off her shoes yet. So when the cocky one grinned and pounced toward the bed, she snatched off one shoe and held it aloft, setting her kneeling stance higher.

"Hey, man, I'd listen to her," the one with the gold tooth said. "You heard about what he did to Barney?"

"Yeah, yeah, I heard that too," the short one said.

She didn't know who Barney was, but the cocky one was discouraged enough to turn to his friends. "That ain't true."

"It is, it is," Gold Canine said. "I heard his girl paid Rushe, paid him to gut Barney like a fish."

"He didn't gut him," the short one said, and peered at her. "He tied him up and slit him open. Just enough to let the rats burrow in and eat him from the inside out... took him hours to die."

"He's not gonna do shit like that in Silver's place, no way," the cocky one said, and whirled around. "I say we test her out."

She didn't wait for him to advance and sprang to her feet on the bed knowing the added height gave her a better vantage point. Raising her shoe high, she smacked it down on the cocky one's head. He howled and bowed down for half a second, then reared up and grabbed her wrist. She kicked out to try freeing herself but lost her shoes in the melee.

While he wrestled her off the bed, she made as much noise and ruckus as she could. She stumbled to the floor and only just managed to get out of the path of his vicious kick aimed at her head.

The other guys were jabbering. One of them was shouting something about Silver, the other wasn't as lucid. She concentrated on returning to a fighting stance, except without her shoes, she had no height and had lost her weapons. The cocky one brought his hand across her face, sending her to the floor again. She spotted a shoe just under the end of the bed and scrambled to grab it.

Using the frame to support herself, she thrashed around, swiping at his kneecap with enough force to send him crashing to the floor beside her. He yelped and cursed, stealing a handful of her hair.

She smacked him in the head with her shoe again and the fucker fell back. Her triumph was short-lived. He cursed at her again and went for the buckle of his belt. Whipping it free of its loops, he balanced his weight on one leg, and clambered to his feet.

Yeah, no way she would stay there and wait for the flogging. She leaped up, but he seized a fistful of her hair, and though she tried to wrestle free, burning pain brought her back down to her knees where he wanted her.

The joy of retribution clamped her attacker's teeth, she sneered on meeting his eye. He could do his worst; she would never let him see her tremble. He brought the belt up, and she gritted her own teeth behind her lips waiting for the pain.

The belt began to descend and then it was gone, barely glancing off her. The hand was wrenched from her hair. She blinked. Rushe. Her love had the guy flat on the wall. He landed one punch, and another, until blood poured from the cocky bastard's mouth. Still, Rushe hit him again.

The short one and Gold Canine had fled, leaving their buddy alone to fight the battle he'd started. She wasn't going to stop Rushe yet. She wanted that bastard to think twice before attacking any woman in the future.

"I'm sorry!" the guy screamed and tried to fight.

Rushe had him by the throat, his arm pressed into the guy's chest, pinning him to the same wall she had been against earlier. Her love growled and punched again before letting the guy fall to the ground.

He backed off. "Apologize to her," Rushe snarled.

"I'm sorry! I'm sorry!" the guy whimpered and tried to crawl toward the exit.

Rushe kicked him to the side, securing him under his boot. "I haven't heard her accept. You're not going anywhere."

Rushe's boot moved higher. Toeing the assailant's chin out of the way, he increased the pressure of his stance on the guy's throat. The cocky bastard wasn't so cocky as he choked and coughed while clawing at the footwear in charge of his fate.

She got to her feet and took a slow breath. "I accept, let him go."

Her love's growl rose as his gaze leaped to her, without releasing the pressure on his prey. He didn't want to free this guy, because Rushe wanted him to suffer for hurting her. When her love huffed and his pupils dilated, it was obvious he was more animal in this second than human.

"Lover," she whispered.

With another grumble, he kicked the guy loose. "No second chances," Rushe barked, and kicked the guy again as he crawled out the ajar door and scrambled to close it, presumably to prevent the predator from attacking again.

Her attention stayed on the door until Rushe blocked her view by clamping his hands on the footrail on either side of her, trapping her against the bed.

"He hurt you."

"Yes," she said, pushing her hair from her shoulder. "But I've been hit in the face before, more so since I met you." Rushe wasn't ready to joke, he bared his teeth in frustration at her request that he release her attacker. "If you hurt him, Silver will be mad, maybe Mercier too. It won't do anything for Serendipity, and it won't do anything for us."

"You are my woman."

"And I'll still be your woman no matter how many bruises I get," she said. "A few scars won't change how you feel about me."

"You pissed him off. That mouth, my mouth, you keep it shut."

"Getting him angry, fighting my corner, it buys time. If I hadn't done that, you'd have walked in on a much worse scene. I told him you'd rip his dick off if he tried to touch me with it."

"I'll rip it off now," he snarled, and his arms bent in a prelude to boosting himself away.

She caught his ribs. "Forget him. I've been without you enough today. I was worried."

"But you stayed here."

"Because I didn't know what I'd be walking into if I came downstairs," she said, caressing his body. "I told you I trust you."

"You're vulnerable here," he said, as though trying to sort through scenarios in his mind.

"I'm safe, Rushe. I'm here. We're together. Please tell me you won't leave me again tonight."

His hand landed on her head. When he stroked down, she smiled. "You fought him."

"You always sound so amazed when you say things like that," she said, ducking down to retrieve her shoe from the floor. "From now on I'm wearing stilettos everywhere we go. I think he'd have thought twice about the belt if I'd put one of those in his ear."

"Shoes," he grumbled, and took the footwear from her to toss it aside.

Reaching over her, he hauled up the duffle to open the top. Stuffing his hand inside, he pulled it out a couple of seconds later to present her with his pocketknife.

"I suppose I should've looked for that before they came in."

"You arm yourself," he said. "Do not let this leave your side. You take it with you everywhere, and do not hesitate to use it. I'll clean up the mess for you."

"How romantic," she said, sliding the knife out of his hand. "With this knife, I'll thee butcher."

"You don't have to kill him," Rushe said. "Just maim him enough to slow him down and leave a trail of blood. Give me a path to follow so I can go finish the job for you."

"Oh, you're such a sweet talker," she said, stretching her arms up to his shoulders. As she was about to pull herself closer, something caught the corner of her eye.

Pushing him aside, she yanked open the duffel and touched the fabric that had drawn her attention. Fingering the material, her eyes misted, and she took them to Rushe. Her stoic, incredible Rushe.

"Rushe," she whispered.

He shrugged. "You love it."

"You hate it…" She pulled the shirt out of the bag. "Because it reminds you of how we met."

Since being carried out of the Waterside Hotel on their last job, she assumed everything left there was lost. Virtually everything they'd owned was in that hotel, in the building where Rushe almost died.

"I sent Eric in that night to get everything. There was sensitive information in that room."

No there wasn't, Rushe would never be so careless as to leave anything personally sensitive lying around. The relevant mission paperwork had been discovered, and most likely destroyed, by those it incriminated.

Sliding her arms into the sleeves of the red and black shirt that drowned her, she brought the crinkled material to her nose, tucking it behind the collar. This was the shirt Rushe had provided for her to sleep in the night they met.

Recalling that offering of comfort warmed her, but he didn't like the reminder of how weak she was then. It only highlighted to him all the things he'd done to her, what they'd been through, and how he'd changed her. She would thank him for every one of those things, he didn't always feel the same way.

"The idea wasn't to hide your body," he said, trying to push the shirt from her shoulders.

She stole his hands. "I want you to make love to me."

"Wearing the shirt?"

She had to smile at the sneer her lover wore. Odd that such a mundane suggestion would be a step too far towards kinky for him.

"I didn't mean that," she said. "I want to ignore the noise, and the people, and the danger—"

"It's the danger that gets you off."

"You get me off."

The slope of his brow told her his thought wasn't far away from hers. Rushe and danger were synonymous.

"I only care about your body and mine," she said.

"Naked. Now."

"Yes, sir."

NINE

USUALLY THE EXPERIENCE of showering together was lengthy, luxurious, and eventful. That morning hadn't been like that. The shower stall was barely big enough for one, so after waiting for Rushe to wash, she'd been left alone to finish her own bathing. On drawing back the shower curtain, Rushe was there, leaning against the door with his arms folded across his broad chest. His obvious grump made her smile.

It could be because they hadn't had sex this morning. More likely, the reminder of their first adventure caused his grouchy mood. He'd had to stand guard for her like this then too. Rushe didn't trust the men there any more than he'd trusted the men in that shack. She was vulnerable just because she was a woman, and the only one there that she'd seen yet.

Theo Silver was supposed to be a pimp, but she hadn't seen any indication of sex for sale when they arrived. Perhaps if she'd been at the party last night, she might have witnessed evidence of it.

Back in the bedroom, Rushe threw clothes at her

as she combed her hair. The act revealed they had somewhere to be, it wasn't like him to choose her wardrobe. Finding out he'd had Eric go back and retrieve their things brought a lump to her throat.

Other things were still in the trunk of their car because she'd heard them rattling around. But he'd put that shirt in their primary duffel.

Thinking about it, another smile curled her lips. As Rushe stuffed everything back into the bag, she sauntered over and pulled herself up to sit on the bed footrail. Leaning in, she kissed his tee-shirt covered shoulder.

He paused. "We've got work to do," he grumbled, and hooked the loops of the duffel.

"Do you think kissing your shoulder is my way of seducing you?"

Slithering her hand around his arm, she reached for his belt buckle, ready to prove just how she would approach him if that had been her motive. Rushe shunted the bag away, snatched her arm, and skimmed her ass along the rail. If he hadn't caught her knees and clamped them against his hips, she'd have lost her balance.

"Get your guard up," he growled. "Don't think about sex."

"I wasn't thinking about sex," she said, tucking her fingers into his pockets. "I was thinking about love."

"What kind of love?" he asked, tipping his chin down.

Obviously, he didn't believe her intentions were innocent. "Hmm, I'm alone in a room with my boyfriend, whom I have pledged my heart and my body to. What kind of love could I be thinking about?"

"You show interest in getting fucked, and someone will take you up on it."

As much as he liked to warn her, to scare her into

submission, she had to sigh. "You're the only one here. Who else is going to take me up on it? The bed bugs?"

"Thought you weren't thinking about sex."

So now he thought he'd caught her out? She laughed. "Lover, not that I'm saying I was, but I'm allowed to fantasize about your body, about having sex with you. Does it make you feel violated to know I do that?"

"You're messing around, and we're in a serious situation."

"Yes," she said, attempting to straighten her face. "Yes, a man and a woman, in love, alone in a bedroom, it's very terrifying… hold me."

He grumbled and nudged her shoulder, sending her back onto the bed. Moments of safety were rare. Although the big picture was oppressive at the moment, she couldn't let him forget that they had each other. It was important to appreciate these times they did share, because they had no idea what was on the horizon. So she let herself laugh, but when he turned on her, melancholy saturated his expression.

"You trust me too much," he muttered.

Sobering, she clambered to her knees. "Don't do that, Lover. Okay, I'm sorry. You're right. You don't have to push me away, and you don't have to do anything stupid."

"You're joking around like we're on vacation."

"I love you, Rushe, and it makes me happy. I'm sorry if I let that show sometimes."

"Don't do that snippy thing," he said, approaching the end of the bed again.

"Me? You're the one telling me I trust you too much. Tell me why I shouldn't trust you? You've died for me, Rushe."

"You want me to do it again?"

"No!"

"Then get your fucking guard up!"

Slamming his hands on the foot bar, he loomed over her, pinning her under that glare.

When she relaxed, she wasn't just risking her own life, she was risking his. "You're right, I'm sorry."

Sometimes the joy of love she felt with him overshadowed the depth of the dilemma they were in. Pushing her shoulders back, she was about to slump when he grabbed her chin and jerked her upward.

Clashing his mouth onto hers, he showed his own love for her in the intensity of that kiss. His lips worked hers, reminding her of the connection they shared. Even if he wasn't as comfortable languishing in it as she was, he still felt she was an extension of him.

On releasing her, he shoved her backward to her haunches. When she noticed the curl of his lips as he turned away, it was clear he hadn't rid himself of the morning's frustration.

He retrieved the duffel from the bed and hefted it to his shoulder. Bringing their possessions with them could indicate they weren't coming back, or it could simply mean he didn't trust anyone there. Not exactly a news flash.

Grabbing her arm, he dragged her off the bed and pulled her toward the door. To free up a hand, he stuck hers into his back jeans pocket, so she'd follow when he took them out of the room, down the hall and the stairs, into the room with the pool table.

Silver was in the same chair he'd been in last night, but Rushe didn't stop to talk to him, or to the other four guys occupying the space.

"Hold up!" Silver said when they were almost in the kitchen. "Take Cody with you."

"Not a chance."

The man who'd shown them to their lodgings the previous night came in their direction, indicating that choice apparently wasn't part of the deal.

"You let him keep an eye on things. You might need backup."

She wasn't naive enough to believe she could be useful combat support for Rushe. But she didn't think this guy, Cody, would be looking out for the best interests of anyone except himself.

"Whatever."

Rushe didn't argue and continued out of the house to the beaten up yard where the car was parked. After tossing the duffel into the trunk, he opened the back passenger door. She wasn't going to question him, but he dropped his mouth to her hair when he turned her to face the car.

"I don't trust him behind you. Seatbelt."

She hadn't shown Rushe she had the knife in her pocket. He'd given it to her and told her to keep it on her, and that was what she planned to do. Propelling her into the backseat, Rushe closed the door and got into the driving seat.

By putting her there, in that position, he was not only protecting her from attack, but situating her in place to protect him if need be.

Rushe's forethought was clear, she was smart enough to recognize when it was in play. If this Cody person tried anything while Rushe was driving, her love's options were limited. In the back, she had optimum placement to defend them.

Rushe put a hand to Cody's headrest to reverse the car, and as he slowed in the angle, he glanced at her. She didn't smile because he was checking her guard, so she made it clear she understood and was prepared to do whatever was needed.

TEN

"YOU GOTTA BE CAREFUL with this guy," Cody said, having spoken for most of the nearly half hour-long drive. "Teague has got a lot of swagger but he's smart too."

"Are you afraid of him?" she asked, filling the silence Rushe wouldn't.

She herself had been guilty of rabbiting on while they traveled. Rushe told her after the fact that it drove him crazy, but he never complained as it was happening. Then again, he never switched off, never stopped gathering information. The chances were he could probably recite back to her more than half of the things she'd said, though she wouldn't recall them herself.

"I ain't afraid of him," Cody said, peering around at her.

The young man had a very expressive mouth, his lips constantly moved when he spoke, more than necessary. But the quirk was endearing. This man was human, and often in their line of work the players were anything but.

"Other people are?" she asked, not prepared to question any gangster's front, human or not.

"Hell, yeah! How do you think he got away with it for so long?"

She didn't know what he'd got away with, but if Silver was sending Rushe to this guy's door, there had to be a reason.

"Has he had other… visits?"

"Yeah, Silver sends guys round all the time. Teague hasn't coughed up yet."

This was about money? If it was Rushe's job to scare this person, it was one he was suited for. How far would he have to go? The previous day, he'd walked into that stucco building with a gun and hadn't had time to talk to anyone. Teague could be about to receive the same treatment.

"Have you visited him?"

"Me? That ain't my job," Cody said. "I—"

"Quiet," Rushe said.

Cody stalled, looked from her to Rushe, then his eyes slunk forward as he dissolved into his seat to face the windshield. She flopped back. It wasn't like she'd been trying to extract information, they were having a conversation. Having Rushe trust her to protect them one minute, and prevent her from learning in the next, was irritating. But, in front of an audience, she couldn't argue with him.

So she let the rest of the journey pass quietly. Not that there was much of it. Rushe pulled into the parking lot of a narrow apartment complex and turned off the engine. When he'd been shooting without hesitation, he'd left the engine running, so this had to be a different scenario.

"If you bring the chick, he'll definitely fuck her," Cody said to Rushe.

"You want to bet," she mumbled.

"Your call, man."

Cody got out of the car but stayed next to it and lit up a cigarette to smoke as he waited for Rushe.

"You're gonna stay here," Rushe said to her.

"If you're going to give me a line about keeping look out or something…" she said. "You can trust me, Rushe."

"I don't know what we're walking into. He could have ten armed guys up there."

Shirking her sulk, she bounced to the edge of her seat to lean between the front two. "Then you're staying here with me. I don't want you walking into a situation like that without someone you trust… I can be useful to you."

"You are."

His focus remained out the windshield, he liked to maintain control. Most of his life was lived behind that mask, letting her peek beneath still pained him.

"For more than sex… You don't think I would take a bullet for you?"

Now his glare snapped around to her. "You don't ever talk like that. Stay."

At least she'd made him angry. He slammed out of the car and marched off across the mass of concrete between their vehicle and the structure, with Cody scurrying to keep up. Puffing out a breath, she sat back and drummed her fingernails on the upholstery.

Everything in her wanted to follow. She wanted to be with him, to be at his side. But she had told him he could do the thug stuff alone. She wasn't scary and wouldn't want to undermine his intimidation. The last thing she needed to be was a liability; they'd been there too many times before.

So quietly seething over the fact she had once again been shunned, she tried to shed her petulance. She was pissed off because he was out there, without her, and he might need her. But she would be useless in a fight, they both knew she'd only be a distraction.

Calmly slowing her breaths, she reminded herself of Rushe's strengths. He could get himself out of tight jams. He'd lived a troubled and dangerous life long before they'd met.

About fifteen minutes passed and having succeeded in calming herself, worry began to take over. Her anxiety this time wasn't about missing out, or over trust issues that might exist between them. Now her concern was what to do if they didn't return.

She had no contacts and no phone. If something happened, she couldn't call for back up and certainly couldn't call the cops. What options were there?

A shout cut into her thoughts. Deep and masculine, but like a scream.

Scanning around, there was no obvious source of the noise, until something falling from the air passed her vision. A dull smack sounded when it hit the ground at the foot of the apartment building, and the yell abruptly ceased.

She was too far away to see details, but she was almost sure that unmoving mass was a body. No one passed by, no one else saw anything or came rushing over. She was torn between the shock of what she'd witnessed and her urge to do something, though she didn't know what. She was still sitting static when Rushe and Cody re-appeared and got back into the car.

Rushe started the engine and pulled out of the lot as if nothing at all had happened. Maybe it hadn't. Maybe she imagined the whole thing.

"Was that—"

"Don't ask," Cody said.

"Seatbelt," Rushe said through gritted teeth.

Without anything better to do, she complied without a word.

ON THE JOURNEY back, Cody had been much quieter, but she was glad of the mental breather. When there was no talking, time in the car often gave her a chance to reflect. From experience, Rushe liked to take the time to think too.

Eventually they got back to Silver's. Rushe parked in the same spot as before. Cody got out and traipsed into the house, but her love lingered at the wheel, so she stayed put. Unsure if he was going to say something, or if he expected her to, she let the silence hang. But they couldn't stay there forever. When he moved to exit, she did too. Both closed their doors at the same time, her love just stood there and didn't head for the house.

A few seconds passed before he looked at her. His eyes were empty, yet filled with something, hope, maybe, or shame.

Stepping into his body, she curled her lips and slid her hand up onto his stubbled jaw. "I trust you," she whispered.

Though their eyes remained locked, his hands skimmed over her hip, and he jolted her back against the car. Bending his knees, he lifted her against the vehicle, and she cupped his face as his mouth devoured hers.

Rushe had never had acceptance in his life, he'd never had trust, not like this. Inside, she saw the soul of a good man, with a good heart, and honest intentions. He just wasn't constrained by the rules of others. Maybe his approach could be brutal, but if Rushe was at your door, if Rushe hurt you, there was a reason for it. She was tolerant of his methods because she believed in him, she trusted him.

"It's been a while since we've done it on the hood," she said, wrapping her arms around his neck until her hands curled around her own elbows.

"I don't share," he growled.

And because she knew for a fact that was the only thing preventing him from taking her there, outside, in broad daylight, she laughed and kissed him again.

"Knock it off!"

Rushe's mouth vanished as he simultaneously released her onto her feet and spun to face the voice, keeping her sandwiched between his spine and the car.

"What?" Rushe demanded.

"We got trouble," Cody said.

Her love glanced at her with ideas of what had been interrupted still flitting across his expression. But he took her hand and led her into the house.

In the living room, Silver was still in his seat. Three other men were in the room already, one of whom was Cody. All looked as pissed as the next.

"My on-site watchman just got himself arrested!"

"Using?" Rushe asked, slipping himself in front of her.

Letting her remain in the room, showed great progress. Back when they'd first met, he would dismiss her from the room when the men started to talk business. Not anymore.

"Yeah," Silver snapped.

"On premises?"

"No! Fuck!"

"Don't think he's that dumb," Cody said.

The riled Silver was angry, Rushe clearly had an idea of what was going on. She didn't have a clue. Except that was no time for questions.

"You gotta get over there."

"No," Rushe said. "That wasn't the deal."

"Fine," Silver said, passive-aggressively cool. "Then the place will be unprotected."

"Send one of these guys."

"Rushe," Silver said, drawling out his name in a way which somehow conveyed a secret message for no one else in the room to understand.

She could almost hear her love grinding his teeth together. "Fine."

"Leave your shit here if you want," Silver said.

"Not a chance."

At breakneck speed, she and Rushe were out of the house. With Cody glued to their heels, the three were in the car again, driving somewhere new.

She didn't know what this new development entailed. Whatever it was, Rushe wasn't happy about it. Having Cody present meant she couldn't question what was happening. Trusting her love was the only option.

ELEVEN

THIS JOURNEY wasn't as long as the first. They drove to the most built-up part of town and through, until they came to a single-story detached building on the outskirts of a neighborhood that didn't seem too savory. A gang of at least twenty men hung around at the corner on the end of the block, all of whom looked their way when Rushe stopped the car up to the storefront.

Half a dozen long blacked-out windows ran from left to right, and then the next six were dressed promising what was inside. Mannequins dressed up in leather and lingerie, inflatable dolls, intimate toys… Yeah, it was a sex store.

Cody got out, like this was nothing, and Rushe followed without delay. Until Rushe opened her door, she'd assumed she was to stay put again.

"Out."

Unable to argue, she did as told. At the last location, she'd desperately wanted to be a part of the job, to be useful. Now, there, the window intimidated her so much that she dreaded to think what could be lurking inside.

Cody went to the store entrance and held it open for her. With a hand on her lower back, Rushe urged her forward, thrusting her into a cornucopia of merchandise she couldn't begin to understand, let alone identify.

Lingerie unlike anything she had seen decorated the walls, shelves offered toys and lubricants, beads and plugs, restraints and paddles. She couldn't close her eyes to it. Two sides were dedicated to pornography, magazines and videos, DVD's and books, everything was explicit, yet Rushe and Cody were unmoved.

Actually, they had moved. They were on the other side of the store while she remained agape in the doorway. Cody shoved aside some hanging beads to carry on.

Rushe held them to scowl back at her. "Come."

She might not have caused his anger, but she got the brunt of it. Scurrying across to him, he shoved her into a short passage where Cody was holding another door. A metal door with a buzzer entry, seemed a strange thing to have at the back of a store. Especially if it was just protecting stock or…

She went through and knew straight away the store was a front, in more ways than one. A dozen women, in various states of undress, loitered around. Though there were no windows, and the space was painted a dark gray, the pink lighting made the place feel cozy, though an unmistakable carnal aura hovered.

To her left were two rows of perpendicular chairs. From there, a corridor lead away from the room, and a curved reception desk at the head of the room was painted the same gray color as the walls. On the other side of that desk, almost straight ahead, was a curtain. She couldn't see what was beyond it.

Cody was at the desk grinning ear to ear, talking to the chest of a young Hispanic woman. Her entry drew attention, but none of the women reacted to her.

Then Rushe came in at her back.

She was used to all sorts of responses when people first saw Rushe. Some people were intimidated, some were scared, or sad, or angry. Some even tried to puff themselves up. But she'd never seen this.

Six of the women, including the one at the reception desk Cody had been talking to, all grinned, shrieked, and rushed toward them.

"Oh my God!"

The women knocked her aside to get to Rushe, they hugged, cooed, and screamed at him with unadulterated delight. He didn't say anything; there wasn't much of a chance, but his expression relaxed enough to reveal he was happy, or at least not sad, to see these women too. He touched a shoulder here, a chin, a cheekbone, stroked the hair of one and tipped aside the head of another to inspect a faded bruise.

"Watchman's room's back here."

Cody's voice was up close, but she couldn't tear her eyes from the strange sight of these women fawning over Rushe.

"What's all the… oh my God!"

A woman wearing nothing but a lace camisole ran from the mouth of the corridor across the room to throw her arms around Rushe.

"Right, Lilah," Rushe said, when the lace-clad blonde didn't let go.

Lilah shook her head and gazed up at him with adoring eyes. "Cody shoulda known better than to bring you here. She ain't here tonight."

Another of the women gasped while the other females fussed. "You're here for Tawny? She's not here. No, she's not here tonight."

"I'm not here for Tawn."

"You taking over?" Lilah asked. "Please tell me

you're coming back."

For the first time, her love lifted his eyes over the top of the women stroking him to set them on her. Her eyes were dry, she couldn't blink and only noticed her chin had been hanging loose when she brought her teeth together with a clack.

The women followed Rushe's gaze.

Lilah stepped away from the group. "You brought us a new thing?" she asked, wandering closer, looking her up and down with a critical but friendly eye. "She's a beaut, she got experience?"

Unsure whether to compare herself to a used car or livestock, she blinked when the woman came so close she had to lean back.

"She ain't for you," Rushe said. "Cody."

"Yeah. Yeah. Yeah."

Cody took hold of her arm and gave her such a pull that she stumbled. "Wait a minute…" she said

"Not now."

Cody kept pulling, and she was still too flabbergasted to argue with Rushe's clipped words. This was a whorehouse, but the women didn't look ill or abused. Other than that one pale bruise Rushe had noticed, there was no sign of harm. Dragged through the curtain, she and Cody went up a narrow hall that opened into a pentagram-shaped hallway.

"Through there you got a bathroom," Cody said pointing to the door to the left. On the right, he opened another door and urged her inside. "This here's the watchman's room. You stay here until Rushe comes."

She opened her mouth, but Cody closed the door before she could speak. The unmistakable snick of a lock followed. As his footsteps disappeared, she rushed to the door and rattled it, but she was locked in.

Waiting for Rushe could mean waiting hours. The space was a decent size with a queen bed, and a couch facing a flat-screen TV. In the corner straight ahead was a fridge with a microwave on top and a couple of kitchen cabinets.

There she was, in another prison. Just like every time before, she hadn't the faintest idea what was going on.

SHE'D TURNED ON the TV to check it worked, but at sounds from outside the room she turned it off. After listening for a while, two things became clear. First, she couldn't make out different voices, let alone individual words. And second, this room shared walls with the reception area, store, and the hallway behind the curtain, which meant she could hear a lot of activity, but no one was actually coming to her.

The linen on the bed hadn't been washed and smelled musty, so she decided against lying on it. The couch was leather and seemed clean enough, so she sat on that and put the TV on again.

The TV was never going to hold her attention. She paced and riled herself into anger. Eventually, she got so bored that she just longed for company. When hunger crept in, she checked the fridge to find an expired jug of milk. The cabinets held nothing but canned soup, and there was no can opener in the place. Whoever bought the soup had apparently taken the can opener with them when they left.

The only windows were frosted narrow slits up high on the wall next to the bed. She couldn't make out any external details. The light faded, dark came in again, and she was still there, alone, without answers.

TWELVE

ON A GROAN of displeasure, she tried to resist the invading arm when it pushed under her shoulder blades, but she was lifted in spite of her feeble protest. It was only when she was laid down and a grubby smell assaulted her senses that she remembered her location.

She immediately opened her eyes and pounced up, away from the smell, shoving Rushe aside in the process.

"It's just me," he muttered. "Do you think I would let a stranger come in here to you?"

She blinked and squeezed her eyes shut as she tried to overcome the transition of asleep to awake.

"The sheets are filthy," she croaked, rubbing her face, trying to find her voice.

"You think 'cause this is a brothel every bed's been used by the product?"

Raising her chin, she re-discovered her anger. "You're going to come in here and get pissy with me? You think if you get mad first, if you're the one to pick the fight, that I'll forget what went on here today? Smell the sheets, asshole, it's not spunk I'm worried about, it's fucking lice," she roared and turned her back on him.

"There's plenty clean."

She sensed more than saw him move.

Whipping around, she stumbled forward a few steps. "Please don't lock me in."

A panic she hadn't processed colored her tone. She rolled her lips into her mouth, trying to belatedly conceal it.

"You were scared," he said, coming back toward her. "You think I brought you to a whorehouse to leave you here?"

She shook her head. When he came into her personal space and dropped a hand to the top of her head, she let him take her other one and tuck it into his pocket.

"You are my woman."

"I know," she said, with a long inhale. "I need to pee."

"Come."

"I don't need you to take me," she snapped and pushed past him to head for the room Cody had pointed out.

Though it didn't make sense why he had when he planned to lock her in.

The restroom was small and functional but blessedly clean. She took time over washing her hands and her face. A gaggle of female voices just outside the door slowed her actions. She actually waited on the other side of the locked restroom door until she heard Rushe's voice.

"Get, the lot of you."

The women laughed and there was more movement. Only when it died down did she open the door. Rushe stood on the other side of the hall, in the bedroom doorway.

She didn't say anything but knew he was watching her. He wanted to judge her mood, to control the situation, and he wanted to anticipate every argument she could throw at him. But she just waited, fixated on his chest, until he moved aside. The bedclothes had been changed. Guess that explained the women and the noise.

"What else do they do for you?"

"Whatever the hell I want," he said. "I've been out there all day having sex."

"Did I say that?" she asked.

She spun as he simultaneously slammed the door. Her hands came up and she stepped forward, frozen at the thought he'd just trapped them.

"We've got a key," he said, fishing one out of his pocket to show her.

"You've got a key! Rushe, I have been in here all day, alone, without a clue about what was going on! I thought we were past this! I thought we had trust! I thought we had—"

"Can we save the earache for another time," he said, dropping to the bed to unlace his boots.

"You're a complete jerk!"

"Whatever," he said, tugging off his tee-shirt and flinging it to the floor.

"You've been here before. How can you exploit these women to line Silver's pockets?"

"Don't judge what you don't know," Rushe spouted her own words back to her.

Locking his fingers behind his head, he lay down on the bed. Her anger receded to a deeper curiosity when she frowned at his jeans. Since they'd been together, he'd never gone to sleep wearing his jeans, or wearing anything for that matter. If she thought about trying to go to bed in as much as a thong, he'd rip the apparel from her and command her to spend the rest of the night making amends for her insult.

"Are there cameras in here?" she asked, scanning for clues.

The only reason he wouldn't initiate intimacy or sex was if he would be expected to perform for an audience, in other words, share her.

Rushe muttered something she didn't hear then said, "Kill the light."

The steam left her funnel. Refusing to engage her meant no argument and no explanation. If he didn't want to talk or have sex, something serious was troubling him.

Putting her own grievances aside, she switched off the light. "Can I take off my clothes?"

"Do what the fuck you want," he grumbled.

"I don't know where we are, Rushe. If we're being watched—"

"This place is under my watch."

"You're here to protect these women?"

The foul mood she'd spent the day entombed in this room with skewed her view of the circumstances. Ridding herself of her clothes, she found her way to the bed and fumbled for his body. Climbing onto him, she pressed her breasts down onto his torso. While lifting her ass to raise her weight off his hips, she loosened his jeans, and curled her fingers around his cock.

"I'm pissed at you," she said with her lips on his pectoral. "I'm not pissed at him."

"Do what you want."

If there had ever been words of water to dowse her fire, he'd just discovered them. Mating there in that place after such a fraught day she'd hoped would bring them both solace. Except he couldn't be less interested. In all their time together, he'd never refused her.

That night, he wasn't denying her, but her lover had never been disinterested. His erection didn't comfort her, his body reacted to hers on instinct. The mind in that unyielding body was constricted with a burden he shouldered alone.

When she tucked her head under his chin, Rushe smoothed her hair away from his stubble in a mechanical, not familiar, caress. Lying together in silence, neither confessed to still being awake, but it took a long time to relax. In the end, only the pulse of his heart against her ribs lulled her to sleep.

THIRTEEN

A SHARP, OBTRUSIVE BELL droned. Before even opening her eyes, she was elbowed aside. Rushe was up off the bed and out of the room. Blinking through the darkness, a small red light above the door flashed, but the bell had ceased.

Activity from somewhere beyond that open door was animated. She slipped off the bed and retrieved the tee-shirt Rushe cast aside earlier. Popping her head through the hole, she got her arms into the sleeves and pulled it down to mid-thigh to cover her body.

Shouting and movement grew louder and more frantic. She crept out of the bedroom on her tiptoes and snuck down the corridor, safe in the knowledge she'd be concealed by the curtain at the end of the passage.

"Don't want to hear it," a female voice, which sounded like Lilah, called out.

"No! She misunderstood, I wasn't—"

"You're out!"

If Rushe's role was to look after these women, part of the job description would be to eject patrons who broke the rules. Letting her curiosity get the better of her, she pulled the curtain aside just enough to see what was going on.

Rushe's back blocked most of her view of the action. He was storming through the door toward the storefront. From the racket, he was clearly dragging the unruly client with him, and the woman continued to berate the guy on the journey through the store.

She glanced at a guy seated in the corner who was pretending to read a magazine while not so discreetly watching the action.

The din stopped abruptly when a door slammed. A few seconds later, Rushe's arm came into view. He was still in the entrance space between store and brothel, again with his back to her.

"You okay?" Rushe asked.

Such a show of placation was unlike her lover. She leaned out, trying to see who he was talking to, but his body shielded the scene. She edged out, letting the curtain flutter shut behind her. Rushe took a step backward to lean on the doorframe, and she momentarily worried about being caught out there. But plenty of women had occupied the reception area in far more revealing attire than she was wearing.

Also, if they were going to be there for an undefined period of time, she didn't plan to spend all those minutes and hours locked away out of sight. She settled her weight back against the wall, without intention of cowering.

"I told you he looked like the type," Lilah said. "Candy has handled worse than that, Rushe. She'll be fine."

He edged aside to let the two women, Lilah and a bleach blonde woman wearing heavy eye make-up, enter reception.

When the three were fully in the reception area

again, the john seated in the corner spoke up. "How much for her?"

"She's done," Lilah said, putting an arm around the bleach blonde.

"Not her," the guy said. "Her."

When the client nodded in her direction, her eyebrows rose. She assumed by his lack of earlier acknowledgement that he hadn't noticed her.

Lilah and the bleach blonde turned. Rushe in his own curiosity did too.

She didn't face the wrath of her lover, she just smiled at the patron. "I'm off duty. Come back another night and maybe you'll get lucky."

"You fucking—"

"Rushe!" she asserted when her love took one stride toward the hapless customer.

This time when Rushe's attention snapped around, she looked him square in the eye. With hope her own glare conveyed her vehemence, she spun around and disappeared through the curtain to return to her room.

For half a second, she wasn't sure he had followed. After a few harsh footfalls, he was in the room, slamming the door. Clouds of gray crashed thunder around them, and that blank stare gave her chills. Now he was angry.

"What the fuck did you think you were doing—"

"There were plenty of other women out there yesterday!" she said.

"And if that guy had decided to take what he wanted while I was busy?"

"You were busy for thirty seconds," she said. "If you had heard me call for you, you'd have come."

"How do you know that?"

"Because I do!"

"Take off the shirt."

"Now you want me naked? Why? Because another man showed interest? You want to scent me?"

With three strides, Rushe's chest met her nose and she leaned back to peer up at him. The nightstand at her back prevented retreat, not that she would run away from his attempt to intimidate.

"I want to see what you've got on under there, what protected my playground from that asshole's reach?"

"Your playground? You weren't interested in playing, or talking, or doing much of anything earlier."

"Take it off," he snarled, his lips curling against his gritted teeth.

She maintained her defiance because this was not a time to flinch under his scrutiny. When he grabbed handfuls of the tee-shirt at her neck she didn't so much as twitch.

The clouds grew thicker around him, and the grate of ripping cotton scratched her skin when he tore the fabric off her body. When he separated the hem, he thrust the material away, tossing it to the floor, leaving her nude.

The span of his two hands reached around her lower ribcage. Pushing the pads of his thumbs to her sternum, he rubbed upward until he palmed her breasts. Still, she maintained eye contact.

"Your pussy is bare."

"That's right."

"You've got a mouth on you, whore." The words were barely whispered, and the gas in his irises swirled when his fingers shifted.

"You want me to do something with it, Lover?" she baited him.

Anger collided with the tingling in her loins, which shimmered north when his hands shrank until his fingertips fooled with the sensitive apexes of her breasts.

"You're gonna do what you're told."

"Maybe," she said, triggering a growl in him. "Try it, thug, ask me to wrap my mouth around your big, hard cock."

"You're a filthy girl; all you can think about is sucking dicks."

Deliberately, she shook her head, causing her hair to flutter forward over her shoulders and tickle his fondling hands.

"Not plural, yours… all I think about is sucking your dick."

His next inhale clenched his fingers, which drew his hands away from her body. Taking pressure from one foot, she dipped to lower herself, but he caught her elbow, preventing her descent.

"Lover?"

Sinking down to sit on the bed, Rushe took her into his lap. "When that bell goes off it means trouble."

Parting his fingers, he combed them through her hair.

"That's why you kept your jeans on," she murmured.

She should've known better than to read anything sinister in the deed. But Rushe could be such a difficult man to interpret. She had learned the importance of picking up on the subtle nuance of his behavior and body language.

"You don't leave this room naked, and when that bell goes off you stay here."

"But—"

"Flick, if I'm watching you, I'm not watching them."

Reading his hidden meaning, she slid her hand the width of his shoulders to rest her arm around him.

"You don't have to prioritize me over them. I

can look after myself. If it comes down to making a choice—"

"You'll stay here…" The sting of his grip bit into her thigh. "If I have to tie you up—"

"You don't have to worry about me. Look how far we've come together."

"I take care of what's mine," he said.

"So do I."

Drifting closer, her lips met his. The pressure eased when he reclined and held her shoulders to maintain the distance between them.

"Sweetheart, we don't wanna do that."

Without meeting her gaze, he exhaled, and lay back and gathered her into their usual sleeping pose.

"You don't want to have sex with me?"

"I'm working. Go to sleep."

Rushe didn't refuse her. Whatever was different there, she didn't like it. The only time he used the endearment "sweetheart" was when he spoke to a female he didn't know, or when he was trying to convey to others, falsely, that they were strangers.

Working had never stopped him from mounting her given the opportunity in the past. His change in attitude gave her a mystery to solve on her own.

FOURTEEN

THE MORNING WAS QUIET. Stillness reeked from every corner and crevice. Rushe had been absent from the room when she awoke. Next to the bed there had been a paper bag with a breakfast bagel in it. Written on the bag in Rushe's handwriting was one word, "stay." After showering, dressing, and sitting alone for an hour, she decided to venture out. If for no other reason than to locate her missing man.

Reception was vacant. The door to the passageway Lilah had emerged from last night was locked, preventing her exploring behind it. She wondered how many women resided through that door, imprisoned, ready to be exploited at Silver's will or whim.

Testing the door for the store, she was surprised to find it open. With no other options, she continued forward. Since she hadn't yet seen another soul, she wasn't content to go back and sit alone in their room.

Slinking through the beads into the store, it was interesting to find the bleach blonde woman from the night before sat behind a narrow glass-fronted counter, poring over a magazine spread open next to the register.

"Rushe ain't here," she said only briefly glancing her way.

The blonde didn't so much as twist in her stool, she just licked a fingertip and scraped one page out of the way to reveal the next one.

"I'm Flick," she said, edging closer to the counter, at the other end of the same wall as the doorway.

"Candy."

"I hope you're alright, after your altercation last night."

Candy tipped her head round toward her. "A john tried to take what he didn't pay for, no big deal."

"Good."

"You one of Silver's girls?"

"No," Flick said.

"Who's paying Rushe?"

If Candy was implying Rushe could be some kind of gigolo that was hilarious. "For sex?"

"That's not Rushe's gig. He's security. So who is it? Your husband? Your brother? You come from money, don't you?"

"What makes you say that?"

"Rushe is expensive. If you're not working to pay off a debt to Silver, Rushe is protecting you from something. That means you've gotta be in serious shit."

"Are you curious or are you worried about what trouble I might have brought here?"

Candy grinned until she snorted out a laugh. "You haven't known Rushe for long if you're still worried about trouble coming for you. Nothing gets past him. If you're in danger after Rushe has taken your case, then Rushe is already dead, and you don't stand a chance against whatever beat him."

So Rushe hadn't told these women of their

relationship. That in itself wasn't surprising, as he'd taught her never to give more details about anything than was absolutely necessary. Also, being that she was Rushe's weak spot, when people found out she could be used against him, they were both put in jeopardy.

"He's here to look after things."

"Yeah," Candy said. "This is Rushe's home."

That was unexpected. "He lives here?"

"Did until a few months back."

"Why did he leave?"

Questioning anyone about her love felt dishonest, but Rushe had taught her the importance of seeking answers when opportunity presented itself.

"Some guy needed help, I guess. Silver had a buddy who wanted something. Rushe only really does his thing for women, so I guess it was some guy's girlfriend or something. We didn't know what, 'cept we knew Rushe would be back. Can't keep him away from Tawny for long."

That name had been mentioned on their arrival. "But she's not here now."

"She'll be back," Candy said, and her smile became sly. "Rushe is more than you can handle, lady, so don't even think about it."

"About what?"

"Walking on the wild side."

"Why would you think I—"

"Tawny would claw out your eyes," Candy said.

"Rushe lived here… with her?"

On a grating electric buzz, the front door opened. Still trying to understand what Candy had said, she anticipated Rushe would come in. He didn't. Cody entered alone.

"What do you want?" Candy barked. "You're to sit outside, that's what Rushe said."

"Got a visitor."

"Not open for business yet," Candy said. "I'm watching the store, and she ain't trading here."

"This is business, not pleasure."

Every muscle in her body tensed at the resonance of the evilly familiar accent coming from behind Cody. Subtly, she relaxed her hand toward her back pocket when Cody stepped to the side.

"Simone," she said., concentrating on the eyes of the sleek and sophisticated blonde.

In her peripheral vision, she noted Candy rising from her perch.

"Where's your bodyguard?" Simone asked.

"None of your business," she replied. "What do you want?"

"I am 'ere to fulfill a promise," Simone said. If she was trying to be friendly, the French mademoiselle missed the mark. "To do you a kindness, to explain how you can make amends and secure a resolution to this unfortunate situation."

"You weren't interested in doing me any favors when we first met. What's changed? Did you panic when you realized the orange jumpsuit clashed with your bottle-blonde hair color?"

"You Americans and your sense of humor," Simone said. "I was not arrested. I was a victim, just like you."

"Really? 'cause I seem to remember you were on the other side of the barricaded door that kept me prisoner."

"Not everything is as it originally seems."

"You won't reel me in," she said, comforted by the lump of Rushe's folded pocketknife in her jeans pocket, indenting her ass. "You were no victim then, and you're no victim now."

"This is not the place to talk, and we must talk."

"I'm not interested in catching up," she said, and

began to turn toward the brothel.

"Where do you plan to go, Felicity? Back into that hovel?"

The thud of the main entrance door catching on the stopper that held it open brought her attention back around. Simone remained in the same spot, but two men, of at least six foot and two hundred something pounds each, came through the entry access and stood as her wings.

"You will come with me," Simone said.

Her smile burst on instinct, and she exhaled a laugh. "You'll have to kill me first."

"That would not be in any of our interests."

"I walk out that door with you, I know exactly what's on the other side of it."

"You're not a pawn anymore, Felicity," Simone said, wearing her own mocking smile. "You're a participant now. You are not a game piece to be manipulated, you are a player who may direct the pieces."

"This isn't a game; lives are at stake. You threaten us and expect us to follow your orders like sheep? Your family is lethal, they're cruel and insane."

"And yours is in peril," Simone said. "If you refuse me, my men will retrieve you, but you are not in physical danger. We have to talk; we need you."

"Need me?"

"I have a mutually beneficial proposition for you. It will resolve the situation for us all."

FIFTEEN

NO ESCAPE lay behind her, reception was the only place she could run to. The women were locked up. The bathroom had no window, and the only windows in their room were fifteen feet up and only a foot high. Getting away from there was not an option.

"You tell me I'm not a pawn," she said to Simone, "and then try to hijack me."

"Rushe wants confirmation that the girl is alive. You may see her now, after that, we will talk. When we are finished, you will be allowed to leave and return here. Holding you against your will would serve no purpose for us. You are unwieldy and inconvenient, not at all obedient or compliant. Do you wish to see the girl or not?"

Serendipity.

Rushe had said he'd requested to see her. "You don't need her."

Though in truth, Serendipity was the ace in the Merciers' hand.

"If that was true," Simone said, "we'd have killed

her."

"Or sold her. I won't put myself in the same situation."

"Lonnie," Simone snipped.

The goon farthest from the door lifted his arm, and an abrupt snap startled them all. Candy cried out and leaped back, blood oozing from her shoulder. It seeped between the woman's clutching fingers, draining from the face hidden behind the crude make-up.

"Fuck!" Cody shouted and rushed over to the bleeding Candy as she fell back against the wall. "You bitch! You shot her! What the fuck!"

These women were Rushe's responsibility, and she was supposed to be his partner. By extension, that technically put them in her charge too.

"You may not be in physical danger. But I did not say the same about those around you. Shall I tell my man to continue?" Simone drawled, aware she had the upper hand.

Exhaling, she gave up hope that Rushe would happen upon the scene. Simone might be a superior bitch, but if the Mercier family wanted Flick dead or kidnapped, they wouldn't have sent this feeble opponent to take on Rushe, or whoever else might have been there protecting her.

If it had been their aim to abduct her, it would've made more sense to do it from her parents' house. Especially since she'd been alone in the Hughes' house on her first night there.

"No," Flick said. "Cody, get Candy help."

"But—"

"Do it."

Striding forward, she felt no fear. Any threat of conflict was nothing she couldn't handle. The two hooligans parted to let Simone exit first, one went out and the other, Lonnie, waited for her to exit in front of him.

If she expected a gang of hoodlums ready to seize her the moment she stepped onto the sidewalk, she was disappointed.

Simone was already beside the driver in the front passenger seat of a sleek black vehicle idling at the curb. Lonnie waited for her to get into the back while his friend went onto the road to get in at the other side, sandwiching her between them in the back seat.

As they got underway, Simone opened the glove box and twisted to hold up a length of black silk. "Lonnie."

The shooter took the silk and wound it around her head in a familiar experience she'd hoped they were beyond. In the past, these journeys had taken hours. Being crammed in between these hulks would make for an unpleasant and uncomfortable trip if it was going to play out the same.

Thoughts of conversation came and went. Rushe had shown how powerful quiet could be. She wouldn't show anyone her hand, displaying emotion would gain her nothing. So she waited, prepared for someone else in the car to break the seal of silence first.

All her assumptions turned out to be false. Less than half an hour later, the car slowed to a halt. At first, she assumed there was a hold up on the road, but the engine ceased, and doors began to open.

The human bread flanking her disappeared. Wasting no time by waiting for permission, she tugged off the blindfold and shuffled out of the car. The road was unfamiliar, but the set up was the same as many residential city streets.

Traversing an alley behind Simone and the driver, she was escorted by the two others from the back of the car. Simone carried on through the door that the driver held ajar until she entered as well. Aiming her down a dark but clean hallway, the three men remained tightly around her, like three points on an arrowhead, as they ascended the stairs.

If this was where Serendipity was being held, it was closer than she'd assumed, either that or something else was going on.

They arrived in an apartment. Perfectly normal. An open plan, large space, with a few doors around it, nothing sinister at all. No gangsters, other than those who had entered with her. With high sash windows that let light flow over the expensive designer furniture, this could be an abode in any European city.

"Follow me," Simone said, leading her toward the window and the wood-framed velvet chaise.

Lonnie passed them to unlock a door. When he pushed it open, she was nervous at the implied invitation for her to enter. But her anxiety fled when a form rose out of a wingback chair inside the room.

Serendipity smiled and rushed forward. "Flick!"

The women met and embraced like old friends. They hadn't spent considerable bonding time together. Their friendship consisted of nothing more than a few minutes of comfort and conversation in an intense situation.

The downtrodden and neglected Serendipity of now had a fuller figure and a brighter complexion, but melancholy still stained her aura.

"Have you seen him?"

"No," she said, allowing Serendipity to lead her past a bed and to the chair in the window she'd vacated. As Serendipity sank down into one, Flick lowered herself into the matching seat angled toward the window. "Rushe went to the hospital and copied some of his notes." She kept her volume low. The door closed, leaving her and Serendipity alone. "He hasn't woken up."

"I punished him," Serendipity said. "He didn't

mean for any of it to happen. He was doing his job. Going undercover was what he did. Bringing those bastards to justice was his mission. He didn't mean for me to get involved, it was never his intention—"

"Don't punish yourself. It wasn't his fault, but it wasn't yours either."

"We had time together. He tried so hard, and I… I punished him."

"You went through a trauma, worse than the rest of us," she said. "He knew it would take time."

Serendipity stared out of the window at the apartment block across the street. A calm came over her, which reminded her of the first view she'd had of the husk of a woman Serendipity was back then. Blank, vacant, void of any emotion, that's how Serendipity had been.

From personal experience, she knew what it was to exist in that state. It often gripped a person when reality overwhelmed them. It was a condition of self-preservation Serendipity had lived in for months.

"Don't let them set you back," she said, edging to the front corner of her seat. "You have to be strong."

"For what? If he doesn't wake up—"

"Jansen needs you to be strong. He loves you. Getting you back was all he could think about. He blamed himself for everything."

"And I wasted our reunion. We've spent months fighting, drifting back together only to crash and lose each other again. He's been so pig-headed about collecting evidence, about trying to find a way to prove that the Merciers were involved. It took over our lives. He was never there, but when he was… I punished him."

"How long have they had you here?" she asked.

"A little more than a week," Serendipity said. "When they took me… I was at the hospital. They knew I would be there."

"Rushe is working for the Merciers. They have him working for a guy called Silver. We're going to get you out of this."

"They want something from Rushe," Serendipity said. "Jerome Mercier is the head of the family, he's Simone's uncle."

"What do they want from Rushe?"

"I don't know. I overheard them talking. Jerome's out of the country. Simone said to one of them that we were staying here until he returns to the US."

"Are they looking after you?"

"Compared to the last time?" Serendipity mustered a smile. "I can't stop thinking about him lying in that hospital bed… Drew always wanted… he just wanted to do what was right. Somehow… he's never had very good luck."

She hadn't known Jansen's first name until now. "He found you, we can't lose hope."

The bedroom door opened to reveal Lonnie standing with Simone.

"You've seen her," Simone said. "She's alive. Now come here."

Seeking Serendipity's hand before her forced departure, she gave it a squeeze in hope it conveyed some solace, no matter how ineffectual it would be.

Without any other choice, she filtered out and back into the living room.

Simone settled on the couch and poured coffee from a French press on the polished walnut table.

She replaced the vessel on its cork coaster and lifted her coffee cup. "Sit," Simone drawled. "We have things to discuss."

SIXTEEN

"YOU CAME TO SILVER'S for me," Flick said. As Lonnie disappeared into an adjoining room, leaving the two women alone, she crossed to sit at the other end of the couch from Simone. "You said Rushe wanted to know Serendipity was alive, but it was me you came for."

"Yes."

"Is your cousin Antoine still with my family?"

"He is. We wouldn't want you to get the idea of doing anything reckless."

"Like what? You have everything you want. Jansen has possible brain damage. Serendipity is your prisoner, and Rushe is running your errands."

"And you expected to pay no price yourself?" Simone asked.

Nothing in her life was ever as it first appeared anymore. "So this is where you bill me? What's the charge?"

"Your involvement led us to where we are today," Simone said, lounging back against the armrest. Each of her words so effortless and casual they could easily have been talking about something as mundane as the weather. "And it will be your involvement that will resolve this situation."

"Will it?" she asked, struggling to restrain her urge to lunge over the couch and throttle the woman who was the cause of so much suffering.

With the bodyguards only a room away and Serendipity locked up, such an action would only get her into trouble.

"Jansen has paid his price and is no longer a threat. Serendipity is here to ensure you pay your share. And you will make sure Rushe pays his."

"What is it you want me to do?" Flick asked.

"Betray him."

"Who?"

"Your lover," Simone said, her lip curling in undisguised pleasure at the idea. "You are an innocent. A little lamb trotting behind the wolf. He will turn on you when he is hungry. You are nothing to him."

"There's nothing you can say that would make me betray Rushe," she said. Ignoring the coffee and the smug European, she rose to her feet. "If I'm not a prisoner, I'm leaving now. Thank you for letting me see Serendipity."

"You have the power to liberate her," Simone said, stalling her. "We have one straightforward task for you. Comply, and everyone will live. We can go back to our business and go our separate ways, all even."

Could it be so simple? She descended onto the couch to hear Simone out. Genuine betrayal might not be an option, but the situation may be able to be manipulated to their advantage. So it would serve her to find out just what Simone was suggesting.

"If you don't want me as a prisoner or in a hospital bed, you must want me doing my part with Rushe. Do you think he will let me lie on my back for your family? Is that what you mean by betrayal?"

"We do not wish you to prostitute yourself in Silver's whorehouse. Silver is nothing to us. Rushe is repaying a debt to Silver that pre-dates his association with our family. That will be settled, and we will be assured of Silver's silence on his knowledge of our acquaintance."

"Then what can you want from—"

"You are going to testify against him," Simone said. "Testify to the brutality of your kidnap, your stay, and your experience with Rushe, the man who violated me… the man who violated you."

"You've accused Rushe of rape? You want him to be the fall guy?"

"It is necessary to underline their coercion of me. Rushe will take responsibility for financing the operation, for being Victor's partner. And he'll be the one to take responsibility for manipulating Jansen, both then and now."

"No," she said on an exhale, understanding what it would mean to have Rushe arrested for the role they were designing for him.

"We've already taken steps to put in place the links between Victor and Rushe, their finances and associations. We have covered all eventualities."

"You're framing him. You want Rushe to go to jail, and you want me to help you put him there."

The left edge of Simone's lips tilted higher. "Yes."

"But Jansen wouldn't have incriminated Rushe."

"Jansen is in no state to be confirming or contradicting anyone's story. You will do this, Felicity. You are going to stand at our side as we watch him go down."

"I won't."

"Rushe is a ruthless man," Simone said. "Like it

or not, he is a criminal. He has been party to wrongdoings. There is plenty that he can be legitimately accused of. He is the greatest threat to us and to others. Getting him off the streets will minimize the chances of future interaction."

"You're afraid of him," she said, figuring it out.

"We are not condemning an innocent man, and you are not defending one. He is not a hero. He is malevolence in a cloak of virtue. You have been bewitched. There will come a time you will see him for what he truly is. With or without you, we will see that he pays for his crimes."

"He's not vicious, and he would never—"

"Without Jansen's testimony, the internal investigation will go away, relieving the pressure on our associates there. Our friends in the police department have already destroyed all evidence linking us to the crime, but they have pressure from their own superiors to worry about. They need to identify and incarcerate an individual to satisfy their own supervisors. Things are teetering on a knife edge. Our police colleagues being discovered before this case is closed would be disastrous."

"What a shame," she said, emphasizing her sarcasm.

"You will corroborate my statement."

"And what about those of the other female captives?"

"Irrelevant, none of them knew the truth."

"But you were seen at Victor's side."

"I admitted that he was a threatening man, who compelled me to act against my will. He and Rushe both did."

She recalled the inky silence that consumed the female hostages until they were shells of their former selves. The prisoners she had met hadn't known the names or features of any of their captors. They hadn't known where they were, or even why they'd been abducted. Simone taunted Serendipity, but the European remained silent around the others.

If Simone had identified herself as a victim, it was likely the cops would accept that claim. They might accept that she was there under duress and only following Victor's instructions in the hope of saving her own threatened life.

"We have destroyed all evidence that has to be destroyed—"

"Including Jansen," she snarled. Jansen, Rushe, and her were the only three people alive who knew the truth. Jansen was no longer in a position to testify or offer any contradiction to whatever fabrication Simone had woven for the authorities.

"Maybe Jansen threatened to stop covering up Rushe's involvement."

"You're going to accuse Rushe of putting Jansen in his current state?"

"The evidence the police need to implicate Rushe is out there. It's only a matter of time before they find it and find him too. We can ensure that they do, when the timing is right."

"I've seen how you take pleasure in watching others squirm, watching them tormented and in pain. Is your family this afraid of him?"

"Now all we need is the testimony of one innocent victim, from a very respectable family, with a lot of credibility. You're a poor, defenseless woman that Rushe took a particular interest in. And for months he has been exploiting you for his pleasure."

"How can you expect me to do this?"

"It will clear the debt and save everyone's lives. You can ask as many questions as you like, but there is only one truth you have to accept. When we deem it time, you will deliver the story of Rushe's brutality against you. All this time you have lived in fear of his tyranny, and he has subjugated you."

"You want me to tell them he has kept me against my will, that he's raped and abused me for the duration of our legitimate relationship? No, I won't listen to any more of this," she said, ascending to head for the door.

"Lonnie!"

She expected violence, or to be restrained, but the men appeared from the other room before she could get to the door.

"Take Miss Hughes back to where we found her," Simone said, maintaining eye contact with her. "You have some time to think, but we will be in touch soon."

Simone turned away to top off her coffee, thus dismissing her. The three men trundled her out of there and piled her into the car. Again, they tied a blindfold around her head, and drove her to the brothel.

She stood on the sidewalk watching the car drive off and knew one thing, she wasn't going back into the building they'd delivered her to. Not yet. As soon as the vehicle left her sight, she turned to walk in the opposite direction.

Still forming a plan, she had no definitive aim, but the last thing she wanted was to be discovered by anyone from Silver's brothel until her thoughts were clearer. To form a distinct goal, and to make an action plan to get her there, she needed help. Picking up her speed, she headed for the heart of town, because there was only one place to go to for information.

SEVENTEEN

CALLING UP AN OLD FRIEND gave her what she needed right now: support. Rushe might not be in the brothel, and he'd been so distant that she couldn't rely on him to listen to her woes. Before she took them to him, she needed to have her own plan of action in place. She needed to show him how seriously she took this situation and what lengths she would go to in order to protect him.

So when she saw her friend Liam approach their pre-arranged meeting point, a little of the weight on her shoulders lessened.

"What's going on?" Liam asked, when he reached her on the corner.

The library he worked at, where she'd originally met him, was more than an hour away by car. But he'd come without question when she'd called from the local library. The time it took Liam to get there gave her a chance to write down the important details on a notepad borrowed from the librarian.

"It's a long story, Liam. Thank you for coming."

Throwing his arms around her, his embrace was tight and almost relieved. "I'm glad you're okay," he said. "When I didn't hear from you again, I thought the worst. I sent the audio to that email address you gave me, and—"

"Thank you, but I didn't call you about that."

"Have you gotten yourself into more trouble?"

"Buy me a coffee, Liam."

After fleeing Victor's gang, she and Rushe had cohabited in an apartment. For the three months they'd lived there, she'd been a regular user of the public library where Liam Hutten worked as a software engineer. In that time, they'd developed a friendship.

Liam was something of a technical whizz and often impressed her with his skills of covert information gathering. Those skills had come in handy during the last assignment she and Rushe had embarked upon.

He had helped them out in a time of need. After recording incriminating evidence on their last job, she and Rushe sent it to Liam. He'd collated and kept it for them until she told him to forward it to another of Rushe's contacts, a man named Eric, one of the two men to hire Rushe for the mission.

Traversing the sidewalk to a nearby diner, they entered and got coffee before she and Liam tucked themselves into a secluded booth in the back corner.

"Where's Rushe?"

"He doesn't know I'm here," she said, hoping her love was safe and wasn't too worried about her.

"You're running from him? Hiding?"

Her eyes fired up to his. "Of course not," she snapped.

"Unless you tell me what's going on, I'll have to keep playing twenty questions," Liam said. "You called me here without notice, so whatever it is, it's important."

She swallowed away her anxiety and curled her

hands around her coffee mug. "I have to tell you a story, the story of how Rushe and I met."

The easy smile, which was usually a permanent feature on the face of the IT expert with the mucky brown hair, was now absent. "Okay."

She appreciated that he sat back calmly and waited, putting no pressure on her to hurry up. She had never told the story, and Rushe would remind her to keep her guard up. Maybe her lover would warn her against trusting Liam, but her friend had come through for them in the past, and right now, she needed guidance.

To bring the situation to a successful end, she had to acknowledge she couldn't do it alone. That didn't mean she had the faintest idea how to bring things to a head. So she sat there opposite Liam and told him everything, the whole story from beginning to the present.

"Jansen was gathering evidence," Liam said after they'd been talking for several hours. "Serendipity told you that?"

"That's right," she said, picking off a corner of the banana muffin Liam bought for them to share.

"So there's something there to find," Liam said. "You have to prove what happened. What really happened."

"That was what I thought too," she said. "But where do we begin? How do we prove beyond any doubt that the Merciers are involved, and that they have the cops in their pockets?"

"They don't have every cop in their pocket," Liam said. "From what you've told me, they're not hugely wealthy. Rushe told you they were mid-level and without great funds. They're not billionaires dallying in human trafficking for fun."

"No."

"They needed the money, they're not infinitely

rich. If that's the case, they've only got a few key members of law enforcement in their pockets. They can't pay off everyone."

"Right."

"Jansen was based somewhere around here in New Jersey. This shack you were at, it was only a few hours' drive from here."

"Yeah," she said.

"Victor's mansion, that's further north than your parents' place, somewhere in Maine, you think. Everything started here and spread out over time. This is far-reaching. There's no way the Merciers have paid every cop to keep their secret."

"We need to find out who they do have on their payroll," she said. "Because whoever it is, they're destroying everything we need."

"No," Liam said, shaking his head and leaning over the table. "We'll have to find that out, sure, but they're not destroying everything, just whatever the cops already have. There has to be more out there, evidence that the cops haven't yet uncovered."

"Jansen's evidence."

"Yeah," Liam said. "If he's pulled all the pieces together, that's great, we're halfway to where we need to be. But he won't have handed it over to the evidence locker if he thinks it's going to disappear from there."

"Who would he give it to? The DA?"

"Maybe, but unless he knows and trusts the DA, he's not going to go anywhere near a place of authority that the Merciers might hear about. You said he tried to go to his own superiors about the mess with Serendipity and word got back to Victor. The guy has got to be paranoid. He's been screwed over from every angle in the past."

"Serendipity didn't say where he kept what he'd uncovered. But if he's already gathered everything, there's nothing left for us to find."

"Not necessarily," Liam said. "Maybe we have to come at this from the other side. Instead of proving the Merciers' guilt, you have to prove Rushe's innocence."

"Before he's been accused of anything?"

"I think they're doing the accusing, and if they're planting evidence, you need to be able to refute it."

"So…" she said, considering what that meant. "We'll retrace every step. I was there, I know what happened. I have to take everything I know and prove Rushe isn't the monster they're going to claim he is."

"Prove that he wasn't the one giving the orders… and that your relationship was consensual from the get-go."

"Right," she said.

"Okay," Liam said, pushing aside the muffin and their cups. "Tell me everything again from the beginning."

EIGHTEEN

THEY TALKED FOR another couple of hours. On leaving the coffeeshop, Liam offered her a ride. She'd opted for a loan of cash for a taxi instead. Night had closed in around them. While she wasn't comfortable accepting a ride and drawing Liam into the danger surrounding the brothel, she also didn't want him walking alone to the less than savory neighborhood the brothel was situated in.

The cab dropped her off and she went to the store door… The unlocked store door, which was a surprise. Then again, customers wouldn't want to be loitering on the sidewalk and drawing attention to themselves. Direct access would be necessary. Getting through the beads to the back door, Flick pushed the button that caused the buzz, and the door was yanked open.

She expected Rushe, she expected fury. Instead, she was faced with a short, black, indifferent man.

"She's fine," Lilah chanted from behind the reception desk, so she was granted entry.

A couple of johns sat quietly. Neither lifted his head when she came in.

"Thanks," Flick said to Lilah. "Is Candy okay?"

"Pissed as hell," Lilah said, picking at her fingernail. "But she's good."

"Good."

"Rushe ain't none too happy either," Lilah said. "He don't like anyone bringing their crap to his girls."

So these were his girls, and Simone was her problem. Any concern she had about his state of mind over her whereabouts that day evaporated.

"Whatever."

She tossed the curtain aside and strode up the hallway, lost in her fogged and tired thoughts. Without first going into the bedroom, she stripped down and went straight into the shower to wash off the day.

Liam was going to find out as much as he could about the Mercier family, Victor's gang, and Theo Silver too. Perhaps more importantly, he was going to probe the internal investigation that suspended Jansen. And the bogus case Simone and the others were perpetrating against Rushe.

Her desperation for answers made her crave the opportunity to do some digging of her own. The only reason she'd left it in Liam's capable hands was so she could come back to Rushe, on the assumption that he may have missed her or been worried. Obviously, that assumption had been wrong.

Without a towel, she couldn't dry off after her shower, but she was too tired to care. Kicking the heap of her clothes from the hall into the bedroom, she ran a comb through her hair before she collapsed onto the bed and went to sleep.

UP, OFF THE BED, off her feet, her back crashed

against something solid. Her upper arms burned against the embers that kept her clamped in the elevated position.

"What the fuck did you think you were doing?"

Dizzy, she fought against the liquid circling her brain, causing her ears to ring. This was Rushe, pinning her to the wall, and he was angry. Blackness surrounded them, it had to be night-time. Quaking from the slumber he'd hauled her from, it took her a few seconds to re-orient herself and recall what was going on.

"Answer me!"

"My job," she croaked and cleared her throat, trying to define her voice. "They shot Candy, I had to go. I saw Serendipity."

"I thought they'd taken you," he growled, his lips never moving. "I thought I'd lost you."

"Yes, I could tell how worried you were when I came in and you were pacing in anxious wait."

"I was out there looking for you, ignoring my responsibility to this place," he snarled. "We got back here and there was blood, a trail from inside to out, and you were gone. What the fuck—"

"Simone's man shot Candy to highlight their power," she said. "I had nowhere to run, Rushe."

"I spoke to Cody, I got in touch with Antoine. Kitten, I was gonna start shooting."

"Simone let me leave as she said she would," she said, struggling against the deepening blaze of his grip. "It wasn't a kidnap, I went voluntarily to get answers and to see Serendipity."

"You didn't come back to me. You left Simone hours ago."

"I didn't know where you were," she said, narrowing her eyes to match the width of his. "I wasn't going to come back in here to sit alone, locked in a room, doing nothing, on the faintest hope that you might deem me worthy enough to talk to eventually. Why have you shut me out again? You trust me, Rushe, I know you do. I thought we were beyond this."

The scorch released. Unprepared for liberation, she tumbled to the floor. Rushe marched ten feet from her and for a moment, there was peace. Then he spun to face her, torture in his countenance like their very early days together.

"You were worried about me," she whispered. "Do you need me to reassure you that I'm okay? That we're okay?"

Rushe understood sex, and the connection when they shared it. In its simplest form, Rushe felt closest to her when their bodies were bonded.

Tumbling forward onto all fours, she stalked toward him, rising to her knees when she reached him. Very slowly, she unbuttoned his jeans and let her eyes drift upwards to his.

"You're hard," she murmured, on liberating his member. "He's missed me."

Leaning forward, she clasped the length of him to her cheek, rubbing back and forth until her eyes closed. She got lost in her bonding with her closest ally. Sliding him across her face, she nuzzled closer, then pushed higher to press him against the column of her throat, humming to send vibrations skittering through him. Urging him upward, she tilted her head to repeat the action with his balls in place against the front of her neck.

When he groaned out in instinct from the pleasure she imparted, she pouted her lips to meet his shaft and drew them up, squeezing her tongue between them. Churning the saliva in her mouth, she lapped his head and suckered in her cheeks around him. Her next instant force of action pulled him into her throat. Pulling back, she milked again, tugging him into her throat and out, in partnership with her tongue flickering the end of him when she withdrew.

"Suck that," he grumbled. "Right there."

Triumph bred a smile, but when she cast her eyes upward again, his eyes were closed. She couldn't remember a time when he'd ever not watched her do this, unless he was asleep. His skull went back, and she closed her curled lips around his bulbous head to suck while pumping her fist up and down his shaft.

"I've missed you," she whispered, consoled they had this time to re-connect.

No sooner had the words passed her lips than he was leaning over her, taking the rigid organ she'd been playing with from her grasp. Snatching her arms, he hauled her up to toss her to the bed.

With a grin, she parted her thighs, expecting to have him join with her in this minute. He didn't. Fury circulated his form, and her frown quickly took place of her glee.

She sat up and scooted to the edge of the bed. "Come here and let me finish."

"No."

"Come on," she said, on half a laugh and reached for him, but he stepped out of her range. "You've never had a problem with my technique before, if I need more practice—"

"This isn't a game, Red!"

Alarm spiked in her chest and shot through her limbs. Slowly, all emotion—pleasure, pain, fear, happiness—it all went away as the icy slurry of terror found every crevice within her.

"What's wrong?"

She managed to snag his loose jeans pocket, but he backed away out of her grasp, going until he hit the back of the couch. Whilst his eyes remained on her, he tucked himself away, the ecstasy of a few seconds ago was now forgotten.

His expression relaxed, freeing him of the anger he entered this space with. "I don't know why I…"

Showing weakness wasn't something Rushe enjoyed, it was so foreign to him that even then, as he looked on her with such confusion, she wasn't sure he knew he was revealing so much of himself.

"Red" was a nickname from when they'd met. Before they'd slept together. Before he knew her hair color at the time wasn't natural.

"It's something about this place," she said. "Something here has changed things between us. Something here is hurting you, Lover. I can feel it in you. I feel your war."

Leaving the bed, she gradually closed in on his position, moving toward him as though he were a scared animal she didn't want to spook.

"You were here before," she said. "Before me, is that it? Did something happen here?" He didn't respond. "You recall what our lives were before we found each other? You can talk to me, Lover… I love you."

The puzzled daze vanished, and his posture adjusted. "There's no place for that here."

On his clipped words, he pivoted, and marched out, slamming the door between them. Rushe had wrestled with demons all his life. Being a loner was an integral part of his identity; he'd confessed himself incapable of love, until there was her.

One of the first things she'd learned about him was not to push him. Coming to terms with what he was now, with her, evidently meant facing who he was before, and the journey he'd gone on to make that transition.

She wouldn't push him. When the time came that he was ready and needed someone to talk to, she would be there, and she had faith he would know that.

Relying on her, trusting her, had been no small feat for him. Traversing the route to the level of trust they had hadn't been easy. It was real and thorough, no shortcuts, no quick fixes, or easy paths. He'd told her she was an extension of him. When the moment was right for him to explain his struggles, he would seek her out. She had faith in him, and in them.

NINETEEN

WAKING UP ALONE to another breakfast bagel on the nightstand, she discovered one great thing about this place. The bed was no more than a box spring and mattress; there was no opportunity available to keep her tied down. No head or footrail existed for Rushe to chain her to in order to keep her immobile.

Struggling to sleep without him was becoming the norm, but he was obviously coming in to check on her because he kept leaving food. Without restraint, she was free to shower and ready herself for the day without any need for permission.

For the first time since they'd been living there, when she moved through the curtain to reception, the doorway to the women's wing was open. Though all she could see was a long, straight passage that ran the length of the building.

Lilah was at the front desk, because it seemed she never had anywhere else to be when she was there. A man she didn't recognize sat beside the store door, but he wasn't a john, not if his casual pose and stocky stance were any indication.

"Going out," she said to no one in particular, and headed for the exit. The unknown man stood and blocked her path. "Have you got a problem?"

"Rushe don't want you going out today," Lilah drawled.

"I don't care what Rushe wants, I have business to take care of."

"He's the boss around here, and when he's with Tawny he's not to be disturbed."

She spun on the spot to see Lilah startled by the abrupt maneuver. "He's on the premises?"

"Well, yeah, but—"

"Tell me what room they're in, or I'll hammer down every door until I find them," she said, spreading on a saccharine-saturated smile as she stormed toward the corridor.

Before Lilah could make it around the reception desk, she was already in the hallway.

"Hold up!"

She knocked on one door, and then the one opposite. All of the doors had numbers, odds on the left and evens on the right.

"Five! They're in five!"

"Thank you," she said to the madam hurrying after her.

The doors she had knocked on began to open, but she had door number five in her sights.

An unexpected entrance would give her the element of surprise, and that wasn't to be underestimated. She was pleased the door opened when she thrust down the handle. Pushing it aside, she found Rushe stretched out on the bed on the far wall of the small room, his hands behind his head.

The laughing blonde beside him, dropped a hand to his abdomen but stopped and cast her eyes to the door when she entered. At the same time, Rushe sat up. Any surprise at her sudden entrance was disguised behind his usual apathetic mask.

Though both were fully clothed, seeing her lover lying in bed with another woman should have delivered a sucker punch to her gut. But her trust in him remained intact. In all honesty, being held prisoner by him was inconvenient and fostered anger, which outweighed any shock or insecurity she might have imagined feeling at beholding the sight in other circumstances.

"Would you ask your man to step aside please?" she said to her love. "I have things to get on with today, and I'd hate to be the cause of bloodshed on two consecutive days… Oh, and at some point, we have to find the time to talk."

People hung behind her, transfixed by the unfolding drama, but Rushe remained fixated on her, and she had no plans to blink first.

"Fuck off," said the blonde on the bed, who she assumed was Tawny. "This is the bitch you're protecting? He's off-duty when he's with me. Nothing's gonna happen to you here. Fuck off!"

"It would be my pleasure," she said. "Call off your man."

Boosting himself up, Rushe came off the bed, and kept on coming until he was at her side. He snatched her arm in his iron grip. Dragging her through the bodies littering the hallway, he got them back to the room where she'd woken up and slammed the door.

"Talk about what?" he hissed through gritted teeth.

"About Simone, and about what she said to me yesterday. I've told you it's important for us to communicate. I don't like it when you withhold things from me. I would never want you to think I'd withhold anything from you."

"You're not even gonna ask me, are you?"

"Ask you what?" she asked.

"About what you just saw."

"I don't know if you realize how serious this is," she said, coming closer. "Do you know what's going on here? What their plan is? We don't have time for the teen angst. I know you're not having sex with her, so I really don't—"

"How do you know?"

"Because I do," she said. "Maybe you have in the past, I don't know, you sure weren't a virgin before we met. Maybe you care for her, and she's important to you, or maybe you just don't want people to know about us. I know they don't know about our relationship. But I won't question your cover while we're on a job, Rushe. This is too important… the most important job yet."

"Do you want to know?"

"Rushe," she said on a sigh. "When you have something to tell me, you will. Until then, I trust your judgement. Now please, I have to go out."

"Where?"

"I saw Liam yesterday, that's where I was after Simone's men dropped me off here," she said, curling her fingers into his pocket. "I asked him to look into the case. Simone didn't give me the specifics of her statement, but I have a good idea what she said. They're trying to frame you for this; they want you to take the rap. She's accused you of some horrible things."

"You have to support what Simone said to the cops?"

"That's what they want," she said. "But if we can find out the story they're selling, we can start to poke holes in it. She alluded to Jansen's statement too. We have to know what he said. If we can find ways to back him up and to disprove—"

"It's too dangerous for you," he said, removing

her hand from his pants, trying to lead her toward the bed.

She snatched her hand back. "If I have to fight my way out of here, I will," she said, leaving no doubt as to her resolve. "Don't work against me. I will do this. I will work to prove your innocence and ensure your freedom. Liam has information, he has my instructions. If you detain me—"

"Close," he snarled, lowering his face toward hers. "Aren't you?"

"You stay here with your adoring fans and be worshipped. The rest of us aren't going to bury our heads in the sand while there's work to be done."

Swerving around him, she left the room and went down the hall. A number of women had gathered in the reception, most notably around Tawny. She went to the store door, and though the same man blocked her path initially, he glanced past her. Nothing was said, but she imagined Rushe nodded his consent because the man stepped aside.

Without doubt of her purpose, she went out onto the street and made her way back toward the library where she'd arranged to meet Liam. If she didn't pick up the pace, she'd be late to their rendezvous, and she desperately wanted to know what he had found out.

TWENTY

SIMONE'S STATEMENT made for harrowing reading. All the statements did. For the first couple of hours while they were at the library, she and Liam poured over the details of the case regarding Victor's gang. Jansen's version of events didn't incriminate Rushe, but they also didn't exonerate him. Actually, the cop had barely mentioned Rushe at all.

That was the way Rushe wanted things, because he didn't want to be on anyone's radar. The only questions Jansen answered about her lover were direct ones and in reference to the given statements of the others. None of his answers had been descriptive. In fact, they'd been rather clipped. If the responses were collated in the right way, then alarmingly, the cagey answers could be construed as Jansen perhaps still being under pressure from Rushe, and still keeping the secret of the scope of his involvement.

Getting the details of the internal investigation hadn't been as easy for Liam. Those records weren't as accessible for some reason.

On the promise of lunch and the use of a telephone, she'd agreed to go back to Liam's place with him. The two-bedroom apartment was larger than she would have imagined, bright and airy, open plan and modern. While the styles were different, the reminder of a sanctuary of private space made her think of the apartment she'd shared with Rushe in their easier days.

"You had a fight, didn't you?" Liam asked, peeking over his laptop on a large desk, perpendicular to his living room window.

"I don't want to talk about Rushe," she said, wrapping her arms around herself to stare out over the city and the ignorant people going on with their oblivious lives.

"You've been pissed off since you showed up this morning."

"And I told you I didn't want to talk about it." Casting her eyes briefly toward his, she then turned to aim for her coffee mug on the dining table.

"Why isn't he here? I know he doesn't like me, but… he's okay with you hanging around with another man?"

"He's not going to hurt you. If you're scared of—"

"I'm not scared," Liam said. "Sure, the guy is scary, you told me that yourself, but… why are you doing this for him if he doesn't care enough to help himself?"

"He cares," she said, sipping the now chilled liquid. "He prioritizes everything and everyone else above himself. But he believes in advance planning. I'm trying to make sure that we're ahead of the game. We know they're going to come for us. We have to know what they know."

"What's he doing right now? What's so much more important than this?"

"He's looking after people who can't look after

themselves. He does big and scary. Information management like this is my part of the partnership. I'll put this together for him."

"We know what they know," Liam said, leaving the desk and picking up the folder of police statements and notes before he approached her. "We can't prove any of it is true or false. Unless we're going to go out there and—"

"Not us," she said, putting the mug back on the table. "You don't know what you're doing in the field. I lived this Liam. I've been to every location and seen every face."

"Not every face," Liam said. "It's dangerous and going out there alone would be insane."

"I don't plan to go alone."

Right on cue, there was a knock on the front door.

Liam glanced over his shoulder then back at her. "You called someone?"

"I told you I needed the telephone."

She went past the computer-pro to the door, opening it as though she had full rights to do so.

"Your boyfriend better be dead, or he'll kill me for meeting you alone."

"We're not alone, Eric."

She smiled at the man whom she had last seen only a couple of weeks ago. Odd that despite dispelling with the trouble, he looked more harassed now than he had then. Eric was broad, built solid, and intrigued by her statement. He sailed past to seek out the other party, while Liam just stared at the new entrant.

"Eric, Liam, Liam, Eric," she said by way of introduction, and closed the front door before heading for the kitchen. "Coffee?"

"This is the guy that…" Liam said.

"Yes," she said.

"Think you know something?" Eric asked with menace.

Flick groaned. "We're all friends here, and here for the greater good."

"Which is what exactly?" Eric asked, marching past Liam to join her in the kitchen as she went through the process of making fresh coffee. "Where's Rushe?"

"Around."

"Oh, great, now you've got cryptic down too. Does he give classes? Talk about technique in bed?"

One corner of her lips crept up. "There isn't much room for talk like that, and don't ask about my boyfriend's sexual proclivities, it's rude."

"You do understand how he feels about you?" Eric asked, dropping a hand onto the countertop to block her route toward the sink, thus stalling her actions.

"You're asking me if I know how Rushe feels about me? I don't understand what—"

"He's gonna kill that guy, whoever the fuck he is," Eric said, with a backward nod in Liam's direction. "He's probably gonna kill me too. What are you doing knocking around in private apartments with other dudes?"

She glanced down, making a pronounced show of checking her apparel. "I am fully clothed. Not everything is about sex… We're actually here to help Rushe, because he won't help himself."

"Oh," Eric said, relaxing a little. "Okay, then."

"Okay, then," she muttered. Eric turned to stride away, taking off his jacket in the process. "Did you think I invited you here for a sex party? I'll try not to be disappointed you're happy I didn't."

"Tell me what's going on."

"Where's Scott?" she asked, while finishing up with the coffee machine.

"Not in the country," Eric said. She caught his

gaze flitting toward Liam. "And not a topic of conversation for public ears."

"Liam is the one who kept the recordings for us and forwarded them to you. Did they get to their intended destination?"

"Yes," Eric said. "You trust him?"

"Yes. What happened…?" she asked, referencing their last case. "With the two of them, did…?"

"One will never see again and the other can't count beyond six using only his hands."

"But I thought—"

"Rushe has the details, he didn't tell you?"

"I didn't ask," she admitted because it was true.

She had thought those men would never get out of the situation she and Rushe left them in, not alive anyway. But some things were worse than death.

"You want to tell me what this is about?" Eric asked.

"Yes, come," she said, gesturing them both to the dining table. "We've got to get ready for a fight."

"WHAT MAKES YOU think she'll remember," Eric said, after she'd laid everything out again, just as she'd done for Liam.

Eric had a lot of questions, but she hadn't answered them all. If Liam and Eric needed the details, they got them, but she wouldn't share all of her memories just to satisfy their curiosity.

"She'll remember," she said, looking to the faces of the two men who sat with her at the dining table in Liam's apartment. "Rushe called you from that motel. We spent the night there. That must have been where he called you from to set up the apartment."

"I know where the motel is, but you're expecting

a desk clerk to remember one couple from months ago."

"She'll remember," she said again. "I was covered in bruises, she noticed. I made a comment about Rushe paying extra for bruises and if there was blood, I'd get a new pair of Manolos. She was so shocked that she couldn't speak, and Rushe scolded me afterward."

"He scolded you?" Liam asked, sounding almost offended by the notion.

"Because my comments made us memorable," she said. "That was the night the cops picked up Simone. The same night Victor died, and Skeeve and all the others. Rushe and I weren't running from the law, and I certainly wasn't under duress. That desk clerk can testify to the fact that Rushe and I were together and happy. He didn't spend the night raping me. He actually took that call with you in the reception, which left me alone. I could've run if I'd wanted to."

"Or he could've tied you down," Eric said.

"He didn't," she said, though the possibility Eric presented wasn't unheard of. "I don't want anyone to ever think that Rushe forced himself on me. I want us to gather all the evidence we can to refute that."

"You can tell the cops yourself if you're ever forced to give a statement," Liam said.

"There's a chance I won't be around to say these things at all. Look at where Jansen is for not playing along. We have to plan for every eventuality. If we stir up enough doubt, get the evidence we need to prove the truth, that's valuable progress. But we have to get the cops on board," she said, and looked to Liam. "You have to get the details on that internal investigation so we know who, if anyone, we can trust."

"I'm on it," Liam said. "I'm doing my best, but not everything is digitized."

"I'll talk to whatever lowlife you want me to," Eric said. "But I ain't going near the cops."

She levelled her attention on him. "Do you want me to go to Rushe and tell him that you upset me?"

"No," Eric said without so much as pausing for breath.

"You'll do what I need you to do," she said. "Rushe almost lost his life for the case you were so determined to recruit him for. If he had died, I'd have gotten to you and your buddy..."

"You said you walked off a street and into Rushe's life," Eric said, letting his admiration shine. "What the hell kinda street did you come from?"

"You have nothing to worry about," she said, snubbing his question and avoiding eye contact with the probably shocked Liam. "There's too much heat around you, your business is illegal, and I wouldn't trust you not to roll over on us anyway."

"Then why am I here?"

"Because two are more effective than one," she said as Rushe once had. "You do the thug stuff. I'm not scary... so I'll deal with it from the other side."

"Other side?" Eric asked.

"The side that requires diplomacy and charm," she said. "We're going over every detail of this again, and then I have a phone call to make. I want both of you clear on the game plan. I reiterate again, this is confidential. Rushe would warn me against trusting either of you, if you prove him right..."

"We get you," Eric said. "That covers us, but do you know what he's gonna do to you when he finds out what we're doing? Lying to him—"

"I'm not allowed to lie to him, not directly," she said. "I can handle Rushe."

"You better hope so," Eric said. "'Cause if you can't and he gets past you—"

"Are you scared?"

Eric clasped his hands together and rested his

weight on his forearms. "I'm not talking about you or me, I'm talking about this." He tipped his head toward the paperwork. "Everything Scott did in that room was on instruction of your boyfriend. I've never seen anything like it. You let your boy off the leash, or he gets away from you… I don't know Silver, or Mercier, but I'll tell you they're serious guys. This could start a war, and someone will get hurt."

"You think Rushe will get hurt?"

"I think you're starting something," Eric said. "And you better be willing to see it all the way through."

"Let's go over this again," she said, keeping her eyes trained to Eric's while reaching for the timeline she'd sketched.

Proving her lover's innocence would hinge on the details. If they got one thing wrong, if things didn't add up, everything could fall apart. She wouldn't let that happen.

TWENTY-ONE

GETTING BACK much later than intended, she walked through the peculiar array of objects filling the store. The items, which had caused her so much shock and outrage initially, were now a part of her everyday life.

Just like the brothel reception. A scantily clad Lilah sat behind the desk. They exchanged a nod of acknowledgement before she went through the curtain and into her bedroom, which promised the solitude and quiet she craved.

The day had been long and tiring. Going through the reports and discussing ideas of how to make things right didn't offer any solace. They still hadn't gotten anywhere concrete. The Merciers had a head start. Their side was at an unprepared disadvantage.

Taking everything off in preparation for bed, she went for a long shower then slid between the sheets alone, as was becoming custom. A minute could have passed as easily as an hour. Somehow, this time, she felt him approach even through her slumber.

The essence of her lover surrounded her, so she

let her moist eyelids part and relaxed her body weight to her back to see him standing at the bedside, watching her. There was no anger in his expression, and no love either. He simply stood, observing her. Her eyes were open, and they had to sparkle in the embers of light breaking through from the narrow windows above. Rushe must have recognized she was awake, but he didn't speak or acknowledge her consciousness.

She felt the urge to reach out and to say something, to communicate with him. For all they'd gone through together, they'd become close and forged a trust she thought was lasting. Her actions since Simone's revelation exposed her desperation to keep them together. To maintain what they'd found, and to prove to him he meant to her just what she meant to him.

But there in the silent room, with two feet between them, the longer he stood there, the more detached from him she felt. She didn't like it.

Elevating her hand, she made a show of shuffling closer without making a sound. Touching the denim on his leg, she registered the texture, smooth and yet coarse in a way that emanated through the material from his skin.

Tensing her abs, she sat, but he didn't move or speak. They couldn't go on like this, and the questions kept building inside of her. Each of them centered more and more on the woman who clearly meant so much to him.

She didn't know who Tawny was, as he'd never mentioned her before. But he'd never mentioned any specific woman from his past. He'd alluded to relationships, at least being intimate with hookers, when she'd asked directly. Maybe this was it. Maybe Tawny was the woman who came before her. It could be that now he was there, faced with his history, he craved the woman from his past more than he wanted her in his future.

She'd been secure with Rushe, but witnessing the gulf widening between them, she began to think herself naive. Tawny could be the one he truly wanted, and she had been too stubborn to see the truth.

Her own hand remained steady on his thigh as his touched her forehead. His fingertips slid back, letting her hair part between them until he combed through her tresses, over her ear, to her cheek, to her chin, holding on to her locks until they slid out of his fingers.

She couldn't let herself slip out of his soul. She belonged to him, and he belonged to her. He gave her an identity; he'd changed who she was. This was what she wanted. This was what her life was meant to be. Giving it up never occurred to her. If she had to walk away from him, she would have no purpose and no identity.

Stretching her fingers, she let them glide upward until his own broad digits got hold of hers to remove her caress. Questions throbbed in her head. She wanted to liberate them but was consumed by the sorrow she felt in him.

Could Tawny be the one he missed? Had being back with her proved to him he wanted to be with her? She couldn't let herself believe it. Rushe belonged to her, she trusted him, even in the times when he didn't trust her.

But they hadn't been intimate since arriving. They'd never had such a long passionless spell. It couldn't be ignored. Rushe had never shied from her physically, and he'd never refused her. He'd always let her take exactly what she wanted. More than that, he'd hankered for her.

Every minute of the day, every time they were together, he proved that desire. With every word he spoke to her, he betrayed how he yearned for her, and that made her feel so powerful. She loved his words, the way he spoke to her. How he couldn't hide the animal that existed in him, the one that wanted her with a singular determination.

She curled around, twisting to plant her feet on the floor on either side of his and up she stood in front of him. Her calves were pressed to the edge of the bed, and she had no room to move. But she didn't want to go anywhere. The silent moment was perhaps the most intimate they'd shared since arriving at Silver's place.

Something was different, Rushe was different, and she didn't know why. If she could foster their intimacy, remind him of their physical connection, she could encourage him to open up. All she had to do was make love with him, and he would remember their bond.

With a concentrated effort, she drew her lips inward, moistened them with her tongue, and pushed up to her tiptoes. Brushing her palm the width of his cheekbone, her fingers touched his hair, and still he didn't move or speak.

"Kiss me, Rushe," she whispered.

He did nothing, his blank eyes just stared. Refusing to take action wasn't like him. In the months they'd spent together, he'd given her confidence. He inspired her to push forward, regardless of her shame or feelings of embarrassment. He taught her there was nothing more important than this, than them.

Taking control, she found the top button of his jeans and pulled until every single one of the fasteners parted.

"You want it," he mumbled.

"Yes," she confessed, hoping this was the moment, the breakthrough, the understanding that he could trust her.

Maybe this was when he would let her in.

Dipping down, he let his mouth meet hers, and parted his lips just enough to give her the taste of him. The heat of it, that moisture, the reassuring dampness of this aching kiss was more than they'd shared in days. But it wasn't him, because this wasn't a kiss of passion, or desire, it wasn't even a kiss of love. It was a kiss of obligation. He didn't want this, and she didn't know how to react to that.

"I want you to fuck me," she murmured.

Pressing her hands against the resistance of his solid chest, she urged her breasts closer, crushing her flesh to his, trying to remind him of the connection they shared.

"Please," she exhaled, mustering the confidence that flailed inside. Matching that fierce stare she'd seen in him so many times, she pinned her gaze to his. "No fucking around. We do it here. We do it fast. We do it now."

Turning her ass to his groin, she grasped his hands around her hips. Leading them to the couch, she bent over it, keeping hold on him as she parted her legs, presenting her naked form for him as open and ready.

"Do it," she said. "Do it like only you can. I need you. I want it now… Rushe, please, make me feel. I have to feel you."

Taking the risk, she loosened her fingers from between his in the hope he would take over. This was a chance he wouldn't pass up if everything was right between them. She needed him to regain control and take what he always wanted from her. Once she was back in his system, she wouldn't let him shake her loose again.

When his digits curled, her lips mimicked the action, and as his grip increased, she thought she could feel him coming back to her.

"Oh your ass," he said, squeezing her just the way he loved to. "High up in the air, right there ready for me. Oh you've got a sweet fucking ass."

Rushe would spank her stupid for it, but she almost wanted to giggle at his words of appreciation out of the sheer delight she felt at hearing them.

"Yes," she breathed, pushing back when he parted her folds and slid his fingers between them, up and down, through the juice that was there for him.

"You're ready, Kitten. All juiced up, all ready to go… You fucking whore."

She whimpered, but his fingers slowed, slowed, and stopped. Then they were gone. She hoped he was about to take her by surprise. That something was about to happen. That this was the instant they'd be together again.

"Do it," she said. "Fuck me, oh God, Rushe."

Fumbling behind her, she tried to seek his hand, but it wasn't there. Her heart beat loud in her ears, every contraction of the organ sent a barb of anguish outward. He was gone. Blood rushed through her veins in a torrent so loud that she heard it, yet she was cold. Her extremities prickled. He'd withdrawn, and there wasn't a fathomable reason for it.

"I can't."

In that second, her heart shattered in a way she'd never known possible. The only time he'd ever been incapable was with Simone. He couldn't function sexually because he didn't want the skinny French chick. He'd been in love with Flick, his Kitten, his woman.

Now they stood there in that brothel, and she felt him slipping away. Rushe said he couldn't. If he couldn't get an erection, it was for one reason and one reason alone, he loved someone else.

Letting her knees bend, they unlocked of their own accord, and she crumpled to the floor in a crouch. Covering her face with both hands, she propped her forehead on the back of the couch and let herself sob aloud; embarrassment be damned.

Rushe couldn't do it, he couldn't be with her. That meant only one thing. A nightmare she had never previously considered had just become reality.

Her instinct was to recoil when his fingertips met her shoulder, but he was stronger and still touched her with entitlement. Curling his digits around the ball of her shoulder, they bit into her with the force he had to use to turn her. He spun her body, and though she complied, she smacked his arm away from her form in the process.

"Don't," she yapped. As her forearm came back down, she noticed something in the way he crouched beside her. "You're hard." Unable to take her eyes from the thick length of him bobbing so proudly between his thighs still on a plateau of denim, she was mesmerized.

"You're offended?" he asked.

"No, I… I don't understand."

"You don't understand?"

"You just said you couldn't," she said. "The only time, the only reason…"

Her anger wouldn't help anyone, and she would just make a fool of herself. Ignoring the rods of agony growing in her throat, she made herself meet his eye.

"It never occurred to me," she admitted. "Not until right now."

"What?"

"That you might… that you might love her more than you love me."

"What the fuck are you talking about?"

"But I don't understand, if you love her…" she murmured. "You have an erection."

Of its own accord, her hand moved forward until her fingers coiled around the length of him. Not in a sexual advance, in a sort of embrace, a comfort, something familiar to hold onto and anchor herself to in this confusing time.

"We can't do it. We can't do it here," he said, taking hold of her wrist to remove her hand.

"Are you withdrawing presumed consent?"

"You think if I wake up to you riding my cock that I'm gonna cry rape?"

"That would be unlikely to happen when you refuse to share my bed with me."

Rushe stood, once again, looking down at her from above. "That's rich, when you've been going to him."

"Don't pretend to be the jealous type. If you thought Liam wanted to touch me, you'd have gone after him already and beat him to a pulp, wouldn't you?" Forcing her knees to take her weight, she straightened her limbs until she stood in front of him. He didn't speak. "Wouldn't you? Rushe? Tell me you would. Tell me I'm your woman."

"He wants you. Don't let your guard down, not for a second."

"What is this?" she beseeched. "What's going on here?"

He walked away. Rushe turned his back and paced away in an action that frustrated her. He didn't like to argue, neither did she, and none of this made any sense.

"What is it you're trying to tell me? What is it I don't understand? Do you love her?" she asked, ignoring the flash of grief that spread out as a ripple from her core.

"Who?" he asked, spinning around. The instant he read her expression, he frowned, and his own torture grew within him. "You're hurt. I'm hurting you."

"Yes." Crossing to the bed, she couldn't hold up her own weight anymore. "I can't breathe," she exhaled, willing herself not to lose it, and not to get emotional.

Becoming hysterical would achieve nothing, it would only upset him. Trying to regain her composure, she pulled her lip between her teeth and tried to set her jaw, still, her chin quivered.

"You know..." she started. "When I thought I'd

lost you… When I thought you were dead… I couldn't breathe. I couldn't breathe, it was… the world stopped turning, and I couldn't stand upright. I couldn't breathe, everything was pain. I fell to the ground, and I didn't want to ever get back up. I lay in that alley, and I'd have stayed there forever. I'd have stayed there forever, Rushe… And now you're here in front of me, and… I don't want to get back up."

Letting her chin fall, moisture seeped out of her eyes. Despite her best attempts to fight, the tears prevailed. He'd disconnected, he wasn't hers, and she didn't know how to get him back.

TWENTY-TWO

BEFORE TUMULTUOUS EMOTION took over, before she let it consume her, she snatched for strength. Rushe gave her power, he made her better. If another man threatened him, he wouldn't collapse, he wouldn't cry. He wouldn't give up.

In a flurry of movement, she opened the drawer, and her hand went inside to seek the knife he'd given her for protection. This wasn't physical protection; it was emotional. Still, protecting herself from pain was her goal all the same.

Surging to her feet, she was intent on exactly what she had to do.

Rushe got hold of her wrist, twisting it until the knife hit the floor. "If I loved her, do you think I would let you hurt her?" he asked. "Do you think I would let anyone hurt the woman I love?"

If she needed confirmation of his feelings, that was it. "I won't let you go to her," she said, determined. Her arm slackened in his hold. "Tell me what I need to do."

The stretch of her fortitude increased with every single second, because this was the man she loved and wanted to be with. She would do anything for him, anything to make him happy, just as he'd promised to do for her.

But he didn't say anything, just remained stoic. She widened her eyes, focusing her burning courage on him, proving she would go to any lengths for him.

"Tell me what I have to do to make you happy."

"Stop it," he growled, baring his teeth.

"Give me a chance to—"

"Stop."

"Please," she said. "It's not fair to expect me to—"

"Kitten! Goddamnit, you are my woman."

Crouching, his arms came to sweep her off the floor into his embrace. His mouth clashed on hers. This was a hungry man, a starving man. One losing grip on his last thread of control. This man kissed as though she held the key to his very existence. His mouth was wide, beckoning hers, desperate for more than she could give. Turned out he would always take what she could offer, crave what she provided, just as she craved him.

With a ragged breath in, her head fell back when he nudged her out the way and kissed down the column of her throat. Twining her legs around his hips, her body merged with his as they collapsed onto the bed. This man wanted her. Her love wanted her.

"You are my woman," he said. "Fuck. This body, I love this body… Your tits, your ass, you're hot, I wanna fuck you. I wanna fuck you until you never forget."

"I couldn't forget," she said.

His mouth was everywhere, her mouth, her neck, her shoulders, her breasts. His hands slid down her arms and up into her hair, back down. Grasping her breasts, he squeezed her nipples, and she whimpered in the ecstasy he provided.

This was a man in love. This wasn't a man holding back, wasn't a man not in love with her. This was her man connecting, seeking her soul. This was exactly the physical breakthrough they needed.

"Talk to me," she pleaded, desperate to hear what he wanted to do with her, because she didn't want to lose this yet.

"Don't ever doubt me again," he said, rasping his teeth over one nipple and then the next.

"I didn't doubt you. I didn't... one day you're going to turn around and see... God, I'm so scared I might lose you."

His mouth ceased in its feast, and he rose to look down at her. "You're fucking crazy," he said. "You're one dumb bitch, you know that?"

"Rushe," she said on a sigh, eager to hear him, to see him, to feel him, to be a part of him.

Coiling her legs higher, she hooked her toes inside the loose waistband of his jeans and pushed down until she'd stripped his jeans away, as far as her legs would let her.

"You're my woman," he said, gazing down on her. "Here, this place, this isn't for love, this isn't for... What we are, and what we have, is not here. It's not for here."

"That's what it is, isn't it? You think it's disrespectful," she said and sighed, almost ready to laugh at her own stupidity. "You think you'd be disrespecting me."

"No, no, it's more than that," he said, clearly frustrated. "This place, a woman like you, you're here because of me, Flick. You shouldn't know places like this exist, let alone be existing here."

"Rushe," she said, sliding her hands up over every ridge of his muscular chest to his shoulders, and across the width of him. She appreciated the strength of him, the security and stability of the man at the core of her universe. "I love you. I want to experience everything with you."

"Just a few days ago…" he said. "We were at your parents… that house, that place… that guy…

"Robert?"

"I saw the way he looked at you."

"You say that about every man."

"You're fucking hot," he grumbled.

"Rushe," she said, as clarity rattled through her. "You've been insecure. You look at where we were, and you look at where we are, and you think that the difference matters. Why can't you see this is what matters? You and me together, talking, being intimate. I don't care where we are, Rushe. I care that we're together. I don't like to be alone. I don't want to go through this without you."

"You are my woman."

"Yes. Are you going to fuck me?"

"You give me everything, Flick," he said. "I don't know why you do it. I don't know why."

"I do it because I love you, because this is what I want, because you are what I want."

"This place is who I am," he said. "This kind of place, this, scum, depravity, deprivation, people, everywhere, all the time…"

"Being all alone in a crowded room," she said when he didn't finish his thought.

"You make me better. But I don't get it, I don't understand what you get. This is who I am. This… it's horrible, it's disgusting, and a woman like you should not be here. You could have anything and anyone you want in the world. Why would you want to be anywhere near scum like me?"

"This isn't about your false opinion of yourself,"

she said. "You don't believe you're good enough for me, and I disagree. This place reminds you of the isolation, of what it was like to be alone; to have no one and nothing. You're a part of something now, you're not alone. You've never had anything to lose before."

"I worry about you every minute of the goddamn day. It ripped me apart to watch you walk outta here today, and yesterday when I thought... But I can't protect you. I can't do it. I've failed every single fucking time."

"You haven't failed," she said. "We go looking for this. This is what we do. Yes, it's dangerous, and yes, we could get hurt. But this isn't a day at the office. We do it because it needs to be done. Nobody else will do it. We do it because it's right. Somebody has to stand up for what's right. This is a privilege, that you share this with me, your life, your work."

"It endangers you."

"Everything endangers us, Rushe," she said. "We all live in danger every day. You and I are just more aware of it than the general population."

His hands moved down her shoulders until he shifted his weight onto his elbows when he hooked them beneath her waist.

"I wanna fuck you."

"You can, you're allowed," she whispered. "Why have you not wanted to touch me?"

"I wanna touch you. You know I wanna touch you. My cock's been thinking about nothing but your pussy, about how good it feels being in there. I couldn't come near you. I couldn't spend the night in here because I couldn't trust myself to do it. I knew you would let me fuck you. I knew you would. I knew you would let me have access to that sweet, little fucking body. But I couldn't do it here."

"Yes, you can. When you're with me, don't think

about them. Don't think about where, or how, or why. Just know that it's right, and it's allowed."

"But when I talk to you—"

"Tell me how you like it," she said. "Do you want me just to lay back and let you work me over? God, you make me horny, I've been so wet for you."

"Are you trying to turn me on?"

"I can feel him," she said, wriggling to let herself get as close to his dick as she could, though he still dominated her and controlled the show. "You can be as dirty as you want, any time you want. You don't disrespect me. I feel respected. I feel powerful when you tell me you want me that much."

"You love the way my cock fills you up, are you empty without it? You're a bad girl."

"I'm a dirty whore."

"You think you can handle it," he said, dropping his lips to her skin to allow the heat of his breath to cascade across her. "Handle what I'm about to do to you. I'm gonna hold you down and make you come. I'm gonna make you scream… I'm gonna give it to you how I like it."

"Yes."

"You can't wait, can you? You want it."

"Yes."

"Oh, my girl, are you gonna show me how much you like it? Scream for me? Speak."

"Yes," she breathed.

He kissed her again, quickly, then his hands were down at her hips, on her thighs, and he rose, pressing his weight against his palms, on her thighs until they burned. He reared up, the length of him slipped to her center, and she knew what was coming next.

Opening her eyes, she looked at him as he looked at her. On lifting her hand toward the glimmer of his smile, which had been absent for so long, he bucked back and surged forward to slam into her all the way to the hilt.

"Oh good God," she gasped as he cursed into the air, filling it with every expletive she'd ever heard and quite a few she hadn't.

"Oh, God," he groaned.

It had been too long.

"Keep going."

"You feel that? You feel where my cock is right now?" he said, gritting his teeth, his voice becoming nothing but a bassy vibration in his chest that rattled through his body, right through her, right through that point of contact where he was inside her, where he belonged.

"Yes."

"You feel that shit?"

"Oh…" She could tell from the way he exhaled after every one of his words just how he was trying to hold onto the control he usually exercised so well.

"Your fucking pussy's wet. Tell me how much you like that shit."

"Oh, yeah," she said. "I like it. I love it. I want you. I love your cock. I love it when you fuck me. I love it—"

"Shut it."

She lifted her torso slightly to dig her nails into the backs of his hands pressed against her thighs. "More."

"You being a cocky little bitch?"

"I want your cock," she said. "I want it right there."

"You feel it? Speak."

"Yes."

"You like being fucked hard, don't you?" he asked. "Say it."

"Oh, I like being fucked hard," she said. "Mm,

Rushe, please…"

"You like being fucked hard and rough. You need a strong guy to work you over. A guy who's just gonna throw you down and fuck you—"

"I don't need a guy," she snarled, cutting him off, which was very unlike her. "I need you. Any other guy tries to touch me, I'll kill him myself."

"You want a bad guy, don't you? I get you off. You like it when I fuck you hard, give it to you rough, don't you?"

"Yes."

He pulled back, and pushed in, out and in, and every time she breathed his name. She said it aloud because she wanted to remember and didn't ever want to forget again. His hands moved from her thighs to her hands, he took them and let his weight fall forward pressing her into the mattress, his body moving up and down, pounding into her faster and harder.

She said his name again. He groaned, fucking faster. Lifting her hips, she met him each time, working her clit against his groin.

"Oh, you filthy fucking whore!"

Coming half out of her passage, he stalled just on the cusp of her orgasm. She swore at him. One beat of his sinister laughter made her eyes pop open, she had him back. That laugh, that smile, those words, they proved he trusted her again.

Just as she smiled, one of his hands left hers to come between them, meeting their point of unity. He rubbed her clit in a circle, smudging the moisture between them, lathering her up until a piercing spike of pleasure fired between her legs, up to her chest and out of her mouth in a long, desperate wail.

He roared, beating backwards and forwards, hammering into her until on one last curse he pushed all the way inside and filled her, every inch of her. Pouring his liquid into her, staining her, he filled the gaping chasm, the starving hunger, that famished spot inside her only he was capable of sating.

Breathing out, he didn't even try to stop panting before he fell down to his side, taking her body with his as he rolled to his back and held her above him.

"I love you," he said into her hair.

She turned her head to him, rubbing her face, her nose, her mouth, her lips, her cheeks, all of herself against him. "I know you do. I love you too."

TWENTY-THREE

THE SULTRY SUCTION on her left breast was as enthusiastic as the ardent massage the other received. He caught her nipple in the joint of his thumb and squeezed until she moaned.

Nothing more than a lustful dream, his hand skimmed down her torso and two of his long, sturdy digits squashed up into her core. The ease of his entry confirmed he'd lubricated his path into her already. The tingling heat between her thighs she'd woken up to had been of his making. His mouth floated up her body until he licked her bottom lip, giving her an intimate taste of where he'd been.

"Morning," he said, not so subtly bringing his knee higher between her legs to urge them apart.

"Shh," she said, aware of her burgeoning grin. "I'm having a really good dream, don't wake me up yet."

"This okay?"

"Don't you dare ask for my consent," she said, letting her hands spread on his biceps.

"Wasn't gonna," he said, and like she was an

object, he took hold of her hips and shifted her into a position more suitable for him, or rather more pleasing because he nestled himself between her thighs. "Are you hungry?"

"Are you going to feed me, Lover?"

"Not what I meant, but sure. If you want a spunk breakfast, that's cheap and easy."

"Like me?" she teased still without opening her eyes.

The head of his cock came so deliciously close to penetration that she purred. But the solid heat of his form left hers, and the bed beside her bounced. Prying her eyelids apart, she rolled her head to see him sprawled beside her.

"Rushe, this is my dream, my scintillating wake-up call," she said. "You're supposed to be arousing me."

"You want me to empty my balls into your belly, Kitten, you don't gotta ask me twice."

Now almost sorry she'd interrupted his seduction, she traced her toes up his calf, until her instep formed around his knee. She slid it down and up while watching the unconscious rhythm of his hand curled around his dick.

He removed her hand from his hip to replace the direct contact around his member with her palm. She let him carry on pumping his fist, using her hand as the sheath that delivered his pleasure.

"Climb on up and ride my cock," he grumbled, but didn't stop the jerking motion.

"I want you to lick me all over first," she taunted, rocking her figure toward him to coil her body around the length of his.

His hand left hers on his dick so he could snatch her thigh and yank it up until it pressed to his balls. But the motion brought her own center against his solid, static thigh. Grinding in, she pressed her nose to the muscle of his arm and opened her mouth when she tilted her head to drag her teeth against him.

"Wrap those pretty lips around my cock, now." Still writhing against him, she reveled in the pinch of her clit trapped between her pubis and his quadriceps. "You're gonna suck me off, Kitten, suck me like your life depends on it."

"My pussy is hungry too," she said, licking his arm and letting her eyes trail up to his as she tightened her grip again.

"Oh, she's gonna get her turn," he growled. Spanning his hand under her hair, he took hold of her chin and tipped her head back as far as it would go. "Open your mouth."

At his request, she parted her lips and his thumb scrubbed across her lower lip to her teeth. He bent his digit between her incisors and forced her jaw further down. Hooking it down into the soft flesh under her tongue, her love coerced her mouth far open until an ache arose beneath her temples.

"You were made for my cock," he said, peering down her throat like she was a show animal. The possessive maneuver got her wriggling closer, this time until her pelvis rounded to mount the front of his thigh. "You pleasing my pussy?" Though he still had hold of her jaw, she managed to nod, but when she tried to avert her attention, he yanked it back to his. "You're gonna show me how much you like that. How grateful you are for my cock? How you want your seat right there on my dick to be permanently reserved?"

He said the words in a snarl, but the ferocity in him was gratitude. Last night she had fixed something in him and brought them back together. There, he proved sharing this intimacy was as important to him as it was to her.

"Rub my cock."

While pumping her hand up and down, Rushe's hand loosened from her face.

"Put your hand in my hair," she murmured. Rushe loved her hair. He was as tactile with it as any other part of her body, and so intent on it at times that his adoration of it was almost sexual.

Sinister triumph lit his eyes, but it made her smile. This was where her power lay. Taking his hand to the top of her head, he spread his fingers wide and loose, capturing as many strands as he could. Twisting her locks, he pressured her down. A sting of pain shot to her nipples, bringing them to pebbled points, which she dragged down the length of him, tickling herself with the bliss of thorny gratification.

He anticipated her mouth, but she paused, relaxing the weight of her breasts against his groin. Wobbling them down, she squirmed closer, enveloping him in her generous cleavage.

"What about your girls," she asked. "They've missed him too." His fingers were still coiled in her hair, but she had the leeway to turn her lips against his abdomen and kiss the grooves of his stomach. "They feel neglected."

"Ain't any part of my woman that's gonna be neglected."

She sighed. "That's what I wanted to hear."

Trailing her tits downward, she slid her clit down over his knee, leaving the intimate scent of herself on his skin. When he growled, she knew he sensed it, but breathing the length of him into her mouth, the pleasure focus flitted.

"You dirty slut," he snarled, loosening then tightening his hold on her hair in time with her ducking and jerking motion. "All that practice and you still love it. You live to suck on my cock, don't you? Speak."

Releasing her concave cheeks with a slurp, she

didn't bother to empty her mouth and held his length against the roof of her mouth with her tongue while nodding.

"Yes," she said, circling her soaked muscle around all of him that she could.

"Lick my balls."

She did as told, then sucked one testicle gently into her mouth.

He groaned as his body spasmed. "Fuck, Kitten."

Straightening her legs, she worked herself on his shin, nipping her clit, wringing her own pleasure as she administered his.

"Don't you come," he ground out through gritted teeth. "Do you get off on sucking my dick?"

"My dick," she said, letting it pop from her mouth to work it with her fist.

He yanked her up. One hand remained in her hair and the other under her arm. Forcing her to her back, he hooked an elbow under her knee and wedged his cock into her pussy, expanding the path for his satisfaction.

"You don't get a say in nothing, you're going to do what you're told. You're gonna scream like the dirty slut you are... You're gonna say thank you for my cock... say it."

"Thank you."

"Thank you, what?"

"Thank you, sir."

"Good girl."

Crushing the head of his dick against her cervix, he slid back through the mire that eased his undulation. His neck thickened as he battered harder until the spurt of his release met the clamp of her passage and they froze together in time, mingled in climax.

"Lover, that was..."

She couldn't find the words because she wasn't

sure if they existed. Though he remained in his habitat within her, she already missed the satiating distension of his thrusting. She wanted him to be in her forever and never wanted to lose him again.

TWENTY-FOUR

AFTER AN UNUSUALLY prolonged make-out session in the shower, Rushe satisfied her another couple of times and then insisted that she get dressed.

"Cody will be here now," he said, taking her hand.

When he moved to leave the sanctuary of their bedroom, she stayed put. "Then we should stay here," she said. "I only have an hour."

"Kitten, we have to talk," he said, touching the top of her head. "And if we stay in here…" His attention lowered to devour the sight of her clothed form. "We have to go out."

The smug coil of gratification made her smile, he'd just betrayed that he wanted her again already.

"Okay."

This time when he went for the door, she let him hook her hand into his back pocket and take her down the hall to reception. That day it was unoccupied. The store was manned, another blonde sat behind the register. Cody stood on the other side of the counter with a goofy grin plastered on his face, until he saw Rushe at least, because then it quickly vanished.

"Move."

This single word from Rushe sent Cody scrambling backwards, and he almost toppled over a display of various butt plugs. The scrawny henchman recovered and ran to the door, literally leaping to the sidewalk.

She was surprised that Rushe didn't speak to the girl. Instead, he took them outside and took hold of Cody's tee-shirt to shove him down into a seat by the door.

"Fink's gonna be over with Barry in twenty minutes, you sit here," Rushe said. "No one in or out."

Cody nodded, and her love strode away with her scampering along in his wake. On the next block, he swung her around into a corner diner. The cracked yellow floor had probably once been white, but the benches facing each other over the blue Formica tables were clean, and the faces seemed indifferent enough.

Rushe unhooked her hand from his pants and took her hip to rotate her around so that he could shunt her into the booth. He began to head for the bench on the opposite side of the table, but she seized his wrist to halt him.

"Sit next to me," she said.

"Why?"

The blank expression and abrupt question curled her lips. "I'm not a company contact; you can put your hand up my skirt while we talk. How many of your colleagues have you been able to do that with in the past?"

He slid in beside her. "You want me to finger fuck you here?"

"Degrees of love, my love," she said, reminding herself she still had things to teach him too.

Gathering his hand from his thigh and into hers, he watched under the table as she held their linked fingers together, there on his knee. His brow came down, and his confusion spurred her on. Stretching her other arm toward him, she curved it around until she found his stubble, and then she scooched in until her thigh pressed to the length of his. She boosted up a little and let their lips meet.

"You're too damn frisky to be out in public," he grumped, noticing the viewing pleasure he got of her breasts from that angle.

"Where's your guard?" she teased and a low rumble quaked from his chest.

"You want coffee?" the server, with the tied back curls, asked on pausing at their table.

"Yeah," Rushe said, still eyeing her cleavage.

"Anything else?" the waitress asked.

"I would like—"

"No."

Rushe cut her off, but the server didn't bother to appear surprised or offended, she just walked off.

"You said we were coming out to breakfast," she said.

"We needed distance."

"Why?"

"Away from that place to talk," he said. "They asked me to take the rap."

Playtime was over, the distance was needed so that they could talk privately. If the Merciers had already put their proposition to him, it made sense why her love hadn't been all that surprised when she revealed the details of her conversation with Simone.

"What did you say?" she asked.

"I told them to go to hell," he said under his brooding brow. "I don't trust any of them and taking me off the street makes you more vulnerable. I need to be around to watch your tail."

"I'm glad you're coming to realize that."

Crossing her legs toward him, she curled into the warmth his form offered. His arm stretched along the back of the booth to tuck her body further into his.

"You do know that if this was as easy as me going inside to keep you safe…"

"You'd do anything to keep me safe," she said, reiterating to him the faith she had both in him and his commitment to her, as she would probably always have to.

"If I'm in there, and you're out here alone—"

"You don't have to explain the insanity of their scheme. They'll only keep doing what they're doing. It won't prevent trouble. Taking you out is their number one goal, because they know getting rid of you makes the rest of us useless. Putting me in the position of testifying against you means I'd have to oppose you, so I couldn't do a thing to help liberate you."

"They'll come for you."

"I know what they want from me, and they won't get it," she said. "I've started to collate everything we need to prove your innocence. No matter what they throw at us, we won't have to worry about the legal side. I'm going to make sure of that. Liam's trying to get the records of the internal investigation regarding Jansen."

"It didn't even occur to you," he stated. "Not for a second."

"What?" she asked, retracing what she had said.

"To squeal on me."

Angling back, she blinked up to meet his eye. Her outrage waned when she saw the slant of his smile. Taking his hand from hers under the table, he coiled his fingers into the ends of her hair until his pressure tilted her head and he compelled their mouths together.

Initiating an isolated kiss was unlike him but

doing so in public was almost unheard of. He broke off the union when the server came over to fill two coffee mugs. Rushe scrutinized her face until the waitress left.

"My woman," he mumbled, lowering his gaze to her cleavage, and loosening his fingers from her locks.

Spreading his bold digits on her smooth thigh, his palm skimmed north under the wisp of her cotton skirt.

Basking in the rediscovery of each other was gratifying, but she had the chance to seek answers from him while they were alone.

"You've been here in this place before, at the brothel," she said, venturing to broach the subject that had been plaguing her.

Rushe read her mind and interpreted the real motive for her statement. "I never fucked Tawny."

"Oh thank God," she sighed, laying a palm on his chest, and letting her head fall against him beside it.

"You could've just asked me," he said, dropping his mouth to the back of her head.

"It's your business. When it's time to tell me things, you do." Turning her head, she kept it resting on his chest under his chin. "I trust you."

"You're something else, you know that?"

"If they got their way, would you still talk dirty to me?"

"From prison?"

"Maybe we could have a conjugal visit," she said, hooking her calf up over his knee.

"Dirty girl," he grumbled. "You ready for more?"

Sliding her hand up, she wound her fingers around his corded neck and let them continue to his jaw so she could direct his mouth down to hers. The sweep of his tongue tempted her to grope for more. It wasn't until he removed her fumbling digits from the buttons of his jeans that she realized she'd subconsciously acted on that thrumming desire.

"When we're through with this case I want you to myself for a month," she said.

"Only a month?" he asked, but she gleaned his teasing.

"You won't get a minute of rest."

"I'm gonna come with you today," he said, toying with her hair again.

"That makes me happy."

"That's what I'm here for, Kitten."

"Will you tell me why you were here before?"

"About five months before the Jansen job," Rushe said. "I tracked her down."

"Tawny?"

"Yeah," he said, opening his fingers and closing them with her locks between. "I'd been trying to track her down for a while. It wasn't a job, so I got side-tracked a lot."

"If it wasn't for a job," she said, "it was personal."

His jaw moved. This was a pivotal moment. Rushe didn't share easily and sharing anything personal was even more difficult for him. It didn't matter that he trusted her. All of his life, he'd relied on no one but himself, it was his default state to be reserved.

"Her mom was the woman in the alley, the one I told you about."

"Oh," she exhaled.

As a youngster, Rushe watched a woman be abducted from an alleyway and had been powerless to prevent it. He found out later the woman was raped and murdered. That single incident prompted Rushe to take on cases in defense of women who were unable to stand up to those who wronged them.

"Does she know?" she asked. "Tawny, does she

know about—"

"No," he said. "I wasn't gonna tell her I let that happen to her mom. She'd never understand." That, and Rushe didn't like talking about it. "Tawny was only a few months old when her mom died. She was in foster care. I didn't even know Tawny existed 'til a few years back when I…"

"When you what?" she asked, caressing his chest.

"I'd put it off for years, but… I did some research on Darlene… the woman from the alley. I wanted to know who she was, that's when I found out about her daughter."

Doing research on subjects was part of what Rushe did, he didn't take anything at face value. It was possible he wanted to know Darlene's history, or maybe he wanted to find out she wasn't as great as she appeared to be when she tried to reach out to him. But he'd got more than he bargained for.

"You came here to help Tawny?" she asked.

"I came to find out if she needed help, if she was okay."

"And she wasn't?"

"She's had it rough," Rushe said. "But she could do worse than Silver."

"You're defending her pimp?"

"Silver looks after his girls, he provides a safe working environment."

"You offer that environment because you owe him a debt."

Rushe tilted his head. "What else did Simone tell you?"

"Just that," she said, "and about their intentions of framing you."

"Do me a favor, Kitten," he said. His fingers glided to the back of her knee to trace circles with barely any pressure. "Don't jump to conclusions, okay? Don't forget what we're about."

"Okay."

His fingers stopped. "Just like that, you comply," he muttered, emanating a subdued awe.

She lifted her eyes to his. "I trust you."

"You're something else, Kit. You take it all in your stride."

"I am your woman," she said, set with her own determination. "I will make you proud."

He took another few seconds to admire her. "I've gotta talk to Cody before we go to your meeting."

Between the booth and the brothel, he didn't let go of her hand. After a few stern words with Cody, her love took her to a vehicle parked at the back of the building. He demanded the address of their destination and they got underway.

She hadn't known Rushe was coming with her that day so hadn't warned Liam. The two men had only met once. Neither had made the best of impressions, which she couldn't really understand because they'd actually agreed with each other.

But wherever she went, there was always the chance she'd be living in Rushe's shadow. It was her home and the place she was most at ease.

TWENTY-FIVE

LIAM OPENED the door with a smile, which dropped to the floor when he noticed the man standing behind her with his arm draped the width of her collarbone.

"Any progress?" she asked, entering without offering any explanation for Rushe's presence.

She would never make excuses for attending anywhere with her protector.

"I found out why we've had trouble with the internal investigation records," Liam said, closing the door when she and Rushe were inside.

The paperwork spread over the dining table drew Rushe's attention. After he scanned the room to take in all the features, he switched their positions, hooking her hand into his back pocket to go over to peruse it.

"Why?" she asked, turning to address a frowning Liam, keeping hold of Rushe's pocket.

Her love liked to have her close, especially in unfamiliar surroundings, and while potential threats loitered. Liam was no threat, Rushe knew it intellectually, but convincing her lover to accept that was a different matter.

"The records were destroyed, a lot of them anyway," Liam said. "Internal Affairs turned up evidence of corruption throughout the chain of command. A couple of captains lost their jobs, actually."

"I'm surprised the department managed to keep it quiet," she said.

"After the first captain lost his job, the second was found destroying evidence of the internal investigation."

"Which is how you found out about evidence that no longer exists," Rushe murmured and took a piece of paper from the table to read it. She looked past him to see it was the timeline she'd laid out. "You wrote this?"

"Yes," she said.

"How did you remember all these details?" Rushe asked.

"It wasn't an everyday occurrence for me," she said. "My memory of events is pretty vivid." Floating closer, she rested her mouth onto his arm. His features relaxed as he read the document again. From the way his body listed toward hers, the reading was cover for his esteem. "I think you've got a good memory of it yourself, Lover."

"There's a bedroom in there if you need it," Liam sniped.

Rushe whipped around so fast she was almost bowled over. Catching his ribcage to steady herself, she soothed his vicious snarl simultaneously.

"Is he upsetting you?" Rushe asked through motionless lips, his eyes burning fury to Liam.

"No," she said. "He's right. We're here to work." Rushe continued to glare over her head. "I'll never say anything incriminating about you, but we have to make damn sure none of the other women do, or that there's any evidence that can be construed to imply any guilt on your part."

"First part of that is finding out what you're guilty of," Liam said.

She struggled to comprehend the accusation in Liam's words, but when she about-faced, he was still the only one there. "You think we're guilty of something?" she asked. "We've talked about this in detail, several times now. If you believed we were in the wrong—"

"He's talking about me, Kit."

Though their bodies still touched and the distance between them was non-existent, the calm understanding Rushe exuded had converted into something else by the time it reached her. Outrage smacked her between the eyes, and she felt in no way calm about it.

"No, look," Liam said. "I don't want to start anything. I just meant—"

"I told you not to be derogatory," she said, angling herself in front of Rushe. "I warned you what would happen if—"

"Get your reins," Liam said, holding up his hands as he traversed toward them. "I apologize, I didn't mean that in the way that it sounded. What I meant was, if there was the possibility, no matter how minute, that there could maybe be evidence out there that could be used to—"

"We shot Shiv," she said, peeking over her shoulder at Rushe.

"Both of you?" Liam asked.

"At different times," she said without taking her focus away from her love.

"He was patched up, and there's no way to prove who pulled the trigger. All the witnesses are dead."

"Except Simone."

"She didn't witness either of us pull a trigger,"

Rushe said.

She noted his words were vague. "Proving you weren't pivotal in the trafficking and that you didn't violate any of those women, those are the main things."

"I'm still trying to trace statements," Liam said. "The whole thing is a mess. Most of what I have is pretty vague in terms of facts. The women describe their individual abductions and their treatment. They don't have a lot of names and dates, just stories of events. But the criminal case has escalated."

"Escalated?" she asked. "What does that mean?"

"There's been plenty of local investigation into Victor's money lending operation. But the testimony of the abducted women, that's all been turned over to the feds."

"Yeah," Rushe grumbled.

"That's great," she said, with a welcome glimmer of hope. "If they're investigating, they'll find out the truth."

"That's not the way it works, Kit," Rushe said.

"They don't seem to care about the internal investigation," Liam said.

"They're not gonna investigate the internal politics of their subordinate colleagues," Rushe said. "They're not gonna care about Jansen or Serendipity, what they care about is where those women were going... But they won't find that out, not if the cops destroyed everything before the feds got involved. Everyone who knew anything is dead, and the paper trail will have been erased. The victims didn't know anything. Victor was far removed from the top of the chain, that was the point of using him."

"They planned to frame him all along?" Liam asked.

"If things went bad, he was a great mark," Rushe said. "A lowlife in over his head, it would've played well."

"Which is why painting you as his partner puts you into the hot seat."

As her head came up, her throat constricted. "Oh God," she said in an exhale.

"What is it?" Liam asked, hurrying the rest of the distance toward her.

Rushe hooked his arm around the front of her shoulders, easing her body back against his.

"That room, that basement, the female abductees saw Victor order you upstairs with Simone. What if she claims that was under duress? What if she claims you had sex? You told them you'd have sex with me… that you'd had sex with me."

"If you tell the cops it was consensual, they'll have no reason to disbelieve that," Liam said. "You're still together now for crissakes, he'd have to be a monster to have been raping you all this time."

"It's not impossible," she said. "They kept Serendipity for months. They could have subjected her to any number of horrors."

"If they can pin the abduction charges on him, coupled with prolonged abuse like that, and possibly murder too… he'll never get out of jail. He'll be in for life."

"Which is why we have to prove he's innocent." No reassurance came from Rushe, he merely expelled a long exhale. "Stop toying and talk," she said, sensing the thoughts rattling through his mind.

"You're both off track. You've missed the most vital factor in all of this."

"Which is?" she asked, knowing he had the most experience in the room.

"Whether the cops, or feds, believe I raped you, or anyone, doesn't matter. The second captain was destroying evidence for a reason. Who was he doing it for?" Rushe asked. "The Merciers? The feds? Was he covering his own ass or somebody else's? And what is it that they don't want us to see?"

"Yeah," Liam exhaled. "You're right. If this is corrupt at all levels, they can frame anything, anyway that they want. We can't trust anyone. We have no way to know if the Merciers are paying off any of the investigating feds either. Evidence be damned, they can destroy it."

"Or fabricate it," Rushe said.

"We can collect it all," Liam said. "But we'd eventually have to turn it over to the authorities. Especially if they already had you in custody and we're trying to get you out."

"And that's when it would start to disappear," Rushe said. "Nothing is secure until we know who is looking over our shoulder."

"But the only person we can trust," she said. "The only cop we can trust is…"

"Jansen," Rushe said.

"The guy in the hospital?" Liam asked, folding his arms. "I thought he went rogue and took on the traffickers in a rage of revenge?"

"They imprisoned his woman," Rushe said. "Can you think of a better reason to want to punish the fuckers?"

"Why didn't he come to us?" Flick said.

"He'd have had no way to get in touch with us," Rushe said. "I'd have told him to go to hell if he called, because if I had a choice, you'd be nowhere near any of this shit."

"Serendipity might know the details of what Jansen was doing," she said. "If I could get back in to talk to her."

"Where were they holding her?"

"In an apartment," she said. "It's in the city. I expected to be traveling for hours, but we weren't. She's in a perfectly normal city apartment."

"Could you find it again?" Rushe asked, turning his mouth against her head when he propped himself down on the table and nestled her in the vee of his thighs.

"No," she said, aware of her crappy sense of direction. "They blindfolded me, and I—"

"It's okay," Rushe said, actually pursing his lips against her. That was a day for kissing, apparently. "Unless I could bust in and take the place to make it completely secure for you, then you wouldn't be going back there anyway."

"We could go to Jansen's apartment, or Serendipity's," she said. "See if there's anything—"

"The cops, or the Merciers, will have already gone through them, I'll bet. But I can get a guy to—"

Rapping on the door had Rushe bolting upright. His body swooped around her, and his arm came around to lock her in place against his back.

"Expecting company?" Rushe demanded. "What have you brought to us, Hutten?"

TWENTY-SIX

"RELAX," SHE ASSUAGED, sliding her hand down his arm. Swerving around him, she went to the door and opened it before Rushe could snatch her and tie her to something.

"I got the—" Eric stopped as soon as he came in and noticed Rushe.

Her lover was already striding across the room, so she hurried to intercept him. Planting her hands on his ribs didn't stall him. She actually slid back a foot and a half on the hardwood flooring before he stopped moving forward.

"What the fuck is he doing here?"

"You said you weren't gonna lie to him," Eric exclaimed, backing toward the exit.

"I didn't, but I didn't get a chance to mention you," she said, trying to decipher the rage displayed in her lover's expression. She hadn't mentioned Eric because she hadn't thought his involvement was a big deal. He hadn't come up in conversation to make him relevant enough to discuss. It hadn't occurred to her to make a point of mentioning him. "I don't understand—"

"Bedroom?" Rushe asked.

Liam pointed to a door further down from the front door on a perpendicular wall. Rushe snatched the back of her neck and spun her around to propel her toward it. Her lover practically threw her into the room. She stumbled as she listened to the door slam.

Whirling around, she was met by him crowding into her personal space.

"Quite a band of men you're assembling, Kitten. Are you building your own little gang?"

"What the hell is your problem?"

"What does working alone mean to you?"

"Lover," she said, but when her fingertips touched his pockets, he batted them away and paced off, keeping his back to her. "Why are you upset?"

"I work alone," he said, pivoting around. "I don't want them out there. I don't trust them."

"You trust me," she said. "If you think I'm going to stand aside and let these lunatic criminals indict you for their misdeeds, you're crazy! No one gets to tear you down!   There is no way I'll stand aside and let that happen! I'll raise a goddamn army if—"

"You'll do what you're told! We don't involve other people. They're gonna screw us over. We don't rely on them; we don't rely on anyone. Eric is careless, you can't trust him, and Hutten doesn't have a clue what he's doing."

Her love didn't shout, but when he was pissed off like this his already deep voice got lower and rumbled up out of him all the way from his diaphragm.

"I need to be able to support you, Rushe. We're not going to run and hide; we're going to fight! You taught me how important it is to stand up for what's right, and this is right."

"We're not sharing our shit with them. I'm not gonna sit there and pretend we're all buddies, 'cause we're not. We don't need them; we don't need anyone."

"There's nothing wrong with asking for help," she said. "Having allies—"

"I won't do it. You don't know what it is to be screwed over and left in the shit. The more people involved, the harder it is to control, to foresee the problems that—"

"We're all here to work together—"

"I won't do it," he said, and turned to aim for the exit.

"You're walking out on me," she said, knowing that the words would stall him. "I'd do anything for you, Rushe, anything in the world. These men are going to help me keep you near to me. They'll help me to do what's right because I can't do it alone. I'm not as strong as you, or as experienced. I need help, Rushe. I won't let you get in the way of me ensuring your freedom."

"I work alone," he grumbled, without turning around.

"I know this is uncomfortable for you. I know you've had to adapt to having me in your life, and that wasn't an easy adjustment for you to make. Accepting help from others goes against your nature, so I'll deal with this, Lover. I won't make this harder for you, but don't make it harder for me, either. If you want to leave, then leave. I won't stop you. But I'm staying here, because fighting for you matters more to me than anything, and I need those men in there to help me do it well."

Bracing herself for what would come next, she couldn't guess as to how he would respond. Anticipating Rushe's actions wasn't always simple, no matter how hard she tried. Often it was more difficult because she didn't have all the relevant data. All she could be sure of was their trust and their love. If Rushe needed space, she would give it to him, every time. Pushing him too hard would only make him rebel, and she wasn't going to risk losing him emotionally again.

Having her doing research and fighting for him was a struggle enough for Rushe to accept. He'd probably have tolerated Liam, because the IT guy didn't have criminal connections and had proved he could keep his mouth shut. Seeing Eric come in to join them had obviously been a step too far and brought matters too close to home for Rushe to be comfortable with.

His hesitation to leave wasn't sustained. His hand rose to the door handle, and he strode out of the bedroom. She followed but made no attempt to chase or harangue him.

"Rushe," Eric said, and began to approach, but her love was enroute for the front door.

"Let him go," she said, stopping to wrap her arms around herself.

Just like that Rushe slammed out of the apartment and left them all in reverberating silence.

"Flick...?" Liam asked.

"We have work to do," she said. "Nothing changes."

Rushe had been there so briefly, but he'd already helped so much. Re-directing their focus to the core of the issue gave her new ideas and new concerns. If physical evidence was irrelevant, people were all that mattered. The Mercier side had a leading edge on the manipulation and intimidation of potential witnesses.

"Where's he going?" Liam asked.

"Forget about Rushe," she said. "Do you know where the police captains are now?"

Moving back to the dining table, she began to gather up the documentation. Suddenly, having so much paper seemed unprofessional and risky.

"I can get their addresses," Liam said. "Do you think they'll talk to you?"

"No," she said. "But I want to know where they are. Jansen had to be onto something, or close. Victor knew when Jansen talked to his superiors, so someone is paying attention."

"He's in the hospital," Eric said, taking hold of one of the chair backs opposite her when she finished stacking the papers.

"I need you to go to Serendipity's today," she said.

"Wait, wait, wait," Eric said. "I don't know what's going on. Who are these police captains?"

"We'll bring you up to speed, but you have to go there today, tonight at the latest, because tomorrow you're taking me home."

"Whoa, what?"

"You came to Rushe for help when Scott needed it, and he said no," she said. "You got him on board, he helped you, and Scott, because of one thing."

"You," Eric sighed.

A moment of nothingness passed.

"What's the deal with you and Rushe?" Liam asked Eric.

"I'll make coffee," she said, unwilling to let Rushe be discussed any further. "Liam, bring us up to speed with what you have on the internal investigation, I'll tell Eric what to look for at Serendipity's."

These men would mobilize for her, but her love struggled to understand their motives. Someone simply wanting to help him out of kindness was alien to him. He relied on the primal instinct of fight or flight. Liam and Eric were there by her request, Rushe couldn't fight them, but his discomfort fired primitive impulses. He had only one other choice - flight.

She'd bring him around to the idea. Just as it had

taken him time to accept their relationship, it would take him time to accept friendship. She couldn't undo a lifetime of conditioning overnight. Until Rushe was open to the concept of outside aid, she would fight on for him.

TWENTY-SEVEN

NOTHING IN THE INFORMATION they had so far was the silver bullet she needed. They weren't going to find anything that would cure them of the disease threatening them. They couldn't approach anyone in the police department or the FBI, because they couldn't trust them. They didn't operate on the right side of the law either, so they couldn't pick up a phone and ask for official help. With all Rushe had been responsible for in his past, any direct contact with the authorities would likely lead to them incriminating him, and that would make things much worse.

If the Merciers found out that she was trying to prove Rushe's innocence, they might speed up their plans to have him arrested. But Rushe had planted a seed in picking out the police captains. She wanted to know what those two men knew.

Because they could run back and report to the Merciers, walking up to them and asking out-right would not be wise. Surveillance was an option, though she would need Rushe's guidance on how to approach that.

An hour or so had passed since her love left. She felt stalled, sluggish, and useless.

"This is so frustrating," she said and sighed. "How can we have all this information, but have none of it be of any use to us?"

"You've gotta consider that…" Eric trailed off.

"What?"

Clasping his hands, he leaned forward in his seat opposite hers. "They have a case. If the cops get hold of Rushe, he's going down for something. He was involved, and he has taken part in criminal acts. Once he's arrested, that's it, game over. Do you see Rushe calmly cooperating while they control his every move?"

He'd be powerless and frustrated. As much as she hated to admit it, Eric had a point. "No."

"The Merciers are going to keep coming at you," Eric said. "Even if you prove Rushe is innocent, or gather enough evidence to prove it, they can still have him arrested. It still causes him a lot of hassle and opens him up to a lot of questions he won't want to answer."

"I know."

"It might not be the best idea to try logicing your way out of this," Eric said.

"What do you suggest?" she asked.

"If you won't do what they want and testify against Rushe," Eric said, "you have to find something they want more than his incarceration."

"Like what?" Liam asked, from his position two place settings up from Eric.

"Money?"

"No." She shook her head. "Rushe said they wouldn't be paid off. He's already working for Silver because Antoine wants him to. If that's not enough…"

"Rushe doesn't work for anyone unless it's a means to an end," Eric said, wearing a frown.

"He's keeping them alive," Liam said. "That

sounds like a legitimate ends to me."

"It's not as simple as that," Eric muttered to himself, while watching her intently. "Nothing's as simple as that where Rushe is concerned."

"We're not here to investigate Rushe, we're here to figure a way out of this mess," she said, casting aside her own curiosity about Rushe's debt to Silver. "Rushe isn't going to take the fall, and I'm not going to roll over on him. Building a legitimate case is seeming less and less feasible, especially without knowing what Jansen knew. We need to speak to witnesses, to try building a case as a safety net, in case the cops do come for Rushe. I want to be prepared for that. But maybe you're right, maybe I can find out if there's anything else that Antoine will settle for instead. There could be another way to make this go away. I won't know unless I ask him."

"Negotiate," Liam said. "Do you think it's wise to try negotiating with a human trafficker? That's dangerous. I mean, who knows what else he could be involved in. You could get hurt."

"I guess Hutten doesn't know what you were doing a couple of weeks ago, huh?"

"Was that a threat?" she asked, narrowing her eyes.

A jolt of horror went through Eric. "No! No, I meant he doesn't know what you're capable of."

She hadn't known the extent of what she was capable of until Rushe died for her. "There must be something else Antoine wants. If he wanted us dead, he'd have done it by now. I have to take the risk and ask him. I wanted to go home to check on my family. But that gives me the cover I need to have a conversation with Mercier. While I'm up there, you can keep digging, Liam."

"Why?" Liam asked. "If you're going to negotiate terms to have them all leave you alone, then—"

"Backup," she said. "I want to know what we're dealing with. I don't trust Antoine. If they're still trafficking, and we can expose their criminal—"

"Wait a minute," Liam said, holding up his hands. "Ensuring your freedom, Rushe's too, that's one thing. But you can't expect to bust open the trafficking they could be involved with."

"You don't even know if it got off the ground after Victor's gang was eliminated," Eric said. "The whole thing could've fallen apart."

"Best case scenario," she said. "But until we know for sure, we have to suspect otherwise. The more we know about them, the more leverage we have. Antoine's family is in France, and I doubt Simone has too many weak spots, unless we threaten to sew her legs together."

Eric laughed, but Liam was horrified. She regretted that her glibness made him feel uncomfortable. Her frustration caused her to lash out with the snide comment, but Liam was too kind to ever consider such insults acceptable.

"I gotta say," Eric said. "You got some set of balls, Flick."

"Yeah," she exhaled, letting her gaze fall to her half-full coffee mug.

The real life testicles she'd lay claim to were too far away. Rushe had been correct about her not feeling right when they weren't together. Even with everything that was going on, she couldn't get her lover out of her mind.

As though the thought had been enough to spur action, the apartment door opened, startling them all. On twisting in her seat, she had no time to seek a weapon or Rushe's knife in her pocket.

But the need for a weapon evaporated when she registered who'd come in. The man who swung the door closed and strode toward her was the most powerful in her arsenal: Rushe.

Her glow surged up to a grin, forcing her onto her feet. When he reached her, she caught his cheeks and her love's forehead descended to hers. After nuzzling her nose with his, he tipped her head and joined their mouths. The simple act conveyed all the apology that she needed.

"Lover," she said on a sigh.

The joy she felt at his concession, at his willingness to be there with her, made her want to shriek. He'd literally been unable to stay away or been so overcome by the instinct to be with her that he'd been unable to resist her gravitational pull.

He grumbled but swooped around, taking her hips, and forcing her into his lap in the chair she'd just vacated. Burying his face in her hair, he rubbed it side to side and splayed his fingers on her ribcage. Urging his palms up over her breasts, he squeezed, then drew them down to her hips, which he hitched back to meet his pelvis.

None of these moves were sexual, as such. He was scenting her, possessing her, reassuring both of them that equilibrium had been restored in their worlds.

"I want you to investigate the captains," she said to Liam, happy that Rushe was still burrowing his face in her locks and caressing her abdomen. Eric's eyes literally bulged. Liam was equally at a loss. "I need their histories."

Liam slanted his head as he peered past her to watch Rushe. "Why?"

"We're not going to get direct answers from them."

"You're going to threaten them?" Liam asked her. "That's risky. I can't support something that might get you hurt. These could be dangerous men."

"See the guy I'm sitting on?" she said, knowing both Eric and Liam were still amazed by Rushe's actions. She herself wasn't immune to that wonder either. "Some would say he's one intimidating S. O. B., yet I've got him eating pussy on command… Do you think I should worry about a couple of cops?"

"I think she'll be set," Eric mumbled.

"These men were corrupted, either through bribery or blackmail," she said. "The Merciers are using something against them. If we can find out what that is, maybe we can alleviate the pressure. We'll find out what we can and watch them until we know if they can be approached. I doubt these guys wanted to lose their jobs.

"All too quickly, you're on a slippery slope. You accept one payment or give in to one threat, and then they've got you. We want their histories because we want to see if we can find a way to help them."

"Help?" Eric asked.

"They could be desperate, and we can offer sympathy. A reassuring shoulder to cry on… so to speak."

"You're dangerous." Rushe's breath warmed the back of her neck, he swept her hair aside to dip her forward and kiss that cozy spot. His hands briefly made contact with her chest again, then he sat back with a nasal inhale, locking his arms around her torso to clamp her against him.

"If we can get them on our side," she said, "we have a chance of getting them to help us, or at least giving us relevant information."

"Fuck, she's smart and sexy as sin," Rushe said, propping his chin on her head and joining the conversation. "You're gonna get the information she wants, Hutten."

"Eric's going to take me to my parents' tomorrow," she said. "I have to check my family is okay and find out if Antoine will accept a settlement."

"A settlement?" Rushe said.

"We'll talk about it alone later," she said, dragging her fingernails up and down the denim on his thighs, that came with a satisfying zipping noise. "Eric will come to ensure my safety."

"I don't want to be responsible for you," Eric balked. "What if something happened to you?"

"I know the risks, you don't have to feel guilty if—"

"It's not you he's worried about," Liam said. "It's himself."

Liam's attention was on her love, who was no doubt glaring. "Rushe has to stay here and do his duty with Silver. Liam, you're going to get details on the captains so when I get back here, I can follow up."

"I'll follow up," Rushe said.

"We need to watch them and get a feel for who they are and if they have weak spots. But if it comes time to approach them… We don't want to intimidate them, we want to disarm them, and gain their confidence," she said. "You're scary, and I'm diplomatic. You can wait in the car this time."

"You're not gonna be alone with these guys," Rushe said, tightening his hold.

"They're more likely to be charmed by the sexy lady than the…" Eric trailed off.

From his whitening complexion, she was sure Rushe was scowling again.

"I think it's time for us to go," she said, picking up all the papers from the dining table.

When she had collected them all, Rushe lifted her up and put her on her feet.

"What are you doing with the paperwork?" Liam asked, as they headed from the table to the door.

"We're going to destroy it," she said. "I don't

want too much left lying around."

"I can shred it," Liam said, holding out a hand.

She gave it to an un-expectant Rushe. "We'll take care of it," she said. Rushe opened the door. "Check that apartment for me, Eric, then pick me up in the morning."

"I haven't agreed to—"

"He'll be there," Rushe said, tucking her hand into his back pocket. "Bright and early, with a smile on his face, and he's gonna bring my girl back without a scratch… Say goodbye."

"Bye," she said and left the abode on Rushe's heels.

TWENTY-EIGHT

HE TOOK HER to the sidewalk and around the corner to where the car was parked in shade.

"You stayed up there," he said, after the car got moving.

"I stuck to my guns," she said, taking her feet from her shoes and wiggling her toes. "You came back."

"I couldn't stay away," he said. "You're my woman, I have to be at your side. You accused me of walking away from you… I won't ever do that. I won't. I had to come back. Where you are is where I'm supposed to be."

"I meant what I said, Rushe, I have no problem dealing with those guys alone. Liam is my friend, and he wants to help. I think he enjoys the challenge and the excitement of it."

"He wants to fuck you."

"He does not," she tsked, leaning over the center console to rub his thigh. "Liam is my friend, there's no reason you should feel threatened—"

"You don't want that guy, Kit," he said. "You'd

never open your legs for him, but that doesn't mean he doesn't want it."

"I disagree."

"You do that."

"No warning about my guard?" she teased.

"Guy looks the type too scared to jerk off, he's never gonna make a move on you. If he tried to force the issue, you'd make a stain out of him. No man touches my woman."

"Why were you so angry to see Eric?"

"He's careless, and I don't get attached," her love said. "I've never worked two consecutive jobs with the same people. I rarely work twice with or for the same party."

"Except me."

"A lot of stuff I do with you that I don't do with other associates."

"Damn right," she soothed, taking her hand to his shoulder. "Do you trust Eric?"

"He's small time. That last job was the most serious thing I've seen him involved in."

"He said you met at a bloodbath."

"He was in the wrong place at the wrong time on that one. He doesn't have a bad bone in him. He's soft, dotes on that kid, makes him vulnerable."

"Gracie," she said, identifying Eric's daughter with an involuntary smile.

"See," Rushe said, glancing at her. "You've never met the kid, and you're soft already."

"Eric's a big burly guy, to think of him with a little bundle of baby is adorable."

"You getting broody?"

"Kids would get in the way of our sex life," she said, noticing they were rounding the corner to the parking area at the back of the brothel.

The future in front of her and Rushe wouldn't

involve children. She'd happily carry his babies if he wanted her to, but then she'd do anything he wanted her to.

Rushe parked and took her out of the car to lead her around the building.

"Should I call my sister to let her know I'm coming?"

Rushe stopped and pinned her to the side wall of the brothel before they reached the frontage. "I don't want you going back there alone."

"They're my family, Rushe. I have to know what's going on. I hate to think of them up there oblivious to the threat, and Lucia… I know that look in her, the way she acted with Antoine—"

"You think he's fucking her?"

She rolled her eyes up to him while landing her hands on his chest. "Women like Lucia aren't fucked," she said.

The concern in his expression dispersed to wry amusement. "Plenty of your prissy little friends like it fast and dirty, I guarantee it."

"My sisters are elegant and proper, Rushe. They make love with respect."

"I've never met a girl as dirty as you, Kit, and I respect the shit out of you."

"Yes, you do," she said, curling her fingers to grip the fabric beneath them. "But you couldn't fuck my sister like you fuck me."

"I couldn't fuck anyone like I fuck you."

"Damn right," she said, levying herself up. "You're mine. Any woman tries to touch you, and I'll end her life. You've been warned."

"If Antoine is screwing your sister, it'll detonate her marriage, and—"

"Not necessarily," she said. "Ninety percent of marriages in that sphere are a sham in one way or another. But I wouldn't want her to get hurt or be made a fool of."

"Why do you care so much?" he asked, genuinely perplexed. "They wanted nothing to do with you. They wanted you to marry that guy, and they let you walk away when they didn't get their way. They'd rather have you out there alone than support you."

"We'll have to send them a thank you gift, because if they hadn't done that, forced me out, I'd never have found you."

"I'd have found you," he said, taking the ends of her hair in between his fore and middle fingers. "You get yourself into enough trouble that you'd have blipped on my radar eventually."

"And if I'd been married by then?"

"Do you think I would've let that stop me from claiming you?" he asked, though they both knew it would.

"Your woman," she beamed.

"That's right."

"I'm going to call my sister to let her know I'm coming, then I'll get the paperwork out of the car. I want to commit as many of the details to memory as possible before we destroy it."

"Why didn't you let Hutten deal with it?"

She shrugged. "I know you like to reduce the chances of error. If we do it, we know it's done right." She paused. "I know you don't trust easily and you've been alone for a long time. But there are good people out there, people we can rely on. If we can trust them and let them use their skills to help us, we can help more women."

"Right now there's only one woman I want to help: you."

"I'm going to put my mind at ease by checking on my family and Eric's going to watch my back. You're going to stay here and keep Tawny and the others safe.”

“You’re forgetting one thing.”

“What?”

“Your crazy statement,” he said, still stroking her hair.

“What?

“A settlement?”

“It’s worth a try,” she shrugged.

“You don’t reason with these people,” Rushe said. “You don’t show them weakness, and you don’t ask them for favors.”

“We can’t get in touch with Simone; she was the one who approached me about incriminating you.”

“Yeah. So?”

“Is it better to tell Antoine I won’t do what they want when I’m in my parents’ house and we’re surrounded by neutral people, or should we idly wait until Simone’s henchmen snatch me off the street again?”

Simone had allowed her to leave that apartment, presumably as a show of trust they were on the same team. It was difficult for her to imagine ever being tempted to ally herself with Simone under any circumstances.

Eventually they would want an answer from her. Simone had told her she had time. When that time was up, she could be approached and cornered again. If things didn’t go their way, the next time the Mercier family might not let her leave so readily.

“I don’t want you to go anywhere alone,” Rushe said. “Nowhere, not here or at your parents,’ okay?”

She nodded. “I’ll be here with you today, I’ll be with Eric and my family tomorrow.”

“You have one night,” Rushe said. “I’ll let you out of my bed for one night. You think about making it any longer, and I’ll come for you, Kit. One night.”

"Can I call you?"

"Phone sex?"

"Degrees of love," she reminded him. "If it goes that way, you know I love to hear you talk dirty. Sometimes I just need to hear your voice. You ground me, Rushe. When I lose my way, if I'm scared or unsure, the only thing that can console me is you."

"Phones are traceable," he said.

"They know where we are anyway."

He wasn't a fan of phones, or any devices, that could be monitored or used to target them, but she missed having a link to him.

Her love must have sensed her disappointment because he took hold of her chin in his brutish way and hiked her attention up to meet his.

"Am I any less yours when I'm not right in front of you? You said that to me. But if you don't want to go—"

"I do," she said.

She should know better than to show weakness or uncertainty in front of anyone. Being honest with Rushe had to be her default position, though, because she had to maintain their trust. She wouldn't give him any reason to doubt her or push her away.

When Rushe saw her tremble, he wanted to step in and fix everything for her. Except, to be useful to him and the work that she did, she had to be able to fight through her anxiety.

"You leave me a number and I'll call."

"You'd do anything in the world for me, even if it means going against your natural impulses," she said. "I make you soft."

"Never been a problem for me where you're concerned, Kitten."

"Care to take me inside and prove it?"

"We've got work to do, whore."

"Work first," she sighed.

"I'll order pizza tonight," he said.

This was his hit for normality. He'd never cook for her or romance her in a traditional way, but pizza, a movie, and a make out session was her perfect night in.

In recent weeks, they'd barely had a chance to breathe, let alone bond. She appreciated him making this effort.

"Okay," she said and nodded. "As long as there's plenty of dessert."

"Have I ever left you hungry?" he asked, crouching to bring his mouth closer to hers.

"Don't tease me, Lover. If you warm me up with your words, I'll expect you to follow through."

"Why do you think I stopped to have this conversation outside? If I get you in that room alone, I'll strip you naked, tie you down, and never let you leave my sight again."

"If we get through this, I promise I'll let you."

"Make your phone call," he said, backing away, scrutinizing her figure. "Mine."

"Yours."

"I'm gonna make you prove that all night long."

"You'll destroy the paperwork when I'm gone?"

"Yes," he said.

She headed toward the front of the building again, sashaying her hips as she went. "We work this afternoon, but tonight is ours."

Being apart set them both uneasy, but they had to complement each other. Part of being a team meant they could cover twice as much ground as one. Rushe could stay and tow the Silver line for Mercier, while she would go to her parents', check on the oblivious hostages, and reason with a madman. It may be a fool's errand, but she would close no doors. Their lives and their unity depended on her being able to strike a bargain.

TWENTY-NINE

THE PIZZA had been ordered, though not much of it was consumed. They'd spent a joyous night wrapped in each other on the couch in their room. For a while, she'd forgotten where they were and the danger that surrounded them. The TV blared, ignored as she lay there under Rushe writhing up against him. His hand massaged her breast and his tongue massaged hers. The peril couldn't have been further from her mind.

It had taken time for Rushe to appreciate the value of a good kiss, and a good make out session, but he understood now and embraced both with gusto. Still, there came a time to step things up. When his hand glided down her waist to her thigh, then up under her skirt, she hoped that time had arrived.

"I love my woman," he grumbled against her cheek, his mouth trailing its way down her throat, and she thought he was aiming for her chest.

"She loves you too," she said, combing her fingers through his hair.

He lifted his head, just briefly enough to catch

her eye, then he flopped back down to sample the other side of her neck. His finger nudged her underwear aside to just trace her opening. She tried to lift her hips to tempt his digit inside, but his pelvis tilted against one of her hips, thus holding her in place.

"I'm practicing taking my time."

"No you're not," she said on a grin, tightening her fists in his hair. "You're trying to infuriate me."

"Is it working?"

When they got the chance to relax, to joke and enjoy each other, nothing in her life could be wrong. Then, the unilluminated room was blasted by red light, and her body wilted.

"What?" he asked, raising his head at the same moment the bell blasted.

Off the couch with a groan of his own, he ran his hands through his hair and went for the door. Her own frustration would be nothing to the fact he had to go out there and do his job while sporting the impressive boner that had been nestled against her not so very long ago. The light continued to flash, but the bell was thankfully silent after that first discharge.

Appreciating Rushe may be a while, or that he might be less in the mood when he returned, she sat up, straightened her top, and stood to flatten out her skirt. The bell only went when there was trouble, when Rushe was needed. After a few seconds she heard a commotion from the reception.

On exiting, her love had left their bedroom door open. She took the liberty of wandering to the hall. With the shouting dying down, she heard the slam of the store door and a melee of female voices. The women there were under the protection of her love, but she knew nothing about any of them.

Leaving them with him tomorrow ensured their safety, but she had no idea who she was leaving her love with. If after she returned, she'd been unsuccessful with Antoine, there was a chance that they would be here for a while. She had to take the time to get to know these women, especially Tawny, who was linked to such a crucial part of Rushe's past.

Pulling back the curtain at the end of the hall, she didn't hide. After all, she didn't want these women to think she was trying to sneak up on them. Lilah wasn't there, nor Candy or Tawny. Although she didn't recognize the women present, it was clear they knew who she was. None of them acknowledged her, though most of them took the time to sneer or glare while the four carried on their conversation.

"Someone's gotta talk to Connie," one woman said, referencing another woman, who she guessed wasn't there.

"Karmel tried," a tall blonde in a pink robe said.

"I did too," said a woman wearing red satin. "I did try to talk to her."

"Silver's gonna go crazy," the first woman said.

"You think Lilah hasn't told him?" Pink Robe said.

"When was the last time any of us spoke to Silver?" Karmel asked. "You gotta talk to Rushe."

"Rushe knows," Pink Robe said, placing a hand against the reception counter. "You think there's shit goes on here he doesn't know about?"

"Kick her out."

"He's not gonna do that," Karmel said.

"She's endangering us all," Red Satin said. "We're all gonna get smudged out."

"What the hell is smudged out?" Pink Robe sneered.

Karmel laughed. "Fucked until we're nothing but stains on the mattress."

"You get your cut," Pink Robe said. "You do

your job and you get paid."

"Who are you talking about?" Flick asked.

The four women who had snubbed her until then all turned slowly in her direction.

"This doesn't concern you," Pink Robe said. "You go back to your safe little space and cry in a corner somewhere."

Her smile was easy but automatic. "I can have a conversation with you and then do that, if you think that's what I do."

"You don't work for a living," Red Satin said. "I ain't never seen a girl under this roof who don't work to earn her keep."

"I pay my way."

"Yeah, I'm sure you've got a rich daddy," Pink Robe said, and twisted her body to block her out. "I vote we talk to Tawny."

"Tawny's not gonna do nothing," Karmel said.

"She can get Rushe to toss Connie out," Pink Robe said.

"Rushe ain't paid to toss out girls," Karmel replied. "He's paid to toss out johns who get rough. He ain't no enforcer, he's a protector. Connie's mess don't mean shit to him."

"It will when he knows Tawny's in danger."

"The only clients who cause trouble are the ones Connie brings in. Tawny ain't never had none of them."

"So we swing it that she does," Pink Robe said and shrugged. "Aren't you sick of just rolling over and taking their shit? These guys think they can do whatever the fuck they want."

"'Cause they can," Red Satin said. "You're in the wrong trade if you're looking for tender respect."

The other three laughed at Pink Robe. "This shit started when she arrived," Pink Robe said, spinning on her. "Connie started the same week that you showed up."

"I don't know Connie," Flick said, aware the other women were watching on. "She's a new girl?"

"Keeps bringing in all these kinky clients," Karmel said. "Guys bent on taking what they want."

"Rushe won't let any of them hurt you," she said.

Karmel snorted out a laugh. "Unless Rushe stands in the room with every one of us while we see every client, there's no chance of guaranteeing that."

"He'd do it for Tawny," Pink Robe muttered.

"He don't want to watch her having sex, he's protective as all hell."

Karmel seemed to be pretty levelheaded. From how she constantly balked and sneered, she couldn't work out if Pink Robe was jealous of Rushe and Tawny's relationship, or resentful of it.

"Why don't you refuse to see Connie's referrals?" Flick asked.

"You don't refuse clients. If you see a girl around here who can pick and choose her johns, then she's a girl who don't need to be here, like you."

"You shouldn't work if you feel unsafe," she said. "Someone should talk to Connie about these men."

"That's what we're talking about," Karmel said, turning her focus to the other girls. "We talk to Lilah, she'll talk to Rushe, and he'll talk to Silver—"

"Yeah, and it will take a month. Who else is gonna get shot in that time?" Pink Robe said.

Again, all glaring eyes were on her. "I'm very sorry about Candy."

"I'm surprised you're still here," Pink Robe said. "Bringing your shit here? Landing it on one of Rushe's girls… your daddy must be paying him a lot."

"Yeah, 'specially since Tawny's not happy about you," Karmel said. "You won't last long now."

"I don't mean anyone here any harm," she said. "I want to help."

"How nice of you," Karmel said as the others laughed.

"Is that so difficult to believe?"

"Look…" Pink Robe said, pushing away from the desk to swagger toward her. "You think you're down here roughing it 'cause you've got a big, bad man looking after you? Do you think this is fun? An adventure? This is our life, this is what we live, so you scurry on back to rich fucking boyfriends and leave us alone."

"My boyfriend doesn't want me to leave here," she said, unintimidated even when Pink Robe stopped only inches from her, towering above her at a height of at least five ten. "And I can be of use."

"We don't need you for nothing. You're a joke around here, no one gives a fuck about you. When you're gone, we'll all forget you in a heartbeat. This is real life, bitch, not a soap opera you can act in while it suits you."

The store door opened, and Rushe came in with another man at his back. When the two men saw Pink Robe looming over her and the others not far behind, they straightened up.

"What's going on?" Rushe asked.

"Nothing," Pink Robe beamed, backing off a step. "Did you get rid of him?"

"Yeah," Rushe said, fixating on her.

"I'm going to bed," she said, meeting Pink Robe's eyes once more to show that there was no fear.

She spun around and made her way back to the bedroom.

THIRTY

IT WASN'T A SURPRISE when Rushe's hand blocked her from closing the door to grant his own entry to the bedroom with her. Only after he was inside did he let her close the door.

"What happened?" he demanded.

"Nothing," she said. "We were just talking."

"Don't you fucking lie to me, Kit. I came here to get the story from you 'cause you don't lie to me."

"I offered to help," she said. "They laughed at me. It's no big deal, Rushe. I hardly expected to win their respect with one conversation."

"Help with what?"

"Connie, this new girl," she said. "She keeps bringing in clients they don't like, and they want something done about it."

"What were you gonna do?" he asked, folding his arms across his chest.

"Talk to Connie, find out where these guys are coming from and what the problem is."

"I don't want you mixed up in this place. Don't

get bogged down in their internal politics."

"I was trying to reach out to them, to show them I'm not the enemy. They already blame me for Candy, and God knows how long we'll be here after… when I get back."

"Don't make friends here," he said, scowling. "You'll get hurt."

"You always worry about me getting hurt," she said. "You're always so worried about me."

He worried about her because he loved her and wanted to protect her. She knew about the work he did and why he did it. But she still felt it necessary to make a point about this place they were in. Her hope was he could explain the distinction she couldn't decipher.

Going for the bills he kept in the nightstand, she retrieved one and brought it to him.

"What's this for?" Rushe asked when she handed him the money.

"Sex."

His eyebrows came up, very rarely had she seen so much of his eyes. "You want to give me money in exchange for sex? That's illegal, sweetheart. And a woman like you shouldn't have to pay for it."

"How would you feel if I told you that a man had offered to pay me for use of my body?"

"Who?" he barked, balling the bill into his raised fist at the same time he strode up to her until their bodies made contact. "What did he look like? When did this happen? Why the fuck didn't you tell—"

She put one hand to his lips and the other into his pocket. "Why is it different for them?" she asked. "Those women through there are exploited for sexual use by men… if I called you one day and told you I was living like that—"

"Why wouldn't you be with me?" he grumbled.

"Hypothetically, Rushe." Her fingers slithered

down to his chest. "The idea of hundreds of men taking turns with me, one after the other, using my body for their own private sexual gratification—"

"Enough," he growled, baring his teeth. "Don't talk about my woman like that."

"They're being used for sex, exploited for profit."

"The profit is theirs, they chose this. You will never have the choice of this lifestyle, I would never allow it."

"It's not right, Rushe," she said, shaking her head. "You know it's not right."

"These women choose to be here. They come and go as they want. This is a safe environment. There are no drugs allowed. There is always a watchman to look out for the girls as they work. It's a simple cash for sex transaction."

"And you're okay with that?"

"I can't tell them what to choose, Kitten," he said. "This is the way of the world. There's nothing we can do about that. No one is hurting them here."

"What about Tawny? Are you okay with her being here?"

"Tawny can't get her shit together for more than twenty minutes," Rushe said. "If she's not here with someone watching her all the time, then she's high."

"She has a drug habit?"

Rushe nodded and ran his hand into her hair. "I tried to get her out of here, I wanted to set her up somewhere."

"What happened?"

"She thought I wanted to get married," Rushe said, deadpan.

She smiled. "So you ran for the hills?"

"No, she thought I was in love with her. She wanted me to be in love with her," he admitted.

From the prickle that crossed his shoulders, it was clear that experience was uncomfortable for him.

"But you weren't?"

"I didn't come here for that," he snarled. "She didn't understand that. I wanted to know she was okay. I was looking out for her, but that was as far as it went."

"For you."

"She seemed in love with me from the second I looked at her," he said. "I made damn sure she knew it wasn't about sex or any relationship."

"You were a bastard," she said, knowing from experience how vicious her love could be when he was trying to maintain barriers between himself and another person.

If his time with Tawny had been so recent to his meeting her, she could understand just why his venom toward her getting attached was so fresh.

"I tried to explain to her that I wasn't capable," he said. "I wasn't interested in love or commitments and relationships."

Knowing what it was to crave this man and have him turn his back on her, she felt sorry for Tawny. But Rushe had really believed he had no capacity for love, and he wouldn't have shied from making that obvious to Tawny.

"She was in love with you."

"She liked the attention," he said. "It didn't matter who I was. The reality of living with a guy like me doesn't induce love… I didn't think it was possible for anyone to love me, just like I thought it wasn't possible for me to love them."

Her instinct was to refer to their relationship. Until he'd met her, he didn't see any long-term attachments in his future. But the story wasn't about them.

"You broke her heart," she said. "Whether the

love was real or not, it hurt her to have you reject her. It's why you never slept with her. You could have, she's a pretty girl. It would've made her feel better for a while. But it would have set an expectation."

"Yeah," he said.

"Did you want to love her? Were you tempted? You could've had a future with her."

"I didn't feel anything when I looked at her," he said. "Other than the obligation I'd felt since I found out she existed."

"That made you feel guilty?"

"No," he said. "I didn't... I had never looked at a woman and wanted anything else. I could look at a hot woman and want sex, but feelings? The emotional shit... it had never happened to me."

"No wonder you pushed at me so hard," she said, briefly pressing her face to his chest. "You must have hated me."

"I wanted to hate you."

"You'd just gone through an emotional time with Tawny, who wanted you, and you'd convinced her you weren't able to love, and then something happened when you looked at me."

"I didn't convince her," Rushe said. "I was as cold and as distant as I could be. I think eventually she accepted it, but sometimes she'd look at me with..."

"Hope."

"She says I'm different now," he said. "Changed... it's been easier to talk to her, to tolerate her. I suppose she's happy to be friends now."

Friends was the word Tawny might use, but Rushe didn't have friends. "So you set her up a new life, and what happened? How did she end up back here?"

"She started using again and got herself into trouble. Eventually I figured the only thing keeping her clean was this place and these girls. She and a few of the other girls live here full-time. There's a kitchen and a social area in the basement where they all hang out."

"There is?"

"Yeah," he said. "Where do you think I slept when I wasn't in here?"

"Tawny doesn't use drugs when she's here?"

"Silver won't have drugs on the premises, as soon as any of the girls try to use, they're out. Johns who try it aren't allowed back. When Tawny ends up on the street, she ends up worse off, mixed up with shady pimps and dealers. Here, they feed her and look after her. She's one of the youngest girls, and…"

"And?"

"I send an allowance every month to make sure they look after her, but she doesn't know that. She doesn't work much."

She would never fail to be amazed by this man's generosity. Technically, there was no requirement for him to look after Tawny at all. His sense of responsibility compelled him to care for the girl who had no one to look out for her. So every month, like a big brother or a protective parent, he went the extra mile to make sure the girl was safe and healthy.

"It's a shame I already love you so much, because I think news like that would've made me fall even harder," she said. "Unfortunately, it's not possible for me to love you more than I already do."

His brows came together as he lowered his chin. "Explain."

"You care about her."

"Kitten, if you think that—"

"Not in a sex way," she said, dropping her hold to his belt. "You lived your whole life with no one looking out for you. But there's so much goodness in you."

"Who knows what her life would've been if I had

stopped those guys."

"Who knows what yours would've been if you hadn't been present in that alley at all."

"You're not angry I'm throwing our money at a lost cause?" he asked.

"She's not a lost cause, no more than you or me. Everyone deserves a break, you're her guardian angel. She's very lucky."

"She's a pain in the ass," he said. "A fucking brat. She's not even a very nice person most of the time."

He tensed as he spoke, and it made her sigh. "You're beating yourself up because you're not fond of her personality. I've got to tell you something, Rushe, and please don't be disappointed by this, but you don't like very many people."

"Only one person."

"Yeah, and if it wasn't for my breasts, I'm not sure even I would qualify sometimes," she teased.

Letting her body drift into his, she wrapped her arms around his ribs. It still took him a few seconds to reciprocate, but eventually his arms relaxed. He locked one wrist in his other hand, encompassing him in her embrace.

"You have to deal with Connie."

"I'll talk to Silver tomorrow," he said, and his mouth sank into her hair.

She closed her eyes thinking about the women in this building, those who revered Rushe and those who feared him. They wanted something done about the clients this new girl was bringing in, but none of them had wanted to talk to Rushe about it. Yet six words on her part was all it took to solve the problem. She had no doubt now Rushe had it in his mind, it would be dealt with.

THIRTY-ONE

ALL THROUGH THE car ride to her parents' she thought about Rushe. Eric talked as they drove; he played the radio and sang along with the tracks that played. He made jokes and stopped at gas stations for food to munch on while they traveled. The usual journeys she took with Rushe were a major contrast to this one with her newest associate.

Eric had filled her in on what he'd found at Serendipity's apartment, which ended up totaling a big fat zero. There was evidence Jansen had been staying there, but nothing written down that indicated any investigation on his part. The computer was gone too, which confirmed what they'd thought: someone had gone through the apartment already. Any evidence that may have been there was long gone now.

"Where's Gracie's mom?" she asked when the radio station switched to the weather and Eric turned the volume down.

"At work, probably," Eric said, attempting to rub powdered sugar away from his thigh.

"No…" She smiled. "I meant, you said you didn't have a steady girl, but you have Gracie, and she's so young—"

"You wanna know how I screwed up?"

"I never said that. I'm curious," she said. "You didn't love her? Was it a one-night stand or one of you screwed around—"

"We're better parents apart," Eric said, forgetting the sugar.

"You don't sound convinced," she said, noting how static his usually animated expression had become.

"Jocelyn is," he said. "She's a great mom, the best."

"You like being a dad?"

"You should see Gracie when I walk in the room. Man, she gets all excited and starts squealing. It's a buzz, and it takes forever to calm her down, she just…"

"Worships you," she said, feeling the burn in her cheeks from the stretch of her smile. "I'd love to meet her."

"I don't think Rushe would like that," Eric said, back in his easy, relaxed state. "He looks at her like she's an alien."

"Rushe has met her?"

"A couple of times," Eric nodded. "Just brief like. I've done some hardware for him in the past. Gracie comes to the store when I've got her."

She tried to picture her lover doing business while a two-year-old weaved in and out of his ankles. She could imagine how uncomfortable he'd be.

"Do you want kids?" Eric asked.

"Not me."

"I've never seen Rushe like that, like he was with you in Hutten's place yesterday. You've got him by the balls."

"You sound happy about that," she said.

"Well, yeah, but not in a bad way. That guy is too uptight, he needs to chill out."

"Would you say that to his face?"

"Not a chance," Eric said, flashing her a smile.

"Have you heard from Scott?"

Scott was Eric's colleague, the second man to hire Rushe for the last job.

"Not recently," Eric said. "Don't expect to for a while. Losing Susie changed him. I think he'll need time to get over it."

"Getting over something like that doesn't seem likely."

"He'll make it, or he won't," Eric said.

"Turn up here," she said, knowing the GPS would direct Eric to the front of the Hughes mansion.

"Is there a back entrance?"

"You're not coming in," she said, pointing ahead. "Pull up there."

Eric did as she directed and put the vehicle in park. "You said to Rushe I was going to look after you."

"If I walk into that house with a guy like you only a few days after leaving it with a guy like Rushe, my mother will have a heart attack… I want you to find that girl, the motel receptionist, just like we talked about."

"I thought we were abandoning the idea of building a legitimate case."

She shook her head and reached into the back seat to snatch her jacket. "We don't know how this will play out. I'm not ready to give up on anything yet. It will take you the rest of the day to drive to that motel in Maine. Find out if anyone has approached or tried to influence her."

"You're gonna go in there alone? Antoine's in there."

"So is half my family, and a dozen phones," she said. "He doesn't do the hard work; he wouldn't physically hurt me. I'm here to have a conversation."

"I'll find the girl and get her to back up your story."

"Good," she said, and went for the door.

"Do you know what you're going to say to him?"

"Antoine? Yeah," she said, curling her fingers around the plastic handle. "Hayden, not so much."

"Hayden? The guy you were dating when you met Rushe?"

"I wasn't dating him." She stood him up, twice, but it wasn't deliberate. "I'm going to call him. He saw Rushe and me together after that night, after Victor and the others died. I introduced Rushe as my boyfriend and told him Rushe had saved me, Hayden can back us up."

"Rushe okay with that?"

"Rushe trusts me. Don't make me regret trusting you."

She left the car and retrieved her bag from the trunk. Eric remained in the same spot and watched her walk down the sidewalk to the alley that led to the back gate of her parents' house. He'd promised to watch her, and to his credit he did so until the very last second she let him.

WITNESSING ANTOINE MERCIER charm and disarm her family was sickening. From the moment she entered the house, her mother, especially, made it clear she was happy Rushe hadn't joined her.

The last thing she would want was for anyone to think she was ashamed of her lover. The only thing that kept him from her side right then was circumstance. But she wasn't going to talk about him. In fact, she said very little to anyone during her time with the family.

It was going to be difficult to find time to talk to Antoine alone. The men didn't actually join the women until dinner time, and then the air was filled with the banality of small talk. Being back there like this made her wonder how she'd lived this life, in this world, for so long.

Nothing there mattered. It mattered to the people there, but when she compared it to her life with Rushe, this seemed to be frivolous, sickeningly so.

A few times throughout the meal Antoine stared at her. He must have things to say to her. At least he would be open to the idea of them talking, which was the first hurdle to overcome.

Vivian and Martin left early. Lucia and her husband, Roger, hung around for longer. They had been waiting for Charles to finish a phone call, but they eventually gave up waiting and decided to leave.

She was unsettled by how her sister's gaze lingered on Antoine, who seemed happy to receive the attention. When her mother went to see the couple off, she deliberately hung back in the hope Antoine would do the same. He did.

When the drawing room door closed, leaving them alone, she and Antoine turned in unison to face each other.

"Your family is very welcoming," he said first.

"Perhaps they wouldn't be if they knew the truth of who you were," she replied. "And what you and your family do for fun."

"You know nothing of my family," Antoine smirked. "Not as I know yours… your sister Lucia is especially friendly."

The European slunk around her and moved back into the body of the room, leaving her with a chill. He'd worn such a smug leer that there was no way she could doubt his intimacy with Lucia. How far did that go?

"Isn't that a risk?" she asked, trying to maintain her mask and not show how the news disturbed her. "If my father finds out you've been trying to seduce his daughter—"

"Your father cares much less about his family than he does about his business."

"Something you can identify with, I'm sure," she said.

Antoine picked up his wine glass by the rim and took it to his lips. "You came here to confirm your family's welfare, did you not?"

"Yes," she said, sauntering toward him.

"They are healthy, and they will continue to be while you and your master work for us."

Referencing Rushe as her master was meant to belittle her, but she'd never feel disrespected in that role. "And if we choose not to?"

Antoine lowered the glass to his side. "You have delivered yourself to me for punishment?"

"I am here to tell you I have no intention of betraying Rushe."

"You could have told my cousin that," Antoine said. "When she came for you."

"And trap myself with her?" she said. "No. I came here to tell you. I'm smart enough to know Simone is only running your errands, just as you run your uncle's."

Antoine put his glass down after another sip. "Do you think we will accept your refusal without consequence?"

She forced herself to move in closer until they were only a foot apart. "This is about good old-fashioned revenge. Dress it up anyway you like, but that's what it comes down to. You don't like Rushe, and he's not intimidated by you."

"No, he is not."

"You want him off the streets so he can't interfere in your operations again. This is about punishing the man who put one over on you. But you cannot take on Rushe. He's trumped you once, and he'll do it again."

"We do not need to take him on," Antoine said, wearing that smirk again. "We have Serendipity. All we need to do is dispense with you. He will be neutralized when you comply."

"I will never stand up against him."

"Then you will lose your life. We will not allow you to further derail our plans."

"Do you think killing me will make Rushe easier to deal with?" she asked, trying not to laugh while making no secret of her amusement. "Others have tried that before…"

"I am not deterred by your present defiance. I believe that you can be persuaded."

"Can I?" she asked, sneering as she looked him up and down.

"Oui," Antoine said. "You are a sensible girl, Felicity, despite your tendency to talk too much. What will your death achieve for your cause?"

"Do you think you can logic me into rolling over on the man I love?"

"You are risking yourself for a man who does not reciprocate your love."

"Simone has tried that line with me already," she said.

"We have heard how distant you are from your lover, how Rushe shuns you in that place. And now you are here, departed from him."

THIRTY-TWO

NEWS OF THE TENSION between her and Rushe in the brothel had traveled back to the Mercier family.

"It's nothing," she said, turning away from Antoine to get away from the nauseating scent of his cologne. "You have spies?"

"We know everything," Antoine said. "We know where your lover is, we know how he spends time with other women in that place. How he favors young Tawny."

Antoine didn't need to know that she and Rushe had mended the almost-rift. "My relationship is my business."

"You will die for a man who makes love to other women? Even when you are in that place, when you are in his bed, he chooses to seek pleasure with other women."

When Antoine's form loomed at her back, her eyes closed. His proximity tempted her to lash out, to scream and injure the man threatening Rushe. She might know her love had never been intimate with the women at Silver's place. Whoever was reporting back obviously didn't.

If they knew Rushe spent time with Tawny or heard about him spending time with her before, it stood to reason the mole would assume sex was involved.

"He does not want you, ma chère," Antoine said, lowering his volume. "My cousin was right, Rushe toys with you for his own amusement. He is not a man to be faithful, and he is not a man to value your life more than his own."

She knew different. "You don't know what you're talking about."

"I think I do," Antoine said. His fingertips touched her shoulder blade and she flinched. She didn't move when he lifted a slice of her hair and smoothed it between his fingers. "You enjoy the danger, and you are overwhelmed by a man with such power. I see how you grew up here and see in you that spirit which craves more."

"There must be something else," she said. "Something else you want from us. Killing us gets you nothing."

Antoine said nothing but continued to hold her hair. He lifted it higher, and she heard him inhale. A quiver of disgust fired through her, but she remained in place.

"An alternative offer," he said. "Actually, you could be more useful than we had initially anticipated."

"Me?" she asked, tipping her chin toward her shoulder. "You think I could be of use to you?"

This news actually excited her, it gave her hope she could somehow save herself and Rushe from the tyranny of this family. On turning, his body was uncomfortably close to hers, but she wouldn't cower, wouldn't let him gain the upper hand or see her tremble.

"Rushe cannot be satisfied with a woman like

you, you know this, don't you?" Antoine asked. "Since your relationship is doomed, perhaps if you would be willing to sacrifice it…"

"You want me to leave him?" she asked, unsure how that tied into what the Merciers could want from her. "Why?"

"You have influence," Antoine said. "Here."

"Here?" she asked, frowning at her parents' drawing room. "I don't understand."

Antoine took half a step back to lift his head and look around the room. "Your family has great influence, power, and connections in this part of the world that could be very useful to me. Our business interests are not sustainable as they stand."

That snap of horror in her spine must have registered to him, but he maintained eye contact, searching her for further reaction. "My family?"

"Spending this time with them has shown me just how they value the material. Your father, your brothers-in-law, they are… pliable."

"You want to corrupt my family? Annex them into your criminal empire?"

"You flatter me. Empire is quite a goal," Antoine said. "I could have sustained interests here. Our families could collaborate."

"So put it to them," she said, hoping he would. "Go and tell my father you want to involve him in the trade of human cargo."

Antoine laughed. She shrank back, surprised by his reaction. "We would not do that. We are still trying to fulfill our potential. Not all our business is illegal, it is important to maintain a respectable facade."

"Which my family can provide," she said. "You want to use my family's credibility, maybe their money, and their network, to give you cover for further disreputable deals?"

It wouldn't be the first time she'd heard of society closing ranks to protect one of their own. If they wanted to support a cohort, they had the money and influence in many spheres to do just that.

"Once this deal is completed, it will be difficult to maintain this level of intimacy with your family, unless I have a personal connection. You may be useful," Antoine said, returning his solemn expression to her.

"Me? I know nothing about the business. I don't have the connections to—"

"No," Antoine said, closing in on her again. "You don't, but you do provide a link to your family; a reason that they would want to be generous with their advantages."

"I don't—"

"You could provide us the perfect cover," he said. "You are an embarrassment to them, Felicity. Your name is not mentioned, here or in any of their circles. They are ashamed of you and your rebellion against the privilege they offer."

"My relationship with my family is not your concern."

What he said was true, that didn't make it any easier to hear.

"You have gallivanted long enough, and your family would very much appreciate you returning here." She remained silent. "You cannot be naive to my suggestion," Antoine said. But she was, until his hand rose, and he brushed the back of his finger down her cheek. "Your family would be very grateful to the man who brought you back and kept you in line."

The clamp of revulsion trapped her lungs inside her ribs and compressed them until she had to gasp for oxygen. "You want me to... you want to use me?"

"If we form a romantic union, we could make an excellent team."

"No," she said, slapping his hand from her face and backing away. "I wouldn't have you near me."

"It is not a sexual contract," Antoine said, undeterred. "I am not interested in your body."

Though from the way his eyes skulked over her figure, she wasn't sure she believed that claim. "You disgust me."

"I care not about that," he said with an unaffected shake of his head

"I won't," she said, regaining her senses. "I won't give you that opportunity."

"Then you are useless to us. Your life will be taken, as will young Tawny's, and we shall have Rushe comply with our wishes. Serendipity will be disposed of. It causes very little disruption to us."

"You want me to come home, to live with you here, and give you access to my family's acquaintances."

"You will not be mistreated," Antoine said. "No one will be injured."

"And Rushe, what happens to him?"

"We shall still expect him to comply with our request. Though we may allow our cousin to imply she was too traumatized to remember the events of her sexual violation accurately."

"I won't leave him and give you an in here."

"You have a choice," he said, reaching up to stroke her shoulder. "You give the police your statement, stand up in court against him, and lose Rushe, a man who would rather be with another woman anyway. Or you come here, lose Rushe, and prove to your family you are dedicated to me."

"No."

"Then you die. Serendipity will die. Tawny will die, and Rushe will go to jail."

In coming to negotiate with Antoine, she had appreciated compromise may be required. They would all have to sacrifice something, but this seemed impossible.

"It won't work. You can't pin this on him."

"With three more dead and the murder weapon in Rushe's possession, he will go to jail."

"You want to frame him for that too?" she asked. "They'll never let him out."

"That would not mean a great loss for the world."

If she wasn't around to fight Rushe's corner, how far would he go to fight for himself? He was so used to fighting for everyone else that he never prioritized himself. The horrible truth was that without her, and Tawny, Rushe would blame himself for the deaths. He'd no doubt give up, believing in some warped way that he deserved to be incarcerated.

"You are thinking about it."

She despised the pleasure in Antoine's tone. "No, no I'm not."

"Tell me how else this can end? What do you wish to offer? Do you think we can walk away, just forget how you disrespected us?"

"We can give you your money back, we can pay back everything—"

Antoine laughed again. "This is beyond money. Your disruption of our cash flow is not what brought us here. You have embarrassed my family, just as you embarrassed your own. You are selfish and irresponsible. You cannot presume others will pay for your mistakes, and Rushe is paying, Serendipity too."

She couldn't expect Antoine to surrender victory, walk away, and receive nothing in return. But if he would not accept monetary reparation then every other price was, in her eyes, too high. There was still a chance they could prove their case legitimately, but as Eric pointed out, if the cops got Rushe in their custody he'd be vulnerable to investigation beyond the Victor case.

She'd negotiate with Antoine, not to give in to his commands or to beg his forgiveness. She had to keep her head. He had made an offer and now she had to counter it, which was how negotiations worked. Antoine asked for the most he wanted, it was her place to offer him the least she could.

"I'll testify against the others," she said. Antoine's expression became curious. "I won't testify against Rushe, but I will give a statement as to what happened. I can incriminate Skeeve, Victor, all the rest of them."

Leaving Rushe out of her testimony wouldn't be too difficult. No one alive had seen them together. Events in the basement of Victor's mansion were open to interpretation, and none of the abducted women knew anything of her and Rushe's relationship.

At the time, after events had unfolded, she had been ready to give a statement. At Rushe and Jansen's urging, she hadn't. They highlighted if she did say anything unfavorable that the Merciers, or corrupt cops, might come after her. But there she was in this situation anyway.

During the ordeal, she hadn't known anything about anyone bankrolling the operation. She'd thought Victor was in charge. It wouldn't be difficult to maintain that line with the cops now. She could plead ignorance to anything beyond Victor's regime.

"We can put everything on Victor, you don't need Rushe."

"That may ensure Rushe's freedom," he said. "But we gain nothing, it's not enough."

She swallowed the wail lodged in her throat. There were no aces up her sleeve, this was it, all she had. She could testify against the others and keep the Mercier family name out of the equation; it was a name she hadn't learned until Antoine showed up there anyway.

"I thought you were a businessman," she said. "Open to negotiation. If you try to extract testimony from me under duress, it won't be favorable for you. If you try to force me to testify against Rushe I'll be sure to include your name, and your cousin's, and your uncle's. If he goes down, you do too."

"Spirited," Antoine said on a smiling exhale. "We shall consider it, your compliance in court to incriminate Victor, and use of your connections here."

He wanted not only her testimony, but also her family. Sacrificing her relationship with Rushe would be a lifelong price for her, and a cost for Rushe too. Maybe Antoine saw that as punishment enough for Rushe.

Antoine could usurp Rushe's woman. The concept of outdoing the man who had undermined him could be tempting for the Frenchman. Or it could just be about money, her family had access to a lot of it, and they could help Antoine accumulate his own through their vast network.

"No."

"Then we shall expect your statement with the police within a week, and you will be accessible to our lawyers."

"You can't expect me to—"

"No! You cannot expect us to! You wish to negotiate, and these are the terms. Do not frolic with the big boys if you cannot afford the stakes."

Her hatred burned into him with the same fire he returned on her, but the door opened, and her mother entered with her father not too far behind. The couple examined her and Antoine's proximity. The curious concern on her mother's face became delight.

"Are you two getting properly acquainted?"

"I'm going to bed," Flick said, unwilling, or maybe unable, to spend any more time in Antoine's company. Before she could get past him, Antoine took her hand and brought it up to his mouth.

"You have many things to consider," he said, wearing too practiced a smile.

"Goodnight," she said, conveying her displeasure enough that he released her.

"No, stay up some more," Beverly said, as Flick went toward the exit.

"No," she said, noticing how her mother's attention kept flitting back and forth between her and Antoine. "Goodnight."

THIRTY-THREE

"I'VE NEVER SEEN YOU SO QUIET."

"What?" she asked, rolling her head on the headrest to look at Eric in the driver's seat.

"We've been in the car for more than an hour, and you've barely said two words. You haven't even asked about what I found out."

"I'm sorry," she said.

"It didn't go well?" Eric asked.

"Which part? The negotiations with Antoine? The telephone conversation with Hayden or the part where my mother hijacked me this morning to tell me it was time to get over my rebellious phase?"

"Isn't twenty-seven old to be in a rebellious phase?" Eric asked. "Are you a late bloomer?"

"I've been rebelling against my mother since I was four years old," she said. "At least that's what she would tell you. She hasn't realized yet, this is just my personality."

"What? Awkward?"

"Non-compliant," she said, smiling for the first

time since before her discussion with Antoine the night before.

The last time she'd smiled was before dinner, during her telephone conversation with Rushe. He'd called her on the Hughes' library line for an update, not that she'd had one then. But it had been bolstering to hear his voice.

"Right," Eric said.

"I'm not even sure she wants me home, she just doesn't like to explain where the youngest Hughes daughter disappeared to. It's not easy to explain that I ran off to live my life independent of the privilege they offered."

"And then you brought home Rushe."

"Yeah," she said, appreciating Eric's smile. "Maybe I was switched at birth."

"Your mom's probably praying for that."

She laughed and sighed out her despondency. "What did you find out?"

"You were right that the girl remembered you," Eric said. "No one's been near her, I guess they don't know about her. They won't be expecting you to build your own case."

"That's good."

"How did things go with Hayden?"

"I called him yesterday afternoon," she said. "To say he was surprised to hear from me is an understatement. I didn't tell him what was going on, but he remembered Rushe, and us together. That's something. He's a stand-up guy. I don't see him lying to the cops or to anyone for that matter."

"So we can build a case?"

Her head rolled to look out the passenger window. "We have witnesses who can speak to our version of events."

"What happened with Antoine?"

"I don't know what to do…" she said. "I don't know how to fix this."

"Have you spoken to Rushe?"

"On the phone," she said. "He called me last night."

"Did you give him the specifics?"

"No," she said, sure Eric was curious about the details. "We spoke before my conversation with Antoine. Worked out for the best because if I'd told Rushe… He needs to be where he is for now. There will be time to talk when I get back to him."

"Liam has the details of the captains. Do you want me to talk to them?"

"I don't know," she said, appreciating that despite saying he never would, Eric was now offering. "I don't know anything anymore."

"Hey now, don't lose it. You're keeping us all going, giving out the orders and demanding we follow through. You're a strong woman."

"Maybe I don't want to be strong anymore," she said.

"You want to walk out on this? On Rushe?"

Even if she did, she would have nowhere to go, and none of them would be any safer. This problem wasn't going away. It didn't matter how far they ran, they would still be found eventually. Antoine had threatened Tawny too, and Serendipity was still in captivity. No amount of fighting would change the fact their position was weak. The Merciers held all the aces.

"You don't walk out on Rushe," she said. "I couldn't walk out on him."

"I don't think he'd let you."

"I really thought I could make things better by talking to Antoine," she said.

"You haven't been in this game long, have you? You don't reason with the bad guy; he's not interested in helping you out. He's interested in helping himself. Did you make him a counteroffer?"

"Yeah."

"And?"

"He countered it," she said, turning to him again. "But giving Rushe the specifics will only make things worse. I can't lie to him, I don't want to lie, but… it's within my power to make this go away."

"That's great, then why are you so…? Isn't that what you wanted?"

"Yes," she said, admitting at least to herself that in a lot of ways Antoine's proposal was a godsend.

Especially if, like he'd implied, it didn't involve sex.

"Have you got to murder someone?"

"No. No one has to die."

"Rushe goes to prison?" She shook her head, gazing at the passing scenery. "What's the problem?"

"He won't let it happen, he just won't."

"Rushe? If he knows it saves everyone's hide…"

"I'm all he has."

"A few weeks ago," Eric said, "you were telling me the job was all he had."

"Things have changed."

"Yeah, dying will do that to a guy."

The future promised between her and Rushe was not one of romance and innocent bliss. But it had been a future she was certain about. Since admitting their love and Rushe telling her he would do anything to make her happy, she had known exactly what she wanted her future to hold: Rushe.

The only thing that could have prevented them from being together was each other, if their feelings had failed, and she had been confident that wouldn't happen. The idea that an outsider could tear them apart, and beyond that, keep them apart, made her ill. But if it meant keeping everyone alive, and keeping everyone free…

She'd promised to do anything for Rushe but convincing him to let her do this would not be easy.

"AND SHE'S BACK," Cody said, when she walked into the brothel reception after Eric dropped her off.

Lilah sat behind the desk. Candy was at her side with her arm in a sling.

She cringed and lowered her bag to her side. "Candy, you're back too."

"I hope you didn't bring any of your friends with you."

"I am so sorry," she said. "For what happened, I really didn't mean… I'm sorry."

Being shot wasn't something an apology could erase. But she couldn't drop to her knees and beg for forgiveness. It wasn't like she was the one who'd pulled the trigger. She also couldn't explain to everyone exactly who Simone was and what she had been doing there that day.

Looking at the three faces, which were all looking at her, her head began to work. Who could the mole be? Antoine knew things that could only have come from someone there.

"Is Rushe here?" she asked.

"Over at Silver's," Cody said. "He'll be back later."

She nodded and dragged her bag toward the curtain. "Hey." She stopped at the sound of Lilah's voice and was confused by the frown the madam wore. "You okay?"

"Yeah," she said, forcing herself to smile, half-hearted though it was.

If she couldn't convince these complete strangers she wasn't troubled, what hope did she have of convincing Rushe? He wasn't there, that gave her some time to gather herself together. Except she'd had the whole car journey with Eric and hadn't managed it yet.

They had stopped at Liam's on the way back to retrieve the information on the police captains, and she had every intention of discussing surveillance with Rushe. Eric promised to check out the guys' addresses that night to give her an idea of any immediate worries. She'd arranged to call him from the library tomorrow to get his report.

Eric had been dedicated to helping, she wasn't sure why. Maybe because he'd been grateful to Rushe for what he did on the last job, and things had very nearly gone very wrong. If Rushe was right that Eric was soft, by Rushe's definition, then he no doubt felt guilt that she and Rushe had experienced most of the peril.

The brothel hadn't seemed like much when Rushe first brought her there, but she was surprisingly glad to be back. The first thing she noticed on entering their bedroom was that her adopted red and black shirt was laid on the bed. The gift was Rushe's equivalent of moonlight and roses.

Daylight was fading. It had been a long couple of days, so she showered her family and the Frenchman off her body and tried to rid them from her thoughts. Crawling into that shirt, she snuggled into the bed and inhaled the scent of her lover lingering on his pillow. He'd be back soon, his presence would help her regain her buoyancy.

AWARENESS OF THE WEIGHT of his body came after she registered his mouth on hers. Sighing, she stretched her arms to the sides before bringing them together to coil them around his neck.

"Just a dream, Kit. Go back to sleep."

"No," she mumbled, rocking her head from side to side while still enjoying the short, frequent kisses he pressed to her lips. "I don't want to sleep through this."

"I didn't want to wake you. It's late, and I have to go out again."

"Rushe," she griped without opening her eyes.

He lifted his hips enough to cup her inner thigh and pull her legs apart. She lay on top of the covers because it was warm. The denim of his jeans scraped her sensitive flesh and the metal of his belt buckle dug in deep. If he was clothed, he wasn't preparing her for his entry. This was just a better, more reassuring position for them to be in. Reiterating that reassurance was the track of his erection nestled in her center.

"You shouldn't have started if you weren't going to finish," she said, touching her tongue to his lip.

"Couldn't help myself," he said. "You're too sweet a package to be left lying here untouched."

"You left me a present lying out. Thank you for my shirt."

It was important for her to acknowledge he had done such a simple, nice thing for her. Giving gifts or being romantic wasn't in his nature. Reinforcing the positive behavior would hopefully lead to a repeat of it in the future.

"I want to hear everything that happened."

"I thought you were going out."

"I am," he said. "When I get back, we're going to talk about it, okay?"

"They threatened Tawny," she admitted.

That was the kind of news that wouldn't wait. If anything happened to the girl and she hadn't said anything to Rushe, she would never forgive herself.

"They what?"

"Someone here is watching us," she said. "Antoine knew that… you hadn't been sharing my bed."

He pulled back, and she opened her eyes to his deepening frown. "Why were you talking about our bed?"

"It doesn't matter," she said. "We can discuss the details later. But I wanted you to know someone here is reporting back. Maybe you already know who it is, I know you know more about what's going on here than I do. But I wanted you to know I knew, just in case. And Tawny should be careful—"

"Tawn will be fine here."

"Okay," she said. "I don't doubt your ability to keep her safe. They think you're sleeping with her, that you've chosen her over me."

"What the fuck—"

"Hey!" she said, locking her arms around his neck to prevent him from leaving his position on top of her. "I'm telling you so that you know what they know, or what they think they do."

"They think I'm screwing around on you?"

"I don't care what they think."

"What the hell right does that fucking—"

"Don't get riled," she said, lifting her head to kiss his jaw. She dragged her teeth on his stubble and lapped out at his bottom lip. "I missed you so much. You and your mouth."

When she urged his face downward, he complied reluctantly, but on pressing her lips to his, she sucked his lip enough to make him open to her. As she traced her tongue on his, Rushe's body began to relax.

She concentrated on every crevice of his mouth, tasting and tickling him slowly. Parting her legs further, she brought them higher until she very gently wound them around his hips, hoping the gradual action wouldn't register, that she could lull him back to calm.

"I wanna take my time, Kit," he murmured, bracing himself above her, sliding a hand from one knee to her ass. "I don't wanna fuck you fast now. I wanna take my time."

"Okay, Lover."

"I'll wake you up when I get back."

She nodded, and he kissed her again. Her arms dropped away when he tried to shift, but her legs stayed locked around him, which brought him back to her with a smile.

"Problem?" she asked with a grin.

He snagged her lip in his teeth. "You'd give me room if I told you I was getting my dick out."

She laughed. "Yes, I would. Right now he likes being where he is."

"And he'll be back there soon. But you've gotta let me go now."

As she relaxed and let his weight depart from hers, the chill that took his place sank into her bones. That last sentence was exactly what she was afraid of.

THIRTY-FOUR

IT TURNED OUT A NIGHT with Rushe was exactly what the doctor ordered. The consequences of her refusal of Antoine's request hung unknown on the horizon. The uncertainty plagued her. Still conflicted over what had happened at her parents' house, she hadn't got into specifics with her love. Neither of them had much inclination toward talking when Rushe returned to her bed.

Her love had kissed every inch of her and made long, slow love to her for hours, until her mind cleared itself of turmoil. They couldn't have fallen asleep more than three hours earlier, but she was invigorated that morning despite the lack of sleep.

Getting down and depressed about what was going on wouldn't help them. It was a new day, and she was going to be proactive and make a difference, no matter how small.

After climbing out of the shower and brushing her hair dry with the blow dryer in the bathroom, she went back to the bedroom entirely naked and grinned at the sight of her man, naked and face down on the bed, snoozing in innocent bliss.

No one could take this away from them. This man had expanded her world and opened up to her when he'd never trusted another soul. He trusted her. She had spent her childhood being overshadowed by her sisters and had never been good enough for her parents. Somehow, she'd always fallen short. For everyone except Rushe. She'd never understood his commitment and loyalty to her, but both were irrefutable.

Bounding over to the bed, she exaggerated the bounce as she crawled toward him on her knees. With a few more bobs on the mattress, she heard him mutter.

"Roll over," she said, slapping her hands to his shoulder blades, throwing a leg over his waist.

"I'm sleeping," he grumbled into the pillow.

"I can see that," she said. "Roll over."

Digging her fingers into his flesh, she massaged her hands up to his neck and across his shoulders.

"No."

"Don't be finicky," she said. "He wants to play with me."

"He doesn't," Rushe mumbled.

Tilting her hips forward, and dragging them lower, she ground her clit down against his spine. She sagged down on him to push her naked breasts into his back.

"I get to play with him anytime I want to," she said, licking the nape of his neck and further down his back as she worked her way lower until her pelvis rested in the dip of his lower back.

"You gotta work for it, Kitten."

"I'll work, I'll work. I'll do all the work." Kissing the breadth of him, she wriggled deeper. "Please roll over, Lover."

He loved to tease her. Over the months as he'd

relaxed into the security of their love, he'd gotten better at it. Part of her role in the relationship was to lighten the mood. He needed a friend, a playmate; he'd never had one before. She wanted to fulfill every role in his life that he'd been deprived the pleasure of.

"No."

"Okay," she said, undeterred.

Flipping her form away from his, she could almost feel his interest being roused. If she looked at his face his eyebrow would be up, though his eyes remained closed. Keeping him guessing stimulated her too. Crawling up the bed, she sucked his earlobe into her mouth, then whispered, so close that her lips touched the shell of his ear.

"Your dick's not the only part of you capable of pleasuring me," she breathed.

While ensuring her breasts remained on either side of his bicep, she slid her fingertips downward, scarcely touching so much as the hair on his forearm until she lifted his wrist. Shifting onto her back, she pressed his arm into her cleavage while her hands took control of his. Resting the heel of his hand on her pubis, she opened her legs, and draped one leg over his butt to spread his fingers against her.

"Feel how wet I am?" she murmured, slipping her fingers between his.

Taking control of two of his fingers, she rubbed them up and down her clit, pushing her hips up and his hand down at the same time.

"Flick your own clit," he said, though his arm remained loose and his hand in her power. "What do you need to get me juiced up for?"

"This," she sighed out.

Elevating her hips, she pressed her finger the length of his, and urged his digit inside her. Her own finger remained on top of his as she wriggled deeper with the two digits acting as one. He didn't move or make a sound, but his chest vibrated. She smiled, undulating up and down against their joint invasion. The tip of his finger twitched against her g-spot, and she gasped. His cool, unaffected act wasn't going to last much longer, but she wanted to push him harder.

Whipping his hand down, she spun to her side, pressing her body to his and bringing his hand up between them, still cradled in both of hers.

Smudging his bottom lip with his moist finger, she dipped her head in to kiss his lips with their fingertips still trapped between them.

Sucking his finger into her own mouth she groaned. "I taste good," she said.

His face relaxed into a smile before he very deliberately licked his lips, still though, his eyes stayed shut. "You're one dirty, fucking 'ho."

"I know," she purred, rolling to her back while embracing his arm as she ran her tongue the length of his digit.

The ease was erased in a cascade of snow when she saw a figure in the doorway, watching them.

"Rushe," she gasped, and immediately pounced off the bed.

Her lover was already up and off the bed behind her, but he stopped as soon as he registered what she'd seen.

"Missed my invite to this party." The figure came into the light, Silver, alone. He closed the door behind him, inviting himself into their shelter. "Love the tits; God was kind to you."

She grabbed Rushe's tee-shirt from the back of the couch and pulled it on to cover her naked form. "They're not for public consumption," she said.

"You have nothing to worry about," Silver said, coming in closer. "But that's enough to make a man fall to his knees and worship."

Glancing at Silver, she found he was looking at Rushe's groin. Before she could process what that meant, Rushe's hand landed on her hip, and he tugged her body in front of his to protect himself from open view.

"You know better than to fuck around with me," Rushe said.

"If wishing made it so," Silver said, but lost interest and wandered around the end of the bed to the other side of it. "You've gotta split."

She couldn't understand why this man, who wanted Rushe to settle his debt, was telling them to leave. If the debt was settled, she would've thought Rushe would have left straight away.

"Got work to do," Rushe said. "I'm going nowhere."

"Leave your tits here if you want," Silver said, lifting his attention to the windows.

Rushe reached past her to whip his jeans from the back of the couch to pull them on.

"His tits go with him," she said, propping her fists on her hips.

"I wouldn't be mouthing off. You're in enough trouble round here," Silver said. "I ain't never had one of my girls shot before."

"I wasn't holding the gun," she said.

Rushe's hands landed on her shoulders. "They've got Tawn in their sights," he said. "I can't carry both of them alone."

"Not when they're likely to kill each other… We'll take care of them," Silver said. "They're on you, man. Those guys were hanging around again last night, spooked Cody and the boys."

"Your minions come running to you scared," she said, "and that grants us an audience with the great Theo Silver?"

Silver smiled, a wide grin that showed his glowing white teeth. "She's a firecracker."

"I'm not bailing, Silver," Rushe said, sliding a hand down her arm to take her hand and draw her back.

He guided her body to behind his and stuck her hand in his back pocket.

"You gotta run," Silver said. "They'll get the drop on you when you don't expect it. As long as you're here, they know where to find you."

Silver couldn't be wild about the idea of cops or the Merciers coming there in pursuit of Rushe or her. That was trouble no lowlife criminal wanted on his doorstep.

"I'm ready for them," Rushe said. "I know it's coming."

"But you'll stay here, protecting these ladies, until the last possible minute. What is wrong with you, dude? You're gonna let them do it? No, you gotta run and keep on going, or they'll put you away forever."

When she thought of Theo Silver, she didn't think of a kind man. She certainly didn't think of a chivalrous one. But their visitor wasn't an evil man intent on collecting a debt.

"What's going on here?" she asked, suddenly aware she didn't have the full picture.

Rushe had told her not to jump to conclusions but hadn't gone on to lead her to any accurate ones.

"Your boyfriend's a wanted man, mixed up in some shady shit."

"She knows," Rushe said.

She was taken aback by his honesty. It wasn't normally their policy to advertise how open they were with each other, or how close they were. The women there, whom they'd been living with full-time, didn't know for sure that she and Rushe were physical with each other, let alone intimate.

"You weren't kidding when you said she was your number two, were you?" Silver said with a serving of incredulity.

"No, I wasn't."

Being dubbed Rushe's second was so humbling she was speechless. In addition, he'd done it to a third party, a stranger. For half a beat, she couldn't grasp the concept at all. Why would Rushe be so open with a man effectively holding them to ransom? Still, she edged in, propping her chest against him, and allowing her lips to make contact with the back of her love's arm.

"We'll look after her, man," Silver said. "You know we will."

She couldn't imagine Silver meant they would care for her in the same way that they did for Tawny, that Rushe would send money each month to secure her a place to stay there.

"I won't work for you," she said. "If you expect me to bend over for your clients—"

"You're a queen, you could own this place here if the girls knew the truth," Silver said to her, as though Rushe wasn't there at all. "Rushe ain't never had a woman, not ever, not a regular one while he's on a job. He's worked for me before."

"She knows," Rushe said again.

"She clearly don't know everything, 'cause she's standing there looking at me like I'm the devil. You tell her my girls are here by choice? I look after these girls. I got respect for the girls in this line of work."

"Silver's mom was an escort," Rushe said, still in front of her. "She was killed by a john when he was fourteen."

"I see what these women go through. My momma had no choice, and she raised me good. Taught me no drugs, no violence. Yeah, I get a cut for running this place, but my girls get a safe place to work, no danger here. I keep 'em safe."

THIRTY-FIVE

THE EASE BETWEEN the men made more sense. They both had a lot of respect for women and seemed interested in protecting them when they were at their most vulnerable.

"If you're such a great guy, why force Rushe to be here? Force him to settle this debt?"

"Your boy and I are playing them for fools. As long as they think we're enemies, and that he don't want to be here, the longer they'll leave him here."

"You're buying us time," she said. "But… why?"

Rushe took her hand from its pouch and backed up until he leaned on the back of the couch, guiding her body into the vee of his thighs.

He draped his arms around her. "I came here to find Tawny, I told you that."

"I thought he was here to cause trouble," Silver said, dropping onto the bed and stretching his legs out as he propped himself up to sit against the wall. "We about near killed each other."

"He thought I was trying to muscle in on his

territory, to take over," Rushe said. "I made it clear Tawny was my only concern."

"Then he found out how we run things here."

Rushe must have realized these women weren't victimized, exploited, or abused. "So you came to the agreement about Tawny?"

"After he tried to take her out and clean her up," Silver said. "Yeah. But she's not level, that girl. Think she thought your man was her shining prince."

A burst of laughter bubbled from her chest. Rushe's arms clenched around her, so she glanced up. "Sorry," she said, and brushed her cheek on his chest as he grazed his lips through her hair.

"Took her time to realize Rushe wasn't interested in love, wasn't capable of it," Silver said. "Least that's what we all thought."

"You know more than all those women," she said. "More than the girls here… more than Tawny?"

"Your secrets are safe," Silver said. "Your boy keeps mine."

The edge of Silver's mouth crept upward. His eyes drifted downward to survey the couple, but it wasn't her figure the pimp was enjoying.

Splaying her fingers on Rushe's bare chest, she rested her face against the heat of his firm, muscular flesh. "Don't worry, Lover. I'll protect you."

Silver laughed, a warm, booming sound that actually set her at ease.

"You two cut it out," Rushe said, lowering his mouth into her hair again.

"You've got a hunk of man there, honey. If you ever feel like sharing…"

"I'm the jealous type," she said. "Sorry."

"Shame."

"Why don't you tell—"

"I got enough guys coming in and out of my crew

regular enough. If I get a reputation of being soft, maybe my girls don't stay as safe."

"It's rough around here," Rushe said. "Silver doesn't always deal with the most understanding of guys."

"All this time I thought…" she didn't finish.

"That I was an evil bastard," Silver said.

"He likes people to think that," Rushe said. "He hams it up well."

"Would've figured you'd tell your lady about me," Silver said. "If she's pissed off, she won't suck your dick for a week… you've still got my number, right?"

The mischief in Silver's voice was obvious. Did he really mean what he said or simply enjoy making Rushe uncomfortable?

"You better watch out, I can be scrappy," she said, twisting enough in Rushe's arms to peek at a smiling Silver through her hair.

"If you've got any influence over that man, you should be telling him to watch his ass," Silver said, getting up and strolling around the bed toward the couple. "We'll watch yours here, 'cause if Tawny ever finds out about this…"

His smile dissolved.

"She'll claw my eyes out, I know, I've been told."

"Who the fuck said that to you?" Rushe asked, growing rigid.

"The same woman who told me I shouldn't walk on the wild side because I wouldn't be able to handle you."

"What I hear, he's the one who can't handle you," Silver said. "You're a wild cat."

"You came here to warn us," she said, twisting her body to lean back on Rushe's chest, twining his arms further around her.

There was something about the thickness of his

solid, shielding embrace that sheltered her from danger and negativity.

"I came here to tell you they're watching," Silver said. "I don't want the girls getting twitchy."

"And?"

Rushe's single word was deep and commanding. He had picked up on something she'd missed.

Silver's shoulders dropped a couple of inches. "He woke up."

Rushe's form grew. Although he kept her in his arms, he took his butt off the back of the couch and rose to his full height. "Jansen?" Rushe asked. Silver nodded and averted his gaze. "Fuck."

"Wait, Jansen is awake?" she asked, trying to get either of the men to look at her. Rushe tightened his embrace to prevent her moving away. "This is great. This is amazing news."

"Maybe," Rushe said.

"How can you say maybe?" she said. When Silver did eventually lift his head, the two men shared a solemn look. "Wait a minute, how do you know anything about Jansen?"

"Silver got me on the Jansen job," Rushe said.

"I had some guys trying to back door drugs into this place a few years back, caused me some trouble," Silver said. "Jansen was working a case and came to me. I gave him information, and he kept the pigs from my door."

"You were an informant," she said.

"I don't mean anyone no harm," Silver said. "You leave me to my business, and I'll leave you to yours."

"Having a relationship with the cops helps keep trouble away," Rushe said.

"So you and Jansen had an association, and Jansen came to you when Victor took Serendipity?"

"Rushe was here with Tawny at the time," Silver said. "He agreed to help Jansen out."

So that was how Rushe had gotten involved in the first place. "Rushe left here to work for Victor?"

"Yeah," Silver said. "Victor called me to check Rushe was legit."

"A reference?" she asked, imagining even criminals liked to check employment history.

"I acted mad," Silver said. "Told Victor that Rushe screwed me over. It gave your boy credibility when I said he'd fucked up one of my girls."

"Sure it did," she said.

Victor wanted to check Rushe was crooked, and Silver gave that confirmation. It made sense now why the Merciers would make an agreement with Silver to send Rushe back until they were ready for him. They thought Silver wanted revenge too, and that Rushe begrudged being there paying for the damage he allegedly did to this fictitious woman.

"Is he talking?" Rushe asked.

Silver shrugged. "That's all I got. I had a guy checking in at the hospital every day or two. He just wanders by and listens to the nurses' talk."

"Okay, we have to go there," she said, casting aside thoughts of getting to the library and calling Eric.

"No," Silver said, taking an involuntary step toward them. "This is gonna change the timetable."

"Timetable?"

"Antoine was waiting for his uncle to get back," Rushe said. "Now that Jansen's awake, if he starts talking…"

"We have to know what he knows," she said. "He'll be devastated to hear about Serendipity, he has to know that we're on the case."

"Yeah," Rushe said. Despite not seeing his face, she could hear his mind working. "You're right. We have to know what he knows."

"I was supposed to talk to Eric today about the captains. It might be best to leave that until later. Jansen can tell us if there's a chance that we can trust them."

"Captains?" Silver asked.

"Don't worry about it," Rushe mumbled, his mind still elsewhere.

So Silver didn't know everything? That was hardly surprising. Rushe wasn't known for sharing more than was necessary, as she'd found out again that day.

"I have to get dressed," she said, digging her nails into Rushe's arm when he didn't release her.

"Not in front of him you don't," Rushe said, sounding more with it than he had a few seconds ago.

"He doesn't care," she said, not that she'd intended to get naked in front of Silver.

The pimp's smile rose again, and he leaned back. "Not me," Silver said. "Get your tits out again."

"He fucks his share of women too," Rushe grumbled. "He'll stick his dick in any hole that passes."

The revelation actually made her smile at Silver. The man she'd written off as flat and one-dimensional actually turned out to be very intriguing.

"I like the way she's looking at me now," Silver said to Rushe, keeping his smiling eyes on her. "Maybe sharing's not such a bad idea anymore, huh? If I fuck you first, can I share your man?"

"Out," Rushe barked.

Silver laughed but sauntered toward the door. "Don't get yourself in more trouble," he said on reaching the exit. "Check it out if you want, but I say you should run, get going before those guys panic and have you in leg irons."

"Thanks for your concern," Rushe grumbled and opened the door. "Out."

Silver ambled on out. Rushe swung the door into

the frame behind him.

"We have to go now. We don't want the cops getting there before us," she said. "We have to tell Jansen about Serendipity—" Rushe turned his intimidating glare on her, but she didn't shrink. "What?"

"Going to the hospital is dangerous."

"I know," she said, peering closer. "So is walking down the street for us these days. Silver is right that this will change their timetable. They could send the cops here if they decide to arrest you—"

"I'm prepared for that."

"I'm not," she said. "You're not allowed to leave me. Who will watch my tail if you're in prison?"

"Eric," Rushe said. "I've given him instructions to—"

"Oh my God," she said, drawing back when he began to approach her. "You've made a contingency plan. You've actually made arrangements. Am I supposed to sit on my ass for the next thirty years while you rot in there?"

"If you want to fuck around—"

"That's not what I'm talking about, and you know it," she said. "You are not going to prison. I will do whatever it takes to prevent it… whatever it takes."

"What does that mean?" he asked, doing some scrutinizing of his own as he kept coming at her.

She backed away. "Nothing," she said, shaking her head quickly and swallowing away her determination.

This wasn't a man to be caged. If she had to give up her liberty for his, she would. As his eyes narrowed, her heart pumped louder because she was sure, she didn't have an ounce of doubt. Rushe would remain free; she would dedicate her life to that conviction.

"We have to go to the hospital," she said. "Get ready."

THIRTY-SIX

HOSPITALS WEREN'T MEANT to be daunting places, at least not in terms of bad guys and danger. Her apprehension only lessened once they parked the car, and she could see the building. This was a place of healing, not of torture. It would be filled with kind, noble people.

If they could talk to Jansen, they could finally get some answers. Visiting was important, it was not a time to be overcome by fear. Rushe had taken her to a diner to call Eric and let him know of the development. Eric would update Liam, and the plan was to regroup later.

After selecting a parking spot on the far side of the lot, they left the car. Rushe took her hand to lead her through the vehicles toward the main building. Because Rushe had been there before, he knew where he was going. On reaching the complex, they went past a vent pumping out steam and down a narrow alley, flanked by two dark brick walls.

The walkway was thirty feet long, but she could see the edge of the automatic doors on the other side of the courtyard beyond. Keeping her sight set on that, every step was one closer to the knowledge that had the potential to set them free. Getting inside would be easy, they had to find Jansen's room, and…

Someone stepped into view at the end of the narrow space. Rushe stopped. They didn't have a chance to retreat because a fire door opened behind them, and eight men came out from inside before they let the door click back to lock.

"Isn't it wonderful news?"

The person at the end of the alley started toward them but stopped fifteen feet away. She wouldn't have expected Antoine to leave his post at her parents' home, but there he was, standing tall in front of them.

"What are you doing here?" she asked.

Rushe put his body in front of hers in a shielding maneuver, but the eight guys gathered in an arc around them from the rear. None of them touched, but they were menacing enough to set her on edge, Rushe too.

"We got the news very early this morning that our associate is conscious, isn't it wonderful?" Antoine asked, without an ounce of delight.

"What do you want?" Rushe asked.

"It is time to satisfy your debt with us. We shall settle your remaining affairs with Silver."

"No," she said.

"We can send the police to Silver's place for you," Antoine said. "Or we make the call here… Were you trying to finish the job you started on Jansen?"

Their intention was to blame everything on Rushe. With enough police corroboration, they would get away with it. If Jansen was no longer a credible witness because of his injuries, he'd be useless. Alternatively, it was possible that when he found out about Serendipity, he would do anything to keep her safe. That could include lying and implicating Rushe. She could jump up and down and proclaim his innocence as much as she liked. If she was alone, she'd be ineffective.

"You expect me to stroll up to the closest cop and turn myself in?" Rushe asked.

"Non," Antoine said on half a laugh. "We expect your lady to phone them."

"Excuse me?"

"Oui, our boys here have rescued you from an attack they witnessed. You are free of the abuse you have lived under. Now you have the chance to tell the police the full story."

She started forward. "Why you fucking—"

Rushe grabbed her shoulders and yanked her back, preventing her from advancing on Antoine.

"You have no choices," Antoine said.

A thwack preceded a curse, then Rushe's hands were gone. She spun to see him land a punch on one guy as another smacked his jaw. Rushe turned but was hit again. Blood sprayed, and a third guy came at Rushe as a fourth brought up the butt of a gun.

"Stop!" she screamed out.

The men desisted, remaining on pause; none released his grip on the other. Blood on Rushe's forehead and the back of his head scared her. All of the guys matched her love in bulk, but he was outmatched in numbers.

"You knew this was coming, ma chère… Your statement is expected."

"I told you I would testify against Victor," she said, spinning around to beseech the European. "Please, I told you I would, I promise you. I'll implicate them all. You won't go to jail. No one will know anything about your family. Please! None of the other women can testify to anything except Victor and his men. I'll corroborate that, and Simone can give her testimony too. Please, Antoine! You don't have to do this."

"Your father would be ashamed of your begging."

"I don't care," she said, aware of the weight of wetness on her lashes. The rabble of men detaining Rushe were a good ten feet behind her. "You can be a reasonable man. This makes sense. Everybody wins. You get to start again, and we get to walk away."

Antoine came closer though remained out of reach. "And I told you it wasn't enough," he hissed.

Flesh smacked flesh, and when she whirled around, two guys got hold of Rushe's arms. They dragged him to the wall as a third thug landed a punch on his chin and another hit his gut. The gang would beat her love to a pulp and then claim they'd done it in defense of her.

"No!" The male faces all came in her direction. "I said, no!"

"Do you think you can do something to prevent us, mademoiselle?" Antoine asked, bringing his body toward hers when she shifted her focus to him.

"You made me an alternative offer," she said, forcing herself to keep her eyes locked to his despite the twist of bitterness in her throat.

"Oui."

"You want my family," she said with increasing determination.

"Oui."

Gritting her teeth, she had to will herself to utter the words. "You can have me," she exhaled. His chin came up. Unable to believe she was going to acquiesce, her soul left her body. "I'll do it. Whatever you want. Set him loose. Leave him alone, and Serendipity, and Jansen… your family will consider the debt paid, never go near any of them again, and I'll do whatever you want."

"Kitten."

She disregarded the growl from a distance behind her. Rushe was out of her view. Far in front of her the haughty, yet intrigued, Antoine.

"Do we have a deal?" she asked.

Less than ten seconds passed, but it felt like a lifetime.

The European's smile curled further. "Take him far from here and let him free."

Antoine's hand came up to caress her face. She had to force herself not to recoil or spit out at him. Movement and shouting flared in the background, but she didn't see Rushe again. Though it broke her heart not to look into his eyes one last time, her own heart would never survive the intangible contact.

"Flick! Kitten! You fucking dumb bitch…!"

The shouting kept up, but when the gang split from the alley the specifics faded.

"You know I have been intimate with your sister," Antoine said.

"Yes."

"I will not be faithful to you. There will be no love… We will know the truth, but your family will not. Their connections will be very useful."

"I know what you want from me, Antoine," she said. "If you and your associates hold up your end of the bargain, I will do the same."

THIRTY-SEVEN

BEING BACK IN HER FAMILY home so soon was unexpected. Until she received word Rushe was still free, she would maintain her frost. Not that she could imagine shirking it after events of the day.

The Frenchman had put her into the back of his car, and they'd been driven all the way back to the Hughes' home immediately.

"I can't believe it," Beverly said, when Flick and Antoine entered the family dining room. "Antoine told us that he would retrieve you, and here you are."

Her mother went so far as to rest a gracious hand on her daughter's elbow.

"He what?" she asked.

Antoine moved in close to her side. "Yes, this feud is just ridiculous. You should embrace your family. We should work through issues with support, as it is not our place to judge each other."

"But you leave and return with our youngest child within a day," Beverly said. "You must be very persuasive."

"I certainly am," Antoine said.

His arm came around her shoulders. Her whole body went rigid as she dampened the urge to scream and lunge around at him. She wanted to smack him in the head, beat him until he begged her for mercy, and then keep on going.

It had taken eight guys to drag Rushe from her side. He'd be back with her as soon as he could be. This wasn't over. Making a scene now wasn't going to improve anything. In fact, there was a good chance it would risk lives.

"I'm going to call your sisters. We'll all have dinner this evening. This is tremendous news; your father will be pleased that you are home to stay."

Beverly brushed her hand upward and vanished from the room in a flurry of silk and sparkling jewels. Beverly Hughes was always turned out to perfection. She wore stylish clothes in expensive fabrics, complemented by the latest jewelry designs and understated makeup. There was no detracting from her beauty or her sophistication.

The door closed.

Instantly, she shoved away from Antoine. "What did you do with him?" she demanded now they were alone for the first time since the incident in the alleyway.

"Rushe is fine."

"I don't believe you," she said, going for the Scotch decanter in the corner and pouring herself a large measure.

"He will remain working with Silver," Antoine said. "We have a few jobs, and he can enforce for us."

"No," she said. "You want my family. You want me here. I'm here on the proviso that no one gets hurt and that you liberate my friends, which includes Rushe. He's tied to nothing, and Serendipity goes free."

"They shall," Antoine said. "As soon as the case

has been dispensed with."

"You're going to keep Serendipity, and keep tabs on Rushe, until the prosecutors have made their case?"

"And accountability has been placed firmly on the shoulders of Victor and his group, yes."

"That could take months."

"Or years," he said, watching her finish the liquor and pour another couple of fingers. "I like my woman to enjoy a drink, though perhaps not of something so potent in such volume."

"Let's get one thing clear: I am not your woman. And Rushe lets me drink in whatever manner I choose."

"I have done you a kindness. My uncle is a rational man, Rushe could be useful."

She was getting tired of hearing people say that about him. "Because he's not squeamish?" she asked, pleased the warmth of alcohol was circling her heart, replacing the hollow ache that had consumed her since the alley.

"You chose to be here, chose to stand with me, at my side, to permit my lingering association with your family."

"As opposed to destroying the man I love? Yes, I did."

"Then you will learn to do as you are told," Antoine said. Narrowing the space between them, he took her glass away as she lifted it toward her lips again. "You are here to play a role, to be my woman, to give me cover for further dealings with your father. We are on the cusp of a crucial deal. My cut, I imagine, will be closely tied to how intimately related I am with your family."

"So I smile at you and laugh at your jokes while you exploit my relatives?"

"This was your proposal; you negotiated this deal," Antoine said. "You wanted an alternative, and this is it. You will testify against Victor, and you will maintain the appearance of an intimate relationship with me. I will make money for your family—"

"And more than a little for yourself."

"It would be naïve of our families not to unite. I promise you that it is in my interest to maintain this alliance with your family. They will be safe and protected, provided they are useful to me, and that you do not threaten our unity. My uncle looks forward to meeting your father."

"No one will believe we're romantically involved."

"You will make them believe," he said, sampling her drink, then swirling the remaining liquid in the base of the tumbler.

"We barely know each other."

"You have proved yourself reckless and impulsive," Antoine said. "They believe you do not always act with good sense. If you found yourself compelled to explore your attraction to me…"

"I am not—"

"You want to be of use to me, as you wish Rushe to be free to be with his whore, do you not?"

Antoine must still believe that Rushe and Tawny were sleeping together.

"I won't have sex with you."

His lips contorted into a smile. "You may be as eager for me as you like, but your family must believe our relationship is sustainable. Our courtship shall be proper, but you will be faithful to me. Your attention will be entirely mine, you will fulfill your duties as I designate them."

"You will never have me," she said, the only man she would be faithful to was Rushe.

"Do not lay a challenge before me. Sex, ma chère, is easy to coerce." He put the glass on the table and brought his body against hers. "You shall serve me as I see fit and obey my every command. Your feelings, in time, may surprise you. You enjoy dangerous men, Felicity. Danger comes in many forms."

He lowered his head as though to kiss her.

Ready to shove away, she elevated her elbows. A sound in the corner raised her attention, and Antoine's too. Charles Hughes stood there in the doorway with shock flaring from his expression, a grinning Beverly next to him.

"Oh my! We did not mean to interrupt," Beverly said, placing her palm on her husband's arm, which was her equivalent of squealing in glee. "We should leave you alone."

"Non," Antoine said, thankfully backing away. "Felicity was on her way to refresh herself after our long journey. She must wash away the past." Though he didn't look at her, she heard the implication of Rushe's name on Antoine's lips and shivered at the idea of ridding herself of the remnants of her love's touch. "The trip was tiring, but she promises to entice me. I find myself intrigued."

"We can intrigue!" Beverly declared. "Come with me, and we shall indulge the men, tempt them as best we can."

"Très bon," Antoine said, bestowing a smug smile on her. "I look forward to it, ma chère."

With no other choice, she left the Frenchman to accept her mother's outstretched hand. Beverly would preen her to what a perfect Hughes woman should epitomize. But Flick didn't want perfumes and face packs, she wanted pizza and her lover.

Antoine couldn't be trusted. She couldn't help but be preoccupied with fears for Rushe's wellbeing. Without her touchstone at her side, she was already beginning to flounder.

THIRTY-EIGHT

TO PREVENT RUSHE'S pain, she'd agree to anything. Her parents were thrilled she was there. Vivian seemed happy about it too. She forced herself to look at Antoine when he spoke but couldn't bring herself to adore him, though it was obviously what he expected of everyone.

As soon as Lucia saw that Antoine remained at Flick's side and that he kept touching her, much to her difficult-to-disguise chagrin, the eldest Hughes child appeared dismayed. No one asked questions about her and Antoine's frequent proximity. That didn't surprise her. Appearances were what mattered in that household. They were beautiful people, admiring and fawning over each other. This was the life she fought to escape from.

Tossing the last of her wine to her throat, she left Antoine's side on the couch and went to the bar for the bottle. She filled her glass and downed half of the sweet liquid without taking a breath.

"Felicity, dear, don't be inappropriate," Charles said.

"Don't worry, Charles. We'll school her again in

more ladylike ways," Beverly said. "We shall remind her what it is to be a Hughes. Please do not be deterred by her crassness, Antoine."

Her family would make no secret of their desire to see her coupled up with the European. So she was being pitched as a marital prospect by her family, again.

"I am not," Antoine said. "And that shall be her last drink."

Keeping her eyes trained to the aloof Antoine posed on her mother's couch, she raised her glass to her lips. He made her sick.

"You can't auction Flick off to Antoine," Lucia said. Had Lucia ever mouthed off? Even in such a delicate way. "Antoine has taste."

Any hint Lucia may have been defending her baby sister was dispersed by that comment.

"Felicity is a very attractive woman," Antoine said. "She has displayed interest that I am aware of. But these are our personal matters."

"Of course, of course," Charles said. "We care—"

A loud crash from beyond the room startled them all into silence. Shouting ensued with a maelstrom of clatters and rabbling. The din came closer, then ceased for half a beat.

"Kitten!"

Inhaling a gasp, her hands fell, the fragile wine glass slipped from her fingers and hit the floor in a splinter of shattering sparkles. She was already moving, already across the room, out the door and running up the hallway toward the lobby. Bursting through the door, she dashed around the staircase. And there he was, spinning to face her.

"Lover," she whimpered, and ran to leap into his arms.

Rushe swept her off the floor, his forearm under

her ass and his other hand cradling the back of her skull.

"What the fuck!" he hollered at her.

His eye was blackened, and his jaw was bruised. He'd been more than cast aside, he'd been beaten. But he was alive, and he was there.

"You came here," she gasped, smudging her mouth to his. "You shouldn't be here; you can't be here."

"We've called the police," a steward said.

She hadn't been aware of the dozen or so others in the foyer. "No," she said, clamping her arms tighter around him. "No police, he's fine, he's allowed here. Lover, you came for me."

"What the fuck did you think you were doing?" Rushe snarled at her, oblivious to the others.

She noticed then how loose his clinch was. His enfolding arms were holding her form back from his ribs. If he hadn't been so focused on her, he might have registered pain on his expression beyond his clenched jaw and gritted teeth.

"They hurt you," she wept, cradling his face. "Oh, Lover, they hurt you."

"We're leaving."

As he turned toward the door, she slithered down him and hooked his pocket. Rushe kept hold of the back of her neck, keeping her body eclipsed in his.

"The police are on their way, ma chère."

The exotic accent froze her in her steps, bringing Rushe to a halt at her back.

"They'll put you away," she exhaled.

"We're leaving," Rushe insisted.

She cast her wet eyes up over her shoulder to her scowling love. "You have to go."

His brows drew closer together, that piercing black stare seared through her. "We are leaving."

"What about Serendipity and Tawny?" she whispered.

Her family was in the room. They'd no doubt believe these names were of women Rushe had dallied with.

"We're leaving." Rushe seemed almost unable to accept her refusal to move.

She only refused because she had to.

Twisting in his arms, she laid her forearms against his torso. "You have to go, and I have to stay. You have a job to do, and so do I."

"No," he said, and dipped to take her off her feet.

Marching for the door, the stewards and staff circled them. The trapped animal in Rushe threatened to emerge. He was ready to lash out and damage the threat to him and his prize.

"There are many witnesses to this kidnap attempt," Antoine drawled.

"This is making it worse," she said. "Be patient, Lover."

"You are my woman."

"Not anymore," Antoine said, approaching their periphery. "She chooses to be here with her family, with me."

Rushe dropped her. She stumbled on her heel, collapsing to the floor as Rushe spun on Antoine to bear down upon the European.

Her love's fist balled.

As it came up, she clambered across the floor. "No!" she shouted. The howl of a siren struck terror into her. "It'll make it worse! Leave him! Please, Rushe!"

He whipped around to look at her. "Kit," he murmured.

"Go," she whispered.

In two strides, he was at her side, bending to snatch her arm and haul her to her feet. "I love you."

Admitting it so openly was a first. She hated to see conflict rage in him. "I know."

The siren grew louder. "I'll come for you. Keep your guard."

In a sweeping crouch, he snatched her head and captured her mouth in a brief but consuming union. All too quickly, he was gone. She closed her eyes to lock up tight the memory of what could be their last moment together to keep it deep within her.

"Shouldn't we stop him?" came a staff voice.

"Good luck trying," Roger said.

She met Antoine's eyes. "Let him go… we let him go."

"He is pained to lose you," Antoine said, coming to her. He brushed her lips with his fingers, wiping away her lover's kiss. "It is done, and there will be no more… oui?"

The salt of her tears touched his fingers, but she had to nod. She was locked in there without other options.

"No more."

"Then we shall dismiss the police," Antoine said. "And put this down to a final, dramatic goodbye."

"But what about—" Charles began.

"We have Felicity to ourselves now," Antoine said. "This marks the end of that chapter. No more drama. We want only family, and he will no longer take up any of our time. He is the past."

With those cold foreign eyes, Antoine made her shiver. If Rushe was the past, Antoine wanted to be her future. There wasn't anything she could do to prevent that disgusting truth from becoming her new reality.

THIRTY-NINE

"IT'S ME."

She waited until everyone had gone to bed, then left a decent interval for everyone to find their slumber. Her two sisters and their husbands had elected to spend the night in her parents' house. Everyone was sufficiently disturbed by Rushe's intrusion that they didn't want to risk going home alone.

Once she was sure everyone would be sleeping, she tiptoed her way down to the family library, seated herself at the cherry wood desk, and picked up the phone.

"Thank God," Liam exhaled down the line. "We were starting to get worried. You called to say you were going to visit Jansen and said you would get back in touch after you'd seen him. That was a lengthy hospital visit."

"Something happened."

"Yeah, we figured that out. What?"

"I'm back at my parents'," she said into the receiver. "They ambushed Rushe and me at the hospital.

They wanted to call the cops, to say that Rushe had been attacking me when Antoine's men stepped in."

"Giving you the chance to be honest about the tyranny you've lived under for all these months?"

"Yeah," she said. "Something like that. I couldn't let them do it."

"I don't understand what that has to do with your parents' house," Liam said. "Did they arrest Rushe?"

"No," she said. "Antoine made me an offer; he made a request of me..."

"During your negotiations?"

"I told him to go to hell at first, but... I'm going to testify against Victor, see that he and his gang are implicated without the Merciers entering the equation."

"I still don't see what that has to do with—"

"Antoine told me that wasn't enough," she admitted, shutting her eyes against the memory of those words. "I offered him that, and he said it wasn't enough."

"No, 'cause he wants you to suffer. All of you."

"When it's done, they'll let Serendipity go, they won't touch Jansen again... Rushe will be free."

"That's too easy. You give a statement, stand up in court, and that's it? No," Liam said, with a note of suspicion. "What else?"

"He wants my family name, their credibility and connections."

"Your family..." At first, Liam didn't follow. "Wait, are you telling me...? You've entered into some sort of sordid arrangement to use yourself to protect the others?"

"It's not sordid," she said. "It's not sexual, I've made that clear to him."

"For crissakes, Flick, you can't... do you think Rushe is going to let that happen? That he'll let you hang off that guy's arm just to better the frog's business prospects?"

She'd never heard Liam use an insulting word to describe anyone. "It's a low price to pay. It makes sense. No one will lose their lives. The threat will be gone, no more pain, no more hurt, and everyone can be free."

"Except you," Liam said. "How long do you expect this to last? Does he want to marry you? Does he expect you to give up the rest of your life?"

"I don't know," she said, as saline rushed to her tongue. "I don't know, Liam. All I know is that I couldn't let them hurt Rushe anymore."

"What is jail time?" Liam said. "Rushe will do—"

"That's why I'm calling you," she said. "I need you to talk to him. Find Eric, then both of you talk to Rushe."

"And tell him what?"

"That this makes sense, and that he has to let me go. I'm not in pain, Liam. I'm healthy. Antoine is not molesting me. The conditions here are perfectly acceptable, excellent in fact. If a person had to choose their own prison, I imagine my mother's home would be a near ideal choice. I won't want for anything here."

"Except freedom. I can't condone this, Flick."

"Rushe will drive himself insane. He'll self-destruct. He'll blame himself for this. If he does something stupid—"

"Like what? Turn himself in?"

"I won't testify against him," she said. "You need to tell him that going to the cops won't do anything to free me. I'll still be here. Antoine will still have me, and there won't be a thing Rushe can do about that from inside a jail cell.

"Someone needs to watch my tail, and he can do that, he can check in with me periodically, just… tell him to stay away from here. He can look from afar if he wants to. Antoine will only be understanding for so long and seeing Rushe will only remind me that I can't… Antoine expects me to be faithful."

She had no intention of being intimate with anyone except Rushe. But she couldn't let her lover think that prospect was on the horizon. If Rushe kept coming back, they would only get into trouble, because she wouldn't be able to resist him. If Antoine decided to be done with her, or if he felt embarrassed when she was caught in a compromising position with Rushe, there was no telling what he would do.

"I thought it wasn't a sexual arrangement."

"I'll be celibate. The request of fidelity is about control," she said. "The point is you have to convince Rushe that coming here will do no good. I still don't trust that Tawny will be safe, or that they'll be kind to Serendipity while they have her. Someone needs to get in touch with Jansen, to tell him what is going on, and to let him know that when Victor's mob officially gets the blame Serendipity will be turned loose."

"You believe that will happen?"

"I believe we have to let Antoine believe we're going to hold up our end of the bargain. As long as his interest in my family remains business-oriented, there's no need for me to go back on my word. They're in danger here too. If I risk his business interests…" She sighed. "All he wants is an in. He's not asking for much more of me than my parents when they wanted me to marry Robert. That arrangement was meant to better the Hughes' business network. The Merciers will have connections that will tempt my father too, and he'll want the cemented association. Antoine has made a big deal of family, so if he has me, he's… family."

"I don't like this."

"Do you think I do?" she asked, the life drained down through her body and out into the roots of the family home. "But everyone's alive, Liam, and everyone is safe. Tell Rushe to stay away. Tell him to keep working. His work is important, and he shouldn't stop helping other women just because we've found ourselves in this mess. Please, Liam, keep him sane, keep him focused. I need to know you and Eric are on this… What's the alternative? Rushe goes to jail, my family is endangered, Tawny and Serendipity too, and why? Because I'm too stubborn to live in a building with my family and feign an interest in a specific man? That's all I have to do."

"What if he decides that he wants more from you?"

"Then he'll be disappointed," she said. "Forcing the issue makes no sense from his position either. I'm a shill. I'm here to sell Antoine to my family. He can have sex with anyone he wants to, it's not like there's a real relationship. This is a business arrangement."

"Convincing Rushe won't be as easy."

She was surprised Liam sounded almost sorry for Rushe when the men hadn't always seen eye to eye.

"I know that," she said. "But Rushe trusts me, and he is logical. You just have to make sure he doesn't act on impulse. Remind him how important his forethought is. Make sure he thinks this through, and he thinks through all his actions. This isn't over. There's a long way to go, and we have to be willing to take our time and get this right."

"A marathon, not a sprint?"

"Exactly," she said. "I want your word, Liam. Please look after him, and make sure he keeps his head."

On a dubious exhale, Liam spoke. "I'll try my best, but I'm not sure he'll listen to me."

"Remind him Tawny needs him, and that he needs to be there to look after her while this is going on. They know Rushe cares for her."

"Who is Tawny?"

"It doesn't matter. Just remind him I'm strong, and I can handle this. Tell him my guard is in place, and it's not going anywhere."

"He's a helluva lucky guy," Liam said.

"I'm the lucky one," she said. "I have your word?"

"Yes."

"Thank you," she said. "And thank you for your help through this. You're a really great guy."

"You can thank me when we get you out of there, because we will get you out of there… somehow."

"I have to go."

She hung up without waiting to hear more. She'd said her piece and trusted Liam to follow through. But she couldn't let herself believe it was going to be an easy fix. She was in deep, and Antoine was the only person there, other than her, who knew the truth. She was alone.

FORTY

THREE WEEKS didn't sound like very long when she said the words in her head. But as she watched her mother and father retreat down the hallway toward their bedroom, she tried to recall a time when she hadn't been locked in this hell and failed.

"You need to rest."

She snatched her hand out of Antoine's and began to stalk toward her own bedroom on unsteady legs. "Don't pretend you care about me."

Spending time with the family was the peak of her torture. At least when she and Antoine were alone, there was no illusion to propagate. When they went out on "dates" Antoine tended to hire a private dining space, which meant he could conduct business and they could ignore each other.

She went into her bedroom and closed the door, falling against the wall as she bent to yank her shoes from her feet, just to have something to throw across the room in frustration.

Antoine had given her no time at all to settle in.

Within the first forty-eight hours of being back in her parents' house, he'd taken her to the cops. He'd declared himself as a "concerned family friend" who had heard her tale of woe and insisted she come forward, despite her fear of retribution.

It was actually easier than she would have thought to convince the cops she was scared for her safety, which apparently prevented her from coming forth sooner. Yet she claimed to be tired of running. The police had spoken to her only briefly, then she'd been quickly turned over to the feds for further questioning. They'd had her in and out a few times and asked her the same questions over and over again. She stuck as close to the truth as she could, only omitting Rushe's name from the story.

Victor and his gang were the focus of the investigation, though it was clear the feds suspected involvement from other parties. Mercier hadn't been happy when she had referenced the "man who protected her" from Skeeve and the others at the shack, but she used her own forethought. Being honest about Rushe, without naming him, would ensure if the Merciers ever tried to have Rushe arrested she could point to him as her protector.

Law enforcement already had her, and her name, on record. It turned out that they had tried to trace her. She explained going into hiding at her protector's insistence and had only recently had the courage to return to her family home.

Antoine had access to a lot of information. A lot more than she and Liam had managed to collate. That wasn't a surprise. The criminal had ties to law enforcement. So her job became to confirm details that implicated Victor. But she basically told the truth about everything... except the sex and the love that followed.

As for her time at home, she could see just how

things with the family were going to play out. Lucia was the only other unhappy person around the dinner table these days, and it was because she didn't sit beside Antoine. She struggled to believe that Lucia had actual feelings for Antoine. Feelings which may be hurt. That could be because she herself despised him so. Lucia's distress was more likely wounded pride. Still, it didn't sit well with her to be at odds with her sister. Not that Lucia ever vocalized her consternation.

Standing in her bedroom, she took a deep breath and reminded herself to stay calm. Every second she missed Rushe. Every single second. The more that passed, the harder it became to tolerate Antoine and the situation. All she thought about, every minute of the day, was her love and his welfare.

Avoiding all contact with Rushe, and the others, had been a deliberate choice on her part. It wouldn't be fair to tell Liam to stay away, then constantly be pestering the men. So she'd made a promise to herself to have one month without contact. After that, she would call to check in with Liam and get news on Rushe.

"You need to learn greater control, ma chère."

She spun around to see Antoine inside her bedroom, the door closed to give them their privacy.

"Get out of here," she said, pointing at the exit behind him.

"Your family is very pleased about our relationship."

Coming toward her, he ignored her request and took her hand from its position in mid-air. She hated it when Antoine held her hand, or when he curled her fingers around his arm. She hated it when he kissed her cheek and stood so close to her with a possessive hand against her spine. She hated it because she hated him.

"Yes, I had realized that," she said, yanking her hand away from his grasp. "Now get out of my bedroom."

"You are beginning to struggle."

"Beginning to?"

"You must learn to hold it together. Your drinking is becoming unacceptable. You are intoxicated every night. Our love should be strengthening now; you should be happy with me," he said. "Are you thinking about him?"

"I think about Rushe every day," she said, meeting his eye without hesitating for one moment to use her love's name.

"He has accepted your separation," Antoine said. "He is enjoying the girl, the whore."

"Maybe."

"He is," Antoine said. "We have news of him; I hear they are very happy together."

She didn't believe him, but there was a chance Rushe wanted Antoine and his cronies to believe he and Tawny were intimate, so she wouldn't fight too hard.

"Then all is well," she said.

Antoine took her hand from her side. "This arrangement benefits us all."

"I've held up my end of the bargain."

"And so have we."

"Good, then," she said. "Please leave my bedroom."

"Why do you fight so hard, ma chère?" he asked, sweeping her hair back over her shoulder and taking her knuckles to his lips. "You do not need to fight me. We are allies here."

"I'm not interested," she said, edging away from the obviously impending seduction. "Your accent doesn't do it for me."

Antoine's features slackened to a smile. "You are not as repulsed by me as you would have me believe. No doubt you wish you were. You are more comfortable with my hands on you now than you were in the beginning."

He still had a hold of her hand, she whipped it away. "Your hands will be the only thing on me, and they are there despite my protests."

"My uncle shall return to the country next week," Antoine said, not discouraged. The news piqued her attention. "I look forward to introducing him to your family."

"You're a snake."

"It's a part of our deal, that our families will work together," Antoine said. "He shall come here for dinner. Our families will meet. And we shall announce to him our engagement."

Her eyes crept up to his at the same rate conceited indulgence spread on his face. He enjoyed torturing her. "Our what?"

Dipping his hand into his pocket, he pulled out a small square box, which he urged into her hand. "You will start to wear the ring tomorrow, because you will be unable to contain your excitement. Thus, you will be announcing our engagement to your own family. This act shall bother me, as I will tell them we had agreed to conceal the joyous news until my uncle's arrival. But you are impulsive and selfish and wish to boast about our union."

"We've known each other for three weeks—"

"As far as your parents are concerned, I have helped you through a difficult time. They believe since I brought you back here, we have discussed your past and your fears for the future. They think you have confided in me, and that we have trust. I offer you security and am intrigued by you. You tend to be swept up in the romantic. Three weeks is a very respectable interval for a couple as in love as we are."

"They believed that?"

"They had no reason not to," Antoine said. "I, of course, will imply that I concealed our physical dalliances to protect your modesty."

"You've told them that we've…"

"I have not told them anything," he said. "But they will assume. I did tell them of your advance toward me the day after the anniversary event."

"All that time ago?"

He reached for her hand again. "It is the reason I came to retrieve you. I knew you were unhappy with that man. It can't be a surprise to you that your parents were disgusted by the idea of Rushe as your partner."

"They weren't worried about me or disgusted by him. They were worried about themselves, and about how it looked for the family."

"Oui," Antoine said. Their relationship might be false, but that meant there was no need to tiptoe around the truth and pretty things up. Antoine saw the truth of her family, and she knew it. "Rushe does not fit in here. I do."

FORTY-ONE

"HE'S A BETTER MAN than you could ever dream to be."

"Ah, perhaps." Antoine laughed. "You are vehemently passionate about a man who cares not for you."

"He cares."

"He does not care that you are here, with me, in my bed."

"I've been nowhere near your bed."

"He does not know that," Antoine said. "How will he react on learning of our engagement?"

She didn't doubt Antoine would make sure that news got back to Rushe. But she had faith in her love.

Squaring her shoulders, she maintained eye contact. "My agreement with you keeps everyone safe and alive. I don't regret it."

"I am glad to hear that," Antoine said. "Because you and I will be allies for many years to come, Felicity."

"My father may not approve of such a hasty betrothal."

"I have no intention of marrying you next week unless it serves my interest. So we may plan on a prolonged engagement," Antoine said. The enjoyment in his face made her cringe. "But the suggestion was your father's. He made very clear to me how he valued my ability to keep you on the straight and narrow."

"My father suggested that you propose marriage to me?" She shouldn't be shocked, but she still didn't understand how such an idea, the idea of marriage without love, could be palatable to anyone. But her family didn't see the truth, only what she and Antoine presented for appearance sake.

"Your father is not a bad man," Antoine said. "He is pragmatic, very sensible, practical and logical… not unlike yourself, Felicity."

"Me?"

"You had an issue with our initial request of you. You were active in seeking a solution that would suit all parties. You did not run. You did not hide. You did not make things worse for anyone by being dramatic. You came to me, and we reached an accord."

"To save the lives and ensure the liberty of those I care about."

"That is your priority," Antoine said. "Your father's is business and money; he is a man tempted by capital. Wealth to him is what Rushe is to you. You were logical and came to me with a sensible solution. You were also wise enough to recognize what was reasonable. This may not be your first choice of location, and I may not be your first choice of husband, but you are not cruelly treated here. This is an arrangement that suits the many and costs only the trivial needs of a few."

She had never considered herself as having shared any qualities with her father, but what Antoine said made sense. For the first time, she began to look at things from the point of view of her family.

"Is Jansen out of the hospital?" she asked, recognizing Antoine was more in touch with the happenings of her comrades than she'd wanted to admit before.

If he was a reasonable man, there was no need for him to withhold details from her. She'd just never asked before.

"No."

"How could you do that to him?" she asked, letting her muscles lose some of their rigor. "How can it be acceptable behavior to you to order such a thing?"

"What of Rushe's past behavior?"

"We're talking about Jansen; you had him beaten," she said. "He could have died, and you live with that on your conscience."

"My uncle makes the decisions in our family," Antoine said.

"So that's it? That's how you absolve yourself? It was someone else's fault?"

"He was spying on us. He threatened our operation, and he could've exposed us."

"He was doing his job," she said.

"As am I."

"Does Simone still stay with Serendipity?"

"Yes," Antoine said and led her toward the ottoman bench at the end of her bed to seat them both. She placed the ring box on the bench beside her thigh. "The women remain together."

"Your cousin is evil."

His palm skimmed up her forearm to her elbow and down again, as he shifted her extremity to his lap. "I am sure there are those who would say the same of Rushe."

"He is a good man and hurts only those who deserve it."

"And who makes that decision?"

His hand carried on up her arm to her shoulder until he touched her jaw.

"I'm not that drunk," she said, slapping his caress away when his thumb made a move to tip her chin.

"I am surprised," he said, when she bounded up off the ottoman. "You have spent most of these last three weeks in a stupor."

"That's what being with a man like you will do to a sane woman," she said, snarling at him.

Antoine was on his feet and coming at her, but she didn't flinch, not even when he grabbed her arms to haul her closer to him.

"You should be grateful to me! You will be grateful."

"I will not," she said. "I will never be."

When he repositioned to pull her higher, she threw her head back and spat forward, spraying his face with her disgust. He roared out and shoved her back, wiping the saliva from his skin.

"You are a cheap whore, nothing to me! That animal suits you."

"Yes," she said with a depraved smile. "He does."

With one stride, Antoine was on her again. "You will wear the ring. You will do what you are told."

"Don't bet on it."

She made for the door, ready to open it and throw him out.

"I will hurt them," he said, halting her. "Lucia will happily fulfill my desires if you will not."

"Leave my sister out of this mess."

"Your sister has desire for me, she craves me. She will do what I wish, what I tell her to. We can make your life difficult."

"What do you think my life is now?"

"You forget the power I have, the lives I control.

If you do not please me…"

And that was why she hated him. Beyond what criminal and debauched activities he took part in. He did have power over her, and she resented it. All of the people who had been drawn into this plot could be controlled by this man and his family, because they had positioned themselves perfectly. They had Serendipity, Jansen couldn't help himself, and Rushe was a victim of his own isolation. The only person who could prevent her love's permanent incarceration was her, there, by doing what Antoine told her to do.

If Rushe was in jail for crimes he did, or didn't, commit, the injustice would be irreversible. Countless women would continue to suffer without the prospect of Rushe being able to continue his work.

"Get the box," Antoine sneered.

Her chest was so tight that she had to haul the oxygen into her quickly rising and falling chest. Everything in her wanted to rebel. She wanted to tell him to go to hell, to spit on him again, and she wanted to hurt him. But the image of Rushe in a maximum-security institution roasted her throat, sending steam to her sinuses.

"Now, Felicity."

Though her hands shook, and her legs struggled to keep her weight, she kept her spine straight and went toward the ottoman and the box she'd left there.

"Pick it up."

All of her focus was on that dreaded cube. The image was crowded away with the sickening clarity of just how ashamed Rushe would be of her if he saw this. There she was, bending to the will of the villain. As she bent to fumble the object into her hand, she could feel Rushe's disappointment quake through her skeleton.

"Open it."

Such simple commands, and yet bile churned in

her stomach, sending blisters of acid upward. Alcohol fogged her mind, she wobbled, and her eyes drifted to the bed. She'd shared that bed with Rushe. They'd been happy and together. Now she stood there holding the promise of another man.

Without looking, she flipped the lid off the box. "Put it on."

She didn't want to. The burn in her throat was the incarcerated scream that begged for liberation, but she couldn't grant that wish. Bringing her attention to the platinum band bearing three diamonds, she immediately wanted to throw the beautifully vile object away.

"Put it on, Felicity."

"I can't."

She remained intent on it but became aware of him storming over. Antoine snatched the box and pulled out the ring, tossing the box aside. Grabbing hold of her hand, he squeezed her knuckles, forcing her fingers straight until he could ram the ring onto her finger.

"You will wear it. And you will be grateful, Felicity." He lowered his head until his breath moistened her hairline. "Or all of you will suffer."

The man left her perimeter and her bedroom, but she wasn't rid of him. Her torture was only just beginning.

FORTY-TWO

JEROME MERCIER WAS NOTHING like she expected. The suave man didn't come off as immediately evil, he was actually sickeningly personable and courteous. Receiving his false platitudes wasn't the worst part of the evening though. The true horror came when she realized Simone was on her uncle's arm. Her father had invited Robert as well, which managed to further compound her indignity.

Now the two families sat together in her father's drawing room, enjoying a drink and perfectly pleasant after-dinner conversations. But she couldn't stop her teeth from chattering. She struggled to focus at all. Words blended and faces fuzzed out. If she hadn't been drinking from the same wine bottles as everyone else, she might have believed herself drugged.

The stinging behind her nose wasn't of tears. It seemed to be connected to the chill that made her shoulders quiver.

"Are you ill, ma chère?" Antoine asked, taking her hand from her knee.

On impulse, she snatched her hand away. "No," she said.

That night at dinner, Antoine made the formal announcement of their engagement.

Her family had seen the ring on her hand and chirped about it all week. Antoine acted suitably unimpressed that she was wearing it, but that only made her want to ram the ring into his eye. The Hughes had agreed to keep the secret of the union until Antoine's family had been told.

This whole situation made her nauseous, especially to see Simone sneering at her. All of the Merciers knew she was in a forced position, yet they fawned over the soon-to-be newest member of their clan. Simone had even gone so far as to announce herself maid of honor, above the Hughes' daughters.

"Excuse me," Flick said.

Not interested in explaining herself to anyone, she left the couch and the drawing room to head for the restroom. Splashing water onto her face, she put thoughts of smudged makeup aside, she had to do something to get more with it. Rushe had been right about her diabolical acting ability. It was easier for her to be somebody else when she had Rushe at her side, or watching her back, to ground her. But there in this place, she felt like an alien in her own body.

"He is an excellent lover."

She swung around to see Simone enter the bathroom with her. "You better not be talking about your uncle or your cousin… though I wouldn't be surprised if that level of depravity existed in your family."

"You speak of my family," Simone said, fastening the lock. "Your family is effectively auctioning you off to my Antoine."

"If you feel like busting them for it, please go ahead," she said with a skeptical shake of her head.

"I speak of Rushe."

"Yes," she said, sighing out and keeping her expression deadpan. "He is a superb lover, and you would definitely know that from all those times you have not had sex with him."

"You pine for a man who is ensconced with another."

"Says you," she said, folding her arms and leaning back against the vanity countertop.

"You must see this as an opportunity. I was disbelieving when I heard of your proposal, and of my uncle's acceptance of it. He is not a vengeful man—" Flick snorted. "He is not. He is a rational man. But he does not like to be disrespected. You and your associates disrespected him."

"What was it you did?" she asked. "You had a responsibility in that house. You were to look after the women, and to report to your uncle. Instead, you spent your time chasing every dick in the place."

"I enjoy men."

"All but one," she said with a glow of pride. "My love wasn't interested. He saw through you and into your black soul."

"You should not be so smug in defending a man who has rejected you."

"The only person in this room who has been rejected by Rushe, is you," she said. "You will not succeed in slating Rushe to me. My opinion of him will remain as it always was."

"You are engaged to my cousin," Simone said, lifting her chin to sneer down her nose. "He is your primary concern, and you will follow his orders."

"Did you come in here trying to scare me?"

"I came in here to remind you that your position is precarious. If my family is disrespected—"

"Antoine does a good job of reminding me every

day of exactly where my responsibilities lie," she said. "All I have to do is look at him to be reminded of what he's costing me."

"You are lucky to have him."

"Oh, God," she said, tempted to laugh. "Yes, I'm grateful, now get the fuck out of here."

"Your mouth has gotten you into trouble before; you do not learn. Do I have to remind you what we are capable of?"

"No," she said. "Your family is capable of manipulation. You exploit others to better your own means."

"Our methods should be your concern now, not our goals. Need I remind you that Serendipity remains in our custody?"

"You do not have to remind me," she said. "But if you hurt her, Jansen will come for you."

"Jansen," Simone scoffed. "He remains in the hospital; he still struggles to move. He is no threat."

"And Rushe? Is he a threat?"

"Not so long as you are here," Simone said with an arched brow. "Not so long as he has his whore to worry about. And if Serendipity was sacrificed…"

Rushe would never forgive himself if any of these women were hurt; three women, and one man trying to protect them all. She didn't want to think of his torment, it would be tearing him apart, and she wasn't at his side to soothe him. She'd failed him.

"If you sacrifice Serendipity, you give up your ace," she said. "Jansen would have nothing left to lose. Rushe can take care of Tawny and knows I can take care of myself."

Simone's lips curved to a superior smirk. "Can you?"

"You can hurt me," she said. "I may not have physical size, but my tolerance level for bullshit is pretty high… as our current situation speaks to."

"The sooner that you forget about Rushe and his whore, the sooner we can all move forward. You will marry Antoine, and we will be a family."

"That's not your concern," she said, narrowing her eyes to examine the European. "You're enjoying this. You came in here to lord it over me. You're actually enjoying every damned second of this, aren't you? What is it that you want? Do you want me to tell you how I miss Rushe, or do you want me to cry on your shoulder about his apparent betrayal with Tawny?"

"You were such a stubborn wench," Simone said, slinking toward her. "You thought you were something so special, thought you were important… now look at you. Pathetic."

"I'm pathetic?" she asked, meeting Simone's eye. "I am here for a greater purpose. You run errands for your uncle and suck cock to validate yourself. You take pleasure in being cruel and perverted. Your existence is entirely reliant upon your uncle's mercy. Does he know what went on with Victor and his men? Does he know you're a whore?" She shifted up onto her feet. "Does he know you opened your legs for those disgusting rapists? Those sickening excuses for human beings who barely made the definition of being male. Anything with a penis is superior to you, because you're nothing but a foul, degenerate slut, ready to drop to her knees and worship even the most nauseating of men. Men who would make any other woman vomit and consider suicide before they'd consider so much as looking at their dicks voluntarily."

Simone's hand flew up and out, catching her across the cheek, snapping her head to the side. Her opponent's visceral reaction wound her lips into a smile. Yes, this was much more productive than sitting in that room with the families, getting acquainted.

"He is an excellent lover," she drawled quietly, bringing her gratification around to Simone slowly. "Do you know what it's like to be worshipped by a man like Rushe? How empowering it is to have him on his knees in front of you, savoring every second he spends with your pussy? To have him so overcome with desire that he'll tear you from the floor, slam you to the wall, and hammer into you fast and rough, because he just can't contain himself? Passion like that is overwhelming. His being craves mine, his cock wants to be inside me constantly. He covets my touch, my yearning, my attention. All I have to do is smile, and he wants me. In fact, all I have to be is present. If I'm near him, all he thinks of is me. Even when we're apart, I consume him. His devotion to me is absolute, and you, ma chère, will never know that adoration, because you… are pathetic."

Skirting around the fuming Frenchwoman, Flick's smile persisted as she unlocked the door and went back to the party. Now it was a party. This farce could be whatever it wanted, the people there could flatter and crawl all over each other. Simone had done her a favor. Now she remembered just how Rushe and she felt, and just how all-encompassing that love was.

They could be thousands of miles apart, they could be universes apart, and their separation could go on for decades. Their devotion was infinite, it was eternal.

FORTY-THREE

AS MUCH AS her mother gushed about wedding dates, she said nothing. Antoine was in no hurry to put anything in stone either. When appropriate, she made the right noises, but kept the details vague and didn't commit to anything.

There was an overarching sense around her parents that if they didn't get the wheels in motion, she would somehow mess up the relationship before it got to the altar. There were worse prospects in the world.

In the week after her encounter with Simone and the big family introductions, Jerome Mercier had been back three times. The men were bonding, and the business was booming. She tried her best to switch off to most of it and kept herself busy in the gym and in the library.

Her stresses had increased over the last week. When she had built up the gumption to call Liam, he hadn't answered the phone. She had tried again twice, neither time had been successful. After the first call, she sent him an email, but it took him four days to get back to her with a message that merely said, "We're all alive." Those words didn't inspire confidence. She wished she had a way to get in touch with Rushe directly, because she needed to hear his voice.

If there was trouble with the men, she wanted to know what it was. Short of asking Antoine and alerting him to her attempts to get in touch with Liam, there was nothing she could do. Antoine hadn't actually told her not to be in touch with Rushe, but it was implied. She didn't communicate with her lover more for Rushe's sanity than for her own. If she was in touch with him and told him just how unhappy she was without him, Rushe would abandon everyone else to be at her side.

Bedtime was approaching. She put her book back on the library shelf, then crossed the room to turn off the lamp. When she was only a few feet from the exit, the phone began to ring.

No one usually called this line; the phone in here seldom rang. Only once had she heard the extension ring, and that was as she sat waiting to hear from Rushe during her overnight stay before this fiasco began. She was the only one to use this room. Her sisters had little interest in spending their day with books, and her father had his own office.

That was the phone she had used to call Liam after she arrived with Antoine. Hope blazed to her lungs.

Rushing across to the desk, she snatched up the handset and brought it close to her mouth. "Liam," she gasped out, knowing it wasn't wise to show her hand if there was a stranger on the other end. Desperation had burst out on its own. Initially, no one said anything, and her hopes were dashed. It had to be a wrong number, or at least it wasn't who she thought it was. "Hello?"

"Kit."

The one syllable paralyzed her legs, and she sank onto the floor there in the library under the desk. "Oh my God," she exhaled. Clutching the receiver with two hands, she tried to bring it closer as though she could hold him against her. "Rushe."

"Are they listening?"

"I don't know," she said, ice clenched her sinuses, instantly watering her eyes. "Oh, Rushe."

"I know I'm not supposed to get in touch with you. I'm trying to respect your wishes, Kitten, I am—"

"No," she hiccupped. "I'm glad you called. I shouldn't be. I'm not allowed to be, but… oh, Lover, I missed your voice."

"Has he touched you?"

"I'm safe, Rushe. I miss you. Tell me what's going on? Are you okay?"

"Simone was here today," he said.

That deep rumble from within him closed her eyes. She propped her temple against the table leg, trying to remember what it was like to feel the vibration of that voice against her.

"She was here last week, I upset her."

"She said you were misguided."

Her smile relaxed. "I told her you were devoted to me."

"I am devoted to you," he said. "I know they've been telling you—"

"I don't care about that," she cut him off. "I don't care about their stories. I love you. I miss you."

"I knew you did," he said with an audible sigh of relief.

Rushe wasn't the type who would immediately strike anyone as insecure. But the part of him that believed he wasn't worthy of her was often more engulfing than she realized.

"They told you different?"

"You're wearing his ring."

She just knew that line was delivered without lip

movement. Her chest grew tighter. "Yes."

"I won't let it happen."

"Lover, you have to—"

"Has he touched you?" Rushe growled.

"No," she said. "I would never let him… I made it very clear to him that I belong to you."

"Has he tried?" She didn't want to answer the question; he had to have sensed her hesitation. "Kitten?"

"No. Anytime he tries to come near me, I remind him how he repulses me."

"Good girl."

"I tried to get in touch with Liam. I wanted to know what was going on. I needed to know how you were. I worry about you, Rushe."

"We got copies of your statements," Rushe said. "You're playing his game."

"And I'll continue to do that," she said. "I will keep us safe."

"They could be listening to this call. But I'm telling you now, and them too, that this isn't over."

"I know that," she murmured, though she didn't know if he meant their relationship or the situation. "I miss you so much. I can't sleep. I don't want to eat. I just want to be back with you. I want things to be right again. This isn't right. Being away from you, like this, I can't breathe, Rushe. I'm trying to be strong, but I miss you so much."

There were a few beats of silence, she feared their link had been lost.

"I want to come and get you."

Which was why communicating throughout this was a bad idea He would want to be proactive in doing whatever it took to ensure her happiness.

"You can't. I wish you could. Tawny would be left open, Serendipity too. We know this is for the best. What's the alternative?"

"He said you weren't my woman."

"You know that's not true," she said. "Am I any less yours when I'm not right in front of you?"

"I want to kiss you," he admitted. "For all the sex I dream about having with you… it's your mouth I miss the most. And your hair, waking up with it spread out all over me. Your heartbeat pounding between those sweet tits against my ribs."

Drawing in a breath, she blew it out silently through circled lips. She wanted to reassure him, to tell him that they would have those things again, that this was only temporary. But she couldn't make that promise. As he'd pointed out, if anyone were listening, she couldn't take the risk that the Merciers would assume they were being duped.

"You're getting better at the romance," she said, forcing herself to smile between the fresh tracks of tears on her cheeks.

"I can only be honest with you, Kit. I didn't realize how much those dumb little things… I didn't know they mattered… I can't think straight without you here."

"Yes, you can," she said, determined he wouldn't doubt himself. "This is what you do. You've always done your job well. I shouldn't affect your ability to do it."

"But you do."

"You're doing it for me," she said. "You're going to work hard for me because it makes me happy to know you're out there doing what you believe in. How is Tawny?"

"Ignorant."

"Eric and Liam?"

"Eric was in Silver's getting his rocks off last night," Rushe said. "Haven't seen Liam in a few days."

Judgement made her frown. "What does Jocelyn say about that?"

"Joce? I don't think she's worried about Liam. He'll turn up."

"That's not what I meant, and—"

"How do you know about her?" Rushe asked.

"Eric talks when he drives. You never told me you'd met Gracie."

"We shouldn't talk about that now," Rushe said.

"No… I hate that there are restrictions on us."

"I hate there's distance between us. You know how I feel about my access to you."

The only thing that should restrict his access to her was her own wishes. If it was within her power, she would never restrict him.

"We're going to be okay, Lover. We're going to survive."

"That's not enough for me anymore."

A sob escaped her lips, she immediately sucked her lips between her teeth to prevent more of her heartache conveying to him. Surviving had been what Rushe's existence was before her, and she gave him more to live for now. She understood what he meant because she too wondered how she had ever lived without him.

"I am your woman, but we can't keep doing this to ourselves. We have to accept where we are, accept what is going on, and make the most of it."

"Make the most of it?" Rushe said. "There is nothing without you."

"Yes, there is. You have a life there, and a job, and Tawny needs you."

"If you think I'm gonna—"

"Get over me, Rushe," she said, aware it was unlikely that would ever happen. "Put me out of your mind and do what is right for the job. Get your guard up, put up those shutters. I'm just a 'ho, remember? A woman you fucked for a while. A dumb little bitch who enjoyed sucking your cock."

"Do you think I could convince myself of that?"

"Yes," she said. "I've seen how you can hold yourself away from things. Why is this different?"

"I don't know," Rushe said. "I've never been like this, but… you're in my head all the time."

"Then put me out of your head, do whatever you need to do to forget about me. I'll survive. No one is hurting me here. I'll take care of things from this side. I'm holding up my end of the deal to keep everyone safe, and I will do whatever it takes to maintain that."

"What is 'whatever it takes'?" he asked.

"You know what it means," she said, trying to set her shoulders and level her tone. "If I have to walk down that aisle or lay down in his bed, I will do it, Rushe. Please make no mistake about that."

"You will not," he snarled. "I won't allow it."

"You can't come here," she said. "They'll arrest you, and you will not achieve your goal. I will still have to do those things."

"You won't," he insisted. "I'll come there now and get you, if you think—"

"I could go to him now," she said. "Go to his bed. Would that make it easier? If you hate me, if I'm damaged and dirty, will that erase your love for me?"

She could never do it, could never go to Antoine. As much because she would be physically sick if he thought about touching her. But angry, Rushe was focused and determined, not distracted and confused.

"You will not go to him. You will not let him touch you. No one touches what is mine."

"I make the decisions on what I do with my body," she said. "You can't stop me, but he can stop you, and I don't want you to give him grounds to do that. Don't you see if he gets you into that jail cell, he'll keep me anyway? If you're in there, what do I have left out here to fight for? If I have to marry him, and live my life with him, I'll do it knowing you are out in the world free and doing good noble work. I am one woman, Rushe. You can easily replace me."

"Don't talk like that," he barked. "I hate when you talk like that."

"I told you where the smart money was if it came down to a choice. I am making that choice for us… You need to be out there. Here, this is where I am supposed to be. This was what my life was meant to be. At least now, after my time with you, it has more meaning. By being here, living here, and spending my life in this society, I have a greater purpose. I'm not here just because my father wants me to improve his family connections. I am here to make sure you can do your work without fear of retribution, retribution that was only brought back to you because of me anyway."

"That's not true."

"If you'd slept with Simone, the Merciers would have had no reason to doubt you," she admitted. "You might have had more time to get Serendipity out yourself."

"Or we all could have died."

"Maybe," she said. "There's no point in arguing about the past. We are here now. Everyone is alive and the only thing we had to give up was our love."

"And that's acceptable to you?"

"If there weren't so many other lives at stake…"

"What?" he asked when her words tailed off.

"I am with Antoine now, Rushe. You have to accept that."

"I won't."

"You have to. That is the way it is and the way it will remain. I will share my life with him, or as much of it as he wants me to… and I'll share my body too."

"No—"

"Goodbye, Rushe."

Every nerve in her body fizzed as she lowered the phone from her ear. Though she could still hear him shouting, she let her thumb drift over the disconnect button to press it, silencing her lover's protests.

Saying the words out loud to Rushe was easier than believing them. But they were words that had to be said. They had to say goodbye because their love incapacitated them. It had got them to there, but it couldn't get them out.

FORTY-FOUR

HER CONVERSATION WITH RUSHE constantly plagued her thoughts, but she didn't know if Antoine, or anyone else in the household, knew that it had happened. Nobody said anything to her about it. Antoine had taken her out for another date the previous night. That date gave him the opportunity to reveal his knowledge of the interaction between her and her love, but he didn't.

However, it was less than forty-eight hours later that Antoine walked into her bedroom after her bedtime shower and demanded she pack her things, because they were leaving. She didn't have time to ask questions but packed up some items in a backpack and met him outside the Hughes' house less than an hour later.

It became clear that her family thought they were going somewhere for a romantic getaway, though Antoine told them the hasty departure was due to urgent, unforeseen business. No romance was involved, but she got the impression the real reason wasn't any kind of official business, either. For one thing, he didn't have to take her anywhere for legal business.

Antoine spent most of the time in the car talking in abstract terms that she didn't care about. He conducted business on the phone and with the associate of his who accompanied them. They were discussing a deal involving some land they wanted to build on, but she didn't pay attention to the specifics.

Night rolled past the window. After a couple of hours traveling, she fell asleep in the back of the car. Sunrise had arrived by the time they reached their destination. She was only awoken when car doors slammed. They were in a parking garage. It was after she clambered out and was led to an elevator that she found out they were in a hotel.

Her lip curled when she caught scent of the fresh linen and shampooed carpets. The smell reminded her too much of the Waterside Hotel, the primary location of their last job. The suite they arrived at was sumptuous and spacious. It gave her distance from Antoine too, he left her in a bedroom and disappeared with his cronies.

Her purpose there hadn't been defined so she washed up, took a nap, and read until it was time to go downstairs for dinner, which she did alone. Being by herself, and with no Rushe to tempt, she didn't bother to go to any effort. She wore skinny jeans and a loose-fitting cotton top that hung over her derriere. She pulled her hair back, tying it high on her head, and put her feet in wide-heeled clog mules.

Dinner was delicious and perfectly prepared for her to enjoy in these luxurious surroundings. She took her time, as the only thing waiting for her upstairs was Antoine and his men. There was no rush… in either sense. After dinner, she ordered another bottle of wine, happier to while away the time down there alone than up there under their scrutiny.

This would be her life now, trailing around the country after a man who couldn't care less about her, or if she was occupied, let alone if she was happy. She craved something to do, something with meaning. She'd found it increasingly difficult to concentrate, there didn't seem to be any point to anything in her life anymore.

The wine helped her lose herself in a now familiar fog that was more comforting than facing reality. Her current bottle was almost finished, and she was considering ordering another, when Antoine came in with his associate in his wake. They came straight to the table, and she was hauled up to her feet by Antoine. Already off balance because of the booze in her system, her knees gave, but he yanked her upright.

"What do you think you're—"

"We have business," Antoine said, and pulled her across the room, through the diners who watched on with interest.

She was dragged to the street, where two limos were parked in a row on the curb. She and Antoine got into the second car with his associate, and then they were moving.

"What is going on?" she asked, trying not to fumble her words over her coiled tongue and slowed senses. Antoine was sneering, knowing her intoxication would irk him, she didn't expect him to be so dramatically angry about it. "Would you tell me what the fuck—"

"You are no lady," Antoine barked. "You sit and you drink, you get yourself into a disgusting state as this, no man would tolerate it."

"No man that I want would have to," she said, spreading her hands on the vacant seats at each of her sides. Antoine and his associate sat in the facing seats with their back to the unseen driver. "I get drunk because the prospect of spending so much as one more second with you sickens me."

"Things are going to be different now. You will

be watched at all times. We will hire you an attendee. Your family will consider this person present to cater for your whims. But his job will be to ensure you maintain an appropriate standard. You will not embarrass us."

She didn't like to be chastised. From the way the associate observed, she could tell he enjoyed watching her put in her place. "What about your behavior? Dragging me around the country for no good reason. You should've left me at my parents' house. We shouldn't be around each other any more than we absolutely have to be. You don't like me, and I don't like you. Let's base our marriage on that."

"Au contraire," Antoine said, shifting to the front edge of the seat to lean across toward her. "We will be spending far more time with each other."

"Why would we—"

"You will be in my bed tonight."

"No," she said, and insects scurried across her skin when she saw how he leered at her chest.

"Yes," he said. "I would not marry a woman I cannot be intimate with. You will obey, and you will ensure my gratification. If I am unhappy, your friends will suffer."

"I told you I would not—"

"You are unreasonable," Antoine said. "You will learn to respect me. Every night you will dedicate yourself to my pleasure until you learn how to behave and do as you are told. You are my subordinate, Felicity. I will not allow you to assume otherwise. I have been patient. We have moved through our courtship, but it is time to consummate our union. You will be happy for the opportunity. You have distressed me with your actions, with your drinking and your attitude; this will teach you your rightful place."

"Teach me?"

"If you are not willing to learn, our arrangement

shall be terminated."

"What got you so pissed off tonight?" she asked, almost ready to spit in his face again. "Did my father call you out for the fraud that you are?"

"I am not fraudulent," Antoine said, resting back in his seat again. "You are conning your family, and you believe that you can play me for a fool… You spoke to your former lover."

She bristled. "How do you know about that?"

"My man overheard you talking in the library," Antoine said, without looking at the associate.

The associate present turned his eyes away from her, revealing all that she needed to know.

"You were listening into my phone call?"

"I am entitled to do whatever I wish with the woman affianced to me," Antoine said. "You told your love that we were intimate, and that you would share your body with me. I intend to take you up on that."

"It wasn't an offer," she said, wondering how much of their phone conversation had been eavesdropped on. "I was trying to keep him from ripping out your entrails through your testicles."

"If he attempts to hurt me, all of you will die."

"It wouldn't make much of a difference to you if we were dead because you'd be dead already. Rushe doesn't want to hurt you, he wants to kill you, and he always gets the man in his crosshairs… eventually."

"Threatening me serves no purpose, these threats are all empty. Rushe cannot hurt me because I have you."

"In body only," she said.

"You wish for him to move on," Antoine said. "To accept the way things are, and we do not want him to complicate matters."

"He's not complicating anything. He's doing what you want him to, he is where you want him to be."

"For now," Antoine said. "We do not trust that he, or your friends, appreciate the full scope of our power."

"Why?" she asked. "Why now? What's changed?"

Antoine's foul mood had come from somewhere, and this trip had been completely unexpected. Something must have happened to cause these changes. Except she couldn't believe a single phone call between her and her lover would cause such consternation.

"There has been a development," Antoine said.

"What development?" she asked, trying not to smile as she thought about how Rushe may have gotten one up on the Merciers.

If there had been a plan in motion, her love wouldn't have shared it with her on the phone, not while they were unsure if there were other ears listening in or not. From what she could gather, Antoine's associate had only eavesdropped. That meant they'd only heard her side of the conversation, though she didn't know how much of it.

She had to be ready for anything. If something had occurred that got the Frenchman this unsettled, it was likely she would be further endangered, or used as some sort of bait.

But she was ready.

Just because she didn't know Rushe's plan didn't mean she wouldn't do all she could to support it. He'd told her once that he trusted her instinct. When all else failed, her instinct was to go to Rushe, to trust him. If she had a role to play, Rushe would make it clear to her when the time was right.

Only now did she take the time to look through the rain-soaked vehicle window trying to see through the artificial light sparkling in the night surrounding them.

As she peered out, she began to pick out familiar features.

There was… the diner where she and Rushe had breakfast.

She sat upright.

Antoine's smirk came back around to her. "He will learn."

The car stopped, she had no time to respond. The door beside her was opened and she was snatched. Catching her heel on the car door sill, she fell onto the sidewalk, scraping her palms in the process. When she was bodily lifted from the curb, she curled her toes to keep her shoes on her feet as she was hefted around her waist and brought up under the arm of one of the goons.

They were outside Silver's brothel. The other car was parked in front of the one Antoine and his associate were currently getting out of and must have been where the goons emerged from so quickly.

"Flick!" Cody's voice pierced the night.

Still, she hung under the arm of the man who had pulled her from the car. She raised her focus to see Cody on his feet by the door, franticly looking between the half dozen men closing in on him.

"Open it," Antoine demanded.

One of his henchmen threw Cody out of the way to shove into the storefront.

Displays were trashed as she was carried through the store toward the back business entrance. She didn't want Rushe to be blindsided but calling out for him might make him react without thinking. Deliberately flailing, she made as much noise as she could, and kicked out to knock over a shelving unit.

"Arrêt!"

Antoine's infuriation only made her fight harder. She was determined they would be heard, and whoever stood on the other side of that door would be prepared.

The first henchman battered the door, and at first no one approached. They may be ignored. What was Antoine's contingency plan? The buzzer rang constantly, and commotion sounded on the other side of the door.

Any sense of accomplishment she felt vanished when another man appeared from the rear of the group carrying a battering ram.

"Why are you doing this?" she beseeched Antoine, who stood calmly a couple of feet from her. "They'll be terrified."

"You answer your own question," Antoine said without looking at her.

Two men, at the head of the group, swung the ram back and hit forth once, and that was all it took. All of the men backed off. She wasn't sure what they expected to happen now they'd desisted in their aggression.

"They'll never voluntarily let you in," she said.

A click from the door accompanied Antoine's smirk, and the door opened from the inside. She recognized the woman who came out, reaching toward Antoine.

"Connie, we may always rely on you to fulfill your role."

Antoine took Connie's outstretched hand to kiss it. At least they knew the identity of the mole. The shady clients she'd been bringing through this business were no doubt Antoine's men, it was no shock they'd been depraved.

Their group advanced, and hope blossomed that maybe Rushe wasn't there at all. The women in reception screeched and scarpered from the six men, along with Antoine and his associate. The only thing immediately obvious to them was they weren't official or altruistic.

Lilah popped up from behind the reception desk. Flick tensed, trying to wriggle free of the man who carried her like a football.

"Silver will kill you! What do you want?" Lilah shouted, though her fear was apparent through her pale skin.

"Silver will be compensated," Antoine said, coming to the front of the group. It was then she saw through the wavering bodies blocking her view that Rushe stood in front of the curtain to the watchman's hallway.

"What the fuck are you doing here?" Rushe asked without displaying an ounce of emotion.

"Paying you a visit," Antoine said, amusement in his tone. "My fiancée and I like to do that."

With a sideways nod, the men parted, giving her an unobstructed view of Rushe, and him a clear view of her. He didn't flinch, but her throat flooded.

"I didn't know," she whispered.

"I think he can tell that, ma chère. You can't stand on your own two feet and went to no effort with your appearance."

"Yeah, 'cause he gives a fuck if I'm dressed in silk," she snarled at Antoine, who didn't acknowledge her.

"Your chambre privée shall be sufficient for our conversation," Antoine said.
Rushe stepped aside and held the curtain. Her love wasn't going to turn his back on Antoine, and she didn't blame him.

FORTY-FIVE

THE GOONS CLOSED in around her, keeping her away from Rushe, as they all filtered up the hallway and into the watchman's bedroom. She was taken to the furthest corner on the other side of the bed and dropped to the floor. She might have stayed there if it wasn't for her transporter snatching her hair to yank her to her feet.

She hissed through the pain and used the wall to support herself as she ascended. When she was up, he grabbed her throat, pinning her back against the wall. Her eyes shut as the rush of alcohol in her system made her abruptly lightheaded.

"Is she high?" That was concern in Rushe's voice despite his attempt to maintain his practiced apathy.

"Drunk," Antoine sighed out. "As she so frequently is."

"I do what it takes to get through the day," she said.

"No one speaks to you now," Antoine barked out, whipping around to glare at her. "Be silent."

Rushe was against the back of the couch with a

man on either side of him. Two in front facing him, watching his every move. She remained in the corner with the fifth man, the sixth stood not too far behind.

Antoine took his place at the end of the bed with his associate behind him.

"You shouldn't have brought me if you didn't want to deal with me," she said.

"You will be quiet," Antoine said, glancing at the man holding her.

She was released and backhanded by a blow that sent her to the floor, her head landed on the perpendicular wall with a thump.

Rushe growled so loudly that it cleared the smog enveloping her. The pound of a punch came before a clatter, and then there was a shuffle of movement.

"Non!" Antoine exclaimed. "We do not wish this to turn into a brawl."

Rushe was posed to fight. One man was on the floor while the other three held her love. She fumbled out for the bed and pulled herself to her knees to show Rushe she was okay. He wouldn't look at her because he was on guard, but he'd catch her in his periphery.

"Enlighten us," she mumbled to Antoine, though aware her words felt slurred. "Why are we here?"

"You will be silent," Antoine said. "You are insignificant, here merely as a tool of manipulation."

"I'd figured that out," she spat out.

"Be silent!" Antoine declared. "On your feet, and we will silence you!"

"I will not!"

"Kitten."

Her eyes flitted to Rushe, who was intent on Antoine, his chin tipped down and those thick shadows blanketing his eyes. He spoke through gritted teeth, with inflexible lips, he was focused. Whatever the business Antoine was there to discuss, Rushe wanted it out in the open.

Moistening her lips, she dragged her legs under her and pushed up to her feet, taking her place quietly in the corner in front of the goons. That wasn't a time for her to be a distraction for Rushe. By aggravating the situation she was enforcing the manipulation they were trying to levy.

Clasping her hands behind her, she rolled her lips into her mouth, and cast her eyes downward. She wouldn't divert Rushe while he worked.

"The woman is uncontrollable. She will not obey me," Antoine said, after an incredulous silence. "How can you make her—"

"She is not your woman," Rushe said. "What's your business here?"

"Where is he?" Antoine said, without further delay.

"Don't know what you're talking about," Rushe said, but she read beyond the denial.

"You do," Antoine said. "I want to know where he is."

"You came all the way here to ask me that? Wasted trip."

"Why do you protect him?" Antoine asked. "We have his woman. Does he not understand the danger she is in? What we can do to her?"

"What you've already done, for all we know," Rushe said. "It's been two weeks since any of us saw Serendipity."

So they were talking about Jansen and Serendipity. Someone else must have seen Serendipity two weeks ago, perhaps further proof of life. She'd been ensconced at her parents' house and had missed so much of the action that she was playing catch up, trying to memorize every detail.

"She is alive, but she doesn't have to stay that

way."

"So kill her," Rushe said. "I don't know where Jansen is."

"He left the hospital late last night, where would he go?"

"What is it he knows? Why do you care where he is? If you've got Serendipity so well protected, it doesn't matter where Jansen is. If the stories are right, the guy can barely walk, so he's no physical threat to your operation."

"Not all threats are physical," Antoine said. "Though I understand that a man like yourself would not necessarily be able to appreciate that."

She inhaled to defend Rushe, but her love's eyes flashed to her, and she clamped her mouth shut. If he didn't want her to speak, she wouldn't. But she didn't like to hear anyone ridicule him. She dropped her chin.

Rushe's attention went back to Antoine.

"You have an odd relationship," Antoine said. "You and young Felicity. She is not easily tamed and is impossible to live with."

"If she's causing you trouble, leave her here when you fuck off."

Antoine laughed. "Yes, that would be very convenient. But being rid of Felicity before our nuptials would put our trials so far to shame. She is difficult but serves her purpose well. Are you going to congratulate us?"

"I don't condone fraud," Rushe sneered.

"You are a man of few morals; I have heard of your work. Does Miss Felicity know the extent of your history? The murders you have been involved in? The torture you have perpetrated? Does she know what you did to the woman here?"

She dug her teeth into her lip, torn between wanting to laugh at the notion Rushe could physically hurt an innocent woman, and being so offended that she wanted to retrieve the knife from her back pocket and gut every man there.

Lashing out would serve no purpose. While Antoine was driving this scenario, it wouldn't matter how many of his thugs she injured, he wouldn't bat an eyelid. The men there were all expendable, present only to ensure that Rushe listened to the Frenchman's taunting.

"Fill her head with all the stories you want to," Rushe said. "You've had time. You didn't need to bring her here to do that."

"No, I didn't," Antoine said. "We are here to make our position clear, and your position."

"What's that?"

"You are no longer a part of her life, or a part of our lives. You are of no use to us. If you cannot provide us information, we will find other uses for your skills. But you are not to contact Felicity again."

"The phone call," Rushe said.

"He overheard me talking," she said, nodding toward Antoine's associate.

"Do not talk to each other," Antoine insisted. "Felicity made it clear to you that you have to move on from her, and your whore here needs you. You satisfy her, and I will satisfy Miss Hughes."

"Will you?" Rushe asked on an almost snicker.

Lifting her head, the faintest glimmer of a smile was on her love's face. It was all swagger and made her think of all the times they played together.

"Yes," Antoine said. "She is a woman that every man should experience at least once, wouldn't you agree?"

For Rushe, the only thing worse than Antoine sampling her would be if Antoine shared her around. "You will respect her."

"She will be my wife," Antoine said. "I will do

with her what I please, as I already do."

"If that's all you're going to do with her, carry on," Rushe said. "You've done nothing with her, and I'm happy for you to keep doing that."

"She came to me," Antoine said. "She understands our arrangement requires some… exertion on her part. We have to make the best of what we have, Felicity has rather voracious needs. You schooled her well for me; I shall savor each of her exquisite talents." Her love said nothing, his lack of reaction was curious. "You are not opposed to our intimacy? You are not discouraged?"

"You have no intimacy," Rushe said. "You came here for information and to rile me, and you've failed twice."

"You speak with confidence," Antoine said, with growing rage. "Felicity will be in my bed tonight, her body on display for my consumption, dedicated to my every indulgence. Do you have any recommendations, anything she is particularly good at?"

"She makes a mean carbonara," Rushe said. "Avoid the chili if you can, she never gets it right." She smiled. "But she'll be disappointed if you don't finish it, though that's true of anything she cooks."

This time when she took her lips into her mouth, she was stifling her laughter. Rushe wasn't worried by the idea of her with Antoine because he knew that she hadn't been. It didn't matter how much the Frenchman tried to taunt him, her love would never believe it.

"You are arrogant," Antoine jeered. "You think you can belittle me, but the woman you try to claim now belongs to me. I shall do what I want with her. Her body is mine to do with what I will, and she will oblige me. Her breasts, her buttocks, all of her belongs to me. Her mouth and her tongue will do as I command."

"She's never been very good at following

instructions," Rushe said.

Antoine fumed and started round the bed, barging one man out of the way and then the one that guarded her. He grabbed her hair and tugged her to his previous position at the end of the bed.

She tried to free herself, but the Frenchman's grip was solid. In her periphery, Rushe was being grabbed, held, and pinned by the four thugs around him.

"Cover him," Antoine demanded of the two men near her.

Her guards dashed to a hostile Rushe. One rounded to clamber on the couch to hold her love back as he struggled to shirk off his would-be captors.

Antoine's associate approached her from behind to knock her knees out. On a yelp, she fell to the floor. The associate took a handful of her hair and yanked her head back against the bulge of his erection. Trying to tussle her way out of his grip made the associate grasp her jaw, and he squeezed until her mouth opened. Before her, Antoine went for his belt and began to unbuckle.

"Regardez!" Antoine shouted, tugging his shirt tails up to reveal his stomach and the ridge of his arousal.

She wouldn't do it. He'd try to force her, and he'd do it with Rushe there watching, but she had no intention of delivering any pleasure to this man. Her love roared out in his attempt to fight off the half dozen men restraining him. She'd told Rushe she could take care of herself, and now she had to prove it.

Fumbling her hands under the tail of her shirt, she stole the knife from her pocket, and flipped it open at the moment Antoine tugged down his underwear.

The associate began to urge her forward. She cried out and thrashed with the knife, dragging the blade up the associate's leg to his thigh in the same motion that she whipped it around and slashed Antoine's groin.

Blood sprayed all around her. The wet heat of it

bathed her face, her chest, her shoulders. It seemed to be everywhere. Everything. So much happened in the same instant. Both men jerked away, bawling in agony. She moved so fast she didn't register how she got on her feet, or how she reached Rushe's side.

"Fuck!" he hollered.

The men who had held him were all in such shock that none pursued her or Rushe straight away.

"Rushe! Rushe!" she panted out his name with every breath.

"I got ya," he said. "I got ya."

Suddenly, she was hooked under Rushe's arm and swooped behind his back. In the same maneuver, her love twisted the knife out of her hand and into his. Doubling over the back of the couch, in her stumbling descent, she steadied herself and pushed back up to her feet when she saw Mercier's associate fall to the floor in front of Rushe, blood pouring from the thick gouge that ran the width of his throat.

"Rushe," she said again, unable to get with it.

He spun and dug the same knife between the ribs of a goon she hadn't seen coming. Withdrawing the blade, Rushe grabbed her hand and yanked her along, pulling her to the reception, where he snatched her hips to lift her up to sit on the desk.

"Get me a towel. Call Silver! Get the guys from the street and get them out of here!"

She didn't know who he was talking to, she didn't even know who else was there. She couldn't see through the blood still blurring her vision.

"Holy fuck!" Cody screamed. "What happened?"

"Get the guys!" Rushe hollered back. "Get those fuckers out of here, all of them, and get that room cleaned out."

"Where the fuck do we—"

"Tawny," she said, trying to order her thoughts.

"Oh God, Rushe, I'm sorry."

"No," he said, clasping her face, bringing her eyes up to unite with his. "I'm proud of you, Kitten. I'm proud of you."

If she could stop the quaking that racked her body, she might have smiled or noticed the shine of honor in his eyes.

"We have to get Tawny," she said. "We have to leave, they'll kill you!"

"We're out of here."

"Go," Lilah said from beside them.

The movement and the noise coming from every angle disoriented Flick.

Rushe picked her up and took her toward the door. "Tawny," she said, slapping a hand on his chest. "They'll—"

"She's not here," Rushe said. "I sent her out last night when Jansen went AWOL. We'll talk later. Right now, we gotta run."

And this time when he took her to the door she didn't object. She curled in as close as she could to him, desperate for the heat he could offer her. The shaking hadn't stopped. Given what she had just done, she wasn't sure that it ever would.

FORTY-SIX

RUSHE REMAINED REMARKABLY composed in the car after he bundled her in and got them moving.

"Where are we going?" she asked, using the towel that had been tossed on her lap when they entered to wipe the blood from her hands. All she succeeded in doing was smearing and spreading the crimson stains.

"Someplace safe," Rushe said. "We'll get cleaned up and get on the road."

"I didn't… it wasn't my intention to…"

"He was bleeding pretty badly, but you didn't sever anything, not that I saw. Mercier will live, but he'll be pissed. His injuries will need attention and care, but that buys us time."

"I'm sorry, Rushe… I couldn't let him… I couldn't—"

"Don't apologize to me," he said, clenching and unclenching his fists around the wheel because he was still wound tight. "I got the guy worked up. If those fuckers hadn't kept hold of me, I'd have gutted him before he got near you. I will finish the job for you,

Kitten. I swear it."

"I've made this worse," she said. "I was supposed to keep my head, to keep my cool. They're going to hurt Serendipity, and—"

"She's the only chip they've got now," Rushe said.

"My family—"

"Antoine is worried about himself tonight. Those guys who were on us were hired muscle, they'll have scattered to the wind already. You're gonna call your parents and tell them the truth of who that bastard is."

"They'll never believe me," she said.

"Injuries like that mean Antoine won't be going near there; he might not be able to go back at all. They don't have to believe you. You just have to scare your folks enough to make them beef up security."

"We have nothing the Merciers want, Rushe. If they try to put you in jail because I... Oh, Rushe, we have nothing to barter with."

"Don't be so sure about that," Rushe said. "We didn't just sit on our asses while you weren't here."

"You have something?"

"I told you it wasn't over. Did you think I would let another man take off with my woman?"

"I didn't know we were coming today," she said. "If I'd known you had a plan—"

"Jansen took off from the hospital last night, but we don't know where he is or what he's doing. He sure wasn't part of any plan. If anyone fucked this job it was him, and when I get my hands on him—"

"Hey," she said, lunging over to touch his thigh. The blood on her consoling hand caught her eye until they locked on the angle of the diamonds protruding from her ring finger.

Recalling the memories of the night Antoine put

the fetter on her made her falter. She had fantasized of doing something to him like she'd done that night. Rushe's hand must have left the wheel because it landed on top of hers and he wrenched the offending piece of jewelry away from her digit. Parting her lips, a blub choked out as their eyes met. Her chest constricted, and she blinked the water from her gaze.

"I don't ever want to see that again," he grumbled, digging it into his watch pocket.

He had to take his gaze back to the road, but his fingers curled around hers and she exhaled, letting herself sink back into the passenger seat.

"I couldn't have let him do it," she muttered, letting her head loll to the side. "At least I didn't use my shoe this time… I'd have sunk my teeth in before I let him enjoy me for one second."

"It was brutal," he said, on an exhale of admiration. "I'll never worry about your fidelity if that's your reaction to the sight of another guy's dick."

"It's not just you they have to be afraid of," she said. "You just remember today if you ever think about screwing around on me. Imagine what I'd do to your floozy."

"You armed yourself, you didn't even know you were going to be in danger, and you armed yourself."

"I don't go anywhere without your knife, you told me not to."

"You followed my instruction?" he asked, apparently not sure he'd heard her right.

"You know what you're talking about," she said. "As long as it doesn't compromise your safety, I'll follow your advice."

"I won't forget you said that," he said. "We've come a long way, you and me."

The chill in her muscles began to subside. "You've been practicing with the romance," she said.

"You've been practicing the danger."

"Lover," she breathed, and his eyes flicked to her. "We're together again. I get to fall asleep in your arms tonight, don't I?"

"Every night," he said. "We won't be separated again."

"I want to know what's going on. What have you all been doing without me here? Where's Tawny?"

Rushe thought ahead as many moves as he could. When Jansen disappeared, he'd foreseen there would be developments, and he'd got Tawny out for her own safety.

"The only thing I'm worried about tonight is you… I want to hear about what you've been through too. But I want you out of those clothes and in a shower first. Safe, warm, and clean, then we'll catch up."

"Will you tell me where we're going?"

"Somewhere you've been before, Kit. You're safe now. You're with me again, and I don't plan to let you go this time."

Five weeks apart was too much. Right then, the idea of five minutes apart was too much. Sitting here in this humid car with the stench of blood infusing the air, she felt love and security for the first time since she'd last been at his side. In finding him again, she had rediscovered herself.

"WHAT THE FUCK, MAN!"

She recognized Silver's voice, but from the convoluted route they'd taken through the woods she'd already known that was where they were headed. The kitchen was empty when Rushe carried her through the back door. Silver was there in their path as soon as they were in the living room with the pool table.

"Who's here?" Rushe demanded.

She tried to take her feet to the floor, but her love was having none of it. He held her tighter, one arm under her thighs and the other around her back. There was absolutely no need for him to carry her, but as soon as her feet touched the dirt of the yard, he'd been at her side swooping her feet out from under her.

"No one, man," Silver said. "I cleared everyone out when Lilah called. What the fuck happened?"

"I don't have time to explain," Rushe said, going toward the door to the stairs. "I'm going to get her clean, and then we're heading out. Call Eric."

"Already done, man, he's on his way. Hutten too, with Tawny. They're all on their way."

"Good," Rushe said, kicking the door out of their path and taking her up the stairs, where Silver did not follow.

"How does Silver know Liam?"

"When I wasn't watching the girls, I had Eric and Liam in there. It was the only way I could be sure there were people on the premises who knew what was going on. I wasn't going to put that on Lilah or the girls."

"So Silver and Liam have met?"

"Yes," Rushe said, only returning her to her feet when they got to the bathroom.

He turned on the shower and took the hem of her top to draw it up. She stalled his hands before he could lift it over her chest. His head tilted when he frowned at her. Would it seem she didn't want him to see her naked or maybe that his entitlement to her body had expired? Neither was the case.

"I've missed a lot."

"You won't miss anything else," he said, releasing her top and taking a step backward. "I'll leave you alone to get clean. Scrub your hair to the root and under your fingernails too. I'll—"

"No," she said, taking his hand when he tried to

shrink closer toward the door. "You need to get clean as well. I've made a mess of you."

Rushe had blood on his clothes, on his hands and arms, as well as on his chin. He might not be as soaked as she was, but the stains wouldn't be missed.

"The stall is tiny, and we—"

"I don't mind getting close," she said, sliding her shoes off her feet. Letting him go, she whisked off her top, and unhooked her bra, allowing both to fall to the floor.

His eyes locked onto her chest and glazed. He'd kept it together through everything. Even when Antoine was in that room taunting him, Rushe had remained on guard. But there, as he fixated on her breasts, a bomb explosion wouldn't distract him.

Taking no time at all, because she didn't want to torment him, she got rid of her jeans and stood there in full naked glory in front of him.

"Join me in the shower, Rushe."

"We shouldn't right now, we're on a clock and we have to—"

"You said that there was time. Everyone believes you and Silver are enemies. No one is looking for us here. We don't have to have sex. If you don't want to—"

Snatching her arms, he strode forward, forcing her back against the wall by the stall. Bending his knees, he smacked his mouth to hers, catching her so completely off guard that no breath had the chance to seep through her lips.

Inhaling through her nose, she linked her arms around his neck and pushed her tongue to his, testing the resistance as she tried to force it out of her mouth and into his. But he fought back, he wanted to be in her, a part of her, and as deep as he could be. Releasing her arms, he dug his fingers into her ass and hauled her up.

The ridge of his erection clashed against her. She

moaned, desperate to know she could still experience this, that she could still experience him. His forearm came under her, and he hoisted her higher, freeing his belt and unbuttoning his jeans.

"Don't you even think about asking for my consent," she snarled.

Lugging her up, he stole her hips and speared her down onto him. There in the middle of this tiny bathroom, with the shower pounding out water a few feet from them, he was in her, filling her void. His cock was buried deep in the space that had craved him so desperately.

"Yes," she screamed out, throwing her head back and caring not an ounce for discretion.

Sex wasn't a priority. People in this place might be worried, Silver might be worried. Liam could be there with Eric, and possibly Tawny too. Still, she threw her arms around Rushe's neck and planted her mouth on his again.

He was there with her, they were together. Nothing would keep them apart, not there in that moment. Rushe kept hold of her hips. For every time he surged forward, he pulled her hips to meet his, working both sides of the union as her heels dug in at his lower back where her ankles were locked.

She wasn't conscious of their locomotion until the spray of the water hit her back, causing her to gasp out. He'd carried them into the water and into the confined space of the shower stall. With his elbows in closer to his body, he kept working her, lifting her up and down on his cock, coming out of her only to propel back in.

The stab of ecstasy on her clit made her suck harder on his tongue, trying to restrain the impending orgasm, because she didn't want this to be over. She'd been so afraid they would never have this again. Now that they did, she didn't want to lose it.

When his head smacked into her cervix the battle was lost. Again, her head went back, his name pulsing from her lips at a dozen decibels. And when she seized the rod within her in an iron grip, her love opened his mouth and clamped it onto her throat, sucking on her flesh until the bruising pain sent a bolt of agony shooting right between her eyes.

The water pounded over them. The tempo wasn't far off the out of sync inhales and exhales they imparted.

"Sorry," he grumbled.

That was the first time she'd heard him apologize. "You should be," she said, bringing her hand up to push his drooping hair away from his forehead. "I've been waiting five weeks for that... what took you so long?"

FORTY-SEVEN

ANY THOUGHT OF embarrassment, or expected scolding, went out of her head when they got to the bottom of the stairs and entered the living room. Silver was there, in his usual reclining chair. But it was Eric she saw first. Liam was also in the room, in the corner, with Tawny on his lap. The sight stopped her and took a moment to register what it could mean.

Rushe had left her in the shower after they'd gotten clean and come down in a towel to get their clothes, or rather have someone retrieve the duffel from the trunk. It might have been five weeks since they'd seen each other, but he still had her things packed there with his. As though the whole separation was just an inconvenient interlude, which she supposed now it had been.

So they dressed, Rushe packed up the rest of their things and brought her down with their duffel ready to go.

"Flick!" Eric and Liam exclaimed simultaneously.

Liam cast Tawny out of his lap and both men came toward her until they were upon her. Liam pulled her into a hug and Eric pushed her shoulder in an awkward attempt at being familiar, but she could tell he was very aware of Rushe.

"Where have you been?" Eric asked. "What did you do? Silver told us about the blood, what happened?"

"My fiancé tried to force himself on me in front of my lover," she said, leaning back against Rushe's torso. "I didn't mean to hurt him. I mean it wasn't my intention, but…"

"It's done now," Rushe said. "We're not talking about it again."

"What comes next?" Liam asked, turning serious eyes over her head to look at Rushe, Eric was also intent.

The men crowded so close that she couldn't see Silver in his seat, or Tawny in hers.

"We keep going as planned," Rushe said. "Have you got Jansen yet?"

Liam shook his head. "I'm working on it."

"Keep working," Rushe said. "But keep moving too, you take Tawny, and—"

"Yeah, yeah, we got it," Eric said. "We'll take care of her. What about Flick?"

He only glanced at her, then his focus went back to Rushe as he awaited instructions.

"I'll take care of her," Rushe said. "Did the guys leave the brothel?"

"Yeah," Silver said. Liam and Eric parted enough to let her catch sight of him. "They got rid of them, dragged them out, dumped them. The guys who came in with them didn't hang around long."

Just as Rushe had told her they wouldn't. He knew the setup and had probably known more than a few guys who hired out their muscles. Technically, he had been one of those guys at one time.

"They'll need medical attention," she said.

"Guys like Mercier have connections," Silver said.

"Half expected him to call you," Eric said over his shoulder to Silver.

These men had shared many secrets with each other.

"Wish he had," Silver said, getting up from his seat. "I'd have told him where to get off."

"Don't worry about them," Rushe said. "They can worry about themselves. We have to worry about keeping our trains on the track."

"What trains?" she asked.

Rushe only placed a hand on the top of her head. "We're getting out of here. We've got to secure the Hughes."

She was surprised that her family was her love's first concern, especially now, and with all they had done to him. Or rather how they had treated him. But her family could be in danger, and she knew that as well as he did. Despite their snub of him, and their disapproval of the relationship, Rushe was willing to take the risk and go back to that place just because he knew it meant something to her.

"I want to hear as soon as you get something on Jansen," Rushe said to Eric, who nodded. "You get us a car?"

Eric held up a key.

Rushe snatched it from him and gave it to her. "You go out, I'll be there in a minute."

She noticed him glance toward Tawny, who had been surprisingly quiet throughout the ordeal. When she bent to lift the duffel, Rushe's attention switched to her, he grabbed the bag out of her hand to thrust it at Eric, who took it because he had no other choice.

"Guess I'll show you to the car," Eric said,

gesturing for Flick to exit.

After Liam gave her another hug, she left the room and the house, leaving Rushe alone with Tawny, Silver and Liam. When she got into the yard, she watched Eric put the luggage in the trunk, but she didn't get in the vehicle.

"How has he been?" she asked.

"Horrendous," Eric said, slamming the lid. "But we all get it. We all get why he's been such a jerk."

"You looked after him," she said. "Thank you."

"I didn't do nothing, darlin'. I kept my head down. Rushe is a good guy, he just doesn't get that."

"You don't have to convince me."

"He loves you too. When he found out that you were engaged to that—"

"It wasn't a choice." She bristled. "I didn't decide to do it out of love."

"We know that," Eric said. "But it's not easy for any guy to think that his woman is with another man."

"Tawny and Liam are close."

"I'll say," Eric said, exhaling a laugh and propping himself on the side of the car as she folded her arms. "They spent a lot of time together when Liam and I were guarding the girls for Rushe. Rushe doesn't like Tawny working, so we keep her distracted, keep her busy and away from the johns. We never paid attention to her and Liam getting together, and then they were screwing, legit like."

"They're sleeping together?"

Eric nodded. "Have been for a couple of weeks, best I can tell. She's a crazy chick, but she sees something she wants, and she gets it. He seems happy about it."

Her eyes drifted downward as her lips curved. She couldn't have imagined a more unlikely couple but somehow, if it made them happy, it worked. "That's... wow."

"It's not a problem for you, is it?"

Her focus darted up to see Eric scowling. "Why would it be a problem? I guess there's an age difference, but it's not inconsiderable, she must be in her early twenties."

"Yeah but, you know, he was…"

"He was what?" she asked.

Eric's expression relaxed. "You guys were into each other, right? If it hadn't been for Rushe, you guys would've hooked up."

"It was never like that," she gaped. "Liam is my friend, and I'm happy for him. I just hope he doesn't get hurt."

"You think she's gonna hurt him? Don't think she's been working at all since they've been together. He's got enough money to support her, I guess."

Eric guessed a lot. Despite all the time they'd spent with each other, and all the things they'd done together, it hadn't occurred to the men to get the truth of their relationships set with each other.

"How is Gracie?"

"Haven't seen her in a while," Eric said, losing his calm and ease. "Figured it was best to stay away while all this was happening."

"I'm sorry you got drawn into it," she said, reaching over to take his hand. "You're a really good guy, Eric. You didn't need to help us, but you did. You're a friend. If you ever need anything from Rushe—"

"You offering out my services?"

Turning in the direction of his voice, she saw Rushe coming down the stairs toward them. "I don't have any of my own to offer," she said.

"None that you're offering any guy, that's for sure."

Eric shifted when Rushe opened the car door and pushed her inside. The men backed away from the vehicle and spoke in mumbles for a couple of minutes, then Rushe was in the car at her side.

"We're going to my parents'?" she asked, as he reversed out.

"Yeah," he said. "Time for you to take me home to Daddy, Kit."

Convincing her parents of who Antoine really was would be difficult. Perhaps not as difficult as it would be convincing them Rushe was a good guy. But she had confidence if they could get through the first hour without anyone calling the cops, progress would be made. They would come around eventually, she hoped.

FORTY-EIGHT

ABOUT HALFWAY BETWEEN Silver's pad and her parents' home, they stopped and spent a few hours in a motel. She'd been reluctant to delay, but Rushe pointed out showing up there stressed would only make things worse. So they stopped, ate, made love, and slept for a couple of hours.

Now they were parked outside the back entrance to the Hughes' house. She'd never been so nervous in her life. What reception would her parents offer? Given they may need to make a hasty departure, they left the duffel in the trunk. She typed in the private code on the sealed keypad to let them into the grounds.

As soon as they were around the perimeter hedges, Rushe took her hand and pulled her to a halt. "You have to be honest with them," he said. "About everything."

"I will be," she said, shuffling in close, still relishing the re-discovered novelty of their proximity.

"It's not gonna be easy, but you can't fudge the details. Start at the beginning and get it all out."

"Surely we can—"

"No," he said. "Lay it out, just like you did on paper in that timeline for Hutten. If your family thinks you're making anything up, or leaving out information, they'll be less likely to believe the story."

"Our world isn't like theirs," she muttered.

"Right," he agreed, picking up the ends of her hair and running it through his fingers. "I'm with you, Kit. Whatever happens in there, I belong to you."

"I know," she said, driving her hands slowly down into his pockets. "I love you. You didn't have to come or be with me here—"

"I'm not leaving you alone again. If they call the cops—"

"We bail," she said. "Together. I won't let you go down for this."

"I'm not sure that would satisfy the Merciers anymore. Antoine is gonna want you. We all screwed him over, but you…"

"Yeah," she said, aware of inflicting such a personal injury. "I lost my knife."

"It's in the duffel," Rushe said. "I put it in my pocket. I wasn't gonna leave the weapon on the scene."

"We have to find Jansen. Did any of you speak to him?"

"No," Rushe said. "He's been in the hospital, and the cops have been all over him."

"They're accusing him of something?" she asked. "Does that mean he's on the run right now?"

"We're not sure," Rushe said. "There's no charges out on him, and no warrant. We think the guarding has been unofficial."

"The Merciers exercising their control?" she asked. "They don't want us near him."

"It's likely he has something incriminating. They went after him first, and they went after him hard."

"Why did they pick then to go after him?"

"We're gonna find out when we find Jansen."

"We should go inside before the grounds-men spot us and panic," she said.

Evening was drifting in toward them. Rushe nodded once and ducked to touch his lips to hers. In that kiss, she felt his own gratification that they were together and his firm resolution he wouldn't let her go again. After tucking her hand into his back pocket, Rushe led her to the house and through the front door without any announcement.

The head steward came into the lobby and paused at the sight of them.

"Are my parents home?" she asked.

"Your mother and sisters are taking tea," the steward said. "Your father and brothers are in the drawing room."

"Thank you," she said.

"Will Mr. Mercier be joining you?" the steward asked, eyeing Rushe.

"No," she said, stepping into her role, appropriate or not. "Mr. Mercier and I are no longer engaged. He assaulted me last night, and he is not to be allowed onto the premises again."

"But—"

"Please notify all employees that anyone who does not follow my instruction or attempts to contact Mr. Mercier, will lose their job, do you understand?"

"Yes, Miss Hughes."

She linked her fingers between Rushe's and started toward the hall that would take them to the men's location.

"Sexy, watching you give out orders in that classy little voice," Rushe muttered. "Where's my dirty little kitten? You gonna bring that voice to bed later?"

Glancing back at him, she smiled at his stoic

expression. Although he didn't convey it explicitly, he was kidding with her. The light-hearted moment was appreciated with so much tension to come, and that tension wouldn't be short-lived.

Entering the formal drawing room without knocking or declaration was against the rules. When she strode in with Rushe, the three males present were stunned into silence.

"I need to tell you a story, Father. We have to get Mother here, Lucia and Vivian too. You all need to hear this."

"This is the man who stormed in here," Charles said, nodding at Rushe. "Where is Antoine?"

"He assaulted me," she said. "I injured him in defense of myself, and we are no longer engaged."

"Now, whatever—"

"No, Father, nothing you can say will change that. He's a fraud, as was our relationship. I'm going to tell you everything. If, when I'm finished, you never wish to see me again, I'll accept that."

"You have disgraced us?"

"Maybe," she said.

"Then why did you return?" Charles asked, sneering at Rushe. "Clearly, you have chosen your suitor, and you cannot expect us to accept—"

"Rushe has been mine since the moment we met," she said. "Nothing has changed since then. In these last five weeks, I have been committed to him as fully as I have always been, and he me."

"You were engaged—"

"It was a lie," she said. "A fabrication. A fraud. I was being blackmailed, coerced by Antoine. He is a criminal who wanted access to our intimate network."

"I don't believe it."

"You're all in danger," she said. "That's why I'm here, why I returned… why we returned, to warn you and do our best to protect you. Right now, all I'm asking is that you listen to the facts. When I'm finished all I'll ask is that you protect yourselves. If you choose, you will never have to see Rushe or me again for as long as you live."

Charles glared at them both in turn but conceded with a nod. "Tell us your story."

The steward was summoned to retrieve the women as she took Rushe to the couch and prepared to settle in. Already she was second guessing their decision to return. Though with her family in danger, they'd had little choice. There was no avoiding it, the story had to be told.

FORTY-NINE

"I DON'T BELIEVE IT," Lucia said.

After they'd all gathered in the drawing room, she told the story and fielded all the questions. Now she braced for the reaction. Her mother said nothing, her brothers in-law seemed blank. Vivian couldn't close her mouth.

Rushe had stuck with her. She'd begun by sitting at his side, but during a particularly heated exchange between her and her father about the truth of Antoine's identity, Rushe had scooped her onto his knee, which actually calmed her down.

It was possible he'd sensed her imminent urge to get up and leave. She'd been on the edge of her seat, bouncing, getting herself more and more worked up. At that point, Rushe seized her hips, put her on his knee, and she'd been perched there ever since. Any initial surprise from the others about his maneuver had long since subsided.

"I know it's difficult to wrap your head around," she said. "But—"

"I'm not an idiot," Lucia snapped. "Antoine is a good man."

"Tell me one good thing he did," she said. The three couches in the room were arranged around the grand, gilded fireplace. She and Rushe occupied one, while the other two accommodated her parents and siblings, each sitting with their respective partners. "Just because he was smug and charming—"

"He knows his stuff," Roger piped up. "He understood the figures, the business contracts—"

"You've never heard of a crook who can read?" she asked. "He's dangerous."

"If he is dangerous," Lucia said. "Why didn't you tell us this when you got here?"

"I knew you wouldn't want to believe me," she said. "I don't exactly have a lot of credibility with you. We've never seen eye to eye. I didn't know his intentions. If I'd come to you with this while he was here calling me a liar, I'd never have been heard. You wanted him to be part of the company, but he's not honest, Father. You have to trust me."

Rushe hadn't said a word yet, not one single word. His hands slid around her hips and back to their previous position. His way of reassuring her, letting her know she wasn't alone.

"This requires consideration," her father said with a deliberating look.

"Charles," Beverly scolded.

Her father didn't flinch. "These accusations are serious. Felicity can't know all the details. There could be some sort of misunderstanding here. I'll make some calls."

His eternal arrogance may actually be her friend for once. Her father hadn't outright dismissed her or called her a liar, but he wouldn't take her word. No doubt he thought she was being an irrational female and questioned the veracity of her claims, but the concept of being made a fool of would mortify him.

Now it had been brought to his attention, he couldn't take the risk of ignoring it. If any of her accusations later turned out to be true, his youngest daughter couldn't show him up. She couldn't have known something he didn't. So Charles Hughes would do his investigating. She just wasn't sure what that would show up.

"You can't be listening to this," Lucia said. "Antoine has been our friend, part of our family."

"What am I?" she asked. "What would be my motivation for lying?"

"Drama," Lucia sniped.

Rushe's fingers dug into her. She slid a hand down to cover his, hopefully soothing him.

"If I wanted drama, I could've taken off with this guy and never bothered any of you again.

"You gave up Antoine to be with that guy?" Lucia asked.

"Actually, I gave up Rushe because Antoine forced me to. I was always Rushe's woman, I always will be."

"What do you know about this man you are with now?" Charles asked.

She wished his question was out of fatherly concern. No way it actually was. "Everything I need to," she said. "Rushe is no threat to this family. He wants nothing from you."

"Except our youngest daughter," Beverly said, giving little away.

"I don't belong to you," she said. "You cast me out, I wasn't a daughter of this family when I met Rushe. This family was not a factor in his decision to be with me, unlike every single other man from my past."

"You apparently attract men with ulterior

motives," Beverly said. "If your story is accurate."

"Like Robert," she said. "You wanted me to marry him because of what he could do for you."

"Is this your attempt at revenge?" her mother asked.

"No, I did as you wanted with Antoine, but I would not be violated. He wanted to manipulate all of you. We have to be united now, or he could hurt us, physically, he could attack us."

"You're being dramatic again," Charles exhaled, displaying his impatience.

"I'm trying to impress upon you how serious this is."

"The most volatile factor here, from what I have seen, is the man that you brought with you today," Charles said. "Why should we trust him?"

"Rushe loves me, he'd do anything to keep me safe and to keep me happy. It's the only reason we're here now because he knows I value your safety."

"We cannot be sure he is reliable," Charles said. "That he will prioritize this family, or your wellbeing—"

"Then you owe him two million dollars," she said, silencing the room. "He paid the ransom you refused to pay."

"He's the guy who paid for your safety even after you were safe?" Vivian recalled.

As understanding settled over the room, even her mother loosened.

Her love's hand pressed into her lower back, maintaining the force it ascended her spine. She pushed back in response to the heavy pressure of his possessive, yet calming, action.

Charles would never understand Rushe's logic, but Roger and Martin were piqued and almost seemed to lean as though trying to gape at her concealed lover.

"Rushe isn't on trial here, no one is," she said,

when Rushe's hand returned to her hip. "All I'm asking is you be on guard. Do your investigation, Father. But don't trust Antoine, none of you, not Simone, or Jerome. Rushe and I will stay a day or two. We'll answer your questions and be here in case there are any developments."

She would appreciate the chance to learn what her father found out. If Antoine got back in touch, she wanted to be there to defend her family. They couldn't possibly be prepared for what may come.

Whatever investigation or plan Rushe had going on, she hoped that they could play their part from there. She didn't want to be separated from her love, not when so much was at stake. While Jansen was out there, a variable hung in the air, but there was hope too. If he had something the Merciers were afraid of, it could bust the case open.

She was protected, Tawny too, but Serendipity was vulnerable. She hoped her actions hadn't endangered the woman's life. Serendipity had already endured so much.

"Bed," Rushe said.

It was still early and not yet time for bed. But they had a lot to talk about. Rushe probably wouldn't be wild on the idea of them staying there. Her family could use the time to process what she'd revealed, so it was best for her and her love to give them some space.

"We're going to rest," she said, taking hold of both of his hands. "It's been a long couple of days. You should all talk, come to terms with this change. Rushe and I aren't going anywhere yet. If you have a problem or want us to leave, then say so now. Rushe and I are a package deal, we will not be parted. But we won't inconvenience you if we are not welcome."

Standing together, she and Rushe waited while their audience examined each other and them.

"Problem?" Rushe's word came at the same time he brought their still joined hands up and wrapped their arms around the front of her shoulders.

"No," Charles said, making eye contact with Rushe for many lingering seconds.

When her father looked to his glass, Rushe took her hand to his pocket, and led her out of the room.

"I'll get our things," he said when they reached the lobby.

She snatched his hand when he tried to go for the door. "Eight, two, five, eight," she said. "That's the security code for the gate, but…"

"But what?"

Slinking in close, she encircled him in her arms. "Give the key to the steward, they'll bring in the car and our things. Don't leave me, Rushe. I've spent too long in this house without you."

"Okay, but business first," he said, reading her mind.

All she could think about was re-learning his mouth. "As long as we're together, I'll do anything, Lover."

"That's why I need reminding we're on a job."

Revealing the truth of her past, and her experience with Rushe, to her family, wasn't something she'd ever thought would happen. But needs must and having Rushe with her made the confessions easier. She'd craved the security of his companionship the whole time they were apart, and she would never take it for granted again.

FIFTY

THEY GOT THEMSELVES and their things into her bedroom. Rushe began to unpack the duffel to check out and inventory their equipment, as he did when trouble was advancing or retreating. She sat on the ottoman, crossed her legs, and watched him lay everything out.

"If I told you a story like that, you'd mobilize in five minutes flat," she said, staring in a trance at his practiced actions.

"What do you think I'm doing right now?" he asked, pulling from the bag what turned out to be the pocketknife she'd used on Antoine.

"No," she said. "I mean if you didn't know the story, and I told you that something like that happened to me."

He took his attention from the knife to tilt his head toward her. "How many stories like that have you got?"

"You're missing the point." She snapped out of her daze. "I'm saying, it's a sad state of affairs that a man I've known for less than a year cares for, and trusts, me more than my own family."

"They don't know you like I do, Kit," he said. "They're bastards, and they've treated you like shit. If you wanna say fuck them, we can walk out the door right now."

"We should leave them to be slaughtered because they were mean to me? That's harsh."

"Do you think they would protect you?"

"It doesn't matter, this is what we do. We help people who can't help themselves. Nasty or nice, this is our job. The fact that I'm biologically related to them is sort of irrelevant. They're clients, let's just look at it that way."

"You're emotionally invested, don't ignore that. I've warned you before," he said, flipping open the knife to inspect it more closely. "We should sterilize the thing, but it's clean enough. I don't want you unprotected." Rushe clicked it shut and tossed it to the end of the bed, just in front of where she sat. "I'd tell you not to hesitate to use it, but I think you've proved yourself."

Reluctant to touch it initially, she got over her funk and picked it up to tuck it into her back pocket again. It had been useful in protecting her. Rushe had been right, as he so frequently was.

"Do you think he'll come here?"

"Not himself," Rushe said. "I think he'll be beyond wanting to connect with your family. Saving face here does nothing for him now. He's lost you, so he's not getting into the family. It makes no sense that he would return when he knows he can't strong arm you into being with him. When you go for a guy like that, Kitten, like you did… there's no way he's lying down next to you to sleep."

"I've always been very nice to your cock," she said, drawing up her knees and folding her hands on them before she rested her chin on her knuckles.

"Especially when you're sleeping."

"That's 'cause you love my cock," he said, unrolling a gun from a shirt.

"I do."

"I've never tried to force it on you either."

"No," she murmured, and replayed the moment she was compelled to kneel in front of Antoine as he unbuckled his belt. "But another man trying it… I'd rather be beaten… or murdered…"

"Hey," he said, tossing the gun aside and coming to the end of the bed to sit at her side, his feet on the floor and his back to the bed. "You're a fighter, and you're not gonna let a fucker like Mercier break your spirit. I won't allow it, Kit. You fought, you made me proud."

"There was so much blood," she exhaled, rolling her cheek to her hands to meet his eyes.

"All his blood was headed that way, and you were in the path of it. You did the right thing."

"I made things worse."

"We're together again," he said, twisting to stroke her hair while laying his other hand on the end of the bed to support his weight. "That's not worse."

"And if it costs Serendipity her life? If she dies because I wouldn't suck his cock?"

Sinking toward her, he traced his lips on hers then licked out to part them. She obliged with her pout. Although he remained close, he didn't kiss her again.

"It would've killed me to see that," he admitted. "You saved my life."

Appreciating his attempts to console her, she sighed and lifted her arms to drape them around his shoulders. Climbing over into his lap, she wrapped her legs around him and leaned back, forcing him to take her waist and her weight.

"You've covered the bed with stuff, how will I

fuck you now?"

"Yeah," he said, bracing her on one arm to use the other to fondle her hair hanging loose behind her. His palm scooped it up into a bunch at the base of her skull. "'Cause a bed's always been a requirement for us."

"You missed my hair," she said.

"You missed my dick."

He bestowed on her such wonder, though he didn't look her in the eye. For some reason he was still awed by the notion she would want to be in his arms.

"I missed your face," she said, cradling it in her hands. "I missed your voice, and your eyes, and your smile, and your hands. I missed your heart, Rushe, and how you make me feel. I love your dick. But even if I could never play with it again, I'd still be right here." Gradually as his gaze came to hers, his brows came down in a frown. "Believe it, Lover."

Something passed over his expression, but he didn't get the chance to speak. She lifted her mouth to his and tried to show him just what love was in a way he would explicitly understand.

She kissed his jaw then nipped his earlobe between her teeth.

"Business first," he said.

She shook her head. "Business later."

Clutching her in his arms, he swooped to the floor and pinned her body down, gripping her wrists in his solid fists. "I got five weeks of frustration to pump out."

"Fill me up," she said, using all her weight to arch up.

She didn't move far, but the action was enough to spur him on.

He liberated her wrists long enough to grab the hem of her top. Shoving it upward, he exposed her breasts and took his time to admire them. Sinking down, his mouth enveloped the cap of one bosom, and he sucked her in, as much of her as would fit in his mouth.

The growl this time came from her, but her attempt to wriggle lower was unsuccessful. Her love reared up, and kneeling at her hips, his shins trapped her thighs against the floor. He leaned forward just enough to press the length of himself against the scorch at her apex, and still she tried to squirm closer.

His expression relaxed until after a few seconds of trying, he smiled at her. "My pussy's gonna purr tonight."

"Do it slow."

"We're gonna do it every way that's been invented… and then make up some of our own."

"Yes, sir."

Her grin came with his groan as he dropped to take her hair in his fists and yank her head back, giving himself access to her throat. "Gonna get you naked first."

There was a knock at the door, and his attention came up enough to briefly make eye contact. Then, in a flash, he was on his feet with her still in his arms. He tucked her onto the bed and slapped the gun into her hand as she pulled down her top to cover herself again.

"Stay," he ordered, and stormed for the door.

It was unlikely to be trouble because they hadn't heard any commotion, but she stayed where he'd put her and reveled in the notion her love put a gun in her hand and then turned his back on her. There was a time he wouldn't have trusted her aim… or her nerve. He hadn't taken the gun with him; he'd given it to her to ensure her safety and trusted her to be his back up.

Rushe opened the door to a steward, who stumbled back at the sight of this man ready to bowl him over. "You're needed downstairs."

"Why?" she asked, climbing off the bed, keeping

the gun in hand.

She only paused to slip her feet back into her ballet pumps as she traversed to join Rushe.

When she reached his position, her love stayed in place, giving her just enough room to peek under his arm. Clearly, he wasn't taking the risk she could be a target, so he reduced the surface area of her someone had to aim at. His form also prevented anyone from getting hold of her if they wanted to pull her out.

"Your father requires your presence," the steward said.

What questions could her family have for her? She relaxed and tucked the gun into the back of Rushe's jeans.

"Stay here," she said to her love. "I'll find out what this is about."

She ducked and was about to squeeze through the narrow gap when Rushe's arm tensed, clamping the door closer to his body, preventing her exit.

"We're a package deal," he said, taking the gun out and putting it on the floor by the door.

With her hand in his pocket, he took her out of the bedroom, and they followed on after the steward. Rushe liked to be prepared for conflict, but she appreciated him not taking the weapon to her family. If her father, if her sisters saw it, it could cause uproar. They weren't against guns as such, and the men had been known to hunt. But a handgun in their house, and after the story they'd been told, would probably be too much.

As soon as they got to the top of the stairs, she knew something wasn't right. It wasn't a compliment to her intuition though. Two uniform cops stood in the lobby with her parents. Her sisters and their husbands loitered in the shadows on the perimeter.

"Stay here," she said to Rushe, brushing her lips against his arm.

In credit to him, Rushe didn't follow her when she went down the stairs. He didn't flee either, not that she expected him to. If the officers thought they could take down Rushe on their own, they'd be mistaken. Having him too close, and intimidating them, wouldn't better their cause.

"What's going on?" she asked when she joined the group of four beside the main entrance. "Is there a problem?"

"Are you Felicity Hughes?" one of the officers asked.

"Maybe," she said. "What do you want?"

"We've had a report of a serious incident."

"Okay," she said, glancing at her ashen mother and stern father. "I'm very sorry to hear that."

Playing it cool was the only thing she could think to do. The alternative was to spin on the spot and scream up at Rushe to run.

"Are you engaged to Antoine Mercier?"

"No," she said, surprised by the question. "Not anymore."

"No," the officer said. "We appreciate that the engagement will have been broken now. But you are Felicity Hughes, and you were with your fiancé last night, weren't you?"

"What business is that of yours?" she asked, being cagey probably only increased the suspicion.

The officer who hadn't yet spoken came closer. She tried to edge away as the other officer stepped in.

"This is an outrage," Beverly said. "Your father and I have been trying to explain to these gentlemen that we are a reputable family. We are respected in this community."

All the name dropping and consternation in the world wouldn't change the fact that she was guilty of the crime they put on her. The thunder of footfalls rose. She didn't have to look to know Rushe was bearing down upon them.

"We have to ask you to come with us," the talking officer said.

"No," she said. "I won't come with you."

This was completely unexpected. It hadn't even occurred to her that something like this might happen. For all the time she'd spent worrying about Rushe in a jail cell, she'd never considered how she'd feel if she were put in one. If it meant saving Rushe, she'd do anything. But they'd just gotten each other back, they needed each other, they were a team. Antoine must have sensed that, or this was his revenge. Apart they were weaker, these last five weeks had proved that.

As soon as she'd walked into the watchman's room with Antoine and his men, her strength had returned. That was where she and Rushe had slept, it had been a temporary haven for her and the man she loved. That room was their turf. She'd put up with Antoine and his crap for weeks. But in Rushe's presence, she could take on the world.

"Felicity Hughes, you are under arrest for the assault of Antoine Mercier."

FIFTY-ONE

"WHERE IS YOUR EVIDENCE?" she asked.

"We've seen the injury and there is a witness."

A witness who was no doubt coerced.

"Rushe," she said, turning to seek him out. "What do I do?"

"Be calm," Rushe said.

On his flat words, she blinked up to see his blank expression. His eyes were nothing but the abyss of his pupils.

Aggravation hung around him, but he called on his uncanny ability to detach and just watched her, imparting on her some of the calm he cultivated in himself. If she asked him to fight, he would, and he'd win. He'd get her out of the clutches of these cops and take her far from there. Being on the run meant sacrificing the security they had there and was probably exactly what Antoine wanted.

"Come here," he said and stepped into her.

Rushe swept his hands over her shoulders and down her back. Under cover of a needlessly dramatic kiss, he stuck his fingers into her back pocket and palmed the knife she'd put there for protection. Having the weapon that caused the assault on her person when she was arrested wouldn't help her case. As usual, despite her terror, her love thought of everything.

"I love you," she said, catching her lip in her teeth when the heat of water scorched her face.

When he drew back his eyes softened in the agony her tears always caused him. "I'm gonna get you out, Kit. You trust me."

She nodded and lowered her head to rub her face against his chest.

"We have to take you into custody now, Miss Hughes," the cop said. "Please put your hands behind your back."

She did as asked, maintaining eye contact with Rushe throughout. She'd give anything in the world for her love to be the one putting the cuffs on her instead of this authoritarian officer. He might be doing his job, but this was an injustice, a tactic adopted by a despicable man. The cop didn't know he was doing the bidding of a criminal. Somehow, that only made it worse.

"You consider her precious cargo, or we'll have a problem," Rushe said, when the cops were done.

The reverberation of his chest soothed her. The cops were being warned, though threatening them couldn't be wise. Rushe kissed the top of her head before she was pulled away from him and led toward the door by the cops as they read her Miranda rights.

"I'm gonna follow you in—"

"No," she cut Rushe, and the cop, off. "It could be a trap. I don't trust them. I don't want you there. You have work to do here."

Her love considered her for a few seconds. On a nasal inhale his head went back, and he pinned the family in his glare. "Go with her. I trust her safety to you. You better not let her down."

"We will not take—"

"I'll go," Lucia cut their mother off.

"You will not," Roger said. "To a jail? A place like that? No. You will not. It's not safe."

"If you're that worried, go with her, dickwad," Rushe said.

Roger would be none too happy about the insult or visiting a police precinct with his delinquent of a sister in-law. But staying there with Rushe would offer him no reprieve.

"Come on," the cop said when the other officer opened the front door.

Keeping her eyes on Rushe for as long as she could, she walked backwards, guided out to the car by the cops. The car door slammed behind her, and her body tensed. She was a prisoner again.

BOOKING SEEMED TO TAKE HOURS. Lucia and Roger weren't present as she had her possessions catalogued and her fingerprints taken. The whole process was numbing. She moved through the instructions as she was given them, watching herself from outside her body.

She'd refused to give a statement against herself but thought it odd Antoine had made the report there in New Hampshire and said the assault had taken place locally. Not having to be extradited from the state made the process easier for her, as bail would be straightforward. But she didn't understand the motivation of the European's unsettling untruth.

Fear wasn't what overwhelmed her, vulnerability did. Rushe was out there, and he'd fight for her, but in there she was ineffectual. Abandoning her wouldn't occur to her love. Being detached from him and the job again so soon made her uneasy. She guessed that was exactly what Antoine wanted.

Antoine wasn't dumb enough to assume his relationship with her was salvageable. The idea of being alone with, or susceptible around her probably repulsed him after her actions. She hoped it did. In fact, she hoped it struck terror into him, though more likely it was rage she inspired.

The cell door closing behind her left her in a state of flux, useless when she had a dozen uses. Helpless when her greatest desire at that moment was to help those she cared about.

She spent her time in that dank cell staring at the concrete floor. After driving herself insane thinking about all the things she couldn't do, she turned her mind to the thousands of other people who must have sat in that place, staring at this floor.

The clunk of the door brought her to her feet. When she saw it was being held open a question about what was going on flavored her tongue, and then she noticed a man in the outer doorway.

"Robert," she whispered, and rushed forward, only to be hampered by the cop blocking her route.

"Take it easy, Miss."

Appearing hysterical wouldn't help her case, but she hadn't appreciated the concentration of adrenaline coursing through her veins.

"What are you doing here?" she asked, being escorted across to Robert by the cop.

"I heard you needed a lawyer," Robert said.

"Lucia called you?"

"Yes. I made a call to get you the best."

Criminal law wasn't Robert's thing, and Lucia could afford to hire an expert lawyer. Though depending on the required retainer, Roger may have balked. Robert wouldn't though. He was decent through and through and would never see an acquaintance left in need. Under other circumstances, she may have been wary about what the gesture meant. But Rushe would pay Robert every cent they owed, even if he had to sell his soul to cover the bill.

"Thank you," she said, still gracious despite her innocent suspicion.

"Turns out to be irrelevant," he said.

"What?"

"Charges have been dropped," the officer said. "Guess your fiancé changed his mind. Domestic incidents make me crazy."

"Let's get you out of here," Robert said. "I'll take you to my place and—"

"No," she said. "I need to go back to my parents. I don't have time to waste. My family could be in danger, I don't want to be away from them."

"Away from them, or away from Rushe?" he asked, wiping the amity from his expression and replacing it with curiosity. "You love him?"

"Yes."

"You love a man who doesn't return your affections?"

Taking a reflexive step backward, she frowned. "I am Rushe's world."

"If that was the case, he would be here," Robert said. "Before him, you would never have been involved in anything criminal. I am concerned for you, Felicity."

"I don't need your concern, or your understanding. I appreciate your help tonight. Rushe will see you're fully repaid if—"

"That's not my concern."

"You're not getting into my underwear."

The groove between his brows furrowed. "That's not my concern either."

"So what is?" she asked.

"If your family is left vulnerable because of—"

"Oh," she said, shifting her weight to her back foot. "You're worried about your business interests. Why am I not surprised?"

"Duke out your tiff at home. I've got real criminals to deal with," the cop said.

More likely he had an appointment with a TV show.

As their eyes locked, Robert stepped out of the doorway. "Let's get out of here," he said.

FIFTY-TWO

IT COULD ONLY have been a few hours since she'd last been at her parents' house, but she craved the sight of her love, his embrace, his solace. Roger was parking the car, because the married steward and housekeeper would be the only two staff left on the premises at that time of night. Parking wasn't part of their duties.

So she walked through her parents' front door with Robert and Lucia on her heels. The last thing she expected to see was Liam and Tawny standing on the stairs, but there they were.

"Flick!" Liam exclaimed when he recognized her. He left Tawny's side and hurried over to sweep her into his arms. "Are you okay?"

"What are you doing here? I thought you guys were…" hiding out, was the end of that sentence. But she couldn't say those words in front of their audience. "Why are you here?"

"Rushe called," Tawny said. Liam moved aside so as not to restrict each woman's view of the other. "He doesn't like me to go far. We were in Boston."

"Strength in numbers," Liam said. "He wanted us here looking out for each other."

"What about Eric?"

"He stayed in New Jersey. He wanted to see Gracie again before…"

"Yeah," she said and glanced at the floor. In the intensity of the situation, it was impossible to know what would happen next. "Rushe wanted you here?"

"Your father assured him there would be increased security," Liam said.

"Increased security?" she asked. Her attention snapped around when a side door opened. Her parents emerged with Vivian. "You've hired extra security?"

"Yes," Charles said. "The men will be here shortly."

"Good," she said. "You have to let Rushe brief them. I know you like to be in charge, and of course you'll be present, but Rushe knows—"

"Rushe has given his instructions to me," Charles said. "He issued them before his departure."

"He left?" she breathed and looked back to the sheepish Liam.

"Jansen paged him. He found out Serendipity's location."

"Rushe is going to help him?" she asked. "To retrieve Serendipity?"

"Yes, Rushe called me after he spoke to Jansen," Liam said. "He was on the road before Tawn and I got here."

"It'll take him all night to get down there," she said. "He has a few hours head start, but if we hurry, we can catch—"

On spinning around to aim for the exit, Robert caught her arm. "If security is coming here and you are in some sort of danger, this is the place you need to stay."

"I'm not staying here," she said, yanking her arm

away from his grasp. "I will not leave Rushe out there alone."

"He made sure you had a lawyer, and that your father had security in place, before he left," Liam said. "You'll never catch up to him… unless you plan to break every speed limit."

"If I have to do that, I will," she said. "I don't give a damn."

"The troopers will when they pull you over," Robert said. "As they will if you plan to speed your way toward this danger."

"Is Eric still down there?" she asked, flipping back around to seek out Liam.

"I haven't been able to get in touch with him," Liam said. "I've been calling, but…"

"He should know what's going on," she said, considering options. Calm was quickly leaving her. "Rushe shouldn't have left me here."

"We thought you'd be in jail all night. Rushe had to help Jansen with Serendipity," Liam said. "Jansen was there for you when you needed—"

"I'm not refuting that," she said. "Of course we should help Jansen. But if Rushe had waited for me to return—"

"Perhaps he didn't want you involved in this danger," Robert interjected.

Despite the volume of people in the room, there wasn't one person on her side. Her parents stood silently with Vivian. Lucia remained by the door. Tawny held her position by the stairway. She didn't know where Roger or Martin were, but her brothers-in-law wouldn't be big advocates for her or her cause. Robert was somewhere a few feet behind her. The last man, Liam, was there in front of her.

She lifted her eyes to his to beseech him. "You know what I'm capable of," she said to him. "You know what lengths I'll go to for Rushe. You're the only one here who has witnessed that firsthand. I have to go to him."

"And if you're arrested again or worse?" Liam asked. "Rushe was adamant about your sister going to the precinct because he didn't trust the cops to keep you safe."

"The cops up here aren't connected with the ones down there in Mercier's pocket."

"Maybe not enough to commit murder," Liam said. "But we can't be sure he isn't purchasing information. If Antoine knows you're out of jail... If he knows Rushe has left here—"

"How could he possibly know that Rushe left?" she snapped. "I have to go."

"I'll come with you," Robert said. "If you need support, I'll be there for you. It wouldn't hurt to have a lawyer with you in case you do run into trouble with law enforcement."

"You're a corporate lawyer," she said. "You deal with contracts and acquisitions."

"That's more law school under my belt than you've got," he said.

"This Antoine guy is dangerous," Liam said. "Flick, you can't take the risk—"

"I have to do something!" she asserted.

"I don't know how all of you can so easily assume that Antoine is a criminal," Lucia's voice floated in from the background.

The clack of her sister's heels on the marble floor signaled her approach.

"Don't defend him!"

Tawny startled the group with her outburst and marched over to Liam's side with rage in her countenance.

"Tawn," Liam said, but she completely ignored

him.

"You have no idea what's going on here," Tawny shouted at Lucia, who was clearly uncomfortable with such an uncouth display. She was still in a state of shock that the young woman, who'd seemed to hate her so much, was pouncing into the fray. "This is a guy who tried to force himself on your sister, and you want us to give him the benefit of the doubt?" Tawny continued. "Nu-uh, not a chance, you give a guy like that a break, and he'll take it. He'll walk all over you forever. Flick here slashed him good; you bet he'll think twice about pressuring any girls in the future. We don't let him away with shit." Diverting the softening anger, Tawny looked to her. "You should go to Rushe."

So she did have an ally after all. "Thank you," she said.

"Tawny, you can't—"

"Yes, I can," Tawny said to Liam. "Rushe has been there for us. It's only right that we should be there for him. If I could be any use—"

"He'll want you safe," Flick said to her. "You stay here."

"You don't think he'll want you safe?" Liam asked, flabbergasted by the women ganging up on him. "You can't go down there. You don't know where they are."

"Rushe must have called Jansen after the page," she said. "I can get the number from the phone memory."

"I have Jansen's phone number," Liam sighed. "Rushe gave it to me... You can't go rushing into this, Flick. If Antoine is still down there, going back to him is insanity. I've heard about what he and his family do, about how they intimidate and torture."

"What do you mean?"

"I spoke to the captains," Liam said. "While you

were here… I went looking for them."

"And?" she asked. "Did they give you evidence of the corruption or the Mercier connection?"

"You could say that," Liam said. "The first captain, the one who was fired, gave me a lot of information about the Merciers. About how they started by paying him off, and how he got drawn in deep before he realized the extent of what the Merciers were into."

"That's great," she said, bolstered by the development. "Gathering information is—"

"He committed suicide the next day," Liam said.

A chill flooded her. "Suicide?"

"Shot himself in the head."

That may or may not have been suicide. She'd seen too much of the evil that existed in this world to take it at face value. "Did you record your conversation with him?"

Liam nodded. "As per Rushe's instructions. But I don't see how that will help us. One man versus whatever the extent of this plot—"

"We need to get the evidence to those conducting the investigation," she said.

"We can't trust them, Rushe knew that."

"Did you find out why the second captain was destroying evidence or rather, who he was destroying it for?"

"No," Liam said. "We haven't been able to find him. He took off with his family. He's married and has an eight-year-old daughter."

"They're vulnerable. It makes sense he would want to get them to somewhere safe." But that only frustrated her. "Jansen has to have something. He must be close."

"You don't know that."

"Why else would the Merciers go for him when they did?"

"Maybe they were sick of him sniffing around."

"Maybe," she said. No one else in the room had said anything for a while, but she was caught up in her conversation with Liam and didn't care about them while progress was being made. "But if he has nothing, and we have nothing…"

"We don't have nothing. We carried on building a case," Liam said. "We have evidence of the truth."

"But nothing overwhelmingly compelling, or you'd have presented it," she said.

"Everyone is safe. Rushe and Jansen will get Serendipity, and—"

"And then what? The Merciers are desperate. They're not going to let us all walk away just because they were bested by us. They'll have no prisoners and nothing to bargain with. Rushe taking the rap isn't enough anymore. They're going to want more."

"More?" Liam asked. "Like what?"

"Blood," she replied.

The word lingered in the air, bouncing between all the bodies, echoing and vibrating while they all came to terms with just what that meant. A knock on the front door shattered the reflection and prevented any further discussion on the subject.

As he was the closest, Robert went to the door, and she watched Liam return to Tawny. The woman looked up at him with big round eyes, the whites glowing in respect. When Liam's fingertips touched her cheekbone, Tawny smiled, which made her smile too.

"It's security."

Charles Hughes spoke. She turned to see a squad of men in black enter. Usually the security professionals her father used were discreet and minimal. The Hughes family had never faced a threat so profound before, security was more often a show piece than a requirement. The drivers were trained in combat and knew how to shoot, they were usually enough of an escort for her and her sisters growing up.

But these guys were different, bulky, and packing weapons. Tattoos on show and some heads were shaved, while others sported facial hair. These weren't standard, premium, elegant security men meant to ward off ardent fans. These were hardened men, who appeared more like criminals than saviors.

She counted the first ten and was surprised to count another ten. While they moved around the perimeter of the room, none of them spoke. Then they began to move in, drawing her family and friends closer into the center of the lobby.

Twenty-two men in total entered. She looked to her father to suggest overkill and was horrified to see his widened gaze and clammy skin. She'd never seen her father scared before, but she was sure that was what the expression revealed.

"These aren't your security guards," she said, at the same time the others in the group were figuring it out.

The men drew even closer, forming a human cordon around the group until all eight were confined.

A silent thrum in the air buzzed like an amp turned up to maximum. A beat of silence interrupted, then another. The pulse became a heartbeat, but no one spoke. She reminded herself of Rushe's patience. Silence was powerful. If she was the one to break it, she'd be revealing her apprehension.

Fighting as hard as she could to don the mask she'd seen Rushe wear, she blanked her expression and slowed her breathing, focusing directly ahead.

"What is going on here?" Charles asked the security man nearest him but got no response.

"Charles?" Beverly asked, less guarded with her fear.

All of the group around her, her allies, were scared, but she forced herself to stand tall. Someone touched her hand, and she resisted the urge to lash out at the contact. Glancing downward, she saw Robert link his fingers between hers. The gesture was meant as consolation. For him or her?

"Ma chère," the rich male accent laced with a perverted delight told her their fear was justified.

Shit.

FIFTY-THREE

BETWEEN THE THICK ARMS of the men surrounding her group, she saw Antoine enter with his cousin, Simone. She'd believed Simone was still with Serendipity, apparently not.

Antoine's gait was slow, shuffling. After only a few steps he stopped. Although he tried to hide it, she saw him wince. Gone was the expensive designer suit. Instead he wore black sweatpants and a hooded sweatshirt that zipped up the front. If he'd had his wound stitched and bandaged, the unrestrictive clothing would be required not to irritate the dressing.

"I hoped you'd have bled out by now," she growled.

"Your aim is not very good," he said. "Flesh wound."

As much as she had no interest in going to jail for attempted murder, she wouldn't have minded causing some lasting damage. Though if the way he stooped was anything to go by, it was possible he was in more pain than he let on.

"What are you doing here?" she asked.

"I came to get my ring back."

"I don't have it," she said.

"This is about an engagement ring?" Robert asked.

"He's being facetious," she said. When Antoine lifted his attention, he only now realized she could see him through the narrow space between biceps. "Rushe isn't here."

"I didn't want Rushe here," Antoine said. "Rushe is on his way to rescue a relatively unprotected Serendipity, because we knew that your friend Jansen would call on him to do so."

"It's a trap," she whispered and tried to push through the human barrier. The goons closed ranks, making it impossible for her to pass and obscuring her view of their captors. "Are you going to kill him, is that the—"

"Non!" Antoine said with a spiteful laugh. "He is going to complete the task that we could not. He will retrieve the evidence Jansen has spent all these months collecting. We did not realize how devious the officer was. He has compelling evidence against me and my family, which we cannot allow to become public."

"What kind of evidence?"

"His trade is investigation," Antoine said. "We should have realized he would know the way to do things. He compiled statements from other officers corroborating his story of the corruption within the ranks. Those statements implicate my family."

"Statements aren't—"

"He had them notarized," Antoine said, with a snarl of disgust. "Apparently he knew a man who could help him."

"So he knows what he's doing," she said, her own satisfaction increased. "You can off as many people as you like, those statements are still admissible."

"Yes. He also collected video evidence of meetings between my associates and his colleagues. One of whom is dead, and the other is missing."

The captains.

"Why are you telling me this now?" she asked. "Why tip your hand?"

"I'm doing nothing of the sort," Antoine said. "When we discovered what Jansen was doing, we took action. We displayed how serious we were about protecting ourselves."

"By hospitalizing him and kidnapping Serendipity."

"Yes."

"And now? Jansen's awake, so you expect Rushe to get that evidence, why? Why not just kill Jansen?"

"The evidence still exists," Antoine said, though it evidently pained him.

"You think Jansen confided in someone," she said. "That the evidence is still a threat to you, even with Jansen out of the picture."

"It's a possibility," Antoine said.

"You want the evidence."

"Your boyfriend and his cohort will rescue Serendipity. He will quickly realize how easy the operation was and suspect there is something wrong here."

"You had Flick arrested to separate her from Rushe," Liam interjected. "You needed them apart. You're going to use Flick against Rushe. Make him retrieve the evidence from Jansen in exchange for Flick's safety."

"Oui."

"We also knew he would secure his pet," Simone chimed in. "He removed her from Silver's, so he had to have her close. But both of you present? This is a coup."

Tawny. They had known that Rushe wanted to keep Tawny safe. Now the Merciers had what they considered to be both of Rushe's women.

"You've freed Serendipity, there's no way for you to control Jansen," she said. "He'll release the evidence to the authorities."

"He will not," Antoine drawled. "Rushe is not going to allow that to happen when his own women are in peril. Rushe will finish the job for us. He will retrieve the evidence."

"You think because he has Jansen's trust, and they've worked together to liberate Serendipity, that Jansen will just hand over the evidence for old times' sake?"

"I am indifferent to Rushe's method," Antoine said.

"You let them have Serendipity. You knew Jansen would contact Rushe for help to free her. But you plan to set them against each other."

"Rushe will do what is necessary if it means saving his pets…"

"We are not his pets!" Tawny declared.

Antoine only laughed. "He enjoys his women with… how you Americans say… spunk?" he said. "That is easily extinguished."

"This is a disgrace, Antoine," Charles Hughes piped up. She could only imagine it was his shock at the turn of events that kept him quiet for so long. "We trusted you. You are a criminal. Felicity told us of your deeds, but we did not believe… this is a disgrace."

"Ah, you were all too easily fooled," Antoine said. "It was not difficult at all. A show of wealth and sophistication, you looked no further than the superficial. A perfect capitalist family. You value money over that of your own children's welfare. It makes you easy to take advantage of, Charles. I am sure I am not the first."

"I can assure you that you are. I pride myself on—"

"Foolish pride!" Antoine snapped.

"You will not think that when my own security team—"

"I am not a fool like you," Antoine said. "The fiancé of your youngest daughter contacted the security firm you hired to cancel the order. We shall not be disturbed."

"Our staff—"

"Have already been detained," Antoine said. "Just as you all shall be."

Antoine must have given a silent instruction. Each of the allied group were grabbed by two opposition security guards. The remaining men held the perimeter around them as they were manhandled toward the formal drawing room.

On arrival, they were each thrust into a seat on one of the couches arranged in front of the fireplace around a low table. Their hands were strapped together at the wrist with cable ties.

"This is your big plan?" she asked when Antoine came in with Simone. The pair traversed toward the window. "You're going to keep us here."

"Yes," Antoine said. "Rushe will come for you, of that I am certain."

"So am I," she said. "But he won't do your bidding."

"He will have no choice, if he plans to keep you and your family alive."

Antoine and Simone went to the chairs arranged in the large window to face into the room. Simone actually supported her cousin as he descended to sit. Such a show of weakness would irritate him, but from how he sat awkwardly in the chair, keeping his body as level as he could, his discomfort was great.

"I should've removed the organ altogether," she strutted. "I'd have saved women all over the world from the displeasure of having you attempt to force it on them."

"You are in a minority, ma chère. Even in this very room there are women who crave me."

She didn't want Antoine's dalliance with Lucia to become public, not in front of her parents, so she didn't push.

At that moment, their greatest hope was her brothers-in-law, Roger and Martin. If they contacted the cops before Rushe returned, it was possible they could be saved without this going forward.

"It can't be your plan to hurt us," Lucia said. Did her sister understand just how dangerous Antoine was? "You would never hurt us. We're your friends."

"We are not friends," Antoine said.

"We have shared each other's company," Robert said. "Lucia is right, this situation is out of hand. Mercier, you cannot—"

"Calme! You snivel, all of you."

"Action would be reckless. Rushing you won't make a difference," she said. "You have too many men for us to take on alone."

"So you will sit quietly and wait," Antoine said. "This is my wish. My men will keep you in line. You will remain here, all of you, and we will wait."

"Where is her husband?" Simone asked, peering at Vivian. "What is his name? Where is he?"

"He left here earlier," Charles said when Vivian remained silent. "He will realize that there is something wrong, and—"

"Oui, c'est une possibilité."

The cousins continued their conversation in their mother tongue. If they hoped to hide their intentions, they underestimated the education of the family. She picked up their concern about being discovered by Martin. More telling was their lack of concern about Roger. He'd been with Lucia that night at the precinct and had dropped them off outside the house. No one had seen him since.

"Where's Roger?" she asked, suddenly concerned for his wellbeing. "What did you do to him?"

"You will call your husband on the telephone," Simone said, ignoring the question.

"Who?" Lucia asked. "Neither of our husbands are here."

She too had to be worried for Roger.

"No one has spoken to you," Simone said. "Bring her the phone!"

A security man went to the phone in the corner and took it to Vivian.

"Phone him," Antoine said. "Tell him to come here to retrieve you. Ask him to come inside."

"You plan to trap him here with us," Vivian said, finding her voice. "I will not be a party to—"

The thug who had brought her the phone lifted his hand and brought it across Vivian's face, much to the audible dismay of the family. Vivian clutched her cheek and looked up into the blank face of her attacker.

"Phone him," Antoine said.

The beep of phone buttons being pressed pierced the dense air. She maintained her gaze on Antoine. After only a few seconds, his eyes crept around to hers as though he had sensed her assault. She would not let him see any weakness, and as she imagined all the things she wanted to do to the man, all the hurt she wished him to experience, the corner of his lips curled.

"You wish me harm," he said. "But I will inflict harm on you, Miss Hughes."

"You have no intention of letting any of us go,"

she said. "Rushe will know that."

"Oh contraire," Antoine said. "Your family may go free. I have no use for them and would not wish to complicate matters for myself."

"So you get your evidence and go? I don't believe it."

Vivian was talking into the phone now, but she maintained her focus.

"Believe what you will," Antoine said. "But it matters not. Once we have the evidence and have destroyed it, we will proceed as originally planned."

"You expect me to testify against Rushe? You plan to try framing him again?"

"He will go to jail for his crimes," Antoine said. "But your testimony will be impossible. Your statements to the police will be sufficient. My cousin will be sure to highlight Rushe's involvement in your violation."

"Rushe didn't violate her!" Tawny called. "He wouldn't violate anyone."

"He's trying to upset you," Liam said. "He's trying to upset us all, just ignore him."

Liam was right. But Antoine's plan was enough to infuriate them. Her family would be held captive long enough to force Rushe to get the evidence Antoine sought from Jansen. Once he had what he wanted, Antoine would eliminate her and her family, of that she had no doubt. Keeping any of them alive made no logical sense.

Rushe would realize that too but would have little choice except to agree to Antoine's plan. If nothing else, it would buy them time. She couldn't see a way out. There were too many men. If they truly had kept the two on-premises staff members hostage as well, there would be no one to get them out.

Vivian was off the phone. Martin would be on his way without any idea what he was walking into.

All of that paled to insignificance when she thought about Rushe. When he and Jansen liberated Serendipity, it would be immediately obvious to him what was going on. He would speed there to get to her. It would be beyond daylight by the time he returned.

As of then, he'd be in his car still driving toward Serendipity. He'd probably be worried about her and her getting out of jail. He didn't know yet that she was stuck, just like the rest of her family. What was worse? She'd gotten them into this.

If she hadn't walked into that bar, Dell's… except even now she couldn't regret it. Rushe had become integral to her existence in such a short space of time. She couldn't imagine life without him, wouldn't imagine it. She trusted him. If anyone could figure a way out of this, it was her love.

FIFTY-FOUR

THE CLOCK TICKED through the silence in the room. Conversation had been abandoned long ago, and though uncomfortable, they weren't mistreated. Held on the couches, facing each other and without the freedom to move or talk, all they could do was wait. She sat nearest the fireplace with her back to the door and next to Robert, who had Lucia on his other side.

Liam was in the center of Tawny and Vivian on the couch opposite hers while her parents sat on the head couch, facing the fireplace. None of her group said anything. They spent most of their time staring at the floor. But Antoine and Simone had spent the last half an hour growing more frustrated in their private conversation.

"You two, go and see," Antoine said to two of his guards, who nodded and disappeared from the room.

The rest of the guards stayed around the edge of the room.

From what she'd picked up from the cousins' foreign language conversation, they were expecting the group holding the staff to report in. But they had not. Antoine's arrogance was their friend. He hadn't been initially worried about the delay in the guards' report. Rushe and his cohorts were hundreds of miles away, so for now they were safe … at least they were supposed to be.

"We've been here for hours, and we'll be here all night," Lucia said. "You can't expect us to—"

"Don't start talking," Simone said. "No one wishes to hear you."

She and Antoine sat removed from the group, looking into the room, in the seats flanking the window seat.

"Antoine," Lucia said. "Please, I know you care about me and the family. You don't have to do any of this. You can still let us go. You can still be a good man, the good man I know that you really are."

"You are naïve," Simone sneered.

"But so eager to please," Antoine said, enjoying every moment of Lucia's public humiliation. "She was easy, the easiest of them all to win over."

"We had a connection," Lucia said, a croak in her tone.

"Your husband was tired of you, and you do love attention, Lucia. Your loose morals gave me the opportunity to gain an ally and gave me an avenue into your family confidence. Exactly as I wanted. I did delight in enjoying your body."

"You are lying," Charles insisted.

"I am not," Antoine said. "I have been intimate with your eldest daughter. Ask her to deny it."

A few seconds of nothing passed. Her gut clenched because his claim was true. Antoine had no reason to lie about it. She'd also seen for herself just how besotted Lucia was and had flagged the attraction to Rushe.

"Lucia?" Beverly said when Lucia didn't issue a denial. Charles's silence gave his grave verdict. "Is it true?"

"One child at least had the courtesy to take her debauchery away from your family home. Though it seems she returned with it… Rushe was quite a scare for this family," Antoine drawled. "Bringing him back here, Felicity, scared your parents so much that they were in desperation. My gracious offer to return you to them, out of his clutches—"

"And into yours," she said.

"You were needlessly difficult. We could've been a team and helped each other. The offer of our union was yours, ma chère."

"I offered you my name, not my body. My body is for Rushe alone."

"As you proved in his bedroom. You made a fatal mistake there, ma chère. Had you done as I requested, none of your family would be threatened."

"You already tried to blame this on me," she said. "This is about your family and about the crime you—"

A bang interrupted her words. All the faces in the room began to look left to right, searching the other occupants for the source of the abrupt sound. But it had come from somewhere else in the house, and there was no mistaking that noise as anything other than a high-caliber gunshot.

"What was that?" Vivian asked.

"I believe your husband must have departed as quickly as he arrived," Antoine said.

Simone laughed again.

Vivian wailed, her mouth opened wide, and her eyes squeezed shut against the declaration of the despicable man holding them hostage. Any remaining doubt as to Antoine's intention in the situation was erased. If Martin had been shot, he had been killed.

"Is that what you did to Roger?" she asked.

"Oh, Roger, oh, non, non," Antoine said.

Vivian continued to cry in great hulking sobs, but all their hands were tied, little solace could be extended to her. Liam sat at Vivian's side, and all he could offer was a pat to the knee. The brief contact was enough to encourage Vivian to turn her face against Liam, who lowered his cheek to rest on her hair as she bawled.

"Where is he?" Lucia demanded, hissing through her teeth, and displaying a unique rage.

"Restrained, with the staff," Antoine said. "We will not eliminate him until this situation is under control. We may need…"

"Another scapegoat," she said. "If he was unhappy in his marriage, maybe it was enough to murder his in-laws. Is that the play?"

"Non, but now you come to mention that idea, it may have merit."

Antoine was already in a precarious position with Rushe. The European's plan and his actions guaranteed he would receive no mercy. As Antoine went back to benign conversation with his cousin, she narrowed her eyes on the Merciers. Rushe always got his man. As much as she didn't know how it would play out, she trusted Rushe would get them through this. After he did, she'd let him follow the trail of figurative blood until Antoine didn't have a drop left. In fact, she'd insist upon it.

FIFTY-FIVE

HOW LONG HAD SHE been staring at the clock on the mantle? The answer should be obvious, but it wasn't. The second hand mesmerized her. It had been at least an hour since the gunshot, and she thought about Rushe on his journey. He'd have reached New Jersey already for sure. They'd probably liberated Serendipity and figured out something else was going on. He could be on his way back to her, either way he'd be frantic.

"You three, take that phone," Antoine barked and pointed to the three guards closest to the device. "Go and check on the others; I will call you in sixty seconds."

The guards took the phone and left. The Frenchman's frustration was becoming apprehension. After the gunshot, he'd sent two guards to help clean up the mess, or rather to confirm the kill. They hadn't returned. Nor had the two sent out to check on the staff guards. It was difficult to get excited about the dwindling number of guards in the room when they were still so outnumbered and outgunned.

"I need to use the bathroom," Tawny said, squirming in her seat.

"We've been here for quite a while," Flick said, wondering at the expression Tawny bestowed on her. "Mercier, you have to—"

"I am not that naïve," Antoine said.

"You'll have us here for hours," she said. "Did you have no plans to let us eat or tend to personal needs?"

Gearing herself up for another fight, her gusto was diverted when a crash came from beyond the room. All eyes sprang to the door. For a tense five seconds, nobody breathed.

"Ce qui se passe?" Simone asked her cousin what was happening.

Fearful of alerting them to her knowledge of their language, Flick didn't flinch.

"Je ne sais pas."

If Antoine didn't know what was happening, this wasn't planned. A smile crept to her face. Her lover's name was on her lips, but she didn't speak it. She turned to look at the wide-eyed Tawny with a smile.

"Maybe the bathroom break can wait," Flick said.

"You! Take your group! Get out there and investigate that sound!" Antoine commanded, and tried to push out of his chair, but was reminded of his injuries and collapsed back.

Simone bounced forward in her chair. With one hand on her wincing cousin's knee, Simone took a bottle of pills from her purse on the floor and held them to Antoine.

"All of them?" Flick asked, watching the five men Antoine had spoken to filter out with their guns drawn.

Antoine swallowed down the pills with the wine

he and Simone had been drinking. "Tais-toi," he sniped, and swiped Simone's hand away from his leg.

"Five guys," Flick said as casually as she could, knowing her attitude would rile him. "You must be uneasy… You send out two, who never come back. Then you send out another two who never return, and now you're sending out five… that's a lot of guys."

"Telephone!" Antoine demanded of Simone, who fumbled a cellphone out of her purse to give her cousin, who immediately dialed.

"I don't think they're going to answer," Flick said, casting her eyes toward the ceiling as she relaxed on the couch.

Five short, sharp gunshots snapped to their ears, and her smile only got wider.

"Putain!" Simone's outburst wasn't appreciated by Antoine.

It was by her. "Maybe you should send out some more guys to see what that was," Flick said.

"Come over here," Antoine said, struggling to get to his feet, even with Simone's help.

Sitting in the same position for so long hadn't done his injury any good.

"You want me to come over there?" Flick asked. A security guy closed in on her to pull her up to her feet. "If I come over there, I'll finish what I started."

"You will not hurt me," Antoine said, using the chair for support. "You will not risk the lives of your family."

The guard began to drag her forward, but she lashed out, digging an elbow into his ribs and her heel into his shin. He cursed at her and hoisted her off the floor. She cried out, digging her fingernails into his arm in hope of being released. Her bound wrists limited her options, but she still kicked and struggled all the way to Antoine's side.

"Keep her behind the chair, against the wall," Antoine said and gestured for two others to cover her as well.

Three men on her alone was actually something of a compliment, but the gun against her temple lessened her glee. One man held her shoulders, one held the gun, and the third seemed ready for her to lash out.

"Has he had enough time?" Simone asked Antoine. "Rushe? Is he here already?"

"We shall find out." Antoine took a few steps toward the door. "You!" he commanded another security guard. "Open the door." The guard did as he was told and swung the door back on its hinges while holding his gun ready. "Stay beside it, you warn us if you see anyone."

"That's your plan?" Flick asked, then was jostled against the wall when she tried to move. "Someone stands there until Rushe walks into his line of fire? If you shoot Rushe, he won't be able to retrieve your evidence."

"He will not be shot," Antoine said. "We held your family for a reason."

"He's taken out half your men already," she said, though couldn't be sure of that.

She couldn't be sure of anything.

"Rushe!" Antoine called toward the door. "We have your ladies! Don't be a coward, you have nothing to fear! We have a proposal!"

"You're going to negotiate by hollering?" Flick asked. "He might not even be out there."

Antoine's eyes remained trained on the door, though his head tipped in her direction. "He's out there. He has a compulsion, which I will never understand, to be near you."

"It's called love," she muttered.

"There is a way out of this!" Antoine shouted at the door again.

The guard at the door collapsed to the floor. It took a few seconds to realize he'd been shot. The only clue was the blood that began to form a puddle beneath him.

Antoine took a reflexive step back.

"Do you want to form an orderly line?" Flick asked.

Antoine couldn't send anyone else out there, because they'd be picked off one by one.

Just then, Rushe appeared in the doorway, his gun outstretched. With three quick shots, he took out three more guards. Ducking back behind the wall, he held his gun around the doorframe, aiming at Antoine.

"You're next," Rushe said.

"We have a proposal," Antoine said.

"No," Rushe replied. "You have a problem. A serious problem. Every man not in this room is dead. My associates and I have cleared out this place. The feds are on their way."

"What?" Antoine faltered. "That's impossible."

Rushe shook his head. "Jansen, and one of my associates, got Serendipity out without me," her love said. "I wasn't halfway to his location when Jansen called and told me it was a trap. I came back, and I've been taking your men out one by one. The Hughes' staff is free, they called the cops. Jansen called the feds."

"He—"

"That's the thing we never figured out, Kit," Rushe said to her, still watching Antoine. "The feds found out about Jansen's off the books investigation. The Merciers took Jansen out when they found out the feds had approached him for the evidence he'd gathered. It was the feds watching Jansen in the hospital. They wouldn't let him out to go to Serendipity, so he had to bail behind their backs."

"The second captain," Liam said, from his place

on the couch.

"Witness protection. He wasn't destroying evidence, he was collecting it," Rushe said. "The feds have known about the Merciers' involvement for months. They've just struggled to put the pieces together."

"They have not!" Antoine asserted.

"They couldn't get a handle on you. They didn't know what you looked like, or where you were… not until you showed up on their doorstep with my woman," Rushe said. "Since then, they've been watching you."

"You walked right into their hands when you took me in to make a statement," Flick said. "Why didn't they arrest him?"

"Jerome was who they wanted," Rushe said. "And they got an eyeball on him when he was invited to your engagement party. They've been monitoring his movements since."

"Oh my God," she said on an exhale.

"They were watching you too, Antoine, which means they were watching my woman," Rushe said. "Also means they weren't looking at me."

"Keeping us apart protected you," Flick said.

"Did me a favor there," Rushe said. "Turns out they lost sight of you the night that Jansen left the hospital. Their operation was frantic. They didn't expect you and Flick to leave here so suddenly. No one knew where you went… until Jansen called them tonight and told them you were here. He has his woman now. There's nothing to stop him handing over everything he has and taking you and your uncle down."

"The feds are on their way?" one of the security guards said.

The guys in black exchanged looks at each other, and at their dead colleagues on the floor.

"You guys have no idea what you've walked

into," Flick said. "Antoine's not going to protect any of you. You're all going to go down for life."

"Fuck that," the security guard said, and started for the door.

He paused at the reminder of Rushe.

"Drop your guns and you can leave," Rushe said. "I've stripped your colleagues out there of their weapons; there's nothing behind me. My associates will let you leave if you don't cause trouble.".

"Associates?" Simone asked. "Jansen is here?"

"And Eric?" Liam asked.

"I sat out there until they had time to arrive," Rushe said. "Someone taught me that backup is important."

She smiled and wished her love would look at her, but she couldn't see him properly because of the men still restraining her.

The guard willingly tossed his gun toward Rushe and took another from his hip. "I'm not going down for that guy."

Rushe let him walk out. He was closely followed by his colleagues, who also discarded their weapons, until the only three men left were the ones on her.

"There are easier ways to grope a woman," Flick said to the guy holding her shoulders. "Ones that won't get you sent to prison for life."

"No," Antoine said. "Don't listen to what she says."

His desperation was showing because he turned his back on Rushe to move toward her. The remaining security guards didn't loiter. All cast their weapons aside except one, who shoved a gun at the Frenchman as he passed. Rushe came into the room when the guards departed and closed the door to seal them all inside.

FIFTY-SIX

"ARE YOU SCARED, Antoine?" she asked, trapped between him and the wall where the security guards had left her. "Can you feel the panic? They're on to you. They've been on to you all along. It's over now."

"Non! Non! It is not!" Antoine snatched hold of her, pulling her body in front of his. "You will call them off," Antoine demanded of Rushe.

"Are you going to run like a scared little puppy?" she growled over her shoulder. "Run and hide, curl in the corner and lick your wounds? Now who is the coward?"

"Tais-toi!"

Telling her to be quiet would achieve nothing, but the volume at which he did it betrayed his panic.

"Set everyone free," Rushe said, taking a knife from his back pocket and tossing it toward Liam.

"Non!" Antoine exclaimed. "Non! Stop!"

"You're outnumbered now," Rushe said. "Your men are gone."

"We will shoot your woman," Antoine said, hauling her higher in front of him.

"You do that, and you'll have no way out."

If Antoine killed her, the triumph would be momentary. He'd have no shield against Rushe. Obviously, the European came to the same conclusion because he began to move for the door. If Antoine thought she would go with him, he was mistaken.

She threw back an elbow and both of them bowed. Throwing her head back, she made contact with Antoine's face, and he released her as he staggered backwards. She fell. The moment she hit the rug, another gunshot sounded. This time the curse was in French.

Whipping her head around, she saw Antoine collapse to the floor, clutching at his shoulder. Simone screamed and ducked to snatch a gun from her purse. After one static moment, she bounded to the seated Tawny, who screamed when Simone heaved to her feet. Using Tawny as a shield, Simone began to retreat toward the unconscious Antoine.

Flick rolled onto her chest, expecting to see Rushe bearing down upon them. Instead, Lucia was the closest person, and she had her arms stretched out in front of her, still connected at the wrist. Somehow, in her sister's hands, was a gun. From the deceased security man lying at her feet, no doubt. Rushe wasn't the shooter. Lucia had been the one to shoot Antoine.

"Lucia," Beverly gasped.

"I guess bad-ass is in the blood," Liam said.

Flick's mouth fell open, but there was no time to be shocked. Before her attention even landed on her love, she was already on her way across the room toward him. It wasn't until she got herself tucked behind him that she took in the scene. Everyone was on their feet, crowded in front of the fireplace. Liam had a gun, Robert too. Both men stood guard at the head of the group.

Antoine remained on the floor. Simone stood in front of him, holding Tawny against her, and pressing a gun under the young woman's jaw. Rushe wouldn't risk firing with Tawny so close to the fray.

"He's down," Rushe grumbled at Simone, his aim trained to her. "What are you going to do now?"

"I could shoot her!" Simone screeched.

The wobble of the weapon in the Frenchwoman's hand was worrying.

"Then we shoot you," Rushe said. "Game over… Or you let her go, and we let you walk… Run back to your uncle and tell him to get ready for prison."

The door opened. Panic brought her around to see who'd joined them. Eric. She relaxed.

"Sorry we're late," Eric said.

Her love remained intent on Simone.

"You just got here?" Flick asked Eric.

"Yeah, sorry."

"But I thought…" She gazed at Rushe's back. "You were bluffing? You took out those men by yourself, you were alone… all of that, and you were bluffing about your 'associates'?"

"The rest was true," Rushe grumbled. "You were in danger. I was done waiting."

So much for infinite patience.

Too many guns were trained on Simone. If their group was led by a lesser man, the woman would never have made it out of there alive. Staying behind Rushe, she peeked around his arm and prayed Simone wouldn't do anything stupid. Rushe might not want to hurt a woman, but there were other guns in the room and nerves were fried.

Was Simone considering hurting Tawny? Maybe for spite, if no other reason. Just then, the Frenchwoman hauled Tawny toward the door. As she traversed the space Rushe moved in an arc, keeping the European in the sights of his gun. Flick mirrored the progress, keeping herself enveloped in Rushe's body heat. The last thing she needed to do was distract him. He had to know she was with him. Although Tawny struggled against the movement, Simone got there.

Tawny was too unwieldy a prisoner, and Simone had no muscle on her bones, taking a hostage wasn't an option. On reaching the exit, Simone propelled Tawny forward and used the cover of the flailing woman to make her escape.

"Should we be letting her go?" Robert asked.

"Jansen's in the lobby, she won't get far," Eric said. "She's got nowhere to run."

Liam was already around her and Rushe. Sweeping Tawny off the floor, Liam carried her to the couch and laid her down. Watching him soothe his girlfriend, who seemed to be rather dazed, made Flick smile. Liam stroked Tawny's hair and kissed her lips. She'd never considered Liam as a lover in the past, but witnessing his care, he was probably very attentive in that department.

Turning to the rest of the room, she was met abruptly by the sight of her own lover, glaring down from his intimidating height above her.

"What?" she asked.

"It's your mouth," he said. "It's always your fucking mouth."

"You love my mouth," she teased, pressing a fingertip to his sternum.

He snatched it into his fist. "When it's full," he growled.

Swooping down, he jammed his tongue against hers and forced all his fury into their kiss.

Hooking one arm under her ribs, he took her off her feet to straighten from his stoop but still maintain their kiss. His other hand caught her head, ensuring the suction formed by their lips remained intact.

"We should get out of here," Eric said.

The voice to their side shattered the fervent moment. Rushe didn't release her, but her head drifted down to his shoulder when he turned to Eric.

"Yeah," Rushe said. "Tawny, come on!"

"You can't leave," Beverly said, stumbling toward them. "The FBI are on their way."

Lucia and Vivian were on the couch, holding each other and crying, while Charles tiptoed around the room with Robert surveying the bloody scene.

"No, they're not," Eric said, and glanced at Rushe.

Flick tsked at him. "You lied about that too?" she asked.

"Jansen will call them now," Rushe said. "I wasn't gonna let him do it while I was standing in the room."

"So the threat was…" She didn't know whether to be impressed or angry. "You plan to take off before they get here? What should we do with Antoine?"

"Nothing," Rushe said, looking beyond all the others to Antoine lying on the floor. The European groaned and rolled over to begin crawling toward the door, picking up speed as his consciousness grew. "I'll take care of that."

"You're going to take him with you?" she asked, burying her face against him.

Rushe lowered his chin to seek her mouth again, but their kiss was brief. "Damn right."

"Antoine is escaping!" Charles declared, glancing at the stain of blood on Beverly's favorite rug beneath where Antoine had been.

The struggling Frenchman was disappearing through the door.

"He won't get far," Flick said.

Jansen was still out there.

"You must go," Charles said to Rushe.

"Father—"

"Yes," he said, cutting off Flick and coming to full height to look at Rushe. "I can have trusted security here within ten minutes. They will take responsibility for the mess here tonight."

"But—"

"Jansen will take responsibility," Rushe said. "News of his injuries were exaggerated to take the heat off, but he's capable of firing a gun. In saving Serendipity, he learned what was happening here tonight. Simone's not going to confess to what went on. I'd be surprised if she said anything at all."

"Very well," Charles agreed. "You must leave quickly. From my understanding, you are all involved in a much greater plot here. If the police become involved in Rushe's life—"

"Yes," Lucia said, thrusting up to her feet. "You have to go or they'll arrest you, and your friends."

"We do not need to mention your presence here tonight," Charles said.

"Why would you do that?" Eric asked. "Why would you cover for Rushe?"

"He saved our lives," Beverly said. "And those responsible will be held accountable for their previous misdeeds."

The sight of her family standing in solidarity with her lover made her blink. Hot drops fell from her lashes.

"You have to stay here, Kit," Rushe said. When he used her hand to whip her around, she had to swallow the sob from her throat. "The cops know you came here with Robert when you left the precinct. You have to stay. Tell the truth about everything, Antoine had you here to coerce your testimony. He held you hostage for the evidence Jansen held."

They could tell the truth of what happened, substituting Rushe's name for Jansen's, who was already involved with the feds.

She sighed. "Rushe."

"Get Antoine," Rushe said, and nodded at Eric, who darted out to do as instructed.

"It's a shame that he escaped, injured," Charles said, holding eye contact with Rushe for a few seconds.

Charles had to feel somewhat responsible for the mess, since he allowed Antoine to enter their fold. Now he was doing what he could to make amends.

She tightened her fingers between Rushe's. "You'll come back?" she croaked.

"Once I've taken care of him properly," Rushe said, with a fixed glare on the door Antoine had used to depart.

"I have to speak to the staff," Charles said.

"They're restrained in the pantry," Rushe said. "I didn't trust any of them."

Lucia had a more personal question. "What about Roger?"

"He's with them, Martin too."

"He's alive?" Vivian shrieked.

Rushe nodded. Charles left the room with Robert not too far behind, and Vivian quickly ran after them.

"Lover," Flick said in a voice so small that his concentration was shattered, but her tears were overwhelming.

"Explain," he said, catching a drip from her chin. "Do you think I won't come back for you?"

"I don't feel right when we're not together… if something happens to you, and…"

"You trust me too much to doubt me, Kit. You promised never to do that again. Stay here and help your family. I'm gonna take this guy and finish the job for you, just like I promised you I would. I won't let you down."

"You never have."

Eric was out the room, her father was taking care of the staff, and presumably of Roger too. All she wanted to do was tuck her hand into Rushe's pocket and follow him out of there. But she couldn't.

In her peripheral vision, she watched Liam take Tawny out. Her troupe was leaving, her gang, her true family, and she was being left behind.

"Get," she murmured, knowing that Rushe was reluctant to leave her.

His features relaxed to a fleeting smile, and he ducked down to kiss her again. Before she could relish their warm joining, he left her. Her love turned and was gone, out of the room and away. She prayed for a swift return because already she was bereft.

"Okay," Lucia said, coming over. "What do we tell the cops?"

FIFTY-SEVEN

HER FATHER WAS COMMANDING in dealing with the cops. Robert certainly did his part keeping everything together. Everyone was required to give a statement, and paramedics checked them all over. Other than minor wounds, everyone was healthy enough.

The crime scene investigators were crawling all over the house by the time the cops finished with the statements, so Charles Hughes ordered everyone to a hotel for the night.

One night ended up being three, but by the time they were allowed back home, the Hughes's house was sparkling clean, as though nothing had taken place there at all.

The feds accepted that Jansen had escaped the hospital to save his woman. And that he discovered that the Merciers were holding the Hughes family hostage for the evidence.

By day five, she was getting antsy, very antsy. She hadn't heard a peep from any of her cohorts, not from Liam, or Tawny, or Eric, none of them. Then as though right on time, a steward knocked on her bedroom door and told her that she had a guest who refused to enter and was waiting for her outside. No prizes for guessing who that was; she couldn't get down the stairs fast enough to satisfy herself.

"You came to the door," she said, when she arrived on the front portico to find Rushe propped against one of the columns flanking the stairs. "Why didn't you come in?"

"I almost didn't come back at all," he said.

Angling her head as her brows came down to a frown, she scrutinized the hardened shell around him. "I was getting nervous about not hearing from you for so long. I assumed you were with Antoine."

"I was," he said. "That's taken care of now."

"Good. Thank you." The blink of surprise cleared his barriers for a split second, but they were quickly erected again. "Why the delay in coming for me? It's been five days; I started to think you'd forgotten about me."

"You've had time to make a decision," he said.

"You think because we were separated for five weeks, and I've been back in this life, that maybe I want it again?"

"I checked out Morse, and he's a good guy. You could have a good life here with your family."

"You are my family," she said. "My parents and sisters are ready to accept us now. We'll never be invited over for Sunday brunch with the neighbors, but… they'll leave us alone, Rushe, let us be together without judgement."

"I don't want their acceptance," he spat out like the words were poison on his tongue. "I want you to have a decent life."

"I have a life with you," she said, barely recognizing the bass of her own tone.

"It's no life for you," he snapped. The strength of his reaction astonished her. "This is what you were always meant to have: security, family, and a guy who can provide for you."

"You're doing what they did. You're asking me to marry a man I don't love and live in a life I don't want. Just like my parents did. As Robert, and my sisters did. Just like Antoine did."

"No," he said. Though the steely resolve remained, she saw his Adam's apple bob when he pushed away from the pillar. "Being away from me is better for you."

"No," she said, bounding forward when he took half a step backward toward the stairs. "If you walk away from me, Rushe, I won't be able to find you."

"Yes, you would," he said. "You're like a bad penny."

"You were supposed to come back to collect me, to accept me, not to push me away."

"You've got fire, sweetheart," he said with a subdued awe. "You faced them all, every time. You never backed down, never once."

"Don't say goodbye to me, Rushe," she murmured. "You'll never forgive yourself."

"It's too late for that."

The touch of his gaze circled her. Even without words, she knew his thoughts. He would never forgive himself for all she'd been through, what he thought he'd put her through, subjected her to.

"You love me."

"Yeah, but I should've fucked Simone. I should've fucked her in that house, and I should've walked away from you. Why couldn't I just walk the fuck away?"

The question may have been rhetorical, but as she carefully crept toward him, she saw the flare of yearning he quickly dampened with self-disgust.

"Do you think I don't love you?"

"I know you do," he said. "But you shouldn't."

"I can't help myself. I have to tell you a secret," she whispered, close enough to let her fingernail graze the stitching of his jeans pocket. "It's something I never thought I'd admit to you, but…"

"What?" he snapped, clearly ready to hear her confess a horrible truth.

"You are an excellent teacher." His own facade faltered to a frown. "You taught me that if something is right, then it's worth fighting for, and this is right, Rushe. Us. You and me. It's right, and I will fight for our relationship."

"You don't have to fight. I want to give you the chance to make your own choice, now, with everything you've seen. When I've tried to get rid of you in the past myself, you've never let me walk away."

"And I never will," she said.

"You always push back and call me out. If I hadn't come back here, you'd have come after me."

He stared at her, into her, absorbing everything he could from her. Then he took his hand to her head and stroked downward, watching his fingertips as they drifted out of her locks.

"I would follow you, yes," she whispered. His eyes floated up to hers. "I wouldn't sit here playing the dutiful wife to some pretty boy because you're not man enough to admit I'm the best thing you've ever had in your life. You're the best thing I've ever had in my life, Rushe, and I'm no coward."

"You saying I am?"

"Yes," she said, in spite of the snarl in his voice. "I think it would be easy to walk away and tell yourself you're doing the right thing, that you're doing what is best for me. But it's a crock of shit. You're scared you might lose me. You're scared that something you do or say will put me in danger or hurt me. You're the only one with the power to hurt me, Rushe, and you're doing it right now by implying I'm not worth fighting for."

"I didn't say that," he grumped and shifted back a step.

"You're a bad guy, Rushe. Isn't that what you think? If you're so evil, why do you spend so much of your life trying to do the right thing? I love you," she said. "I want to be with you."

"How can you possibly…" he grumbled through gritted teeth, his eyes blazing with self-loathing. "After everything that went on here, everything you saw… what you saw me do… what you know I did… Do you know how long Antoine took to die…? He felt pain in every second that I had him."

"You didn't do it for fun, Rushe. I don't care how much pleasure you took in torturing Antoine; he deserved it. He treated all of us horribly: me, you, Lucia, my family… our family… He was selling innocent women for profit and loving every moment of it. All you did was show him the other side. That's what you always do, isn't it? Show the perpetrator what it's like to be the victim. He deserved it, Lover, and I'm proud of you." His whole body came up against the column when he backed away further. She stalked forward and dug her hands deep into his pockets, pushing her body flat onto his. "I love you. I'm proud of you, and I won't ever be ashamed. Nothing you could ever do would disgust me, or repulse me, because I trust the essence of who you are. You are my man."

"Flick—"

"Say it, Rushe… Please… say you are my man."

The thump of hope from her heart and dread from her gut collided in her diaphragm. The clash pulsed in every silent second that passed between them. The glow of her eyes met the dull uncertainty of his.

"You might be big and scary on the outside, Rushe," she said. "But you're not invincible. I'm the only one around here who'll remind you of that. And I'd never lie to you. If you tried to ditch me… I'd get myself into so much trouble, you'd be forced to come back to bail me out."

"Yeah?"

She nodded and sunk her hands deeper as she squeezed her breasts together against him. "Then when I was safe, you'd be angry at me for getting myself into hot water, so you'd fuck some sense into me."

"That never works."

"I think it does," she said. "I think you fuck it into me and out of you. What sense would there be in trying to walk away from the only woman on the planet who can satisfy you? You'd never be able to have sex with another woman, because you'd never know if I was going to walk into the room and catch you at it. I've already threatened her life, whoever she is, and I don't give you permission, let's get that clear now. No one touches my stuff… and after we had sex you wouldn't be able to leave me again, because you'd remember how much you love me… and how hot the sex is."

"I never forgot either," he grumbled.

"I know."

"I told you if you came with me, you would get hurt."

"And I told you I didn't care. You're worth the risk. How many times do you think I would get hurt if I was out there alone looking for you? But it wouldn't stop me from doing it."

"You're crazy," he mumbled. "You'd take all those risks to track a man who doesn't want to be found? A man who isn't worth it."

"Oh, he's worth it."

"How do you know?"

"Because I do," she said, allowing a smile to pierce her face. "You know I won't be happy without you, Lover. And you'd do anything to make me happy."

"You still wanna be with me. You actually still wanna… that's your decision?"

"The only thing that's different is there are a few less depraved individuals walking this earth. You've done humanity a favor. I could never be ashamed of you, Rushe. Please don't offend me anymore by assuming I'm interested in changing who you are. I want you to stay the same as you were the moment we met. I don't want to live my life in fear of losing you, either your physical being, or the truth of your soul."

Considering her for a long moment, he eventually sucked in a nasal breath. "There's someone I want you to meet."

"Okay," she said.

"The first guy I killed, he was raping a woman in New York, I just… it was an accident, but… I wasn't sorry."

She rested all her weight onto him. "He was committing a crime. You saved her."

"I ran off," Rushe said. "I wasn't hanging around for no cops… A couple of weeks later, she walked into the shelter where I was staying. I didn't know it was her, I wasn't paying any attention until she came up with this guy… her father. I didn't know who she was until he told me, and I thought I was dead. I was ready to run, but he got hold of me, and… thanked me. They didn't call the cops."

"They were grateful."

"He gave me money, a couple hundred bucks. I thought I'd won the lottery."

"How old were you?"

"Fourteen, maybe fifteen…"

"Did you get close?" she asked. "Do you want to tell me the story?"

"It'll take a while," he said, taking his hand to the top of her head with uncharacteristic caution. "If you ever change your mind, I'll never—"

"Yes, you will," she said. "Or you better. If I start to doubt how much I'm worth to you and try to walk away, you better be damn ready to fight for me. We're a team, a package deal, remember? There is no me without you."

"Doubt your worth," he said, threading his fingers down through her hair until they rested against her breast. "You're the best thing I've ever had in my life."

She sensed his wit but chose to ignore it. "Don't forget it, buddy… Come inside, I'll get my things together and we'll leave."

"I'll wait in the car."

The bubble of uncertainty, of mistrust, that she'd had when he said things like that in the past grew until it burst. "In the car?"

"I'm not subtle, sweetheart. If I was gonna take off, I'd toss you aside and do it now."

"But why—"

"It doesn't pay to get attached, Kit."

Not changing who he was meant accepting some things would always remain the same. Her family had let her down when they cast her out. Rushe would never forget that. He'd never trust them, and her own doubts about how she didn't fit with her family intensified when she sat in that house with them.

Yes, it was nice to know they wouldn't be as judgmental of Rushe, because there was a chance their paths would cross again. But she didn't want the life the Hughes offered; it didn't make her happy.

So she went inside alone, gathered her

possessions, and said her goodbyes. She and Rushe had their own life to get on with. No matter what that entailed, as long as they were together, she'd always be happy.

EPILOGUE

"HEY! Guys paid to stick it up your ass in the eighteen nineties," Tawny said, when Rushe reached the side of the couch she and Tawny were sitting on.

"What are you doing?" Rushe asked.

"Reading."

"Why?" Rushe asked.

"Because it's fun," Tawny said.

She peeked over her shoulder, drawing her eyes to her love. "I read all the time," she said to him. "You told me it was sexy."

"Yeah, but you're…" Both women twisted to look up at him. "Forget it," he said. "You, upstairs."

"Me?" she asked, though he was very obviously glaring at her.

On a nod, he about-faced and started out of the open plan recreational and residential area in the basement of Silver's brothel.

Leaping up, she hurried around the couch to catch up with him. She caught hold of his back pocket just as he went through the swing door to the stairs.

They emerged in reception, bypassing Lilah behind the front desk filing her fingernails. Rushe didn't stop. He went through the curtain and traversed into the watchman's room, where they'd been living for the last three weeks.

As soon as the door was closed, he took hold of her waist, bumped her back against the wall, and brought his body to hers.

"Lover," she said, grinning, as he scowled down at her. "Tawny and I were bonding, as I told you I wanted us to do. I thought this was important. I thought you wanted to talk to me or something."

"My dirty little kitten loves her words."

"She loves your words."

"You're gonna take off your clothes and get onto our bed."

"What are you going to do?" she asked, hooking her hands onto his buckle.

"Watch. I'm gonna watch you. You're gonna get on the bed and spread those hot legs, let me see that lush little spot I love."

"Are you going to fuck me?"

"I'm gonna eat you," he said. "Snack on that juicy cunt you're gonna lube up for me, while I watch your sweet whimpers that make those tits shake."

"Rushe—"

Barely backing off, he spun her around and pressed her body to the wall with the weight of his.

Easing his hips back slightly, he took hold of her ass and squeezed. "My woman, hot, sweet, sexy," her love grumbled the words. Clenching and stroking, he squatted, his thighs on either side of hers. His erection dug into her butt as he took her skirt in his fists and pulled it up, all the while rubbing his face in her hair. "You're gonna ride me tonight. You'll keep going 'til you can't stand anymore, you understand? Speak."

"Yes."

"Yes, what?"

"Yes, sir."

Whirling her around, he urged her toward the bed. She stumbled, unable to keep up with his long strides, so he whipped her off her feet.

"What is that?" she asked, digging her nails into him when she noticed the top of their duffel poking over the back of the couch.

"We're heading out, you and me, tomorrow."

"Why?"

He tossed her onto the bed. "Because we're drifters, Kit. We're too comfortable here. Now, strip."

"So we're going to turn our backs on our friends?"

"That's exactly what we're going to do."

"Rushe," she said, thrusting herself up to prop her weight on her palms. "We are loyal people. We are not going to… don't you dare look at me like that."

The shutters of indifference were cast over his face. He stood there at the foot of the bed, waiting. "Take off your clothes."

"I'm not going to have sex with you while you're being a jerk." His head tilted as his eyes squinted a fraction. "Yes, okay, admittedly, you're always a jerk, but usually it's sexy. Running away isn't sexy, Rushe." At the same time he drew breath through his nose, he began to unbuckle his belt. "I thought I was supposed to get naked, what are you doing?"

"Your mouth needs a distraction from giving me earache."

"I'm not going to suck you off," she said, crossing her legs and folding her arms. "Not while you're being an arrogant bastard."

"I'm always an arrogant bastard. You fell in love with this arrogant bastard."

"Do you know Liam and Tawny are in a fight?"

"What the hell has that got to—"

"He wants her to move away from here," she said. "I don't think she's confident enough to do that, because she gets bored in a nine to five. If she ends up back on drugs, she'll lose him. But if she stays here, she'll lose him too."

"So they're breaking up, who gives a fuck?" Rushe asked. "Either show me your tits or get my dick in your mouth."

"Don't you see, they need us," she said, surging onto her knees to walk down the bed and tuck her hands into his pockets, leaning on him. "Serendipity and Jansen are going through a difficult time, and Eric's really worried about Gracie. I still haven't met her. I'd love to meet her."

"You care about these people," he scowled at her, and took his hand to her head.

"Of course I care about them, Lover. They're our friends."

"I don't have friends."

Still, he hadn't realized. "Don't look now, but I think those people care about you too. We have a life here, Rushe."

"You want to live in a brothel? Permanently?"

"Not permanently," she said and shrugged. "But there's nothing wrong with it now, is there? You gave Silver the diamond Antoine gave to me, he'll be sweet on us for a while."

"We're here doing him a favor."

"Keeping an eye on Tawny still," she said. Rushe was concerned about the people there, and the ones who'd helped them through the case, even if he didn't admit it. "We'll move on when the time is right, but that time isn't now."

"You want to stay."

"I go where you go," she said. "If you feel that strongly about it, if you need to move on—"

"I want you to be happy," he said. "If you get hurt by people I brought into your life—"

"That's what this is about? You didn't introduce me to Liam, I found him on my own. Eric found me; you were nothing to do with our first conversation. And being here, Tawny, it all leads back to me walking into Dell's. Have a little faith. We're going to be okay."

For a long spell, he just fixated on her eyes. "You've got to make it worth my while."

Her lips curled and she pushed in tight against him. "I think I can do that."

Extricating herself from him, she shuffled back a few inches on her knees and pulled her top off over her head to reveal she wasn't wearing any underwear.

Immediately, his shutters vanished. "Now I'm tempted," he said, as she unfastened her skirt and got to her feet on the bed. "We need to get a new bed though, something I can tie you to."

"I'm not going anywhere," she said, walking to the edge of the bed to push down her skirt.

When she could reach no further, her love took over and removed it before grabbing her hips to keep her on her feet.

"I'm taking no chances."

Skimming his hands across the front of her pelvis, he separated her folds enough to lean in and suck her clit. She sighed out his name and let her hands fall into his hair, but he snatched her knees and yanked her legs, sending her to her back with a whoop.

She laughed, recovering from his surprise maneuver. "I'm naked again."

"And I'm not."

"Just the way you like it," she said, caressing her own body, because he remained standing at the end of the bed. "For the art?"

"That's right." After his gaze had consumed her, it locked onto hers. "We can stay… for now."

"Thank you."

"Show me your pussy."

Pressing the soles of her feet together, she dragged them up and let her knees part to present for him. Once again, he examined her.

"Don't you ever get tired of looking?"

"Yeah," he said, gathering his tee-shirt at the back of his neck to pull it off. After casting it aside, he dropped down onto the bed and brought his mouth to her center to breathe hot, arousing breaths against her. "That's when I do this."

Flicking his tongue on her clit loosened her whole body. He tantalized every crevice, kissing and licking her until she couldn't stop saying his name. The time he took, the delectable care, over every millimeter of her flesh made her whimper in a torturous agony of ecstasy that unconsciously led her fingers to her clit, as he lapped her opening. When her digits grazed his forehead, he sat up.

"What the fuck do you think you're doing?" he asked, swiping her hand away.

She pushed up, trying to writhe closer. In such a fuddle of endorphins, she struggled to focus. "I want you," she said on an exhale. "I'm ready."

"I say when you're ready."

"If you don't get your dick inside me within the next thirty seconds, I'm going out there to pay the next john who walks in to come in here and finish me off."

Rushe growled and reared up over her, resting his body weight on her, forcing her into the mattress. "My woman… you want to watch me gut him? Is that what you need to get you off?"

"No, I'll do it myself when he's through," she

said. "No one who touches your stuff will stay breathing for long."

"Damn right," he said, and relieved her of some of his weight. "Open."

Her thighs were already apart, but she elevated them from the bed to his hips, giving him complete access. "I love you," she said, stroking his shoulders.

"I know."

His smile distracted her so much that she didn't register him lifting his own hips. In one slick move, he plunged into her, drawing a satisfied sigh from each of them.

Their unity made her smile join his. As he began to move in and out of her, she matched his easy pace. It wasn't long before the rapture built and she began to move faster, urging him to do the same as she whispered out his name. Clawing her hands down his back, she curled in and bucked out with the pulse of his name sounding from her chest.

"Done yet?" he asked, though his own speed actually increased.

"More," she yelped, gripping his shoulders until her fingernails were ready to draw blood. "More, Rushe, I always want more!"

He delivered, sending her into orgasm again, then once more, before he bent her legs and pushed his weight to her shins as he drove into her and spurted his own climax.

"Oh, you're so good at that," she breathed, when his damp form collapsed beside hers.

He pulled her against him. "We get in a lot of practice, Kitten."

"And long may that continue," she said, turning her face to kiss him.

A knock made them both sit up. As her love darted off the bed to pull on his jeans, she wondered if they'd ever be able to just enjoy each other without the constant threat of interruption. Her lover tossed her his tee-shirt, and she donned it as he stood at the door and waited for her to be decent. Then with a nod when she was, Rushe opened the door.

Jansen stood there with a grin on his face. It was clear the ex-cop knew what they'd been doing.

"Jansen," she said and clambered off the bed to run toward him as he entered.

Jansen held up his hands to stall her. "No physical contact," he said, looking Rushe up and down. "I know where you've just been."

She was amused by the joke, Rushe wasn't. "What do you want?"

"I came to check in on my favorite crime-fighting duo," Jansen said. "And to tell you the feds have Jerome in custody, Simone too. The DA is pushing ahead with the case. We're really gonna win this one. Antoine's still at large; no one's found him." From the look Jansen laid on Rushe, he knew as well as her that Antoine would never be found.

"Checking we're still here?" Rushe asked.

"You guys could've split when you found out what happened to me and Serendipity, but you didn't. You stuck around, and that probably saved her life. I'll never forget that."

"Rushe isn't one for emotional shows of gratitude, but you're welcome," she said. "You were there for me when I needed it."

"Yeah."

"Serendipity, how is she?" Flick asked.

"She's different now," he said. "She's…"

"What?" Rushe asked.

"Grateful?" she suggested with a smile.

"Yeah, how did you know that?"

"Almost losing the man you love puts life into

perspective," she said, sliding an arm around Rushe to hook his opposite pocket.

"We're working on it, but I feel good about it, better than I did before."

"That's 'cause you took care of business," Rushe said. "No more looking over your shoulder."

"What will you do now that you've left law enforcement?" she asked.

Jansen shrugged. "Private sector maybe, I hear it's lucrative."

"Comes with its own set of problems," Rushe said.

Her love's hand drifted down to squeeze her ass just as the red light above the door flashed and the alarm blasted. He kissed the top of her head, then strode out of the room.

"There's still time, you know," Jansen said.

"Time for what?"

"You can come with me, testify."

Her smile stretched wider, but she shook her head. "There are too many questions I can't answer. Being Rushe's woman makes things… complicated."

"We can work it out, bring these guys to justice together."

"Once a cop…? I trust you to ensure justice."

"I've got to ask," he said after an accepting nod.

"What?"

"Would you do it again? Walk into Dell's, knowing what you do now. After everything you've been through… Would you still walk into Dell's, in spite of Rushe's warning not to?"

Taking her attention to the floor, she reflected on her life from that day to this one, but she didn't have to ponder her answer. "Yes."

"You're sure? You have no doubts? He's been worth it?"

"Worth everything I've experienced in the past, and whatever awaits us in the future, yes."

"You're really something, Felicity Hughes."

"It's Felicity Jones now, and he's the one who's something," she said. "I can't wait to see where my adventure with him leads us next."

"You're going to keep going? No settling down?"

"Settling down?" she said and grinned. "Where's the adventure in that?"

Thank you for reading this tale!
If you can, please take the time to review.

~

Ask your local library for more Scarlett Finn novels!

~

For all things Scarlett Finn
check out:

www.scarlettfinn.com